Domes of Fire

David Eddings was born in Washington in 1931 and grew up near Seattle. He graduated from the University of Washington and went on to serve in the US Army. Subsequently he worked as a buyer for the Boeing Company and taught college-level English. *High Hunt*, his first novel, was a contemporary adventure story, but he soon began a spectacular career as a fantasy writer with his bestselling series *The Belgariad*. He consolidated his immediate success with two more enormously popular series, *The Malloreon* and *The Elenium*.

The Belgariad

Book One: *Pawn of Prophecy*
Book Two: *Queen of Sorcery*
Book Three: *Magician's Gambit*
Book Four: *Castle of Wizardry*
Book Five: *Enchanters' End Game*

The Malloreon

Book One: *Guardians of the West*
Book Two: *King of the Murgos*
Book Three: *Demon Lord of Karanda*
Book Four: *Sorceress of Darshiva*
Book Five: *The Seeress of Kell*

The Elenium

Book One: *The Diamond Throne*
Book Two: *The Ruby Knight*
Book Three: *The Sapphire Rose*

The Tamuli

Book One: *Domes of Fire*
Book Two: *The Shining Ones*
Book One: *The Hidden City*

High Hunt
The Losers

SCIENCE
FICTION
FANTASY

DAVID EDDINGS

Domes of Fire

The Tamuli
BOOK ONE

HarperCollins*Publishers*

HarperCollins Science Fiction & Fantasy
An Imprint of HarperCollins*Publishers*
77–85 Fulham Palace Road,
Hammersmith, London W6 8JB

This paperback edition 1994
3   5   7   9   8   6   4

Previously published in paperback by Grafton 1993

First published in Great Britain by
HarperCollins*Publishers* 1992

ISBN 0 586 21313 9

Set in Palatino

Printed in Great Britain by
HarperCollinsManufacturing Glasgow

Domes of Fire

Prologue

– Excerpted from Chapter Two of *The Cyrga
Affair: An Examination of the Recent Crisis.*
Compiled by the Contemporary History Department
of the University of Matherion.

It was quite obvious to the Imperial Council at this point
that the empire was facing a threat of the gravest nature
– a threat which his Imperial Majesty's government
was ill-prepared to confront. The empire had long
relied upon the armies of Atan to defend her interests
during the periodic outbreaks of incidental civil disorder
which are normal and to be expected in a disparate population ruled by a strong central authority. The situation
facing his Majesty's government this time, however,
did not appear to arise from spontaneous demonstrations by a few malcontented hotheads spilling out into
the streets from various university campuses during
the traditional recess which follows final examinations.
Those particular demonstrations can be taken in stride,
and order is usually restored with a minimum of bloodshed.

The government soon realized that this time, however, things were different. The demonstrators were not
high-spirited schoolboys, for one thing, and domestic
tranquillity did not return when classes at the universi-
ties resumed. The authorities might still have main-
tained order had the various disruptions been the result
of ordinary revolutionary fervour. The mere presence of

Atan warriors can dampen the spirits of even the most enthusiastic under normal circumstances. This time, the customary acts of vandalism accompanying the demonstrations were quite obviously of paranormal origin. Inevitably, the imperial government cast a questioning eye at the Styrics in Sarsos. An investigation by Styric members of the Imperial Council whose loyalty to the throne could not be questioned, however, quite clearly indicated that Styricum had had no part in the disturbances. The paranormal incidents were obviously coming from some as yet to be determined source and were so widespread that they could not have emanated from the activities of a few Styric renegades. The Styrics themselves were unable to identify the source of this activity, and even the legendary Zalasta, pre-eminent magician in all of Styricum though he might be, ruefully confessed to total bafflement.

It was Zalasta, however, who suggested the course ultimately taken by his Majesty's government. He advised that the empire might seek assistance from the Eosian continent, and he specifically directed the government's attention to a man named Sparhawk.

All imperial representatives on the Eosian continent were immediately commanded to drop everything else and to concentrate their full attention upon this man. It was imperative that his Majesty's government have information about this Sparhawk person. As the reports from Eosia began to filter in, the Imperial Council began to develop a composite picture of Sparhawk, his appearance, his personality and his history.

Sir Sparhawk, they discovered, was a member of one of the quasi-religious orders of the Elene Church. His particular order is referred to as 'The Pandion Knights'. He is a tall, lean man of early middle years with a battered face, a keen intelligence and an abrupt, even abrasive manner. The Knights of the Elene Church are

2

fearsome warriors, and Sir Sparhawk is in the forefront of their ranks of champions. At the time in the history of the Eosian continent when the four orders of Church Knights were founded, the circumstances were so desperate that the Elenes set aside their customary prejudices and permitted the Militant Orders to receive instruction in the arcane practices of Styricum, and it was the proficiency of the Church Knights in those arts which helped them to prevail during the First Zemoch War some five centuries ago.

Sir Sparhawk held a position for which there is no equivalent in our empire. He was the hereditary 'Champion' of the royal house of the Kingdom of Elenia. Western Elenes have a chivalric culture replete with many archaisms. The 'Challenge' (essentially an offer to engage in single combat) is the customary response of members of the nobility who feel that their honour has been somehow sullied. It is amazing to note that not even ruling monarchs are exempt from the necessity of answering these challenges. In order to avoid the inconvenience of responding to the impertinences of assorted hotheads, the monarchs of Eosia customarily designate some highly-skilled (and usually widely-feared) warrior as a surrogate. Sir Sparhawk's nature and reputation is such that even the most quarrelsome nobles of the kingdom of Elenia find after careful consideration that they have not *really* been insulted. It is a credit to Sir Sparhawk's skill and cool judgement that he has seldom even been obliged to kill anyone during these affairs, since, by ancient custom, a severely incapacitated combatant may save his life by surrendering and withdrawing his challenge.

After his father's death, Sir Sparhawk presented himself to King Aldreas, the father of the present queen, to take up his duties. King Aldreas, however, was a weak monarch, and he was dominated by his sister, Arissa, and by Annias, the Primate of Cimmura, who was also Princess Arissa's surreptitious lover and the father of her bastard son, Lycheas. The Primate of Cimmura, who was the *de facto* ruler of Elenia, had hopes of ascending the throne of the Archprelacy of the Elene Church in the Holy City of Chyrellos, and the presence of the stern and moralistic Church Knight at the court inconvenienced him, and so it was that he persuaded King Aldreas to send Sir Sparhawk into exile in the Kingdom of Rendor.

In time, King Aldreas also became inconvenient, and Primate Annias and the Princess poisoned him, thus elevating Princess Ehlana, Aldreas' daughter, to the throne. Though she was young, Queen Ehlana had received some training from Sir Sparhawk as a child, and she was a far stronger monarch than her father had been. She soon became more than a mere inconvenience to the Primate. He poisoned her as well, but Sir Sparhawk's fellow Pandions, aided by their tutor in the arcane arts, a Styric woman named Sephrenia, cast an enchantment which sealed the queen up in crystal and sustained her life.

Thus it stood when Sir Sparhawk returned from exile. Since the Militant Orders had no wish to see the Primate of Cimmura on the Archprelate's throne, certain of the champions of the other three orders were sent to assist Sir Sparhawk in finding an antidote or a cure which could restore Queen Ehlana to health. Since the queen had denied Annias access to her treasury in the past, the Church Knights reasoned that should she be restored, she would once again deny Annias the funds he needed to pursue his candidacy.

Annias allied himself with a renegade Pandion named Martel, and this Martel person was, like all Pandions, skilled in the use of Styric magic. He cast obstacles, both physical and supernatural, in Sparhawk's path, but

4

Sir Sparhawk and his companions were ultimately successful in discovering that Queen Ehlana could only be restored by a magical object known as 'The Bhelliom'.

Western Elenes are a peculiar people. They have a level of sophistication in worldly matters which sometimes surpasses our own, but at the same time, they have an almost childlike belief in the more lurid forms of magic. This 'Bhelliom' we are told, is a very large sapphire which was laboriously carved into the shape of a rose at some time in the distant past. The Elenes here insist that the artisan who carved it was a *Troll*. We will not dwell on that absurdity.

At any rate, Sir Sparhawk and his friends overcame many obstacles and were ultimately able to obtain the peculiar talisman, and (they claim) it was successful in restoring Queen Ehlana – although one strongly suspects that their tutor, Sephrenia, accomplished that task unaided, and that the apparent use of the Bhelliom was little more than a subterfuge she used to protect her from the virulent bigotry of western Elenes.

When the Archprelate Cluvonus died, the Hierocracy of the Elene Church journeyed to Chyrellos to participate in the 'election' of his successor. Election is a peculiar practice which involves the stating of preference. That candidate who receives the approval of a majority of his fellows is elevated to the office in question. This, of course, is an unnatural procedure, but since the Elene clergy is ostensibly celibate, there is no non-scandalous way the Archprelacy can be made hereditary. The Primate of Cimmura had bribed a goodly number of high churchmen to state a preference for him during the deliberations of the Hierocracy, but he still fell short of the needed majority. It was at this point that his underling, the aforementioned Martel, led an assault on the Holy City, hoping thereby to stampede the Hierocracy into electing Primate Annias. Sir Sparhawk and a limited number of Church Knights were able to keep Martel away from the Basilica where the Hierocracy was deliberating. Most of the city of Chyrellos, however, was severely damaged or destroyed during the fighting.

As the situation reached crisis proportions, help arrived for the beleaguered defenders in the form of the armies of the western Elene kingdoms. (Elene politics, one notes, are quite robust.) The connection between the Primate of Cimmura and the renegade Martel came to light as well as the fact that the pair had a subterranean arrangement with Otha of Zemoch. Outraged by the perfidy of the man, the Hierocracy rejected his candidacy and elected instead one Dolmant, the Patriarch of Demos. This Dolmant appears to be competent, though it may be too early to say for certain.

Queen Ehlana of the Kingdom of Elenia was scarcely more than a child, but she appeared to be a strong-willed and spirited young woman. She had long had a secret preference for Sir Sparhawk, though he was more than twenty years her senior; and upon her recovery it had been announced that the two were betrothed. Following the election of Dolmant to the Archprelacy, they were wed. Peculiarly enough, the queen retained her authority, although we must suspect that Sir Sparhawk exerts considerable influence upon her in state as well as domestic matters.

The involvement of the Emperor of Zemoch in the internal affairs of the Elene Church was, of course, a *casus belli*, and the armies of western Eosia, led by the Church Knights, marched eastward across Lamorkand to meet the Zemoch hordes poised on the border. The long-dreaded Second Zemoch War had begun.

Sir Sparhawk and his companions, however, rode

north to avoid the turmoil of the battlefield, and they then turned eastward, crossed the mountains of northern Zemoch and surreptitiously made their way to Otha's capital at the city of Zemoch, evidently in pursuit of Annias and Martel.

The best efforts of the empire's agents in the west have failed to reveal precisely what took place at Zemoch. It is quite certain that Annias, Martel and Otha himself perished there, but they are of little note in the pageant of history. What is far more relevant is the incontrovertible fact that Azash, Elder God of Styricum and the driving force behind Otha and his Zemochs, *also* perished, and it is undeniably true that Sir Sparhawk was responsible. We must concede that the levels of magic unleashed at Zemoch were beyond our comprehension and that Sir Sparhawk has powers at his command such as no mortal has ever possessed. As evidence of the levels of violence unleashed in the confrontation, we need only point to the fact that the city of Zemoch was utterly destroyed during the discussions.

Clearly, Zalasta the Styric had been right. Sir Sparhawk, the prince consort of Queen Ehlana, was the one man in all the world capable of dealing with the crisis in Tamuli. Unfortunately, Sir Sparhawk was not a citizen of the Tamul Empire, and thus could not be summoned to the imperial capital at Matherion by the emperor. His Majesty's government was in a quandary. The emperor had no authority over this Sparhawk, and to have been obliged to appeal to a man who was essentially a private citizen would have been an unthinkable humiliation.

The situation in the empire was daily worsening, and our need for the intervention of Sir Sparhawk was growing more and more urgent. Of equal urgency was the absolute necessity of maintaining the empire's dignity.

7

It was ultimately the Foreign Office's most brilliant diplomat, First Secretary Oscagne, who devised a solution to the dilemma. We will discuss his Excellency's brilliant diplomatic ploy at greater length in the following chapter.

PART ONE

Eosia

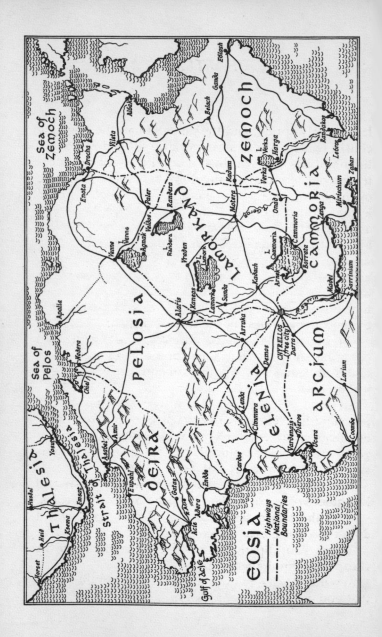

CHAPTER 1

It was early spring, and the rain still had the lingering chill of winter. A soft, silvery drizzle sifted down out of the night sky and wreathed around the blocky watchtowers of Cimmura, hissing in the torches on each side of the broad gate and making the stones of the road leading up to the gate shiny and black. A lone rider approached the city. He was wrapped in a heavy traveller's cloak and rode a tall, shaggy roan horse with a long nose and flat, vicious eyes. The traveller was a big man, a bigness of large, heavy bone and ropy tendon rather than of flesh. His hair was coarse and black, and at some time his nose had been broken. He rode easily but with the peculiar alertness of the trained warrior.

The big roan shuddered absently, shaking the rain out of his shaggy coat as they approached the east gate of the city and stopped in the ruddy circle of torchlight just outside the wall.

An unshaven gate guard in a rust-splotched breastplate and helmet and with a patched green cloak hanging negligently from one shoulder came out of the gate house to look inquiringly at the traveller. He was swaying slightly on his feet.

'Just passing through, neighbour,' the big man said in a quiet voice. He pushed back the hood of his cloak.

'Oh,' the guard said, 'it's you, Prince Sparhawk. I didn't recognise you. Welcome home.'

'Thank you,' Sparhawk replied. He could smell the cheap wine on the man's breath.

'Would you like to have me send word to the palace that you've arrived, your Highness?'

11

'No. Don't bother them. I can unsaddle my own horse.' Sparhawk privately disliked ceremonies – particularly late at night. He leaned over and handed the guard a small coin. 'Go back inside, neighbour. You'll catch cold if you stand out here in the rain.' He nudged his horse and rode on through the gate.

The district near the city wall was poor, with shabby, run-down houses standing tightly packed beside each other, their second storeys projecting out over the wet littered streets. Sparhawk rode up a narrow, cobbled street with the slow clatter of the big roan's steel-shod hooves echoing back from the buildings. The night breeze had come up, and the crude signs identifying this or that tightly-shuttered shop on the street-level floors swung creaking on rusty hooks.

A dog with nothing better to do came out of an alley to bark at them with brainless self-importance. Sparhawk's horse turned his head slightly to give the wet cur a long, level stare that spoke eloquently of death. The empty-headed dog's barking trailed off and he cringed back, his rat-like tail between his legs. The horse bore down on him purposefully. The dog whined, then yelped, turned and fled. Sparhawk's horse snorted derisively.

'That make you feel better, Faran?' Sparhawk asked the roan.

Faran flicked his ears.

'Shall we proceed then?'

A torch burned fitfully at an intersection, and a buxom young whore in a cheap dress stood, wet and bedraggled, in its ruddy, flaring light. Her dark hair was plastered to her head, the rouge on her cheeks was streaked and she had a resigned expression on her face.

'What are you doing out here in the rain, Naween?' Sparhawk asked her, reining in his horse.

12

'I've been waiting for you, Sparhawk.' Her tone was arch, and her dark eyes wicked.

'Or for anyone else?'

'Of course. I *am* a professional, Sparhawk, but I still owe you. Shouldn't we settle up one of these days?'

He ignored that. 'What are you doing working the streets?'

'Shanda and I had a fight,' she shrugged. 'I decided to go into business for myself.'

'You're not vicious enough to be a street-girl, Naween.' He dipped his fingers into the pouch at his side, fished out several coins and gave them to her. 'Here,' he instructed. 'Get a room in an inn someplace and stay off the streets for a few days. I'll talk with Platime, and we'll see if we can make some arrangements for you.'

Her eyes narrowed. 'You don't have to do that, Sparhawk. I can take care of myself.'

'Of *course* you can. That's why you're standing out here in the rain. Just do it Naween. It's too late and too wet for arguments.'

'This is two I owe you, Sparhawk. Are you absolutely sure . . . ?' She left it hanging.

'Quite sure, little sister. I'm married now, remember?'

'So?'

'Never mind. Get in out of the weather.' Sparhawk rode on, shaking his head. He liked Naween, but she was hopelessly incapable of taking care of herself.

He passed through a quiet square where all the shops and booths were shut down. There were few people abroad tonight, and few business opportunities. He let his mind drift back over the past month and a half. No one in Lamorkand had been willing to talk with him. Archprelate Dolmant was a wise man, learned in doctrine and Church politics, but he was woefully ignorant of the way the common people thought. Sparhawk had patiently tried to explain to him that sending a Church Knight out to gather information was a waste of time, but Dolmant had insisted, and Sparhawk's oath obliged him to obey. And so it was that he had wasted six weeks in the ugly cities of southern Lamorkand where no one had been willing to talk with him about anything more serious than the weather. To make matters even worse, Dolmant had quite obviously blamed the knight for his own blunder.

In a dark side-street where the water dripped monotonously onto the cobblestones from the eaves of the houses, he felt Faran's muscles tense. 'Sorry,' he said quietly. 'I wasn't paying attention.' Someone was watching him, and he could clearly sense the animosity which had alerted his horse. Faran was a war-horse, and he could probably sense antagonism in his veins. Sparhawk muttered a quick spell in the Styric tongue, concealing the gestures which accompanied it beneath his cloak. He released the spell slowly to avoid alerting whoever was watching him.

The watcher was not an Elene. Sparhawk sensed that immediately. He probed further. Then he frowned. There were more than one, and they were not Styrics either. He pulled his thought back, passively waiting for some clue as to their identity.

The realisation came as a chilling shock. The watchers were not human. He shifted slightly in his saddle, sliding his hand toward his sword-hilt.

Then the sense of the watchers was gone, and Faran shuddered with relief. He turned his ugly face to give his master a suspicious look.

'Don't ask me, Faran,' Sparhawk told him. 'I don't know either.' But that was not entirely true. The touch of the minds in the darkness had been vaguely familiar, and that familiarity had raised questions in Sparhawk's mind, questions he did not want to face.

14

He paused at the palace gate long enough to firmly instruct the soldiers not to wake the whole house, and then he dismounted in the courtyard.

A young man stepped out into the rain-swept yard from the stable. 'Why didn't you send word that you were coming, Sparhawk?' he asked very quietly.

'Because I don't particularly like parades and wild celebrations in the middle of the night,' Sparhawk told his squire, throwing back the hood of his cloak. 'What are you doing up so late? I promised your mothers I'd make sure you got your rest. You're going to get me in trouble, Khalad.'

'Are you trying to be funny?' Khalad's voice was gruff, abrasive. He took Faran's reins. 'Come inside, Sparhawk. You'll rust if you stand out here in the rain.'

'You're as bad as your father was.'

'It's an old family trait.' Khalad led the prince consort and his evil-tempered warhorse into the hay-smelling stable where a pair of lanterns gave off a golden light. Khalad was a husky young man with coarse black hair and a short-trimmed black beard. He wore tight-fitting black leather breeches, boots and a sleeveless leather vest that left his arms and shoulders bare. A heavy dagger hung from his belt, and steel cuffs encircled his wrists. He looked and behaved so much like his father that Sparhawk felt again a brief, brief pang of loss. 'I thought Talen would be coming back with you,' Sparhawk's squire said as he began unsaddling Faran.

'He's got a cold. His mother – and yours – decided that he shouldn't go out in the weather, and I certainly wasn't going to argue with them.'

'Wise decision,' Khalad said, absently slapping Faran on the nose as the big roan tried to bite him. 'How are they?'

'Your mothers? Fine. Aslade's still trying to fatten Elys

up, but she's not having too much luck. How did you find out I was in town?'

'One of Platime's cut-throats saw you coming through the gate. He sent word.'

'I suppose I should have known. You didn't wake my wife, did you?'

'Not with Mirtai standing watch outside her door, I didn't. Give me that wet cloak, my Lord. I'll hang it in the kitchen to dry.'

Sparhawk grunted and removed his sodden cloak.

'The mail shirt too, Sparhawk,' Khalad added, 'before it rusts away entirely.'

Sparhawk nodded, unbelted his sword and began to struggle out of his chain-mail shirt. 'How's your training going?'

Khalad made an indelicate sound. 'I haven't learned anything I didn't already know. My father was a much better instructor than the ones at the chapterhouse. This idea of yours isn't going to work, Sparhawk. The other novices are all aristocrats, and when my brothers and I outstrip them on the practice field, they resent it. We make enemies every time we turn around.' He lifted the saddle from Faran's back and put it on the rail of a nearby stall. He briefly laid his hand on the big roan's back, then bent, picked up a handful of straw and began to rub him down.

'Wake some groom and have him do that,' Sparhawk told him. 'Is anybody still awake in the kitchen?'

'The bakers are already up, I think.'

'Have one of them throw something together for me to eat. It's been a long time since lunch.'

'All right. What took you so long in Chyrellos?'

'I took a little side trip into Lamorkand. The civil war there's getting out of hand, and the Archprelate wanted me to nose around a bit.'

'You should have got word to your wife. She was just

16

about to send Mirtai out to find you.' Khalad grinned at him. 'I think you're going to get yelled at again, Sparhawk.'

'There's nothing new about that. Is Kalten here in the palace?'

Khalad nodded. 'The food's better here, and he isn't expected to pray three times a day. Besides, I think he's got his eye on one of the chambermaids.'

'That wouldn't surprise me very much. Is Stragen here too?'

'No. Something came up, and he had to go back to Emsat.'

'Get Kalten up then. Have him join us in the kitchen. I want to talk with him. I'll be along in a bit. I'm going to the bathhouse first.'

'The water won't be warm. They let the fires go out at night.'

'We're soldiers of God, Khalad. We're all supposed to be unspeakably brave.'

'I'll try to remember that, my Lord.'

The water in the bathhouse was definitely on the chilly side, so Sparhawk did not linger very long. He wrapped himself in a soft white robe and went into the dim corridors of the palace and to the brightly-lit kitchens where Khalad waited with the sleepy-looking Kalten.

'Hail, Noble Prince Consort,' Kalten said drily. Sir Kalten obviously didn't care much for the idea of being roused in the middle of the night.

'Hail, Noble Boyhood Companion of the Noble Prince Consort,' Sparhawk replied.

'Now there's a cumbersome title,' Kalten said sourly. 'What's so important that it won't wait until morning?'

Sparhawk sat down at one of the work tables, and a white-smocked baker brought him a plate of roast beef and a steaming loaf still hot from the oven.

17

'Thanks, neighbour,' Sparhawk said to him.

'Where have you been, Sparhawk?' Kalten demanded, sitting down across the table from his friend. Kalten had a wine flagon in one hand and a tin cup in the other.

'Sarathi sent me to Lamorkand,' Sparhawk replied, tearing a chunk of bread from the loaf.

'Your wife's been making life miserable for everyone in the palace, you know.'

'It's nice to know she cares.'

'Not for any of the rest of us it isn't. What did Dolmant need from Lamorkand?'

'Information. He didn't altogether believe some of the reports he's been getting.'

'What's not to believe? The Lamorks are just engaging in their national pastime – civil war.'

'There seems to be something a little different this time. Do you remember Count Gerrich?'

'The one who had us besieged in Baron Alstrom's castle? I never met him personally, but his name's sort of familiar.'

'He seems to be coming out on top in the squabbles in western Lamorkand, and most everybody up there believes that he's got his eye on the throne.'

'So?' Kalten helped himself to part of Sparhawk's loaf of bread. 'Every baron in Lamorkand has his eyes on the throne. What's got Dolmant so concerned about it this time?'

'Gerrich's been making alliances beyond the borders of Lamorkand. Some of those border barons in Pelosia are more or less independent of King Soros.'

'Everybody in Pelosia's independent of Soros. He isn't much of a king. He spends too much time praying.'

'That's a strange position for a soldier of God,' Khalad murmured.

'You've got to keep these things in perspective,

18

Khalad,' Kalten told him. 'Too much praying softens a man's brains.'

'Anyway,' Sparhawk went on. 'If Gerrich succeeds in dragging those Pelosian barons into his bid for King Friedahl's throne, Friedahl's going to have to declare war on Pelosia. The Church already has a war going on in Rendor, and Dolmant's not very enthusiastic about a second front.' He paused. 'I ran across something else, though,' he added. 'I overheard a conversation I wasn't supposed to. The name Drychtnath came up. Do you know anything about him?'

Kalten shrugged. 'He was the national hero of the Lamorks some three or four thousand years ago. They say he was about twelve feet tall, ate an ox for breakfast every morning and drank a hogshead of mead every evening. The story has it that he could shatter rocks by scowling at them and reach up and stop the sun with one hand. The stories might be just a little bit exaggerated, though.'

'Very funny. The group I overheard were all telling each other that he's returned.'

'That'd be a neat trick. I gather that his closest friend killed him. Stabbed him in the back and then ran a spear through his heart. You know how Lamorks are.'

'That's a strange name,' Khalad noted. 'What does it mean?'

'Drychtnath?' Kalten scratched his head. '"Dreadnought", I think. Lamork mothers do that sort of thing to their children.' He drained his cup and tipped his flagon over it. A few drops came out. 'Are we going to be much longer at this?' he asked. 'If we're going to sit up talking all night, I'll get more wine. To be honest with you though, Sparhawk, I'd really rather go back to my nice warm bed.'

'And your nice warm chambermaid?' Khalad added.

'She gets lonesome,' Kalten shrugged. His face grew

19

serious. 'If the Lamorks are talking about Drychtnath again, it means that they're starting to feel a little confined. Drychtnath wanted to rule the world, and any time the Lamorks start invoking his name, it's a fair indication that they're beginning to look beyond their borders for elbow room.'

Sparhawk pushed back his plate. 'It's too late at night to start worrying about it now. Go back to bed, Kalten. You too, Khalad. We can talk more about this tomorrow. I really ought to go pay a courtesy call on my wife.' He stood up.

'That's all?' Kalten said. 'A courtesy call?'

'There are many forms of courtesy, Kalten.'

The corridors in the palace were dimly illuminated by widely-spaced candles. Sparhawk went quietly past the throne-room to the royal apartments. As usual, Mirtai dozed in a chair beside the door. Sparhawk stopped and considered the Tamul giantess. When her face was in repose, she was heart-stoppingly beautiful. Her skin was golden in the candlelight, and her eyelashes were so long that they touched her cheeks. Her sword lay in her lap with her hand lightly enclosing its hilt.

'Don't try to sneak up on me, Sparhawk.' She said it without opening her eyes.

'How did you know it was me?'

'I could smell you. All you Elenes seem to forget that you have noses.'

'How could you possibly smell me? I just took a bath.'

'Yes. I noticed that too. You should have taken the time to let the water heat up a little more.'

'Sometimes you amaze me, do you know that?'

'You're easily amazed, Sparhawk.' She opened her eyes. 'Where have you been? Ehlana's been nearly frantic.'

'How is she?'

'About the same. Aren't you ever going to let her

20

grow up? I'm getting very tired of being owned by a child.' In Mirtai's own eyes, she was a slave, the property of the Queen Ehlana. This in no way hindered her in ruling the royal family of Elenia with an iron fist, arbitrarily deciding what was good for them and what was not. She had brusquely dismissed all the queen's attempts to emancipate her, pointing out that she was an Atan Tamul, and that her race was temperamentally unsuited for freedom. Sparhawk tended strongly to agree with her, since he was fairly certain that if she were left to follow her instincts, Mirtai could depopulate several fair-sized towns in short order.

She stood up, rising to her feet with exquisite grace. She was a good four inches taller than Sparhawk, and he felt again that odd sense of shrinking as he looked up at her. 'What took you so long?' she asked him.

'I had to go to Lamorkand.'

'Was that your idea? or somebody else's?'

'Dolmant sent me.'

'Make sure Ehlana understands that right from the start. If she thinks you went there on your own, the fight will last for weeks, and all that wrangling gets on my nerves.' She produced the key to the royal apartment and gave Sparhawk a blunt, direct look. 'Be *very* attentive, Sparhawk. She's missed you a great deal, and she needs some tangible evidence of your affection. And don't forget to bolt the bedroom door. Your daughter might be just a little young to be learning about certain things.' She unlocked the door.

'Mirtai, do you *really* have to lock us all in every night?'

'Yes, I do. I can't get to sleep until I know that none of you is out wandering around the halls.'

Sparhawk sighed. 'Oh, by the way,' he added, 'Kring was in Chyrellos. I imagine he'll be along in a few days to propose marriage to you again.'

21

'It's about time,' she smiled. 'It's been three months since his last proposal. I was beginning to think he didn't love me any more.'

'Are you ever going to accept him?'

'We'll see. Go wake up your wife, Sparhawk. I'll let you out in the morning.' She gently pushed him on through the doorway and locked the door behind him.

Sparhawk's daughter, Princess Danae, was curled up in a large chair by the fire. Danae was six years old now. Her hair was very dark, and her skin as white as milk. Her dark eyes were large, and her mouth a small pink bow. She was quite the little lady, her manner serious and very grown-up. Her constant companion, nonetheless, was a battered and disreputable-looking stuffed toy animal named Rollo. Rollo had descended to Princess Danae from her mother. As usual, Princess Danae's little feet had greenish grass-stains on them. 'You're late, Sparhawk,' she said flatly to her father.

'Danae,' he said to her, 'you know you're not supposed to call me by name like that. If your mother hears you, she's going to start asking questions.'

'She's asleep,' Danae shrugged.

'Are you really sure about that?'

She gave him a withering look. 'Of course I am. I'm not going to make any mistakes. I've done this many, many times before, you know. Where have you been?'

'I had to go to Lamorkand.'

'Didn't it occur to you to send word to mother? She's been absolutely unbearable for the last few weeks.'

'I know. Any number of people have already told me about it. I didn't really think I'd be gone for so long. I'm glad you're awake. Maybe you can help me with something.'

'I'll consider it – if you're nice to me.'

22

'Stop that. What do you know about Drychtnath?'

'He was a barbarian, but he was an Elene, after all, so it was probably only natural.'

'Your prejudices are showing.'

'Nobody's perfect. Why this sudden interest in ancient history?'

'There's a wild story running through Lamorkand that Drychtnath's returned. They're all sitting around sharpening swords with exalted expressions on their faces. What's the real significance of that?'

'He was their king several thousand years ago. It was shortly after you Elenes discovered fire and came out of your caves.'

'Be nice.'

'Yes, father. Anyway, Drychtnath hammered all the Lamorks into something that sort of resembled unity and then set out to conquer the world. The Lamorks were very impressed with him. He worshipped the old Lamork Gods, though, and your Elene Church was a little uncomfortable with the notion of a pagan sitting on the throne of the whole world, so she had him murdered.'

'The Church wouldn't do that,' he said flatly.

'Did you want to listen to the story? or did you want to argue theology? After Drychtnath died, the Lamork priests disembowelled a few chickens and fondled their entrails in order to read the future. That's really a disgusting practice, Sparhawk. It's so messy.' She shuddered.

'Don't blame me. I didn't think it up.'

'The "auguries", as they called them, said that one day Drychtnath would return to take up where he'd left off and that he'd lead the Lamorks to world domination.'

'You mean they actually believe that?'

'They did once.'

23

'There are some rumours up there of backsliding – reversion to the worship of the old Pagan Gods.'

'It's the sort of thing you'd expect. When a Lamork starts thinking about Drychtnath, he automatically hauls the old Gods out of the closet. It's so foolish. Aren't there enough *real* Gods for them?'

'The old Lamork Gods aren't real, then?'

'Of course not. Where's your mind, Sparhawk?'

'The Troll-Gods are real. What's the difference?'

'There's all the difference in the world, father. Any child can see that.'

'Why don't I just take your word for it? And why don't you go back to bed?'

'Because you haven't kissed me yet.'

'Oh. Sorry. I had my mind on something else.'

'Keep your eye on the important things, Sparhawk. Do you want to have me wither away?'

'Of course not.'

'Then give me a kiss.'

He did that. As always she smelled of grass and trees. 'Wash your feet,' he told her.

'Oh bother,' she said.

'Do you want to spend a week explaining those grass-stains to your mother?'

'That's all I get?' she protested. 'One meagre little kiss and bathing instructions?'

He laughed, picked her up and kissed her again – several times. Then he put her down. 'Now scoot.'

She pouted a little and then sighed. She started back toward her bedroom, negligently carrying Rollo by one hind leg. 'Don't keep mother up all night,' she said back over her shoulder, 'and *please* try to be quiet. Why do you two always have to make so much noise?' She looked impishly back over her shoulder. 'Why are you blushing, father?' she asked innocently. Then she

24

laughed and went on into her own room and closed the door.

He could never be sure if his daughter really understood the implications of such remarks, although he was certain that one level at least of her strangely layered personality understood quite well. He made sure that her door was latched and then went into the bedroom he shared with his wife. He closed and bolted the door behind him.

The fire had burned down to embers, but there was still sufficient light for him to be able to see the young woman who was the focus of his entire life. Her wealth of pale blonde hair covered her pillow, and in sleep she looked very young and vulnerable. He stood at the foot of the bed looking at her. There were still traces of the little girl he had trained and moulded in her face. He sighed. That train of thought always made him melancholy, because it brought home the fact that he was really too old for her. Ehlana should have a young husband – someone less battered, certainly someone handsome. He idly wondered where he had made the mistake that had so welded her affection to him that she had not even considered any other possible choice. It had probably been something minor – insignificant even. Who could ever know what kind of effect even the tiniest gesture might have on another?

'I know you're there, Sparhawk,' she said without even opening her eyes. There was a slight edge to her voice.

'I was admiring the view.' A light tone might head off the incipient unpleasantness, though he didn't really have much hope of that.

She opened her grey eyes. 'Come over here,' she commanded, holding her arms out to him.

'I was ever your Majesty's most obedient servant.' He grinned at her, going to the side of the bed.

'Oh, *really*?' she replied, wrapping her arms about his neck and kissing him. He kissed her back, and that went on for quite some time.

'Do you suppose we could save the scolding until tomorrow morning, love?' he asked. 'I'm a little tired tonight. Why don't we do the kissing and making up now, and you can scold me later?'

'And lose my edge? Don't be silly. I've been saving up all sorts of things to say to you.'

'I can imagine. Dolmant sent me to Lamorkand to look into something. It took me a little longer than I expected.'

'That's not fair, Sparhawk,' she accused.

'I didn't follow that.'

'You weren't supposed to say that yet. You're supposed to wait until after I've demanded an explanation before you give me one. Now you've gone and spoiled it.'

'Can you ever forgive me?' He assumed an expression of exaggerated contrition and kissed her on the neck. His wife, he had discovered, loved these little games.

She laughed. 'I'll think about it.' She kissed him back. The women of his family were a very demonstrative little group, he decided. 'All right then,' she said. 'You've gone and spoiled it anyway, so you might as well tell me what you were doing, and why you didn't send word that you'd be delayed.'

'Politics, love. You know Dolmant. Lamorkand is right on the verge of exploding. Sarathi wanted a professional assessment, but he didn't want it generally known that I was going there at his instruction. He didn't want any messages explaining things floating around.'

'I think it's time for me to have a little talk with our revered Archprelate,' Ehlana said. 'He seems to have a little trouble remembering just who I am.'

26

'I don't recommend it, Ehlana.'

'I'm not going to start a fight with him, my love. I'm just going to point out to him that he's ignoring the customary courtesies. He's supposed to *ask* before he commandeers my husband. I'm getting just a little weary of his imperial Archprelacy, so I'm going to teach him some manners.'

'Can I watch? That might just be a very interesting conversation.'

'Sparhawk,' she said, giving him a smouldering look, 'if you want to avoid an official reprimand, you're going to have to start taking some significant steps to soften my displeasure.'

'I was just getting to that,' he told her, enfolding her in a tighter embrace.

'What took you so long?' she breathed.

It was quite a bit later, and the displeasure of the Queen of Elenia seemed to be definitely softening. 'What did you find out in Lamorkand, Sparhawk?' she asked, stretching languorously. Politics were never really very far from the queen's mind.

'Western Lamorkand's in turmoil right now. There's a count up there – Gerrich, his name is. We ran across him when we were searching for Bhelliom. He was involved with Martel in one of those elaborate schemes devised to keep the Militant Orders out of Chyrellos during the election.'

'That speaks volumes about this count's character.'

'Perhaps, but Martel was very good at manipulating people. He stirred up a small war between Gerrich and Patriarch Ortzel's brother. Anyway, the campaign appears to have broadened the count's horizons a bit. He's begun to have some thoughts about the throne.'

'Poor Freddie,' Ehlana sighed. King Friedahl of

Lamorkand was her distant cousin. 'You couldn't *give* me that throne of his. Why should the Church be concerned, though? Freddie's got a large enough army to deal with one ambitious count.'

'It's not quite so simple, love. Gerrich has been concluding alliances with other nobles in western Lamorkand. He's amassed an army nearly as big as the king's, and he's been talking with the Pelosian barons around Lake Venne.'

'Those bandits,' she said with a certain contempt. '*Anybody* can buy them.'

'You're well-versed in the politics of the region, Ehlana.'

'I almost have to be, Sparhawk. Pelosia fronts my northeastern border. Does this current disturbance threaten us in any way?'

'Not at the moment. Gerrich has his eyes turned eastward – toward the capital.'

'Maybe I should offer Freddie an alliance,' she mused. 'If general war breaks out in the region, I could snip off a nice piece of southwestern Pelosia.'

'Are we developing territorial ambitions, your Majesty?'

'Not tonight, Sparhawk,' she replied. 'I've got other things on my mind tonight.' And she reached out to him again.

It was quite a bit later, almost dawn. Ehlana's regular breathing told Sparhawk that she was asleep. He slipped from the bed and went to the window. His years of military training made it automatic for him to take a look at the weather just before daybreak.

The rain had abated, but the wind had picked up. It was early spring now, and there was little hope for decent weather for weeks. He was glad that he had reached home when he had, since the approaching day looked unpromising. He stared out at the torches flaring and tossing in the windy courtyard.

As they always did when the weather was bad, Sparhawk's thoughts drifted back to the years he had spent in the sun-blasted city of Jiroch on the arid north coast of Rendor where the women, all veiled and robed in black, went to the well in the steely first light of day and where the woman named Lillas had consumed his nights with what she chose to call love. He did not, however, remember that night in Cippria when Martel's assassins had quite nearly spilled out his life. He had settled that score with Martel in the Temple of Azash in Zemoch, so there was no real purpose in remembering the stockyard of Cippria nor the sound of the monastery bells which had called to him out of the darkness.

That momentary sense of being watched, the sense that had come over him in the narrow street while he had been on his way to the palace still nagged at him. Something he did not understand was going on, and he fervently wished that he could talk with Sephrenia about it.

CHAPTER 2

'Your Majesty,' the Earl of Lenda protested, 'you can't address this kind of language to the Archprelate.' Lenda was staring with chagrin at the piece of paper the queen had just handed him. 'You've done everything but accuse him of being a thief and a scoundrel.'

'Oh, did I leave those out?' she asked. 'How careless of me.' They were meeting in the blue-carpeted council chamber as they usually did at this time of the morning.

'Can't you do something with her, Sparhawk?' Lenda pleaded.

'Oh, Lenda,' Ehlana laughed, smiling at the frail old man, 'that's only a draft. I was a little irritated when I scribbled it down.'

'A *little*?'

'I know we can't send the letter in its present form, my Lord. I just wanted you to know how I really felt about the matter before we rephrase it and couch it in diplomatic language. My whole point is that Dolmant's beginning to overstep his bounds. He's the Archprelate, not the emperor. The Church has too much authority over temporal affairs already, and, if someone doesn't bring Dolmant up short, every monarch in Eosia will become little more than his vassal. I'm sorry gentlemen. I'm a true daughter of the Church, but I *won't* kneel to Dolmant and receive my crown back from him in some contrived little ceremony that has no purpose other than my humiliation.'

Sparhawk was a bit surprised at his wife's political maturity. The power structure on the Eosian Continent had always depended on a rather delicate balance between the authority of the Church and the power of the various kings. When that balance was disturbed, things went awry. 'Her Majesty's point may be well-taken, Lenda,' he said thoughtfully. 'The Eosian monarchies haven't been very strong for the last generation or so. Aldreas was –' He groped for a word.

'Inept,' his wife coolly characterised her own father.

'I might not have gone quite *that* far,' he murmured. 'Wargun's erratic, Soros is a religious hysteric, Obler's old, and Friedahl reigns only at the sufferance of his barons. Dregos lets his relatives make all his decisions, King Brisant of Cammoria is a voluptuary and I don't even know the name of the current King of Rendor.'

'Ogyrin,' Kalten supplied, 'not that it really matters.'

'Anyway,' Sparhawk continued, sinking lower in his chair and rubbing the side of his face thoughtfully, 'during this same period of time, we've had a number of very able churchmen in the Hierocracy. The incapacity of Cluvonus sort of encouraged the patriarchs to strike out on their own. If you had a vacant throne someplace, you could do a lot worse than put Emban on it – or Ortzel – or Bergsten, and even Annias had a very high degree of political skill. When kings grow weak, the Church grows strong – too strong sometimes.'

'Spit it out, Sparhawk,' Platime growled. 'Are you trying to say we should declare war on the Church?'

'Not today, Platime. We might want to keep the idea in reserve, though. Right now I think it's time to start sending some signals to Chyrellos, and our queen may be just the one to send them. After the way she stampeded the Hierocracy during Dolmant's election, I think they'll listen very carefully to just about anything she says. I don't know that I'd soften her letter all *that* much, Lenda. Let's see if we can get their attention.'

Lenda's eyes were very bright. '*This* is the way the

game's supposed to be played, my friends,' he said enthusiastically.

'You *do* realise that it's altogether possible that Dolmant didn't realise that he was stepping over the line,' Kalten noted. 'Maybe he sent Sparhawk to Lamorkand as the interim preceptor of the Pandion Order and completely overlooked the fact that he's also the prince consort. Sarathi's got a lot on his mind just now.'

'If he's *that* absent-minded, he's got no business occupying the Archprelate's throne,' Ehlana asserted. Her eyes narrowed, always a dangerous sign. 'Let's make it very clear to him that he's hurt my feelings. He'll go out of his way to smooth things over, and maybe I can take advantage of that to retrieve that Duchy just north of Vardenaise. Lenda, is there any way we can keep people from bequeathing their estates to the Church?'

'It's a long-standing custom, your Majesty.'

'I know, but the land originally comes from the crown. Shouldn't we have *some* say in who inherits it? You'd think that if a nobleman dies without an heir, the estate would revert back to me, but every time there's a childless noble in Elenia, the churchmen flock around him like vultures trying to talk him into giving *them* the land.'

'Jerk some titles,' Platime suggested. 'Make it a law that if a man doesn't have an heir, he doesn't keep his estate.'

'The aristocracy would go up in flames,' Lenda gasped.

'That's what the army's for,' Platime shrugged, 'to put out fires. I'll tell you what, Ehlana, you pass the law, and I'll arrange a few very public and very messy accidents for the ones who scream the loudest. Aristocrats aren't very bright, but they'll get the point – eventually.'

'Do you think I could get away with that?' Ehlana asked the Earl of Lenda.

'*Surely* your Majesty's not seriously considering it?'

'I have to do *something* Lenda. The Church is eating up my kingdom acre by acre, and once she takes possession of an estate, the land's removed from the tax rolls forever.' She paused. 'This could just be a way to do what Sparhawk suggested – get the Church's attention. Why don't we draw up a draft of some outrageously repressive law and just "accidentally" let a copy fall into the hands of some middle-level clergyman. It's probably safe to say that it'll be in Dolmant's hands before the ink's dry.'

'That's really unscrupulous, my Queen,' Lenda told her.

'I'm so glad you approve, my Lord.' She looked around. 'Have we got anything else this morning, gentlemen?'

'You've got some unauthorised bandits operating in the mountains near Cardos, Ehlana,' Platime rumbled. The gross, black-bearded man sat with his feet upon the table. There was a wine flagon and goblet at his elbow. His doublet was wrinkled and food-spotted, and his shaggy hair hung down over his forehead, almost covering his eyes. Platime was constitutionally incapable of using formal titles, but the queen chose to overlook that.

'Unauthorised?' Kalten sounded amused.

'You know what I mean,' Platime growled. 'They don't have permission from the thieves' council to operate in that region, and they're breaking all the rules. I'm not positive, but I think they're some of the former henchmen of the Primate of Cimmura. You blundered there, Ehlana. You should have waited until you had them in custody before you declared them outlaws.'

'Oh well,' she shrugged. 'Nobody's perfect.' Ehlana's relationship with Platime was peculiar. She realised that he was unable to mouth the polite formulas of the nobility, and so she accepted a bluntness from him that would have offended her had it come from anyone else.

For all his faults, Platime was turning into a gifted, almost brilliant counsellor, and Ehlana valued his advice greatly. 'I'm not surprised to find out that Annias' old cronies have turned to highway robbery in their hour of need. They were all bandits to begin with anyway. There have always been outlaws in those mountains, though, so I doubt that another band will make all that much difference.'

'Ehlana,' he sighed, 'you're the same as my very own baby sister, but sometimes you're terribly ignorant. An authorised bandit knows the rules. He knows which travellers can be robbed or killed and which ones have to be left alone. Nobody gets too excited if some over-stuffed merchant gets his throat cut and his purse lifted, but if a government official or a high-ranking nobleman turns up dead in those mountains, the authorities have to take steps to at least make it *appear* that they're doing their jobs. That sort of official attention is very bad for business. Perfectly innocent criminals get rounded up and hanged. Highway robbery's not an occupation for amateurs. And there's another problem as well. These bandits are telling all the local peasantry that they're not really robbers, but patriots rebelling against a cruel tyrant – that's you, little sister. There's always enough discontent among the peasants to make some of them sympathetic toward that sort of thing. You aristocrats haven't any business getting involved in crime. You always try to mix politics in with it.'

'But my dear Platime,' she said winsomely, 'I thought you knew. Politics *is* a crime.'

The fat man roared with laughter. 'I love this girl,' he told the others. 'Don't worry too much about it, Ehlana. I'll try to get some men inside their band, and when Stragen gets back, we'll put our heads together and work out some way to put those people out of business.'

'I knew I could count on you,' she said. She rose to

her feet. 'If that's all we have, gentlemen, I have an appointment with my dressmaker.' She looked around. 'Coming, Sparhawk?'

'In a moment,' he replied. 'I want to have a word with Platime.'

She nodded and moved toward the door.

'What's on your mind, Sparhawk?' Platime asked.

'I saw Naween last night when I rode into town. She's working the streets.'

'Naween? That's ridiculous! Half the time she even forgets to take the money.'

'That's what I told her. She and Shanda had a falling-out, and she was standing on a street corner near the east gate. I sent her to an inn to get her out of the weather. Can we make some kind of arrangement for her?'

'I'll see what I can do,' Platime promised.

Ehlana had not yet left the room, and Sparhawk sometimes forgot how sharp her ears were. 'Who's this Naween?' she asked from the doorway with a slight edge to her voice.

'She's a whore,' Platime shrugged, 'a special friend of Sparhawk's.'

'*Platime!*' Sparhawk gasped.

'Isn't she?'

'Well, I suppose so, but when you say it that way –' Sparhawk groped for the right words.

'Oh. I didn't mean it that way, Ehlana. So far as I know, your husband's completely faithful to you. Naween's a whore. That's her occupation, but it doesn't have anything to do with her friendship – not that she didn't make Sparhawk some offers – but she makes those offers to everybody. She's a very generous girl.'

'Please, Platime,' Sparhawk groaned, 'don't be on my side any more.'

'Naween's a good girl,' Platime continued to explain

to Ehlana. 'She works hard, she takes good care of her customers and she pays her taxes.'

'*Taxes?*' Ehlana exclaimed. 'Are you telling me that my government encourages that sort of thing? Legitimises it by taxing it?'

'Have you been living on the moon, Ehlana? Of course she pays taxes. We all do. Lenda sees to that. Naween helped Sparhawk once while you were sick. He was looking for that Krager fellow, and she helped him. Like I said, she offered him other services as well, but he turned her down – politely. She's always been a bit disappointed in him about that.'

'You and I are going to have a long talk about this, Sparhawk,' Ehlana said ominously.

'As your Majesty wishes,' he sighed as she swept coolly from the room.

'She doesn't know very much about the real world, does she, Sparhawk?'

'It's her sheltered upbringing.'

'I thought *you* were the one who brought her up.'

'That's right.'

'Then you've only got yourself to blame. I'll have Naween stop by and explain it all to her.'

'Are you out of your mind?'

Talen came in from Demos the next day, and he rode into the courtyard with Sir Berit. Sparhawk and Khalad met them at the stable door. The prince consort was making some effort to be inconspicuous until such time as the queen's curiosity about Naween diminished. Talen's nose was red, and his eyes looked puffy. 'I thought you were going to stay at the farm until you got over that cold,' Sparhawk said to him.

'I couldn't stand all that mothering,' Talen said, slipping down from his saddle. 'One mother is bad enough, but my brothers and I have two now. I don't think I'll ever be able to look another bowl of chicken soup in the face again. Hello, Khalad.'

'Talen,' Sparhawk's burly young squire grunted. He looked critically at his half-brother. 'Your eyes look terrible.'

'You ought to see them from in here.' Talen was about fifteen now, and he was going through one of those 'stages'. Sparhawk was fairly certain that the young thief had grown three inches in the past month and a half. A goodly amount of forearm and wrist stuck out of the sleeves of his doublet. 'Do you think the cooks might have something to eat?' the boy asked. As a result of his rapid growth, Talen ate almost constantly now.

'I've got some papers for you to sign, Sparhawk,' Berit said. 'It's nothing very urgent, but I thought I'd ride in with Talen.' Berit wore a mail shirt, and he had a broadsword belted at his waist. His weapon of choice, however, was still the heavy war-axe slung to his saddle.

'Are you going back to the chapterhouse?' Khalad asked him.

'Unless Sparhawk has something he wants me for here.'

'I'll ride along with you then. Sir Olart wants to give us more instruction with the lance this afternoon.'

'Why don't you just unhorse him a few times?' Berit suggested. 'Then he'll leave you alone. You could do it, you know. You're already better than he is.'

Khalad shrugged. 'It'd hurt his feelings.'

'Not to mention his ribs, shoulders and back,' Berit laughed.

'It's a bit ostentatious to outperform your instructors,' Khalad said. 'The other novices are already a little sulky about the way my brothers and I have outstripped them. We've tried to explain, but they're sensitive about the fact that we're peasants. You know how that goes.' He looked inquiringly at Sparhawk. 'Are you going to need me for anything this afternoon, my Lord?'

'No. Go ahead on out and dent Sir Olart's armour a bit. He's got an exaggerated notion of his own skill. Give him some instruction in the virtue of humility.'

'I'm *really* hungry, Sparhawk,' Talen complained.

'All right. Let's go to the kitchen.' Sparhawk looked critically at his young friend. 'Then I guess we'll have to send for the tailor again,' he added. 'You're growing like a weed.'

'It's not my idea.'

Khalad started to saddle his horse, and Sparhawk and Talen went into the palace in search of food. It was about an hour later when the two of them entered the royal apartment to find Ehlana, Mirtai and Danae sitting by the fire. Ehlana was leafing through some documents. Danae was playing with Rollo, and Mirtai was sharpening one of her daggers.

'Well,' Ehlana said, looking up from the documents, 'if it isn't my noble prince consort and my wandering page.'

Talen bowed. Then he sniffed loudly.

'Use your handkerchief,' Mirtai told him.

'Yes, ma'am.'

'How are your mothers?' Ehlana asked the young man. Everyone, perhaps unconsciously, used that phrasing when speaking to Talen and his half-brothers. In a very real sense, though, the usage reflected reality. Aslade and Elys mothered Kurik's five sons excessively and impartially.

'Meddlesome, my Queen,' Talen replied. 'It's not really a good idea to get sick in that house. In the last week I think I've been dosed with every cold remedy known to man.' A peculiar, squeaky noise came from somewhere in the general vicinity of the young man's midsection.

38

'Is that your stomach?' Mirtai asked him. 'Are you hungry again?'

'No. I just ate. I probably won't get hungry again for at least fifteen minutes.' Talen put one hand to the front of his doublet. 'The little beast was being so quiet I almost forgot it was there.' He went over to Danae, who was tying the strings of a little bonnet under the chin of her stuffed toy. 'I've brought a present for you, Princess,' he said.

Her eyes brightened. She set Rollo aside and sat waiting expectantly.

'But no kissing,' he added. 'Just a "thank you" will do. I've got a cold, and you don't want to catch it.'

'What did you bring me?' she asked eagerly.

'Oh, just a little something I found under a bush out on the road. It's a little wet and muddy, but you can dry it out and brush it off, I suppose. It's not much, but I thought you might like it – just a little.' Talen was underplaying it for all he was worth.

'Could I see it, please?' she begged.

'Oh, I suppose so.' He reached inside his doublet, took out a rather bedraggled grey kitten and sat it on the floor in front of her. The kitten had mackerel stripes, a spiky tail, large ears and an intently curious look in its blue eyes. It took a tentative step toward its new mistress.

Danae squealed with delight, picked up the kitten and hugged it to her cheek. 'I *love* it!!' she exclaimed.

'There go the draperies,' Mirtai said with resignation. 'Kittens always want to climb the drapes.'

Talen skilfully fended off Sparhawk's exuberant little daughter. 'The cold, Danae,' the boy warned. 'I've got a cold, remember?' Sparhawk was certain that his daughter would grow more skilled with the passage of time and that it wouldn't be very long until Talen would no longer be able to evade her affection. The kitten had been no more than a gesture, Sparhawk was certain – some spur-of-the-moment impulse to which Talen had given no thought whatsoever. It rather effectively sealed the young man's fate, however. A few days before, Sparhawk had idly wondered where *he* had made the mistake that had permanently attached his wife's affection to him. He realised that this scruffy-looking kitten was Talen's mistake – or at least one of them. Sparhawk mentally shrugged. Talen would make an adequate son-in-law – once Danae had trained him.

'Is it all right, your Majesty?' Talen was asking the queen. 'For her to have the kitten, I mean?'

'Isn't it just a little late to be asking that question, Talen?' Ehlana replied.

'Oh, I don't know,' he said impudently. 'I thought I'd timed it just about right.'

Ehlana looked at her daughter, who was snuggling the kitten against her face. All cats are born opportunists. The kitten patted the little girl's cheek with one soft paw and then nuzzled. Kittens are expert nuzzlers.

'How can I say no after you've already given it to her, Talen?'

'It *would* be a little difficult, wouldn't it, your Majesty?' The boy sniffed loudly.

Mirtai rose to her feet, put her dagger away and crossed the room to Talen. She reached out her hand, and he flinched away.

'Oh, stop that,' she told him. She laid her hand on his forehead. 'You've got a fever.'

'I didn't get it on purpose.'

'We'd better get him to bed, Mirtai,' Ehlana said, rising from her chair.

'We should sweat him first,' the giantess said. 'I'll take him to the bathhouse and steam him for a while.' She took Talen's arm, firmly.

40

'You're not going into the bathhouse with me!' he protested, his face suddenly aflame.

'Be quiet,' she commanded. 'Send word to the cooks, Ehlana. Have them stir up a mustard plaster and boil up some chicken soup. When I bring him back from the bathhouse, we'll put the mustard plaster on his chest, pop him into bed and spoon soup into him.'

'Are you going to just stand there and let them do this to me, Sparhawk?' Talen appealed.

'I'd like to help you, my friend,' Sparhawk replied, 'but I've got my own health to consider too, you know.'

'I wish I was dead,' Talen groaned as Mirtai pulled him from the room.

Stragen and Ulath arrived from Emsat a few days later and were immediately escorted to the royal apartment. 'You're getting fat, Sparhawk,' Ulath said bluntly, removing his ogre-horned helmet.

'I've put on a few pounds,' Sparhawk conceded.

'Soft living,' Ulath grunted disapprovingly.

'How's Wargun?' Ehlana asked the huge blond Thalesian.

'His mind's gone,' Ulath replied sadly. 'They've got him locked up in the west wing of the palace. He spends most of his time raving.'

Ehlana sighed. 'I always rather liked him – when he was sober.'

'I doubt that you'll feel the same way about his son, your Majesty,' Stragen told her dryly. Like Platime, Stragen was a thief, but he had much better manners.

'I've never met him,' Ehlana said.

'You might consider adding that to your next prayer of thanksgiving, your Majesty. His name's Avin – a short and insignificant name for a short and insignificant fellow. He doesn't show very much promise.'

'Is he really that bad?' Ehlana asked Ulath.

'Avin Wargunsson? Stragen's being generous. Avin's a little man who spends all his time trying to make sure that people don't overlook him. When he found out that I was coming here, he called me to the palace and gave me a royal communication to bring to you. He spent two hours trying to impress me.'

'Were you impressed?'

'Not particularly, no.' Ulath reached inside his surcoat and drew out a folded and sealed sheet of parchment.

'What does it say?' she asked.

'I wouldn't know. I don't read other people's mail. My guess is that it's a serious discussion of the weather. Avin Wargunsson's desperately afraid that people might forget about him, so every traveller who leaves Emsat is loaded down with royal greetings.'

'How was the trip?' Sparhawk asked them.

'I can't really say that I'd recommend sea travel at this time of year,' Stragen replied. His icy blue eyes hardened. 'I want to have a talk with Platime. Ulath and I were set upon by some brigands in the mountains between here and Cardos. Bandits are supposed to know better than that.'

'They aren't professionals,' Sparhawk told him. 'Platime knows about them, and he's going to take steps. Were there any problems?'

'Not for us,' Ulath shrugged. 'The amateurs out there didn't have a very good day, though. We left five of them in a ditch, and then the rest all remembered an important engagement somewhere else.' He went to the door and looked out into the hall. Then he closed the door and looked around, his eyes wary. 'Are there any servants or people like that in any of your rooms here, Sparhawk?' he asked.

'Mirtai and our daughter is all.'

'That's all right. I think we can trust them. Komier sent me to let you know that Avin Wargunsson's been in contact with Count Gerrich down in Lamorkand. Gerrich's taking a run at King Friedahl's throne, and Avin's not quite bright. He doesn't know enough to stay out of the internal squabbles in Lamorkand. Komier thinks there might just possibly be some sort of secret arrangement between them. Patriarch Bersten's taking the same message to Chyrellos.'

'Count Gerrich's going to start to irritate Dolmant if he doesn't watch what he's doing,' Ehlana said. 'He's trying to make alliances every time he turns around, and he knows that's a violation of the rules. Lamork civil wars aren't supposed to involve other kingdoms.'

'That's an actual rule?' Stragen asked her incredulously.

'Of course. It's been in place for a thousand years. If the Lamork barons were free to form alliances with nobles in other kingdoms, they'd plunge the continent into war every ten years. That used to happen until the Church stepped in and told them to stop.'

'And you thought *our* society had peculiar rules,' Stragen laughed to Platime.

'This is entirely different, Milord Stragen,' Ehlana told him in a lofty tone. '*Our* peculiarities are matters of state policy. Yours are simply good common sense. There's a world of difference.'

'So I gather.'

Sparhawk was looking at all three of them when it happened, so there was no doubt that when *he* felt that peculiar chill and caught that faint flicker of darkness at the very outer edge of his vision, they did as well.

'Sparhawk!' Ehlana cried in alarm.

'Yes,' he replied. 'I know. I saw it too.'

Stragen had half-drawn his rapier, his hand moving with cat-like speed. 'What is it?' he demanded, looking around the room.

'An impossibility,' Ehlana said flatly. The look she gave her husband was a little less certain, however. 'Isn't it, Sparhawk?' Her voice trembled slightly.

'I certainly thought so,' he replied.

'This isn't the time to be cryptic,' Stragen said.

Then they all relaxed as the chill and the shadow passed.

Ulath looked speculatively at Sparhawk. 'Was that what I thought it was?' he asked.

'So it seems.'

'Will someone please tell me what's going on here?' Stragen demanded.

'Do you remember that cloud that followed us up in Pelosia?' Ulath said.

'Of course. But that was Azash, wasn't it?'

'No. We thought so, but Aphrael told us that we were wrong. That was after you came back here, so you probably didn't hear about it. That shadow we just saw was the Troll-Gods. They're inside the Bhelliom.'

'Inside?'

'They needed a place to hide after they'd lost a few arguments with the Younger Gods of Styricum.'

Stragen looked at Sparhawk. 'I thought you told me that you'd thrown Bhelliom into the sea.'

'We did.'

'And the Troll-Gods can't get out of it?'

'That's what we were led to believe.'

'You should have found a deeper ocean.'

'There aren't any deeper ones.'

'That's too bad. It looks as if someone's managed to fish it out.'

'It's logical, Sparhawk,' Ulath said. 'That box was lined with gold, and Aphrael told us that the gold would keep Bhelliom from getting out on its own. Since the Troll-Gods can't get out of Bhelliom, they were down there too. Somebody's found that box.'

'I've heard that the people who dive for pearls can go down quite deep,' Stragen said.

'Not *that* deep,' Sparhawk said. 'Besides, there's something wrong.'

'Are you just now realising that?' Stragen asked him.

'That's not what I mean. When we were up in Pelosia, you could all see that cloud.'

'Oh, yes,' Ulath said fervently.

'But before that – when it was just a shadow – only Ehlana and I could see it, and that was because we were wearing the rings. This was definitely a shadow and not a cloud, wasn't it?'

'Yes,' Stragen admitted.

'Then how is it that you and Ulath could see it too?'

Stragen spread his hands helplessly.

'There's something else too,' Sparhawk added. 'The night I came home from Lamorkand, I felt something in the street watching me – several somethings. They weren't Elene or Styric, and I don't think they were human. That shadow that just passed through here felt exactly the same.'

'I wish there was some way we could talk with Sephrenia,' Ulath muttered.

Sparhawk was fairly certain that there *was* a way, but he was not free to reveal it to any of them.

'Do we tell anybody else about this?' Stragen asked.

'Let's not start a panic until we find out some more about it,' Sparhawk decided.

'Right,' Stragen agreed. 'There's always plenty of time for panic later – plenty of reason too, I think.'

The weather cleared over the next few days, and that fact alone lifted spirits in the palace. Sparhawk spent some time closeted with Platime and Stragen, and then the two thieves sent men into Lamorkand to investigate the situation there. 'That's what I should have done in the first place,' Sparhawk said, 'but Sarathi wouldn't give me the chance. Our revered Archprelate has a few blind spots. He can't seem to get it through his head that *official* investigators aren't going to ever really get to the bottom of things.'

'Typical aristocratic ineptitude,' Stragen drawled. 'It's one of the things that makes life easier for people like Platime and me.'

Sparhawk didn't argue with him about that. 'Just tell your men to be careful,' he cautioned them. 'Lamorks tend to try to solve all their problems with daggers, and dead spies don't bring home very much useful information.'

'Astonishing insight there, old boy,' Stragen said, his rich voice dripping with irony. 'It's absolutely amazing that Platime and I never thought of that.'

'All right,' Sparhawk admitted, 'maybe I was being just a little obvious.'

'We saw that too, didn't we, Platime?'

Platime grunted. 'Tell Ehlana that I'm going to be away from the palace for a few days, Sparhawk.'

'Where are you going?'

'None of your business. There's something I want to take care of.'

'All right, but keep in touch.'

'You're being obvious again, Sparhawk.' The fat man scratched his paunch. 'I'll talk with Talen. He'll know how to get in touch with me if the queen really needs me for something.' He groaned as he hauled himself to his feet. 'I'm going to have to lose some weight,' he said half to himself. Then he waddled to the door with that peculiarly spraddle-legged gait of the grossly obese.

'He's in a charming humour today,' Sparhawk noted.

'He's got a lot on his mind just now,' Stragen shrugged.

'How well-connected are you in the palace at Emsat, Stragen?'

'I have some contacts there. What do you need?'

'I'd like to put some stumbling blocks in the way of this accommodation between Avin and Count Gerrich. Gerrich's beginning to get a little too much influence in northern Eosia. Maybe you ought to get word to Meland in Acie as well. Gerrich's making alliances in Pelosia and Thalesia already. It doesn't seem reasonable that he'd overlook Deira, and Deira's a little chaotic right now. Ask Meland to keep his eyes open.'

'This Gerrich's really got you concerned, hasn't he?'

'There are some things going on in Lamorkand that I don't understand, Stragen, and I don't want Gerrich to get too far ahead of me while I'm trying to sort them out.'

'That makes sense – I suppose.'

Khalad came to his feet with his eyes slightly unfocused and with a thin dribble of blood coming out of his nose.

'You see? You over-extended again,' Mirtai told him.

'How did you do that?' Sparhawk's squire asked her.

'I'll show you. Kalten, come here.'

'Not me,' the blond Pandion refused, backing away.

'Don't be foolish. I'm not going to hurt you.'

'Isn't that what you told Khalad before you bounced him off the flagstones?'

'You might as well do as I tell you, Kalten,' she said. 'You'll wind up doing it in the end anyway, and it won't be nearly as painful for you if you don't argue with me. Take out your sword and stab me in the heart with it.'

'I don't want to hurt you, Mirtai.'

'*You?* Hurt *me?*' Her laugh was sardonic.

'You don't have to be insulting about it,' he said in an injured tone, drawing his sword.

It had all begun when Mirtai had passed through the palace courtyard while Kalten was giving Khalad some instruction in swordsmanship. She had made a couple

47

of highly unflattering comments. One thing had led to another, and the end result had been this impromptu training session, during which Kalten and Khalad learned humility, if nothing else.

'Stab me through the heart, Kalten,' Mirtai said again.

In Kalten's defence it should be noted in passing that he really *did* try. He made a great deal of noise when he came down on his back on the flagstones.

'He made the same mistake you did,' Mirtai pointed out to Khalad. 'He straightened his arm too much. A straight arm is a locked arm. Always keep your elbow slightly bent.'

'We're trained to thrust from the shoulder, Mirtai,' Khalad explained.

'There are a lot of Elenes, I suppose,' she shrugged. 'It shouldn't be all that hard to replace you. The thing that makes me curious is why you all feel that it's necessary to stick your sword all the way through somebody. If you haven't hit the heart with the first six inches of the blade, another yard or so of steel going through the same hole won't make much difference, will it?'

'Maybe it's because it looks dramatic,' Khalad said.

'You kill people for show? That's contemptible, and it's the sort of thinking that fills graveyards. Always keep your blade free so that you're ready for your next enemy. People fold up when you run swords through them, and then you have to kick the body off the blade before you can use it again.'

'I'll try to remember that.'

'I hope so. I rather like you, and I hate burying friends.' She bent, professionally peeled Kalten's eyelid back and glanced at his glazed eyeball. 'You'd better throw a bucket of water on our friend here,' she suggested. 'He hasn't learned how to fall yet. We'll go into that next time.'

'*Next* time?'

'Of course. If you're going to learn how to do this, you'd better learn how to do it right.' She gave Sparhawk a challenging look. 'Would you like to try?' she asked him.

'Ah – no, Mirtai, not right now. Thanks all the same, though.'

She went on into the palace, looking just slightly pleased with herself.

'You know, I don't think I really want to be a knight after all, Sparhawk,' Talen said from nearby. 'It looks awfully painful.'

'Where have you been? My wife's got people out looking for you.'

'Yes. I saw them blundering around out in the streets. I had to go visit Platime in the cellar.'

'Oh?'

'He picked up something he thought you ought to be aware of. You know those unauthorised bandits in the hills near Cardos?'

'Not personally, no.'

'Funny, Sparhawk. Very funny. Platime's found out that somebody we know is sort of directing their activities.'

'Oh? Who's that?'

'Can you believe that it's Krager? You should have killed him when you had the chance, Sparhawk.'

CHAPTER 3

The fog drifted in from the river not long after the sun went down that evening. The nights in Cimmura were always foggy in the spring when it wasn't raining. Sparhawk, Stragen and Talen left the palace wearing plain clothing and heavy traveller's cloaks and rode to the southeast quarter of town.

'You don't necessarily have to tell your wife I said this, Sparhawk,' Stragen noted, looking around with distaste, 'but her capital's one of the least attractive cities in the world. You've got a truly miserable climate here.'

'It's not so bad in the summer-time,' Sparhawk replied a little defensively.

'I missed last summer,' the blond thief said. 'I took a short nap one afternoon and slept right through it. Where are we going?'

'We want to see Platime.'

'As I recall, his cellar's near the west gate of the city. You're taking us in the wrong direction.'

'We have to go to a certain inn first.' Sparhawk looked back over his shoulder. 'Are we being followed, Talen?' he asked.

'Naturally.'

Sparhawk grunted. 'That's more or less what I expected.'

They rode on with the thick mist swirling around the legs of their horses and making the fronts of the nearby houses dim and hazy-looking. They reached the inn on Rose Street, and a surly-appearing porter admitted them to the inn yard and closed the gate behind them.

'Anything you find out about this place isn't for

general dissemination,' Sparhawk told Talen and Stragen as he dismounted. He handed Faran's reins to the porter. 'You know about this horse, don't you, brother?' he warned the man.

'He's a legend, Sparhawk,' the porter replied. 'The things you wanted are in the room at the top of the stairs.'

'How's the crowd in the tavern tonight?'

'Loud, smelly and mostly drunk.'

'There's nothing new about that. What I meant, though, was how many of them are there?'

'Fifteen or twenty. There are three of our men in there who know what to do.'

'Good. Thank you, Sir Knight.'

'You're welcome, Sir Knight.'

Sparhawk led Talen and Stragen up the stairs.

'This inn, I gather, isn't altogether what it seems,' Stragen observed.

'The Pandions own it,' Talen told him. 'They come here when they don't want to attract attention.'

'There's a little more to it than that,' Sparhawk told him. He opened the door at the top of the stairs, and the three of them entered.

Stragen looked at the workmen's smocks hanging on pegs near the door. 'We're going to resort to subterfuge, I see.'

'It's fairly standard practice,' Sparhawk shrugged. 'Let's get changed. I'd sort of like to get back to the palace before my wife sends out search parties.'

The smocks were of blue canvas, worn and patched and with a few artfully-placed smudges on them. There were woollen leggings as well and thick-soled workmen's boots. The caps were baggy affairs, designed more to keep off weather than they were for appearance.

'You're going to have to leave that here,' Sparhawk said, pointing at Stragen's rapier. 'It's a little obvious.'

The big Pandion tucked a heavy dagger under his belt.

'You know that there are people watching the gate of the inn, don't you, Sparhawk?' Talen said.

'I hope they enjoy their evening. We aren't going out through the gate, though.' Sparhawk led them back down to the inn yard, crossed to a narrow door in a side wall and opened it. The warm air that boiled out through the doorway smelled of stale beer and unwashed bodies. The three of them went inside and closed the door behind them. They seemed to be in a small storeroom. The straw on the floor was mouldy.

'Where are we?' Talen whispered.

'In a tavern,' Sparhawk replied softly. 'There's going to be a fight in just a few minutes. We'll slip out into the main room during the confusion.' He went to the curtained doorway leading out into the tavern and twitched the curtain several times. 'All right,' he whispered. 'We'll mingle with the crowd during the fight, and after a while, we'll leave. Behave as if you're slightly drunk, but don't over-do it.'

'I'm impressed,' Stragen said.

'I'm more than impressed,' Talen added. 'Not even Platime knows that there's more than one way out of that inn.'

The fight began not long after that. It was noisy, involving a great deal of shouting and pushing and finally a few blows. Two totally uninvolved and evidently innocent by-standers were knocked senseless during the course of the altercation. Sparhawk and his friends smoothly insinuated themselves into the crowd, and after ten minutes or so, they reeled out through the door.

'A little unprofessional,' Stragen sniffed. 'A staged fight shouldn't involve the spectators that way.'

'It should when the spectators might be looking for something other than a few tankards of ale,' Sparhawk disagreed. 'The two who fell asleep weren't regular patrons in the tavern. They might have been completely innocent, but then again, they might not. This way, we don't have to worry about them trailing along behind us.'

'There's more to being a Pandion Knight than I thought,' Talen noted. 'I may like it after all.'

They walked through the foggy streets towards the rundown quarter near the west gate, a maze of interconnecting lanes and unpaved alleys. They entered one of those alleys and went through it to a flight of muddy stone stairs leading down. A thick-bodied man lounged against the stone wall beside the stairs. 'You're late,' he said to Talen in a flat voice.

'We had to make sure we weren't being followed,' the boy shrugged.

'Go on down,' the man told them. 'Platime's waiting.'

The cellar hadn't changed. It was still smoky and dim, and it was filled with a babble of coarse voices coming from the thieves, whores and cutthroats who lived there.

'I don't know how Platime can stand this place,' Stragen shuddered.

Platime sat enthroned on a large chair on the other side of a smoky fire burning in an open pit. He heaved himself to his feet when he saw Sparhawk. 'Where have you been?' he bellowed in a thunderous voice.

'Making sure that we weren't followed,' Sparhawk replied.

The fat man grunted. 'He's back here,' he said, leading them toward the rear of the cellar. 'He's very interested in his health at the moment, so I'm keeping him more or less out of sight.' He pushed his way into a small, closet-like chamber where a man sat on a stool nursing a tankard of watery beer. The man was a small,

53

nervous-looking fellow with thinning hair and a cring-
ing manner.

'This is Pelk,' Platime said. 'He's a sneak-thief. I sent
him to Cardos to have a look around and to see what
he could find out about some people we're interested
in. Tell him what you found out, Pelk.'

'Well sir, good masters,' the weedy man began, 'it tuk
me a goodly while to git close to them fellers, I'll tell the
world, but I made myself useful, an' they finally sort of
assepted me. They was all sorts of rigimarole I had to
go thoo – swearin' oaths an' gettin' blindfolded the first
couple times they tuk me to ther camp an all, but after
a while, they kinda let down ther guard, an' I come an'
went purty much as I pleased. Like Platime prob'ly tole
you, we figgered at first they wuz jist a buncha amachoors what didn't know nothin' about the way things
is supposed to be did. We sees that sorta thing all the
time, don't we, Platime? Them's the kind as gits therselves caught an' hung.'

'And good riddance to them,' Platime growled.

'Well sir,' Pelk continued, 'like I say, me'n Platime,
we figgered as how them fellers in the mountings was
jist a buncha them amachoors I tole you about – fellers
what'd took up cuttin' th'oats fer fun an' profit, don't
y'know. As she turns out, howsomever, they was
more'n that. Ther leaders was six er seven noblemen as
was real disappointed 'bout the way the big plans of the
Primate Annias fell on ther faces, an' they was powerful
unhappy 'bout what the queen had writ down on the
warrants she put out fer 'em – nobles not bein' accustomed to bein' called them sorta names.

'Well sir, t' short it up some, these here noblemen all
run off into the mountings 'bout one jump ahead of the
hangman, an' they tuk t' robbin' travellers t' make ends
meet an' spent the resta ther time thinkin' up nasty
names t' call the queen.'

'Get to the point, Pelk,' Platime told him wearily.

'Yessir, I wuz jist about to. Well now, it went on like that fer a spell, an' then this here Krager feller, he come into camp, an' some of them there nobles, they knowed him. He tole 'em as how he knowed some furriners as'd help 'em out iffn they'd raise enough fuss here in Elenia t' keep the queen an' her folks from gittin' too curious 'bout some stuff what's goin' on off in Lamorkand. This here Krager feller, he sez as how this stuff in Lamorkand might just could be a way fer 'em all t' change the way ther forchunes bin goin' since ol' Annias got hisself kilt. Well, sir, them dukes an' earls an' such got real inner-ested at that point, an' they tole us all t' go talk t' the local peasants an' t' start runnin' down the tax-collectors an' t' say as how it ain't natural fer no country t' be run by no woman an' the like. We wuz supposed t' stir up them peasants an' t' git 'em t' talkin' among therselves 'bout how the people oughtta all git together an' thow the queen out an' the like, an' then them nobles, they caught a few tax collectors an' hung 'em an' give the money back t' the folks it'd been stole from in the first place, an' them peasants, they wuz all happy as pigs in mud 'bout that.' Pelk scratched at his head. 'Well sir, I guess I've said m'piece now. At's the way she stands in the mountlings now. This here Krager feller, he's got some money with 'im, an' he's mighty free with it, so them nobles what's bin on short rations is gettin' down-right fond of 'im.'

'Pelk,' Sparhawk told him, 'you're a treasure.' He gave the man several coins, and then he and his friends left the cubicle.

'What are we going to do about it, Sparhawk?' Platime asked.

'We're going to take steps,' Sparhawk replied. 'How many of these "liberators" are there?'

'A hundred or so.'

'I'll need a couple dozen of your men who know the country.'

Platime nodded. 'Are you going to bring in the army?'

'I don't think so. I think a troop of Pandions might make a more lasting impression on people who think they have grievances against our queen, don't you?'

'Isn't that just a bit extreme?' Stragen asked him.

'I want to make a statement, Stragen. I want everybody in Elenia to know just how much I disapprove of people who start plotting against my wife. I don't want to have to do it again, so I'm going to do it right the first time.'

'He didn't *actually* talk like that, did he, Sparhawk?' Ehlana asked incredulously.

'That's fairly close,' Sparhawk told her. 'Stragen's got a very good ear for dialect.'

'It's almost hypnotic, isn't it?' she marvelled, 'and it goes on and on and on.' She suddenly grinned impishly. 'Write down "happy as pigs in mud", Lenda. I may want to find a way to work that into some official communication.'

'As you wish, your Majesty.' Lenda's tone was neutral, but Sparhawk knew that the old courtier disapproved.

'What are we going to do about this?' the queen asked.

'Sparhawk said that he was going to take steps, your Majesty,' Talen told her. 'You might not want to know too many details.'

'Sparhawk and I don't keep secrets from each other, Talen.'

'I'm not talking about secrets, your Majesty,' the boy replied innocently. 'I'm just talking about boring unimportant little things you shouldn't really waste your time

56

on.' He made it sound very plausible, but Ehlana looked more than a little suspicious.

'Don't embarrass me, Sparhawk,' she warned.

'Of course not,' he replied blandly.

The campaign was brief. Since Pelk knew the precise location of the camp of the dissidents, and Platime's men knew all the other hiding places in the surrounding mountains, there was no real place for the bandits to run, and they were certainly no match for the thirty black-armoured Pandions Sparhawk, Kalten and Ulath led against them. The surviving nobles were held for the queen's justice and the rest of the outlaws were turned over to the local sheriff for disposition.

'Well, my Lord of Belton,' Sparhawk said to an earl crouched before him on a log, with a blood-stained bandage around his head and his hands bound behind him. 'Things didn't turn out so well, did they?'

'Curse you, Sparhawk.' Belton spat, squinting up against the afternoon's brightness. 'How did you find out where we were?'

'My dear Belton,' Sparhawk laughed, 'you didn't *really* think you could hide from my wife, did you? She takes a very personal interest in her kingdom. She knows every tree, every town and village and all of the peasants. It's even rumoured that she knows most of the deer by their first names.'

'Why didn't you come after us earlier then?' Belton sneered.

'The queen was busy. She finally found the time to make some decisions about you and your friends. I don't imagine you'll care much for these decisions, old boy. What I'm really interested in is any information you might have about Krager. He and I haven't seen each other for quite some time, and I find myself yearning for his company again.'

Belton's eyes grew frightened. 'You won't get anything from me, Sparhawk,' he blustered.

'How much would you care to wager on that?' Kalten asked him. 'You'd save yourself a great deal of unpleasantness if you told Sparhawk what he wants to know, and Krager's not so loveable that you'd really want to go through that in order to protect him.'

'Just talk, Belton,' Sparhawk insisted implacably.

'I – I *can't*!' Belton's sneering bravado crumbled. His face turned deathly pale, and he began to tremble violently. 'Sparhawk, I beg of you. It means my life if I say anything.'

'Your life isn't worth very much right now anyway,' Ulath told him bluntly. 'One way or another, you *are* going to talk.'

'For God's sake, Sparhawk! You don't know what you're asking!'

'I'm not *asking*, Belton.' Sparhawk's face was bleak.

Then, without any warning or reason, a deathly chill suddenly enveloped the woods, and the mid-afternoon sun darkened. Sparhawk glanced upward. The sky was very blue, but the sun appeared wan and sickly.

Belton screamed.

An inky cloud seemed to spring from the surrounding trees, coalescing around the shrieking prisoner. Sparhawk jumped back with a startled oath, his hand going to his sword-hilt.

Belton's voice had risen to a screech, and there were horrible sounds coming from the impenetrable darkness surrounding him – sounds of breaking bones and tearing flesh. The shrieking broke off quite suddenly, but the sounds continued for several eternal-seeming minutes. Then, as quickly as it had come, the cloud vanished.

Sparhawk recoiled in revulsion. His prisoner had been torn to pieces.

'Good God!' Kalten gasped. 'What happened?'

'We both know, Kalten,' Sparhawk replied. 'We've seen it before. Don't try to question any of the other prisoners. I'm almost positive they won't be allowed to answer.'

There were five of them, Sparhawk, Ehlana, Kalten, Ulath and Stragen. They had gathered in the royal apartments, and their mood was bleak.

'Was it the same cloud?' Stragen asked intently.

'There were some differences,' Sparhawk replied. 'It was more in the way it felt rather than anything I could really pin down.'

'Why would the Troll-Gods be so interested in protecting Krager?' Ehlana asked, her face puzzled.

'I don't think it's Krager they're protecting,' Sparhawk replied. 'I think it has something to do with what's going on in Lamorkand.' He slammed his fist down on the arm of his chair. 'I *wish* Sephrenia were here!' he burst out with a sudden oath. 'All we're doing is groping in the dark.'

'Would you be opposed to logic at this point?' Stragen asked him.

'I wouldn't even be opposed to astrology just now,' Sparhawk replied sourly.

'All right.' The blond Thalesian thief rose to his feet and began to pace up and down, his eyes thoughtful. 'First of all, we know that somehow the Troll-Gods have got out of that box.'

'Actually, you haven't really proved that, Stragen,' Ulath disagreed. 'Not logically, anyway.'

Stragen stopped pacing. 'He's right, you know,' he admitted. 'We've been basing that conclusion on a guess. All we can say with any logical certainty is that we've encountered something that looks and feels like a manifestation of the Troll-Gods. Would you accept that, Sir Ulath?'

'I suppose I could go that far, Milord Stragen.'

'I'm so happy. Do we know of anything else that does the same sort of things?'

'No,' Ulath replied, 'but that's not really relevant. We don't know about everything. There could be dozens of things we don't know about that take the form of shadows or clouds, tear people all to pieces and give humans a chilly feeling when they're around.'

'I'm not sure that logic is really getting us anywhere,' Stragen conceded.

'There's nothing wrong with your logic, Stragen,' Ehlana told him. 'Your major premise is faulty, that's all.'

'You too, your Majesty?' Kalten groaned. 'I thought there was at least one other person in the room who relied on common sense rather than all this tedious logic.'

'All right then, Sir Kalten,' she said tartly, 'what does your common sense tell you?'

'Well, first off, it tells me that you're all going at the problem backwards. The question we should be asking is what makes Krager so special that something supernatural would go out of its way to protect him? Does it really matter *what* the supernatural thing is at the moment?'

'He might have something there, you know?' Ulath said. 'Krager's a cockroach basically. His only real reason for existing is to be stepped on.'

'I'm not so sure,' Ehlana disagreed. 'Krager worked for Martel, and Martel worked for Annias.'

'Actually, dear, it was the other way around,' Sparhawk corrected her.

She waved that distinction aside. 'Belton and the

60

others were all allied to Annias, and Krager used to carry messages between Annias and Martel. Belton and his cohorts would almost certainly have known Krager. Pelk's story more or less confirms that. That's what made Krager important in the first place.' She paused, frowning. 'But what made him important *after* the renegades were all in custody?'

'Backtracking,' Ulath grunted.

'I beg your pardon?' The queen looked baffled.

'This whatever-it-is didn't want us to be able to trace Krager back to his present employer.'

'Oh, that's obvious, Ulath,' Kalten snorted. 'His employer is Count Gerrich. Pelk told Sparhawk that there was somebody in Lamorkand who wanted to keep us so busy here in Elenia that we wouldn't have time to take any steps to put down all the turmoil over there. That *has* to be Gerrich.'

'You're just guessing, Kalten,' Ulath said. 'You could very well be right, but it's still just a guess.'

'Do you see what I mean about logic?' Kalten demanded of them. 'What do you want, Ulath? A signed confession from Gerrich himself?'

'Do you have one handy? All I'm saying is that we ought to keep an open mind. I don't think we should close any doors yet, that's all.'

There was a firm knock on the door, and it opened immediately afterward. Mirtai looked in. 'Bevier and Tynian are here,' she announced.

'They're supposed to be in Rendor,' Sparhawk said. 'What are they doing here?'

'Why don't you ask them?' Mirtai suggested pointedly. 'They're right out here in the corridor.'

The two knights entered the room. Sir Bevier was a slim, olive-skinned Arcian, and Sir Tynian a blond, burly Deiran. Both were in full armour.

'How are things in Rendor?' Kalten asked them.

61

'Hot, dry, dusty, hysterical,' Tynian replied. 'Rendor never changes. You know that.'

Bevier dropped to one knee before Ehlana. Despite the best efforts of his friends, the young Cyrinic Knight was still painfully formal. 'Your Majesty,' he murmured respectfully.

'Oh, do stand up, my dear Bevier,' she smiled at him. 'We're friends, so there's no need for that. Besides, you creak like a rusty iron-works when you kneel.'

'Overtrained, perhaps, your Majesty,' he admitted.

'What are you two doing back here?' Sparhawk asked them.

'Carrying dispatches,' Tynian replied. 'Darrellon's running things down there, and he wants the other preceptors kept abreast of things. We're also supposed to go on to Chyrellos and brief the Archprelate.'

'How's the campaign going?' Kalten asked them.

'Badly,' Tynian shrugged. 'The Rendorish rebels aren't really organised, so there aren't any armies for us to meet. They hide amongst the population and come out at night to set fires and assassinate priests. Then they run back into their holes. We take reprisals the next day – burn villages, slaughter herds of sheep and the like. None of it really proves anything.'

'Do they have any kind of a leader as yet?' Sparhawk asked.

'They're still discussing that,' Bevier said dryly. 'The discussions are quite spirited. We usually find several dead candidates in the alleys every morning.'

'Sarathi blundered,' Tynian said.

Bevier gasped.

'I'm not trying to offend your religious sensibilities, my young friend,' Tynian said, 'but it's the truth. Most of the clergymen he sent to Rendor were much more interested in punishment than in reconciliation. We had a chance for real peace in Rendor, and it fell apart

62

because Dolmant didn't send somebody down there to keep a leash on the missionaries.' Tynian set his helmet on a table and unbuckled his sword-belt. 'I even saw one silly ass in a cassock tearing the veils off women in the street. After the crowd seized him, he tried to order me to protect him. *That's* the kind of priests the church has been sending to Rendor.'

'What did you do?' Stragen asked him.

'For some reason I couldn't quite hear what he was saying,' Tynian replied. 'All the noise the crowd was making, more than likely.'

'What did they do to him?' Kalten grinned.

'They hanged him. Quite a neat job, actually.'

'You didn't even go to his defence?' Bevier exclaimed.

'Our instructions were very explicit, Bevier. We were told to protect the clergy against unprovoked attacks. That idiot violated the modesty of about a dozen Rendorish women. That crowd had plenty of provocation. The silly ass had it coming. If that crowd hadn't hanged him, I probably would have. That's what Darrellon wants us to suggest to Sarathi. He thinks the Church should pull all those fanatic missionaries out of Rendor until things quiet down. Then he suggests that we send in a new batch – a slightly less fervent one.' The Alcione Knight laid his sword down beside his helmet and lowered himself into a chair. 'What's been happening here?' he asked.

'Why don't the rest of you fill them in?' Sparhawk suggested. 'There's someone I want to talk with for a few minutes.' He turned and quietly went back into the royal apartment.

The person he wanted to talk with was not some court functionary, but rather his own daughter. He found her playing with her kitten. After some thought, her Royal little Highness had decided to name the small animal 'Mmrr', a sound which, when she uttered it, sounded so much like the kitten's purr that Sparhawk usually couldn't tell for sure which of them was making it. Princess Danae had many gifts.

'We need to talk,' Sparhawk told her, closing the door behind him as he entered.

'What is it now, Sparhawk?' she asked.

'Tynian and Bevier just arrived.'

'Yes. I know.'

'Are you playing with things again? Are you deliberately gathering all our friends here?'

'Of course I am, father.'

'Would you mind telling me why?'

'There's something we're going to need to do before long. I thought I'd save some time by getting everybody here in advance.'

'You'd probably better tell me what it is that we have to do.'

'I'm not supposed to do that.'

'You never pay any attention to any of the *other* rules.'

'This is different, father. We're absolutely not supposed to talk about the future. If you think about it for a moment, I'm sure you'll see why. Ouch!' Mmrr had bitten her finger. Danae spoke sharply with the kitten – a series of little growls, a meow or two and concluding with a forgiving purr. The kitten managed to look slightly ashamed of itself and proceeded to lick the injured finger.

'Please don't talk in cat, Danae,' Sparhawk said in a pained tone. 'If some chambermaid hears you, it'll take us both a month to explain.'

'Nobody's going to hear me, Sparhawk. You've got something else on your mind, haven't you?'

'I want to talk with Sephrenia. There are some things I don't understand, and I need her help with them.'

'I'll help you, father.'

64

He shook his head. 'Your explanations of things always leave me with more questions than I had when we started. Can you get in touch with Sephrenia for me?'

She looked around. 'It probably wouldn't be a good idea here in the palace, father,' she told him. 'It involves something that might be hard to explain if someone overheard us.'

'You're going to be in two places at the same time again?'

'Well – sort of.' She picked up her kitten. 'Why don't you find some excuse to take me out for a ride tomorrow morning? We'll go out of the city and I can take care of things there. Tell mother that you want to give me a riding lesson.'

'You don't have a pony, Danae.'

She gave him an angelic smile. 'My goodness,' she said, 'that sort of means that you're going to have to give me one, doesn't it?'

He gave her a long, steady look.

'You *were* going to give me a pony eventually anyway, weren't you, father?' She gave it a moment's thought. 'A white one, Sparhawk,' she added. 'I definitely want a white one.' Then she snuggled her kitten against her cheek, and they both started to purr.

Sparhawk and his daughter rode out of Cimmura not long after breakfast the following morning. The weather was blustery, and Mirtai had objected rather vociferously until Princess Danae told her not to be so fussy. For some reason, the word 'fussy' absolutely enraged the Tamul giantess. She stormed away, swearing in her own language.

It had taken Sparhawk hours to find a white pony for his daughter, and he was quite convinced after he had that it was the only white one in the whole town. When

Danae greeted the stubby little creature like an old friend, he began to have a number of suspicions. Over the past couple of years, he and his daughter had painfully hammered out a list of the things she wasn't supposed to do. The process had begun rather abruptly in the palace garden one summer afternoon when he had come around a box hedge to find a small swarm of fairies pollinating flowers under Danae's supervision. Although she had probably been right when she had asserted that fairies were really much better at it than bees, he had firmly put his foot down. After a bit of thought this time, however, he decided not to make an issue of his daughter's obvious connivance in obtaining a specific pony. He needed her help right now, and she might point out with a certain amount of justification that to forbid one form of what they had come to call 'tampering' while encouraging another was inconsistent.

'Is this going to involve anything spectacular?' he asked her when they were several miles out of town.

'How do you mean, spectacular?'

'You don't have to fly or anything, do you?'

'It's awkward that way, but I can if you'd like.'

'No, that's all right, Danae. What I'm getting at is would you be doing anything that would startle travellers if we went out into this meadow a ways and you did whatever it is there?'

'They won't see a thing, father,' she assured him. 'I'll race you to that tree out there.' She didn't even make a pretence of nudging her pony's flanks, and despite Faran's best efforts, the pony beat him to the tree by a good twenty yards. The big roan warhorse glowered suspiciously at the short-legged pony when Sparhawk reined him in.

'You cheated,' Sparhawk accused his daughter.

'Only a little.' She slid down from her pony and sat

cross-legged under the tree. She lifted her small face and sang in a trilling, flute-like voice. Her song broke off, and for several moments she sat blank-faced and absolutely immobile. She did not even appear to be breathing, and Sparhawk had the chilling feeling that he was absolutely alone, although she clearly sat not two yards away from him.

'What is it, Sparhawk?' Danae's lips moved, but it was Sephrenia's voice that asked the question, and when Danae opened her eyes, they had changed. Danae's eyes were very dark; Sephrenia's were deep blue, almost lavender.

'We miss you, little mother,' he told her kneeling and kissing the palms of his daughter's hands.

'You called me from half-way round the world to tell me that? I'm touched, but . . .'

'It's something a little more, Sephrenia. We've been seeing that shadow again – the cloud too.'

'That's impossible.'

'I sort of thought so myself, but we keep seeing them all the same. It's different, though. It feels different for one thing, and this time it's not just Ehlana and I who see it. Stragen and Ulath saw it too.'

'You'd better tell me exactly what's been happening, Sparhawk.'

He went into greater detail about the shadow and then briefly described the incident in the mountains near Cardos. 'Whatever this thing is,' he concluded, 'it seems very intent on keeping us from finding out what's going on in Lamorkand.'

'Is there some kind of trouble there?'

'Count Gerrich is raising a rebellion. He seems to think that the crown might fit him. He's even going so far as to claim that Drychtnath's returned. That's ridiculous, isn't it?'

Her eyes grew distant. 'Is this shadow you've been

seeing exactly the same as the one you and Ehlana saw before?' she asked.

'It feels different somehow.'

'Do you get that same sense that it has more than one consciousness in it?'

'That hasn't changed. It's a small group, but it's a group all the same, and the cloud that tore the Earl of Belton to pieces was definitely the same. Did the Troll-Gods manage to escape from Bhelliom somehow?'

'Let me think my way through it for a moment, Sparhawk,' she replied. She considered it for a time. In a curious way she was impressing her own appearance on Danae's face. 'I think we may have a problem, dear one,' she said finally.

'I noticed that myself, little mother.'

'Stop trying to be clever, Sparhawk. Do you remember the Dawn-men who came out of that cloud up in Pelosia?'

Sparhawk shuddered. 'I've been making a special point of trying to forget that.'

'Don't discount the possibility that the wild stories about Drychtnath may have some basis in fact. The Troll-Gods can reach back in time and bring creatures and people forward to where we are now. Drychtnath may very well indeed have returned.'

Sparhawk groaned. 'Then the Troll-Gods have managed to escape, haven't they?'

'I didn't say that, Sparhawk. Just because the Troll-Gods did this once doesn't mean that they're the only ones who know how. For all I know, Aphrael could do it herself.' She paused. 'You could have asked *her* these questions, you know.'

'Possibly, but I don't think I could have asked her *this* one, because I don't think she'd know the answer. She doesn't seem to be able to grasp the concept of limitations for some reason.'

'You've noticed,' she said dryly.

'Be nice. She's my daughter, after all.'

'She was my sister first, so I have a certain amount of seniority in the matter. What is it that she wouldn't be able to answer?'

'Could a Styric magician – or any other magician – be behind all this? Could we be dealing with a human?'

'No, Sparhawk, I don't think so. In forty thousand years there have only been two Styric magicians who were able to reach back into time, and they could only do it imperfectly. For all practical purposes what we're talking about is beyond human capability.'

'That's what I wanted to find out for sure. We're dealing with Gods then?'

'I'm afraid so, Sparhawk, almost certainly.'

CHAPTER 4

Preceptor Sparhawk:

It is our hope that this finds you and your family in good health.

A matter of some delicacy has arisen, and we find that your presence is required here in Chyrellos. You are therefore commanded by the Church to proceed forthwith to the Basilica and to present yourself before our throne to receive our further instruction. We know that as true son of the Church you will not delay. We shall expect your attendance upon us within the week.

Dolmant, Archprelate.

Sparhawk lowered the letter and looked around at the others.

'He gets right to the point, doesn't he?' Kalten observed. 'Of course Dolmant never was one to beat around the bush.'

Queen Ehlana gave a howl of absolute fury and began beating her fists on the council table and stamping her feet on the floor.

'You'll hurt your hands,' Sparhawk cautioned.

'How *dare* he?' she exploded. 'How *dare* he?'

'A bit abrupt, perhaps,' Stragen noted cautiously.

'You will ignore this churlish command, Sparhawk!' Ehlana ordered.

'I can't do that.'

'You are *my* husband and *my* subject! If Dolmant wants to see you, he'll ask *my* permission! This is outrageous!'

'The Archprelate *does* in fact have the authority to summon the preceptor of one of the Militant Orders to

Chyrellos, your Majesty,' the Earl of Lenda diffidently told the fuming queen.

'You're wearing too many hats, Sparhawk,' Tynian told his friend. 'You should resign from a few of these exalted positions you hold.'

'It's that devastating personality of his,' Kalten said to Ulath, 'and all those unspeakable gifts. People just wither and die in his absence.'

'I forbid it!' Ehlana said flatly.

'I have to obey him, Ehlana,' Sparhawk explained. 'I'm a Church Knight.'

Her eyes narrowed. 'Very well then,' she decided, 'since Dolmant's feeling so authoritarian, we'll *all* obey his stupid command. We'll go to Chyrellos and set up shop in the Basilica. I'll let him know that I expect him to provide me with adequate facilities and an administrative staff – at *his* expense. He and I are going to have this out once and for all.'

'This promises to be one of the high points in the history of the Church,' Stragen observed.

'I'll make that pompous ass wish he'd never been born,' Ehlana declared ominously.

Nothing Sparhawk might say could in any way change his wife's mind. If the truth were to be known, however, he did not really try all that hard, because he could see her point. Dolmant *was* being high-handed. He tended at times to run roughshod over the kings of Eosia and so the clash of wills between the Archprelate and the Queen of Elenia was probably inevitable. The unfortunate thing was that they were genuinely fond of each other, and neither of them was opposing the other out of any petty vanity or pride. Dolmant was asserting the authority of the Church, and Ehlana that of the Elenian throne. They had become institutions instead of people. It was Sparhawk's misfortune to be caught in the middle.

He was absolutely certain that the arrogant tone of the Archprelate's letter had not come from his friend but from some half-drowsing scribe absent-mindedly scribbling formula phrases. What Dolmant had most probably said was something on the order of, 'Send a letter to Sparhawk and tell him I'd like to see him.' That was *not*, however, what had arrived in Cimmura. What had arrived had set Ehlana's teeth on edge, and she went out of her way to make the impending visit to Chyrellos as inconvenient for the Archprelate as she possibly could.

Her first step was to depopulate the palace. *Everybody* had to join her entourage. The queen needed ladies-in-waiting. The ladies-in-waiting needed maids. They all needed grooms and footmen. Lenda and Platime, who were to remain in Cimmura to maintain the government, were left almost unassisted.

'Looks almost like an army mobilising, doesn't it?' Kalten said gaily as they came down the palace stairs on the morning of their departure.

'Let's hope the Archprelate doesn't misunderstand,' Ulath murmured. 'He wouldn't really believe your wife was planning to lay siege to the Basilica, would he, Sparhawk?'

Once they left Cimmura, the gaily-dressed Elenian Court stretched out for miles under a blue spring sky. Had it not been for the steely glint in the queen's eyes, this might have been no more than one of those 'outings' so loved by idle courtiers. Ehlana had 'suggested' that Sparhawk, as acting preceptor of the Pandion Order, should also be suitably accompanied. They had haggled about the number of Pandions he should take with him to Chyrellos. He had held out at first for Kalten, Berit and perhaps one or two others, while the queen had been more in favour of bringing along the entire order. They had finally agreed upon a score of black-armoured knights.

It was impossible to make any kind of time with so large an entourage. They seemed almost to creep across the face of Elenia, plodding easterly to Lenda and then southeasterly toward Demos and Chyrellos. The peasantry took the occasion of their passing as an excuse for a holiday, and the road was usually lined with crowds of country people who had come out to gawk. 'It's a good thing we don't do this very often,' Sparhawk observed to his wife not long after they had passed the city of Lenda.

'I rather enjoy getting out, Sparhawk.' The queen and princess Danae were riding in an ornate carriage drawn by six white horses.

'I'm sure you do, but this is the planting season. The peasants should be in the fields. Too many of these royal excursions could cause a famine.'

'You really don't approve of what I'm doing, do you, Sparhawk?'

'I understand why you're doing it, Ehlana, and you're probably right. Dolmant needs to be reminded that his authority isn't absolute, but I think this particular approach is just a little frivolous.'

'Of course it's frivolous, Sparhawk,' she admitted quite calmly. 'That's the whole point. In spite of all the evidence he's had to the contrary, Dolmant still thinks I'm a silly little girl. I'm going to rub his nose in "silly" for a while. Then, when he's good and tired of it, I'll take him aside and suggest that it would be much easier on him if he took me seriously. That should get his attention. Then we'll be able to get down to business.'

'Everything you do is politically motivated, isn't it?'

'Well not quite *everything*, Sparhawk.'

They stopped briefly in Demos, and Khalad and Talen took the royal couple, Kalten, Danae and Mirtai to visit their mothers. Aslade and Elys mothered everyone impartially. Sparhawk strongly suspected that this was one of the main reasons his wife quite often found excuses to travel to Demos. Her childhood had been bleak and motherless, and anytime she felt insecure or uncertain, some reason seemed to come up why her presence in Demos was absolutely necessary. Aslade's kitchen was warm, and its walls were hung with burnished copper pots. It was a homey sort of place that seemed to answer some deep need in the Queen of Elenia. The smells alone were enough to banish most of the cares of all who entered it.

Elys, Talen's mother, was a radiant blonde woman, and Aslade was a kind of monument to motherhood. They adored each other. Aslade had been Kurik's wife, and Elys his mistress, but there appeared to be no jealousy between them. They were practical women, and they both realised that jealousy was a useless kind of thing that never made anyone feel good. Sparhawk and Kalten were immediately banished from the kitchen, Khalad and Talen were sent to mend a fence, and the Queen of Elenia and her Tamul slave continued their intermittent education in the art of cooking while Aslade and Elys mothered Danae.

'I can't remember the last time I saw a queen kneading bread-dough,' Kalten grinned as he and Sparhawk strolled around the familiar dooryard.

'I think she's making pie-crusts,' Sparhawk corrected him.

'Dough is dough, Sparhawk.'

'Remind me never to ask you to bake me a pie.'

'No danger there,' Kalten laughed. 'Mirtai looks very natural, though. She's had lots of practice cutting things – and people – up. I just wish she wouldn't use her own daggers. You can never really be sure where they've been.'

'She always cleans them after she stabs somebody.'

'It's the idea of it, Sparhawk,' Kalten shuddered. 'The thought of it makes my blood run cold.'

'Don't think about it then.'

'You're going to be late, you know,' Kalten reminded his friend. 'Dolmant only gave you a week to get to Chyrellos.'

'It couldn't be helped.'

'Do you want me to ride on ahead and let him know you're coming?'

'And spoil the surprise my wife has planned for him? Don't be silly.'

They were no more than a league southeast of Demos the next morning when the attack came. A hundred men, peculiarly dressed with strange weapons, burst over the top of a low knoll bellowing war-cries. They thundered forward on foot for the most part; the ones on horseback appeared to be their leaders.

The courtiers fled squealing in terror as Sparhawk barked commands to his Pandions. The twenty black-armoured knights formed up around the queen's carriage and easily repelled the first assault. Men on foot are not really a match for mounted knights.

'What's that language?' Kalten shouted.

'Old Lamork, I think,' Ulath replied. 'It's a lot like Old Thalesian.'

'Sparhawk!' Mirtai barked. 'Don't give them time to regroup!' She pointed her blood-smeared sword at the attackers milling around at the top of the knoll.

'She's got a point,' Tynian agreed.

Sparhawk quickly assessed the situation, deployed some of his knights to protect Ehlana and formed up the remainder of his force.

'Charge!' he roared.

It is the lance that makes the armoured knight so devastating against foot-troops. The man on foot has no defence against it, and he cannot even flee. A third of the attackers had fallen in the initial assault, and a score fell victim to the lances during Sparhawk's charge. The knights then fell to work with swords and axes. Bevier's lochaber axe was particularly devastating, and he left wide tracks of the dead and dying through the tightly packed ranks of the now-confused attackers.

It was Mirtai, however, who stunned them all with a shocking display of sheer ferocity. Her sword was lighter than the broadswords of the Church Knights, and she wielded it with almost the delicacy of Stragen's rapier. She seldom thrust at an opponent's body, but concentrated instead on his face and throat, and when necessary, his legs. Her thrusts were short and tightly controlled, and her slashes were aimed not at muscles, but rather at tendons. She crippled more than she killed, and the shrieks and groans of her victims raised a fearful din on that bloody field.

The standard tactic of armoured knights when deployed against foot-troops was to charge with their lances first and then to use the weight of their horses to crush their unmounted opponents together so tightly that they became tangled with their comrades. Once they had been rendered more or less helpless, slaughtering them was easy work.

'Ulath!' Sparhawk shouted. 'Tell them to throw down their weapons!'

'I'll try,' Ulath shouted back. Then he roared something incomprehensible at the milling foot-troops.

A mounted man wearing a grotesquely decorated helmet bellowed something in reply.

'That one with the wings on his helmet is the leader, Sparhawk,' Ulath said, pointing with his bloody axe.

'What did he say?' Kalten demanded.

'He made some uncomplimentary remarks about my

nother. Excuse me for a moment, gentlemen. I really ought to do something about that.' He wheeled his horse and approached the man with the winged helmet, who was also armed with a war axe.

Sparhawk had never seen an axe-fight before, and he was somewhat surprised to note that there was far more finesse involved than he had imagined. Sheer strength accounted for much, of course, but sudden changes of the direction of swings implied a level of sophistication Sparhawk had not expected. Both men wore heavy round shields, and the defences they raised with them were more braced than might have been the case had they been attacking each other with swords.

Ulath stood up in his stirrups and raised his axe high over his head. The warrior in the winged helmet raised his shield to protect his head, but the huge Thalesian swung his arm back, rolled his shoulder and delivered an underhand blow instead, catching his opponent just under the ribs. The man who seemed to be the leader of the attackers doubled over sharply, clutching at his stomach, and then he fell from his saddle.

A vast groan rolled through the ranks of the attackers still on their feet, and then, like a mist caught by a sudden breeze, they wavered and vanished.

'Where did they go?' Berit shouted, looking around with alarm.

But no one could answer. Where there had been two score foot-troops before, there was now nothing, and a sudden silence fell over the field as the shrieking wounded also vanished. Only the dead remained, and even they were strangely altered. The bodies were peculiarly desiccated – dry, shrunken and withered. The blood which had covered their limbs was no longer bright red, but black, dry and crusty.

'What kind of spell could do that Sparhawk?' Tynian demanded.

'I have no idea,' Sparhawk replied in some bafflement. 'Someone's playing, and I don't think I like the game.'

'Bronze!' Bevier exclaimed from nearby. The young Cyrinic Knight had dismounted and was examining the armour of one of the shrivelled dead. 'They're wearing bronze armour, Sparhawk. Their weapons and helmets are steel, but this mail shirt's made out of bronze.'

'What's going on here?' Kalten demanded.

'Berit,' Sparhawk said, 'ride back to the mother house at Demos. Gather up every brother who can still wear armour. I want them here before noon.'

'Right,' Berit replied crisply. He wheeled his horse and galloped back the way they had come.

Sparhawk looked around quickly. 'Up there,' he said, pointing at a steep hill on the other side of the road. 'Let's gather up this crowd and get them to the top of that hill. Put the courtiers and grooms and footmen to work. I want ditches up there, and I want to see a forest of sharpened stakes sprouting on the sides of that hill. I don't know where those men in bronze armour went, but I want to be ready in case they come back.'

'You can't order *me* around like that!' an overdressed courtier exclaimed to Khalad in an outraged tone of voice. 'Don't you know who I am?'

'Of course I do,' Sparhawk's young squire replied in an ominous tone of voice. 'You're the man who's going to pick up that shovel and start digging. Or if you prefer, you can be the man who's crawling around on his hands and knees picking up his teeth.' Khalad showed the courtier his fist. The courtier could hardly miss seeing it, since it was about an inch in front of his nose.

'It's almost like old times, isn't it?' Kalten laughed. 'Khalad sounds exactly like Kurik.'

Sparhawk sighed. 'Yes,' he agreed soberly, 'I think

78

he's going to work out just fine. Get the others, Kalten. We need to talk.'

They gathered beside Ehlana's carriage. The queen was a bit pale, and she was holding her daughter in her arms.

'All right,' Sparhawk said. 'Who were they?'

'Lamorks, evidently,' Ulath said. 'I doubt that anybody else would be able to speak Old Lamork.'

'But why would they be speaking in that language?' Tynian asked. 'Nobody's spoken in Old Lamork for a thousand years.'

'And nobody's worn bronze armour for even longer,' Bevier added.

'Somebody's using a spell I've never even heard of before,' Sparhawk said. 'What are we dealing with here?'

'Isn't that obvious?' Stragen said. 'Somebody's reaching back into the past – the same way the Troll-Gods did in Pelosia. We've got a powerful magician of some kind out there who's playing games.'

'It fits,' Ulath grunted. 'They were speaking an antique language; they had antique weapons and equipment; they weren't familiar with modern tactics; and somebody obviously used magic to send them back to wherever they came from – except for the dead ones.'

'There's something else too,' Bevier added thoughtfully. 'They were Lamorks, and part of the upheaval in Lamorkand right now revolves around the stories that Drychtnath's returned. This attack makes it appear that those stories aren't just rumours and wild concoctions dreamed up late at night in some ale-house. Could Count Gerrich be getting some help from a Styric magician? If Drychtnath himself has actually been brought into the present, *nothing's* going to pacify the Lamorks. They go up in flames at just the mention of his name.'

'That's all very interesting, gentlemen,' Ehlana told

them, 'but this wasn't just a random attack. We're a goodly distance from Lamorkand, so these antiques of yours went to a great deal of trouble to attack *us* specifically. The real question here is why?'

'We'll work on finding an answer for you, your Majesty,' Tynian promised her.

Berit returned shortly before noon with three hundred armoured Pandions, and the rest of the journey to Chyrellos had some of the air of a military expedition.

Their arrival in the Holy City and their stately march through the streets to the Basilica was very much like a parade, and it caused quite a stir. The Archprelate himself came out onto a second-floor balcony to watch their arrival in the square before the Basilica. Even from this distance, Sparhawk could clearly see that Dolmant's nostrils were white and his jaw was clenched. Ehlana's expression was regal and coolly defiant.

Sparhawk lifted his daughter down from the carriage. 'Don't wander off,' he murmured into her small ear. 'There's something I need to talk with you about.'

'Later,' she whispered back to him. 'I'll have to make peace between Dolmant and mother first.'

'That'll be a neat trick.'

'Watch, Sparhawk – and learn.'

The Archprelate's greeting was chilly – just this side of frigid – and he made it abundantly clear that he was just dying to have a nice long chat with the Queen of Elenia. He sent for his first secretary, the Patriarch Emban, and rather airily dropped the problem of making arrangements for Ehlana's entourage into the fat churchman's lap. Emban scowled and waddled away muttering to himself.

Then Dolmant invited the queen and her prince consort into a private audience chamber. Mirtai stationed herself outside the door. 'No hitting,' she told Dolmant and Ehlana as they entered.

The small audience chamber was draped and carpeted in blue, and there were a table and chairs in the centre.

'Strange woman that one,' Dolmant murmured looking back over his shoulder at Mirtai. He took his seat and looked at Ehlana with a firm expression. 'Let's get down to business. Would you like to explain this, Queen Ehlana?'

'Of course, Archprelate Dolmant.' She pushed his letter across the table to him. 'Just as soon as you explain this.' There was steel in her voice.

He picked up the letter and glanced at it. 'It seems fairly straightforward. Which part of it didn't you understand?'

Things went downhill from there rather rapidly.

Ehlana and Dolmant were on the verge of severing all diplomatic ties when the Royal Princess Danae entered the room dragging the Royal Toy Rollo by one hind leg. She gravely crossed the room, climbed up into the Archprelate's lap and kissed him. Sparhawk had received quite a few of the kind of kisses his daughter bestowed when she wanted something, and he was well-aware of just how devastatingly potent they were. Dolmant didn't really have much of a chance after that. 'I should have read through the letter before I had it dispatched, I suppose,' he admitted grudgingly. 'Scribes sometimes overstate things.'

'Maybe I over-reacted,' Ehlana conceded.

'I had a great deal on my mind.' Dolmant's excuse had the tone of a peace-offering.

'I was irritable on the day when your letter arrived,' Ehlana countered.

Sparhawk leaned back. The tension in the room had noticeably relaxed. Dolmant had changed since his elevation to the Archprelacy. Always before, he had been a self-effacing man, so self-effacing in fact that his colleagues in the Hierocracy had not even considered him for the highest post in the Church until Ehlana had pointed out his many sterling qualities to them. The irony of that fact was not lost on Sparhawk. Now, however, Dolmant seemed to speak with two voices. The one was the familiar, almost colloquial voice of their old friend. The other was the voice of the Archprelate, authoritarian and severe. The institution of his office seemed to be gradually annexing their old friend. Sparhawk sighed. It was probably inevitable, but he regretted it all the same.

Ehlana and the Archprelate continued to apologise and offer excuses to each other. After a while they agreed to respect one another, and they concluded their conference by agreeing to pay closer attention to little courtesies in the future.

Princess Danae, still seated in the Archprelate's lap, winked at Sparhawk. There were quite a number of political and theological implications in what she had just done, but Sparhawk didn't really want to think about those.

The reason for the peremptory summons which had nearly led to a private war between Ehlana and Dolmant had been the arrival of a high-ranking emissary from the Tamul Empire on the Daresian continent, that vast land-mass lying to the east of Zemoch. Formal diplomatic relations between the Elene Kingdoms of Eosia and the Tamul Empire of Daresia did not exist. The Church, however, routinely dispatched emissaries with ambassadorial rank to the imperial capital at Matherion, in some measure because the three western-most kingdoms of the empire were occupied by Elenes, and their religion differed only slightly from that of the Eosian Church.

The emissary was a Tamul, a man of the same race as Mirtai, although she would have made at least two of him. His skin was the same golden bronze, his black hair touched with grey and his dark eyes were uptilted at the corners.

'He's very good,' Dolmant quietly cautioned them as they sat in one of the audience chambers while Emban and the emissary exchanged pleasantries near the door. 'In some ways he's even better than Emban. Be just a little careful of what you say around him. Tamuls are quite sensitive to the nuances of language.'

Emban escorted the silk-robed emissary to the place where they all sat. 'Your Majesty, I have the honour to present his Excellency, Ambassador Oscagne, representative of the imperial court at Matherion,' the little fat man said, bowing to Ehlana.

'I swoon in your Majesty's divine presence,' the ambassador proclaimed with a florid bow.

'You don't really, do you, your Excellency?' she asked him with a little smile.

'Well, not really, of course,' he admitted with absolute aplomb. 'I thought it might be polite to say it, though. Did it seem unduly extravagant? I am unversed in the usages of your culture.'

'You'll do just fine, your Excellency,' she laughed.

'I must say, however, with your Majesty's permission, that you're a devilishly attractive young lady. I've known a few queens in my time, and the customary compliments usually cost one a certain amount of wrestling with one's conscience.' Ambassador Oscagne spoke flawless Elenic.

'May I present my husband, Prince Sparhawk?' Ehlana suggested.

'The legendary Sir Sparhawk? Most assuredly, dear lady. I've travelled half-round the world to make his acquaintance. Well met, Sir Sparhawk.' Oscagne bowed.

'Your Excellency,' Sparhawk replied, also bowing.

Ehlana then introduced the others, and the ongoing exchange of diplomatic pleasantries continued for the better part of an hour. Oscagne and Mirtai spoke at some length in the Tamul tongue, a language which Sparhawk found quite musical.

'Have we concluded all the necessary genuflections in courtesy's direction?' the ambassador asked at last. 'Cultures vary, of course, but in Tamuli three-quarters of an hour is the customary amount of time one is expected to waste on polite trivialities.'

'That seems about right to me too,' Stragen grinned. 'If we overdo our homage to courtesy, she becomes a bit conceited and expects more and more obeisance every time.'

'Well said, Milord Stragen,' Oscagne approved. 'The reason for my visit is fairly simple, my friends. I'm in trouble.' He looked around. 'I pause for the customary gasps of surprise while you try to adjust your thinking to accept the notion that anyone could possibly find any fault in so witty and charming a fellow as I.'

'I think I'm going to like him,' Stragen murmured.

'You would,' Ulath grunted.

'Pray tell, your Excellency,' Ehlana said, 'how on earth could anyone find reason to be dissatisfied with you?' The ambassador's flowery speech was contagious.

'I exaggerated slightly for effect,' Oscagne admitted. 'I'm not really in all that much trouble. It's just that his Imperial Majesty has sent me to Chyrellos to appeal for aid, and I'm supposed to couch the request in such a way that it won't humiliate him.'

Emban's eyes were very, very bright. He was in his natural element here. 'I think the way we'll want to proceed here is to just lay the problem out on the table for our friends in bold flat terms,' he suggested, 'and then they can concentrate on the real issue of avoiding embarrassment to the imperial government. They're all unspeakably clever. I'm sure that if they put their heads together, they'll be able to come up with something.'

Dolmant sighed. 'Was there no one else you could

have selected for my job, Ehlana?' he asked plaintively.

Oscagne gave the two of them a questioning look.

'It's a long story, your Excellency,' Emban told him. 'I'll tell you all about it someday when neither of us has anything better to do. Tell them what it is in Tamuli that's so serious that his Imperial Majesty had to send you here to look for help.'

'Promise not to laugh?' Oscagne said to Ehlana.

'I'll do my best to stifle my guffaws,' she promised.

'We've got a bit of civil unrest in Tamuli,' Oscagne told them.

They all waited.

'That's it,' Oscagne confessed ruefully. 'Of course I'm quoting the emperor verbatim – at his instruction. You'd almost have to know our emperor to understand. He'd sooner die than overstate anything. He once referred to a hurricane as a "little breeze" and the loss of half his fleet as a minor inconvenience.'

'Very well, your Excellency,' Ehlana said. 'Now we know how your emperor would characterise the problem. What words would *you* use to describe it?'

'Well,' Oscagne said, 'since your Majesty is so kind as to ask, "catastrophic" *does* sort of leap to mind. We might consider "insoluble", "cataclysmic", "overwhelming" – little things like that. I really think you should give some consideration to his Majesty's request, my friends, because we have some fairly strong evidence that what's happening on the Daresian continent may soon spread to Eosia as well, and if it does, it's probably going to mean the end of civilisation as we know it. I'm not entirely positive how you Elenes feel about that sort of thing, but we Tamuls are more or less convinced that some effort ought to be made to fend it off. It sets such a bad precedent when you start letting the world come to an end every week or so. It seems to erode the confidence people have in their governments for some reason.'

CHAPTER 5

Ambassador Oscagne leaned back in his chair. 'Where to begin?' he pondered. 'When one looks at the incidents individually, they almost appear trivial. It's the cumulative effect that's brought the empire to the brink of collapse.'

'We can understand that sort of thing, your Excellency,' Emban assured him. 'The Church has been on the brink of collapse for centuries now. Our Holy Mother reels from crisis to crisis like a drunken sailor.'

'Emban,' Dolmant chided gently.

'Sorry,' the fat little churchman apologised.

Oscagne was smiling. 'Sometimes it seems that way, though, doesn't it, your Grace,' he said to Emban. 'I'd imagine that the government of the Church is not really all that much different from the government of the empire. Bureaucrats need crisis in order to survive. If there isn't a crisis of some kind, someone might decide that a number of positions could be eliminated.'

'I've noticed the same sort of thing myself,' Emban agreed.

'I assure you, however, that what we have in Tamuli is not some absurd little flap generated for the purposes of making someone's position secure. I'm not exaggerating in the slightest when I say that the empire's on the brink of collapse.' His bronze face became thoughtful. 'We are not one homogeneous people as you here in Eosia are,' he began. 'There are five races on the Daresian continent. We Tamuls live to the east, there are Elenes in the west, Styrics around Sarsos, the Valesians on their island and the Cynesgans in the centre. It's probably not natural for so many different kinds of people to all be gathered under one roof. Our cultures are different, our religions are different, and each race is sublimely convinced that it's the crown of the universe.' He sighed. 'We'd probably have been better off if we'd remained separate.'

'But, at some time in the past someone grew ambitious?' Tynian surmised.

'Far from it, Sir Knight,' Oscagne replied. 'You could almost say that we Tamuls blundered into empire.' He looked at Mirtai, who sat quietly with Danae in her lap. 'And that's the reason,' he said, pointing at the giantess.

'It wasn't my fault, Oscagne,' she protested.

'I wasn't blaming you personally, Atana,' he smiled. 'It's your people.'

She smiled. 'I haven't heard that term since I was a child. No one's ever called me "Atana" before.'

'What's it mean?' Talen asked her curiously.

'Warrior,' she shrugged.

'Warrioress, actually,' Oscagne corrected. He frowned. 'I don't want to be offensive, but your Elene tongue is limited in its ability to convey subtleties.' He looked at Ehlana. 'Has your Majesty noticed that your slave is not exactly like other women?' he asked her.

'She's my friend,' Ehlana objected, 'not my slave.'

'Don't be ignorant, Ehlana,' Mirtai told her crisply. 'Of course I'm a slave. I'm supposed to be. Go on with your story, Oscagne. I'll explain it to them later.'

'Do you really think they'll understand?'

'No. But I'll explain it anyway.'

'And there, revered Archprelate,' Oscagne said to Dolmant, 'there lies the key to the empire. The Atans placed themselves in thrall to us some fifteen hundred years ago to prevent their homicidal instincts from obliterating their entire race. As a result, we Tamuls have the finest army in the world – even though we're basically a non-violent people. We tended to win those incidental little arguments with other nations which crop up from time to time and are usually settled by negotiation. In our view, our neighbours are like children, hopelessly incapable of managing their own affairs. The empire came into being largely in the interests of good order.' He looked around at the Church Knights. 'Once again, I'm not trying to be offensive, but war is probably the stupidest of human activities. There are much more efficient ways to persuade people to change their minds.'

'Such as the threat to unleash the Atans?' Emban suggested slyly.

'That does work rather well, your Grace,' Oscagne admitted. 'The presence of the Atans has usually been enough in the past to keep political discussion from becoming too spirited. Atans make excellent policemen.' He sighed. 'You noted that slight qualification, I'm sure. I said, "in the past". Unfortunately, that doesn't hold true any more. An empire comprised of disparate peoples must always expect these little outbreaks of nationalism and racial discord. It's the nature of the insignificant to try to find some way to assert their own importance. It's pathetic, but racism is generally the last refuge of the unimportant. These outbreaks of insignificance aren't normally too widespread, but suddenly all of Tamuli is in the throes of an epidemic of them. Everyone's sewing flags and singing national anthems and labouring over well-honed insults to be directed at "the yellow dogs". That's us, of course.' He held out his hand and looked at it critically. 'Our skins aren't really yellow, you know. They're more . . .' He pondered it.

'Beige?' Stragen suggested.

'That's not too flattering either, Milord Stragen.' Oscagne smiled. 'Oh, well. Perhaps the emperor will appoint a special commission to define our skin tone once and for all.' He shrugged. 'At any rate, incidental outbreaks of nationalism and racial bigotry would be no real problem for the Atans, even if they occurred in every town in the empire. It's the unnatural incidents that cause us all this concern.'

'I thought there might be more,' Ulath murmured.

'At first, these demonstrations of magic were directed at the people themselves,' Oscagne went on. 'Every culture has its mythic hero – some towering personality who unified the people, gave them national purpose and defined their character. The modern world is complex and confusing, and the simple folk yearn for the simplicity of the age of heroes when national goals could be stated simply and everyone knew precisely who he was. Someone in Tamuli is resurrecting the heroes of antiquity.'

Sparhawk felt a sudden chill. 'Giants?' he asked.

'Well.' Oscagne considered it. 'Perhaps that is the proper term at that. The passage of the centuries blurs and distorts, and our cultural heroes tend to become larger than life. I suppose that when we think of them, we *do* think of giants. That's a very acute perception, Sir Sparhawk.'

'I can't actually take credit for it, your Excellency. The same sort of thing's been happening here.'

Dolmant looked at him sharply.

'I'll explain later, Sarathi. Please go on, Ambassador Oscagne. You said that whoever's stirring things up in Tamuli started out by raising national heroes. That implies that it's gone further.'

'Oh, yes indeed, Sir Sparhawk. Much, much further. Every culture has its hobgoblins as well as its heroes. It's the hobgoblins we've been encountering – monsters, afreets, werewolves, vampires – all those things adults use to frighten children into good behaviour. Our Atans can't cope with that sort of thing. They're trained to deal with men, not with all the horrors the creative genius of aeons has put together. That's our problem. We have nine different cultures in Tamuli, and suddenly each one of them has taken to pursuing its traditional historic goals. When we send in our Atans to restore order and to re-assert imperial authority, the horrors rise up out of the ground to confront them. We can't deal with it. The empire's disintegrating, falling back into its component parts. His Imperial Majesty's government hopes that your Church can recognise a certain community of interest here. If Tamuli collapses back into nine warring kingdoms, the resulting chaos is almost certain to have its impact here in Eosia as well. It's the magic that has us so concerned. We can deal with ordinary insurrection, but we're unequipped to deal with a continent-wide conspiracy that routinely utilises magic against us. The Styrics at Sarsos are baffled. Everything they try is countered almost before they can set it in motion. We've heard stories about what happened in the City of Zemoch, and it is to you personally that I must appeal, Sir Sparhawk. Zalasta of Sarsos is the pre-eminent magician in all of Styricum, and he assures us that you are the only man in all the world with enough power to deal with the situation.'

'Zalasta may have an exaggerated idea of my abilities,' Sparhawk said.

'You know him?'

'We've met. Actually, your Excellency, I was only a very small part of what happened at Zemoch. When you get right down to it, I was hardly more than a channel for power I couldn't even begin to describe. I was the instrument of something else.'

'Be that as it may, you're still our only hope. Someone is quite obviously conspiring to overthrow the empire. We *must* identify that someone. Unless we can get to

90

the source of all of this and neutralise it, the empire will collapse. Will you help us, Sir Sparhawk?'

'That decision's not mine to make, your Excellency. You must appeal to my queen and to Sarathi here. If they command me, I'll go to Tamuli. If they forbid it, I won't.'

'I'll direct my enormous powers of persuasion at them, then,' Oscagne smiled. 'But even assuming that I'm successful – and there's little doubt that I shall be – we're still faced with an almost equally serious problem. We must protect his Imperial Majesty's dignity at all costs. An appeal from one government to another is one thing, but an appeal from His Majesty's government to a private citizen on another continent is quite another. *That* is the problem which must be addressed.'

'I don't see that we have any choice, Sarathi,' Emban was saying gravely. It was late evening. Ambassador Oscagne had retired for the night, and the rest of them, along with Patriarch Ortzel of Kadach in Lamorkand, had gathered to give his request serious consideration. 'We may not entirely approve of some of the policies of the Tamul Empire, but its stability is in our vital interest just now. We're fully committed to our campaign in Rendor. If Tamuli flies apart, we'll have to pull most of our armies – and the Church Knights – out of Rendor to protect our interests in Zemoch. Zemoch's not much of a place, I'll grant you, but the strategic importance of its mountains can't be overstated. We've had a hostile force in those mountains for the past two thousand years, and that fact has occupied the full attention of our Holy Mother. If we allow some other hostile people to replace the Zemochs, everything Sparhawk achieved in Otha's capitol is lost. We'll go right back to where we were six years ago. We'll have to abandon Rendor again and start mobilising to meet a new threat from the east.'

'You're stating the obvious, Emban,' Dolmant told him.

'I know, but sometimes it helps to lay everything out so that we can all look at it.'

'Sparhawk,' Dolmant said then, 'if I were to order you to Matherion but your wife ordered you to stay home, what would you do?'

'I'd probably have to go into a monastery to pray for guidance for the next several years.'

'Our Holy Mother Church is overwhelmed by your piety, Sir Sparhawk.'

'I do what I can to please her, Sarathi. I am her true knight, after all.'

Dolmant sighed. 'Then it all boils down to some sort of accommodation between Ehlana and me, doesn't it?'

'Such wisdom can only have come from God,' Sparhawk observed to his companions.

'Do you mind?' Dolmant said tartly. Then he looked at the Queen of Elenia with a certain resignation. 'Name your price, your Majesty.'

'I beg your pardon?'

'Let's not tiptoe around each other, Ehlana. Your champion's put my back to the wall.'

'I know,' she replied, 'and I'm so impressed with him that I can barely stand it. We'll have to discuss this in private, revered Archprelate. We wouldn't want Sir Sparhawk to fully realise his true value, now would we? He might begin to get the idea that we ought to pay him what he's actually worth.'

'I hate this,' Dolmant said to no one in particular.

'I think we might want to touch briefly on something else,' Stragen suggested. 'The Tamul Ambassador's story had a certain familiar ring to it – or was I the only one who noticed that? We've got a situation going on in Lamorkand that's amazingly similar to what's happening in Tamuli. The Lamorks are all blithely convinced that Drychtnath's returned, and that's almost identical to the situation Oscagne described. Then, on our way here from Cimmura, we were set upon by a group of Lamorks who could only have come from antiquity. Their weapons were steel, but their armour was bronze, and they spoke Old Lamork. After Sir Ulath killed their leader, the ones who were still alive vanished. Only their dead remained, and they seemed to be all dried out.'

'And that's not all,' Sparhawk added. 'There were some bandits operating in the mountains of western Eosia. They were being led by some of Annias' former supporters, and they were doing all they could to stir up rebellious sentiments among the peasantry. Platime managed to get a spy into their camp, and he told us that the movement was being fuelled by Krager, Martel's old underling. After we rounded them up, we tried to question one of them about Krager, and that cloud we saw on our way to Zemoch engulfed the man and tore him all to pieces. There's something afoot here in Eosia, and it seems to be coming out of Lamorkand.'

'And you think there's a connection?' Dolmant asked him.

'It's a logical conclusion, Sarathi. There are too many similarities to be safely ignored.' Sparhawk paused, glancing at his wife. 'This may cause a certain amount of domestic discontent,' he said regretfully, 'but I believe we'd better think very seriously about Oscagne's request. Someone's harrowing the past to bring back people and things that have been dead for thousands of years. When we encountered this sort of thing in Pelosia, Sephrenia told us that only the Gods were capable of that.'

'Well, that's not entirely true, Sparhawk,' Bevier corrected him. 'She did say that a few of the most powerful Styric magicians could also raise the dead.'

'I think we can discount that possibility,' Sparhawk disagreed. 'Sephrenia and I were talking about it once, and she told me that in the forty thousand years of Styric history, there have only been two Styrics who had the capability, and then only imperfectly. This raising of heroes and armies is happening in nine nations in Tamuli and at least one here in Eosia. There are just too many similarities for it to be a coincidence, and the whole scheme – whatever its goal – is just too complex to have come from somebody who doesn't have an absolute grasp on the spell.'

'The Troll-Gods?' Ulath suggested bleakly.

'I wouldn't discount the possibility. They did it once before, so we know that they have the capability. Right now, though, all we have are some suspicions based on some educated guesses. We desperately need information.'

'That's my department, Sparhawk,' Stragen told him. 'Mine and Platime's. You're going to Daresia, I assume?'

'It's beginning to look that way.' Sparhawk gave his wife an apologetic look. 'I'd gladly let someone else go, but I'm afraid he wouldn't know what he's looking for.'

'I'd better go with you,' Stragen decided. 'I have associates there as well as here in Eosia, and people in our line of work can gather information much more quickly than your people can.'

Sparhawk nodded.

'Maybe we can start right there,' Ulath suggested. He looked at the Patriarch Ortzel. 'How did all these wild stories about Drychtnath get started, your Grace? Nobody's reputation really lasts for four thousand years, no matter how impressive he was to begin with.'

'Drychtnath is a literary creation, Sir Ulath,' the severe blond churchman replied, smiling slightly. Even as Dolmant's ascension to the throne had changed him, so Ortzel had been changed by living in Chyrellos. He no longer seemed to be the rigid, provincial man he had been in Lamorkand. Although he was by no means as worldly as Emban, he had nonetheless reacted to the sophistication of his colleagues in the Basilica. He smiled occasionally now, and he appeared to be developing a sly, understated sense of humour. Sparhawk had met with him on several occasions since Dolmant had ordered the cleric to Chyrellos, and the big Pandion found that he was actually beginning to like the man. Ortzel still had his prejudices, of course, but he was now willing to admit that points of view other than his own might have some small validity.

'Somebody just made him up?' Ulath was saying incredulously.

'Oh, no. There *was* somebody named Drychtnath four thousand years ago. Probably some bully-boy with his brains in his biceps. I'd imagine that he was the usual sort – no neck, no forehead and nothing even remotely resembling intelligence between his ears. After he died, though, some poet struggling with failing inspiration seized on the story and embellished it with all the shop-worn conventions of the heroic epic. He called it *The Drychtnathasaga*, and Lamorkand would be far better off if the poet had never learned to read and write.' Sparhawk thought he detected some actual flashes of humour there.

'One poem could hardly have *that* kind of impact, your Grace,' Kalten said sceptically.

'You underestimate the power of a well-told story, Sir Kalten. I'll have to translate as I go along, but judge for yourself.' Ortzel leaned back with his eyes half-closed. 'Hearken unto a tale from the age of heroes,' he began. His harsh, rigid voice became softer, more sonorous as he recited the ancient poem. 'List, brave men of Lamork-land to the exploits of Drychtnath the smith, mightiest of all the warriors of yore.

'Now as all men know, the Age of Heroes was an age of bronze. Massive were the bronze swords and the axes of the heroes of yore, and mighty were the thews of the men who wielded them in joyous battle. And none there was in all the length and breadth of Lamorkland mightier than Drychtnath the smith.

'Tall was Drychtnath and ox-shouldered, for his labour moulded him even as he moulded the glowing metal. Swords of bronze wrought he, and spears as keen as daggers, and axes and shields and burnished helms and shirts of mail which shed the foeman's blows as they were no more than gentle rain from on high.

'And lo, warriors from all of dark-forested Lamorkland gladly gave good gold and bright silver beyond measure in exchange for Drychtnath's bronze, and the mighty smith waxed in wealth and in strength as he toiled at his forge.'

Sparhawk tore his eyes from Ortzel's face and looked around. The faces of his friends were all rapt. The Patriarch of Kadach's voice rose and fell in the stately cadences of bardic utterance.

'Lord,' Sir Bevier breathed as the patriarch paused, 'it's hypnotic, isn't it?'

'That's always been its danger,' Ortzel told him. 'The rhythm numbs the mind and sets the pulse to racing. The people of my race are susceptible to the emotionality of *The Drychtnathasaga*. An army of Lamorks can be whipped into a frenzy by a recitation of some of the more lurid passages.'

'Well?' Talen said eagerly. 'What happened?'

Ortzel smiled rather gently at the boy. 'Surely so worldly a young thief cannot be stirred by some tired old poem?' he suggested slyly. Sparhawk nearly laughed aloud. Perhaps the change in the Patriarch of Kadach had gone further than he had imagined.

'I like a good story,' Talen admitted. 'I've never heard one told that way before, though.'

'It's called "felicity of style",' Stragen murmured. 'Sometimes it's not so much what the story says, but how it says it.'

'Well?' Talen insisted. 'What happened?'

'Drychtnath discovered that a giant named Kreindl had forged a metal that could cut bronze like butter,' Ortzel replied. 'He went to Kreindl's lair with only his sledge-hammer for a weapon, tricked the secret of the new metal out of the giant and then beat out his brains with the sledge. Then he went home and began to forge the new metal – steel – and hammered it out into weapons. Soon every warrior in Lamorkand – or Lamorkland as they called it in those days – had to have a steel sword, and Drychtnath grew enormously wealthy.' He frowned. 'I hope you'll bear with me,' he apologised. 'Translating on the spot is a bit difficult.' He thought a while and then began again. 'Now it came to pass that the fame of the mighty smith Drychtnath spread throughout the land. Tall was he, a full ten span, I ween, and broad were his shoulders. His thews were as the steel from his forge, and comely were his features. Full many a maid of noble house yearned for him in the silences of her soul.

'Now as it chanced to happen in those far-off days of yore, the ruler of the Lamorks was the aged King Hygdahl, whose snowy locks bespoke his wisdom. No son on life had he, but a daughter, the child of his eld, fair as morning dew and yclept Uta. And Hygdahl was sore troubled, for well he wot that when his spirit had been gathered to the bosom of Hrokka, strife and contention would wrack the lands of the Lamorks as the heroes vied with one another for his throne and for the hand of fair Uta in marriage, for such was the twin prize which would fall to the hand of the victor. And so resolved King Hygdahl at last to secure the future of realm and daughter with one stroke. And caused he to be sent word to every corner of his vasty realm. The fate of Lamorkland and of bright-eyed Uta would be decided by trial at arms. The mightiest hero in all the land would win wealth, wife and dominion by the strength of his hands.' Ortzel paused in his translation.

'What's a span?' Talen asked.

'Nine inches,' Berit replied. 'It's supposed to be as far as a man can stretch out the fingers of one hand.'

Talen made the quick computation in his head. 'Seven and a half feet?' he said incredulously. 'He was seven and a half feet tall?'

'It may be slightly exaggerated,' Ortzel smiled.

'Who is this Hrokka?' Bevier asked him.

'The Lamork War-God,' Ortzel explained. 'There was a period at the end of the bronze age when the Lamorks reverted to paganism. Obviously, Drychtnath won the trial-at-arms, and he didn't even kill too many other Lamorks in the process.' Then Ortzel took up his recitation. 'And so it was that Drychtnath the smith, mightiest hero of antiquity, won the hand of bright-eyed Uta and became King Hygdahl's heir.

'And when the wedding-feast was done, went Hygdahl's heir straightway to the King. "Lord King," quotha, "since I have the honour to be the mightiest warrior in all the world, it is only meet that the world fall into my hands. To that end shall I bend mine efforts once Hrokka hath called thee home. I will conquer the world and subdue it and bend it to my will, and I will lead the heroes of Lamorkland e'en unto Chyrellos. There will I cast down the altars of the false God of that Church which doth, all womanly, hold strength in despite and weakens warriors with her drasty preaching. I spurn her counsel, and will lead the heroes of Lamorkland forth to bear back to our homes in groaning wains the loot of the world.''

'Happily heard Hygdahl the hero's words, for Hrokka, Sword-Lord of Lamorkland, glories in battle-strife and doth inspire his children to love the sound of sword meeting sword and the sight of sparkling blood bedewing the grass. "Go forth, my son, and conquer," quotha, "Punish the Peloi, crush the Cammorians, destroy the Deirans, and forget not to bring down the Church which doth pollute the manhood of all Elenes with her counsels of peace and lowly demeanour."

'Now when word of Drychtnath's design reached the Basilica of Chyrellos, the Church was troubled and trembled in fear of the mighty smith, and the princes of the Church took counsel one with the other and resolved to spill out the life of the noble smith, lest his design dispossess the Church and win her wealth to wend in wains Lamorkward, there to bedeck the high-built walls of the conqueror's mead-hall. Conspired they then to send a warrior of passing merit to the court of Hygdahl's heir to bring low the towering pride of dark-forested Lamorkland.

'In dissembling guise this traitorous warrior, a Deiran by birth – Starkad was his name – made his way to Drychtnath's mead-hall, and mildly made he courteous greeting to Hygdahl's heir. And beseeched he the hero of Lamorkland to accept him as his vassal. Now Drychtnath's heart was so free of deceit and subterfuge that he could not perceive perfidy in others. Gladly did he accept Starkad's seeming friendship, and the two were soon as brothers even as Starkad had designed.

'And as the heroes of Drychtnath's hall laboured, Starkad was ever at Drychtnath's right hand, in fair weather and foul, in battle and in the carouse which is battle's aftermath. Tales he spun which filled Drychtnath's heart with mirth, and for the love he bare his friend did the mighty smith gladly bestow treasures upon him, bracelets of bright gold and gems beyond price. Starkad accepted Drychtnath's gifts in seeming gratitude and ever, like the patient worm, burrowed he his way ever deeper into the hero's heart.

'And at the time of Hrokka's choosing was wise King Hygdahl gathered into the company of the Immortal Thanes in the Hall of Heroes, and then was Drychtnath king in Lamorkland. Well were laid his plans, and no sooner had the royal crown been placed upon his head than he gathered his heroes and marched north to subdue the savage Peloi.

'Many were the battles mighty Drychtnath waged in the lands of the Peloi, and great were the victories he won. And there it was in the lands of the horse-people that the design of the Church of Chyrellos was accomplished, for there, separated from their friends by legions of ravening Peloi, Drychtnath and Starkad wrought slaughter upon the foe, bathing the meadow's grass with the blood of their enemies. And there, in the full flower of his heroism, was mighty Drychtnath laid full low. Seizing upon a lull in the struggle when all stood somewhat apart to gather breath and strength to renew the struggle, the deceitful Deiran found his opportunity and drove his cursed spear, sharper than any dagger, full into his lord's broad back.

'And Drychtnath felt death's cold touch as Starkad's bright steel pierced him. And turned he then to face the man he had called friend and brother. "Why?" quotha, his heart wrung more by the betrayal than by Starkad's stroke.

'"It was in the name of the God of the Elenes," quoth Starkad with hot tears streaming from his eyes, for in truth loved he the hero he had just slain. "Think not that it was I who have smitten thee to the heart, my brother, for it was not I, but our Holy Mother Church which hath sought thy life." So saying, he raised once more his dreadful spear. "Defend thyself, Drychtnath, for though I must slay thee, I would not murder thee."

'Then raised noble Drychtnath his face. "That will I not do," quotha, "for if my brother have need of my life, I give it to him freely."

'"Forgive me," quoth Starkad, raising again his deadly spear.

'"That may I not do," quoth the hero. "My life mayest thou freely have, but never my forgiveness."

'"So be it then," quoth Starkad, and, so saying, plunged he his deadly spear full into Drychtnath's mighty heart.

'A moment only the hero stood, and then slowly, as falls the mighty oak, fell all the pride of Lamorkland, and the earth and the heavens resounded with his fall.'

There were tears in Talen's eyes. 'Did he get away with it?' he demanded fiercely. 'I mean, didn't one of Drychtnath's other friends pay him back?' The boy's face clearly showed his eagerness to hear more.

'Surely you wouldn't want to waste your time with some tired, worn-out old story that's been around for thousands of years?' Ortzel said. He feigned some astonishment, but there was a sly twinkle in his eye. Sparhawk covered his own smile with his hand. Ortzel had definitely changed, all right.

'I don't know about Talen,' Ulath said, 'but I would.' There were obviously some strong similarities between the culture of present-day Thalesia and that of ancient Lamorkland.

'Well, now,' Ortzel said, 'I'd say that some bargaining might be in order here. How many acts of contrition would the two of you be willing to give our Holy Mother in exchange for the rest of the story?'

'Ortzel,' Dolmant reproved him.

The Patriarch of Kadach held up one hand. 'It's a

perfectly legitimate exchange, Sarathi,' he said. 'The Church has used it many times in the past. When I was a simple country pastor, I used this exact method to ensure regular attendance at services. My congregation was known far and wide for its piety – until I ran out of stories.' Then he laughed. They were all a bit startled at that. Most of them were fairly sure that the stern, unbending Patriarch of Kadach didn't even know how. 'I was only teasing,' he told the young thief and the gigantic Thalesian. 'I wouldn't be too disappointed, however, if the two of you gave the condition of your souls some serious thought.'

'Tell the story,' Mirtai insisted. Mirtai was also a warrior, and also, it appeared, susceptible to a stirring tale.

'Do I sense the possibility of a convert here?' Ortzel asked her.

'What you're sensing is the possibility of failing health, Ortzel,' she said bluntly. Mirtai never used titles when she spoke to people.

'All right then,' Ortzel laughed again and continued with his translation.

'Hearken then, O men of Lamorkland, and hear how Starkad was paid. Some tears then shed he over his fallen brother, then turned he his raging wrath upon the Peloi, and they fled screaming from him. Straightway left he the strife-place and journeyed even to the Holy City of Chyrellos, there to advise the princes of the Church that their design was done. And when they had gathered all in the Basilica which is the crown of their o'erweening pride, recounted Starkad the sad tale of the fall of Drychtnath, mightiest hero of yore.

'And gloated then the soft and pampered princes of the Church at the hero's fall, thinking that their pride and power and position were safe, and spake they each in praise of Starkad and offered him good gold beyond measure for the deed he had done.

'Cold, however, was the hero's heart, and he looked upon the little men he had served, recalling with tears the great man he had slain at their bidding. "Lordlings of the Church," quotha then. "Think ye that mere gold will satisfy me as payment for what I have done in your behalf?"

'"But what else may we offer thee?" they asked in great perplexity.

'"I would have Drychtnath's forgiveness," quoth Starkad.

'"But that we may not obtain for thee," they said unto him, "for dreaded Drychtnath lieth low in the House of the Dead from whence no man returneth. Pray, mighty hero, tell us what else we may offer thee in recompense for this great service thou hast provided us."

'"But one thing," quoth Starkad in deadly earnest.

'"And that is what?" they asked.

'"Your heart's blood," quoth Starkad. And, so saying, sprang he to the massy door and chained it shut with chains of steel that none might escape him. Then drew he forth Hlorithn, Dread Drychtnath's bright blade, which he had brought with him to Chyrellos for just this purpose. And then took the hero Starkad his payment for the deed he had done on the plains of the Peloi.

'And when he had finished collecting that which was owed him, the Church of Chyrellos lay headless, for not one of her princes saw the setting of the sun that day, and sorrowing still that he had slain his friend, Starkad sadly took his leave of the Holy City and never returned there more.

'But it is said in dark-forested Lamorkland that the oracles and the auguries speak still of the mighty Drychtnath and of the day when the War-God Hrokka will relent and release the spirit of Drychtnath from his service as one of the Immortal Thanes in the Hall of

103

Heroes that he may come once more to Lamorkland to take up again that grand design. Then how the blood will flow, and then how the kings of the world will tremble as once again the world shakes beneath the mighty stride of Dread Drychtnath the Destroyer, and the crown and throne of the world shall lie in his immortal grip, as was from the beginning intended.' Ortzel's voice fell silent, indicating that he had reached the end.

'That's all?' Talen protested vehemently.

'I skipped over a great number of passages,' Ortzel conceded, 'battle descriptions and the like. The Lamorks of antiquity had an unhealthy fascination with certain kinds of numbers. They wanted to know how many barrels of blood, pounds of brains and yards of entrails were spilled out during the festivities.'

'But the story doesn't end right,' Talen complained. 'Drychtnath was the hero, but after Starkad murdered him, *he* turned into the hero. That isn't right. The bad people shouldn't be allowed to change over like that.'

'That's a very interesting argument, Talen – particularly coming from you.'

'I'm not a bad person, your Grace, I'm just a thief. It's not the same at all. At least the churchmen all got what was coming to them.'

'You have a long way to go with this one, Sparhawk,' Bevier observed. 'We all loved Kurik like a brother, but are we really sure that his son has the makings of a Church Knight in him?'

'I'm working on that,' Sparhawk replied. 'So that's what Drychtnath's all about. Just how deeply do the commons in Lamorkand believe in the story, your Grace?'

'It goes deeper than belief, Sparhawk,' Ortzel replied. 'The story's in our blood. I'm wholly committed to the Church, but when I hear *The Drychtnathasaga*, I become an absolute pagan – for a while at least.'

'Well,' Tynian said, 'now we know what we're up against. We have the same thing going on in Lamorkand as we have in Rendor. We've got heresies springing up all around us. It still doesn't solve our problem, though. How are Sparhawk and the rest of us going to be able to go to Tamuli without insulting the emperor?'

'I've solved that problem already, Tynian,' Ehlana told him.

'I beg your Majesty's pardon?'

'It's so simple that I'm almost ashamed of you all that you didn't think of it first.'

'Enlighten us, your Majesty,' Stragen said. 'Make us blush for our stupidity.'

'It's time for the western Elene Kingdoms to open communications with the Tamul Empire,' she explained. 'We *are* neighbours, after all. It's politically very sound for me to make a state visit to Matherion, and if you gentlemen are all very nice to me, I'll invite you to come along.' She frowned. 'That was the least of our problems. Now we'll have to address something far more serious.'

'And what is that, Ehlana?' Dolmant asked her.

'I simply don't have a thing to wear, Sarathi.'

CHAPTER 6

Sparhawk had learned to keep a tight rein on his emotions during the years since his marriage to the Queen of Elenia, but his smile was slightly fixed as the meeting broke up. Kalten fell in beside him as they all left the council chamber. 'I gather that you're less than pleased with our queen's solution to the problem,' he observed. Kalten was Sparhawk's boyhood friend, and he had learned how to read that battered face.

'You might say that, yes,' Sparhawk replied tightly.

'Are you open to a suggestion?'

'I'll listen.' Sparhawk didn't want to make any promises at this point.

'Why don't you and I go down into the crypt under the Basilica?'

'Why?'

'I thought you might want to vent certain feelings before you and your wife discuss the matter. You're a bit savage when you're angry, Sparhawk, and I'm really very fond of your wife. If you call her an idiot to her face, you'll hurt her feelings.'

'Are you trying to be funny?'

'Not in the least, my friend. I feel almost the same way about it as you do, and I've had a very colourful education. When you run out of swear-words, I'll supply some you might not have heard.'

'Let's go,' Sparhawk said, turning abruptly down a side corridor.

They passed through the nave quickly, perfunctorily genuflecting to the altar in passing, and descended into

106

the crypt that contained the bones of several aeons' worth of Archprelates.

'Don't bang your fists on the walls,' Kalten cautioned as Sparhawk began to pace up and down, swearing and waving his arms in the air. 'You'll break your knuckles.'

'It's a total absurdity, Kalten!' Sparhawk said after he had shouted profanities for several minutes.

'It's worse than that, my friend. There's always room in the world for absurdities. They're sort of fun actually, but this is dangerous. We have no way of knowing what we're going to encounter in Tamuli. I love your wife dearly, but having her along is going to be inconvenient.'

'Inconvenient?'

'I'm trying to be polite. How does "bloody hindering awkward" strike you?'

'It's closer.'

'You'll never persuade her to stay home though. I'd give that up as a lost cause before I even started. She's obviously made up her mind, and she outranks you. You probably ought to try to put the best face on it – avoid the embarrassment of being told to shut your mouth and go to your room.' Sparhawk grunted.

'I think our best approach is to talk with Oscagne. We'll be taking the most precious thing in Elenia to the Daresian continent where things are far from tranquil. Your wife's going there is a personal favour to the Emperor of Tamuli, so he's obligated to protect her. An escort of a few dozen legions of Atans meeting us at the Astel border might be looked upon as a sign of his Majesty's appreciation, wouldn't you say?'

'That's really not a bad idea, Kalten.'

'I'm not *totally* stupid, Sparhawk. Now, Ehlana's going to expect you to rant and rave and wave your arms at her. She's ready for that, so don't do it. She *is* going along. We've lost that fight already, wouldn't you say?'

'Unless I chain her to the bed.'

'There's an interesting idea.'

'Never mind.'

'It's tactically unsound to fight a last stand unless you're trapped. Give her that victory, and then she'll owe you one. Use it to get her to agree not to do *anything* while we're in Tamuli without your express permission. That way we can keep her almost as safe as she'd be if she stayed home. There's a good chance that she'll be so happy that you didn't scream at her that she'll agree without thinking it all the way through. You'll be able to restrict her movements when we get there – at least enough to keep her out of danger.'

'Kalten, sometimes you amaze me,' Sparhawk told his friend.

'I know,' the blond Pandion replied. 'This stupid-looking face of mine is very useful sometimes.'

'Where did you ever learn so much about manipulating royalty?'

'I'm not manipulating royalty, Sparhawk. I'm manipulating a woman, and I'm an expert at that. Women are born negotiators. They love these little trades. If you go to a woman and say, "I'll do this for you if you do that for me," she'll almost always be willing to talk about it at least. Women *always* want to talk about things. If you keep your eye on what you really want, you'll almost always come out on top.' He paused. 'Metaphorically speaking of course,' he added.

'What are you up to, Sparhawk?' Mirtai asked him suspiciously when he approached the suite of rooms Dolmant had provided for Ehlana and her personal retinue. Sparhawk carefully let the smug expression slide from his face and assumed one of grave concern instead.

'Don't try to be clever, Sparhawk,' she told him. 'If you hurt her, I'll have to kill you, you know.'

'I'm not going to hurt her, Mirtai. I'm not even going to yell at her.'

'You're up to something, aren't you?'

'Of course I am. After you lock me inside, put your ear to the door and listen.' He gave her a sidelong look. 'But you do that all the time anyway, don't you?'

She actually blushed. She jerked the door open. 'Just get in there, Sparhawk!' she commanded, her face like a thundercloud.

'My, aren't we testy tonight?'

'Go!'

'Yes, ma'am.'

Ehlana was ready for him, that much was fairly obvious. She was wearing a dressing-gown of a pale rose that made her look particularly appealing, and she had done things with her hair. There was a barely noticeable tightness about her eyes, though.

'Good evening, love,' Sparhawk said calmly. 'Tedious day, wasn't it? Conferences can be so exhausting at times.' He crossed the room, pausing to kiss her almost perfunctorily in passing, and poured himself a glass of wine.

'I know what you're going to say, Sparhawk.' she said.

'Oh?' He gave her an innocent look.

'You're angry with me, aren't you?'

'No. Not really. What made you think I'd be angry?'

She looked a bit less sure of herself. 'You mean you're not? I thought you'd be raging by now – about my decision to pay a state visit to Tamuli, I mean.'

'No, actually it's a very good idea. Of course we'll have to take a few precautions to ensure your safety, but we always have to do that, so we're sort of used to it, aren't we?'

'What kind of precautions are we talking about here?' Her tone was suspicious.

'Nothing all that extreme, dear. I don't think you should go walking in the forest alone or visiting thieves' dens without some sort of escort. I'm not talking about anything out of the ordinary, and you're used to certain restrictions on your movements already. We'll be in a strange country, and we don't know the people. I know that you'll trust me to sort of nose things out, and that you won't argue with me if I tell you that something's too dangerous. We can all live with that, I'm sure. You pay me to protect you, after all, so we won't have any silly little squabbles about security measures, now will we?' He kept his tone mild and sweetly reasonable, giving her no reason to raise any questions about exactly what he had in mind when he spoke of 'security measures'.

'You know much more about that sort of thing than I do, my love,' she conceded, 'so I'll leave all that entirely in your hands. If a girl has a champion who just happens to be the greatest knight in the world, she'd be foolish not to pay attention to him, now wouldn't she?'

'My feelings exactly,' he agreed. It was a small victory, to be sure, but when one is dealing with a queen, victories of any kind are hard to come by.

'Well,' she said, rising to her feet, 'since we're not going to fight, why don't we go to bed?'

'Good idea.'

The kitten Talen had given to Princess Danae was named Mmrr, and Mmrr had one habit that particularly irritated Sparhawk. Kittens like to have company when they sleep, and Mmrr had found that when Sparhawk slept, he curled up slightly and that the space just behind his knees was a perfect place for her to nest. Sparhawk customarily slept with the covers pulled tightly around his neck, but that was no real problem. A cold, wet nose touched to the back of his neck caused him to flinch away violently, and that involuntary movement would always open just enough of a gap for an enterprising kitten. Mmrr found the whole process quite satisfactory and even rather amusing.

Sparhawk, however, did not. It was shortly before dawn when he emerged from the bedroom, tousled, sleepy-eyed and just a bit out of sorts.

Princess Danae wandered into the large central room absently dragging Rollo behind her. 'Have you seen my cat?' she asked her father.

'She's in bed with your mother,' he replied shortly.

'I should have known, I suppose. Mmrr likes the way mother smells. She told me so herself.'

Sparhawk glanced around and then carefully closed the bedroom door. 'I need to talk with Sephrenia again,' he said.

'All right.'

'Not here, though. I'll find someplace.'

'What happened last night?'

'We have to go to Tamuli.'

'I thought you were going to do something about Drychtnath.'

'I am – in a way. It seems that there's something – or someone – over on the Daresian continent that's behind Drychtnath. I think we'll be able to find out more about him there than we ever would here. I'll make arrangements to have you taken back to Cimmura.'

She pursed her small mouth. 'No, I don't think so,' she said. 'I'd better go along with you.'

'That's absolutely out of the question.'

'Oh, Sparhawk, *do* grow up. I'm going along because you're going to need me when we get there.' She negligently tossed Rollo over into a corner. 'I'm also going because you can't stop me. Come up with some reason

111

for it, Sparhawk. Otherwise you'll have to explain to mother how it is that I managed to get ahead of you when you all find me sitting in a tree alongside a road somewhere. Get dressed father, and go find a place where we can talk privately.'

Some time later, Sparhawk and his daughter climbed a narrow, spiralling wooden staircase that led to the cupola atop the dome of the Basilica. There was quite probably no more private place in the world, particularly in view of the fact that the wooden stairs leading up to the little bell-tower did not so much creak as they did shriek when anyone began to climb them.

When they reached the unenclosed little house high above the city, Danae spent several minutes gazing out over Chyrellos. 'You can always see so much better from up high like this,' she said. 'It's just about the only reason I've ever found for flying.'

'Can you really fly?'

'Of course. Can't you?'

'You know better, Aphrael.'

'I was only teasing you, Sparhawk,' she laughed. 'Let's get started.' She sat down, crossed her legs and lifted her little face to sing that trilling song she had raised back in Cimmura. Then again, her eyes closed and her face went blank as the song died away.

'What is it *this* time, Sparhawk?' Sephrenia's voice was a bit tart.

'What's the matter, little mother?'

'Do you realise that it's the middle of the night here?'

'It *is*?'

'Of course it is. The sun's on your side of the world now.'

'Astonishing – though I suppose it stands to reason if you think about it. Did I disturb you?'

'Yes, as a matter of fact you did.'

'What were you doing so late at night?'

'None of your business. What do you want?'

'We'll be coming to Daresia soon.'

'What?'

'The emperor asked us to come – well, he asked *me* actually. The rest are sort of tagging along. Ehlana's going to make a state visit to Matherion to sort of give us all an excuse for being there.'

'Have you taken leave of your senses? Tamuli's a very dangerous place right now.'

'Probably not much more than Eosia is. We were attacked by ancient Lamorks on our way here to Chyrellos from Cimmura.'

'Perhaps they were just modern-day Lamorks dressed in ancient garb.'

'I rather doubt that, Sephrenia. They vanished when their attack began to fail.'

'All of them?'

'Except for the ones who were already dead. Would a little logic offend you?'

'Not unless you drag it out.'

'We're almost positive that the attackers really were ancient Lamorks, and Ambassador Oscagne told us that someone's been raising antique heroes in Daresia as well. Logic implies that this resurrection business is originating in Tamuli and that its goal is to stir up nationalistic sentiments in order to weaken the central governments – the empire in Daresia and the Church here in Eosia. If we're right about the source of all of this activity being somewhere in Tamuli, that's the logical place to start looking for answers. Where are you right now?'

'Vanion and I are at Sarsos in eastern Astel. You'd better come here, Sparhawk. These long-distance conversations tend to blur things.'

Sparhawk thought for a moment, trying to remember

113

the map of Daresia. 'We'll come overland then. I'll find some way to get the others to agree to that.'

'Try not to take too long, Sparhawk. It's really very important that we talk face to face.'

'Right. Sleep well, little mother.'

'I wasn't sleeping.'

'Oh? What *were* you doing?'

'Didn't you hear what she told you before, Sparhawk?' his daughter asked him.

'Which was what?'

'She told you that it was none of your business what she was doing.'

'What an astonishingly good idea, your Majesty,' Oscagne said later that morning when they had all gathered once again in Dolmant's private audience-chamber. 'I'd have never thought of it in a million years. The leaders of the subject nations of Tamuli don't go to Matherion unless they're summoned by his Imperial Majesty.'

'The rulers of Eosia are less restrained, your Excellency,' Emban told him. 'They have total sovereignty.'

'Astonishing. Has your Church no authority over their actions, your Grace?'

'Only in spiritual matters, I'm afraid.'

'Isn't that inconvenient?'

'You wouldn't believe how much, Ambassador Oscagne,' Dolmant sighed, looking at Ehlana reproachfully.

'Be nice, Sarathi,' she murmured.

'Then no one is really in charge here in Eosia? No one has the absolute authority to make final decisions?'

'It's a responsibility we share, your Excellency,' Ehlana explained. 'We enjoy sharing things, don't we Sarathi?'

'Of course.' Dolmant said it without much enthusiasm.

'The rough-and-tumble, give-and-take nature of Eosian politics have a certain utility, your Excellency,' Stragen drawled. 'Consensus politics gives us the advantage of bringing together a wide range of views.'

'In Tamuli, we feel that having only one view is far less confusing.'

'The Emperor's view? What happens when the emperor happens to be an idiot? Or a madman?'

'The government usually works around him,' Oscagne admitted blandly. 'Such imperial misfortunes seldom live very long for some reason, however.'

'Ah,' Stragen said.

'Perhaps we should get down to work,' Emban said. He crossed the room to a large map of the known world hanging on the wall. 'The fastest way to travel is by sea,' he noted. 'We could sail from Madel in Cammoria out through the Inner Sea and then around the southern tip of Daresia and then up the east coast to Matherion.'

'We?' Sir Tynian asked.

'Oh, didn't I tell you?' Emban said. 'I'll be going along. Ostensibly, I'll be Queen Ehlana's spiritual advisor. In actuality, I'll be the Archprelate's personal envoy.'

'It's probably wiser to keep the Elenian flavour of the expedition,' Dolmant explained, 'for public consumption, anyway. Let's not complicate things by sending two separate missions to Matherion simultaneously.'

Sparhawk had to move quickly, and he didn't have much to work with. 'Travelling by ship has certain advantages,' he conceded, 'but I think there's a major drawback.'

'Oh?' Emban said.

'It satisfies the requirements of a state visit, right enough, but it doesn't do very much to address our *real* reason for going to Tamuli. Your Excellency, what's likely to happen when we reach Matherion?'

'The usual,' Oscagne shrugged. 'Audiences, banquets, reviewing troops, concerts, that giddy round of meaningless activity we all adore.'

'Precisely,' Sparhawk agreed. 'And we won't really get anything done, will we?'

'Probably not.'

'But we aren't going to Tamuli for a month-long carouse. What we're *really* going there for is to find out what's behind all the upheaval. We need information, not entertainment, and the information's probably out in the hinterlands, not in the capital. I think we should find some reason to go across country.' It was a practical suggestion, and it rather neatly concealed Sparhawk's *real* reason for wanting to go overland.

Emban's expression was pained. 'We'd be on the road for months that way.'

'We can get as much done as we'll accomplish in Matherion by staying home, your Grace. We *have* to get outside the Capital.'

Emban groaned. 'You're absolutely bent on making me ride a horse all the way from here to Matherion, aren't you, Sparhawk?'

'You could stay home, your Grace,' Sparhawk suggested. 'We could always take Patriarch Bergsten instead. He'd be better in a fight anyway.'

'That will do, Sparhawk,' Dolmant said firmly.

'Consensus politics are very interesting, Milord Stragen,' Oscagne observed. 'In Matherion, we'd have followed the course suggested by the Primate of Ucera without any further discussion. We try to avoid raising the possibility of alternatives whenever possible.'

'Welcome to Eosia, your Excellency,' Stragen smiled.

'Permission to speak?' Khalad said politely.

'Of course,' Dolmant replied.

116

Khalad rose, went to the map and began measuring distance. 'A good horse can cover ten leagues a day, and a good ship can cover thirty – if the wind holds.' He frowned and looked around. 'Why is Talen never around when you need him?' he muttered. 'He can compute these numbers in his head. I have to count them up on my fingers.'

'He said he had something to take care of,' Berit told him.

Khalad grunted. 'All we're really interested in is what's going on in Daresia, so there's no need to ride across Eosia. We could sail from Madel the way Patriarch Emban suggested, go out through the Inner Sea and then up the east coast of Zemoch to –' He looked at the map and then pointed. 'To Salesha here. That's nine hundred leagues – thirty days. If we were to follow the roads, it'd probably be the same distance overland, but that would take us ninety days. We'd save two months at least.'

'Well,' Emban conceded grudgingly, 'that's something, anyway.'

Sparhawk was fairly sure that they could save much more than sixty days. He looked across the room at his daughter, who was playing with her kitten under Mirtai's watchful eye. Princess Danae was quite frequently present at conferences where she had no real business. People did not question her presence for some reason. Sparhawk knew that the Child Goddess Aphrael could tamper with the passage of time, but he was not entirely certain that she could manage it so undetectably in her present incarnation as she had when she had been Flute.

Princess Danae looked back at him and rolled her eyes upward with a resigned expression that spoke volumes about his limited understanding, and then she gravely nodded her head.

Sparhawk breathed somewhat easier after that. 'Now we come to the question of the queen's security,' he continued. 'Ambassador Oscagne, how large a retinue could my wife take with her without raising eyebrows?'

'The conventions are a little vague on that score, Sir Sparhawk.'

Sparhawk looked around at his friends. 'If I thought I could get away with it, I'd take the whole body of the militant orders with me,' he said.

'We've defined our trip as a visit, Sparhawk,' Tynian said, 'not an invasion. Would a hundred armoured knights alarm his Imperial Majesty, your Excellency?'

'It's a symbolic sort of number,' Oscagne agreed after a moment's consideration, 'large enough for show, but not so large as to appear threatening. We'll be going through Astel, and you can pick up an escort of Atans in the capitol at Darsas. A sizeable escort for a state visitor shouldn't raise too many eyebrows.'

'Twenty-five knights from each order, wouldn't you think, Sparhawk?' Bevier suggested. 'The differences in our equipment and the colours of our surcoats would make the knights appear more ceremonial than utilitarian. A hundred Pandions by themselves might cause concern in some quarters.'

'Good idea,' Sparhawk agreed.

'You can bring more if you want, Sparhawk,' Mirtai told him. 'There are Peloi on the steppes of Central Astel. They're the descendants of Kring's ancestors. He might just want to visit his cousins in Daresia.'

'Ah yes,' Oscagne said, 'the Peloi. I'd forgotten that you had those wild-men here in Eosia too. They're an excitable and sometimes unreliable people. Are you certain that this Kring person would be willing to accompany us?'

'Kring would ride into fire if I asked him to,' Mirtai replied confidently.

'The Domi is much taken with our Mirtai, your Excellency,' Ehlana smiled. 'He comes to Cimmura three or four times a year to propose marriage to her.'

'The Peloi are warriors, Atana,' Oscagne noted. 'You would not demean yourself in the eyes of your people were you to accept him.'

'Husbands take their wives more or less for granted, Oscagne,' Mirtai pointed out with a mysterious little smile. 'A suitor, on the other hand, is much more attentive, and I rather enjoy Kring's attentions. He writes very nice poetry. He compared me to a golden sunrise once. I thought that was rather nice.'

'You never wrote any poetry for me, Sparhawk,' Ehlana accused her husband.

'The Elene language is limited, my Queen,' he responded. 'It has no words which could do you justice.'

'Nice try,' Kalten murmured.

'I think we all might want to spend a bit of time on some correspondence at this point,' Dolmant told them. 'There are all sorts of arrangements to be made. I'll put a fast ship at your disposal, Ambassador Oscagne. You'll want to advise your emperor that the Queen of Elenia's coming to call.'

'With the Archprelate's permission, I'll communicate with my government by dispatch rather than in person. There are social and political peculiarities in various parts of the empire. I could be very helpful in smoothing her Majesty's path if I went with her.'

'I'll be very pleased to have a civilised man along, your Excellency,' Ehlana smiled. 'You have no idea what it's like being surrounded by men whose clothes have all been tailored by blacksmiths.'

Talen entered the chamber with an excited expression on his face.

'Where have you been?' The question came from several parts of the room.

'It's such a comfort to be so universally loved that my activities arouse this breathless curiosity,' the boy said with an exaggerated and sardonic bow. 'I'm quite overwhelmed by this demonstration of affection.'

Ambassador Oscagne looked quizzically at Dolmant.

'It would take far too long to explain, your Excellency,' Dolmant said wearily. 'Just keep a close watch on your valuables when that boy's in the room.'

'Sarathi,' Talen protested. 'I haven't stolen a single thing for almost a week now.'

'That's a start, I suppose,' Emban noted.

'Old habits die hard, your Grace,' Talen smirked. 'Anyway, since you're all dying to know, I was out in the city sort of nosing around, and I ran across an old friend. Would you believe that Krager's here in Chyrellos?'

PART TWO

Astel

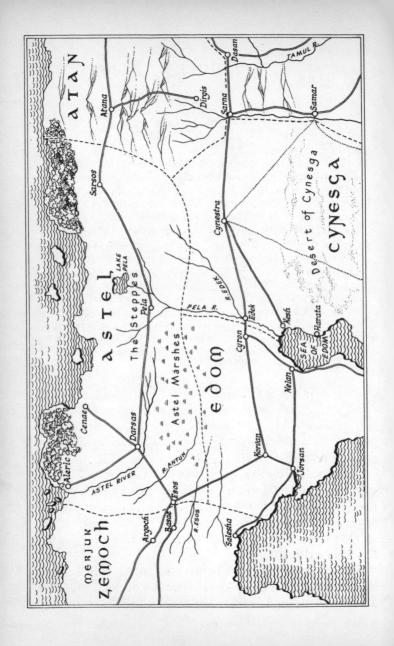

CHAPTER 7

Komier,

    My wife's making a state visit to Matherion in Tamuli. We've discovered that the present turmoil in Lamorkand is probably originating in Daresia, so we're using Ehlana's trip to give us the chance to go there to see what we can find out. I'll keep you advised. I'm borrowing twenty-five Genidian Knights from your local chapterhouse to serve as a part of the honour guard.

    I'd suggest that you do what you can to keep Avin Wargunsson from cementing any permanent alliances with Count Gerrich in Lamorkand. Gerrich is rather deeply involved in some kind of grand plan that goes far beyond the borders of Lamorkand itself. Dolmant probably wouldn't be too displeased if you, Darrellon and Abriel can contrive some excuse to go to Lamorkand and step on the fellow's neck. Watch out for magic, though. Gerrich's getting help from somebody who knows more than he's supposed to. Ulath's sending you more details.

    – Sparhawk.

'Isn't that just a little blunt, dear?' Ehlana said, reading over her husband's shoulder. She smelled very good.

'Komier's a blunt sort of fellow, Ehlana,' Sparhawk shrugged, laying down his quill, 'and I'm not really very good at writing letters.'

'I noticed.' They were in their ornate apartments in one of the Church buildings adjoining the Basilica where they had spent the day composing messages to people scattered over most of the continent.

'Don't you have letters of your own to write?' Sparhawk asked his wife.

'I'm all finished. All I really had to do was send a short note to Lenda. He knows what to do.' She glanced across the room at Mirtai, who sat patiently snipping the tips off Mmrr's claws. Mmrr was not taking it very well. Ehlana smiled. 'Mirtai's communication with Kring was much more direct. She called in an itinerant Peloi and told him to ride to Kring with her command to ride to Basne on the Zemoch-Astel border with a hundred of his tribesmen. She said that if he isn't waiting when she gets there, she'll take it to mean that he doesn't love her.' Ehlana pushed her pale blonde hair back from her brow.

'Poor Kring,' Sparhawk smiled. 'She could raise him from the dead with a message like that. Do you think she'll ever really marry him?'

'That's very hard to say, Sparhawk. He does have her attention, though.'

There was a knock at the door, and Mirtai rose to let Kalten in. 'It's a beautiful day out there,' the blond man told them. 'We'll have good weather for the trip.'

'How are things coming along?' Sparhawk asked him.

'We're just about all ready.' Kalten was wearing a green brocade doublet, and he bowed extravagantly to the queen. 'Actually, we *are* ready. About the only things happening now are the usual redundancies.'

'Could you clarify that just a bit, Sir Kalten?' Ehlana said.

He shrugged. 'Everyone's going over all the things everyone else has done to make sure that nothing's been left out.' He sprawled in a chair. 'We're surrounded by busybodies, Sparhawk. Nobody seems to be able to believe that anybody else can do something right. If Emban asks me if the knights are all ready to ride about one more time, I think I'll strangle him. He has no idea at all about what's involved in moving a large group of people from one place to another. Would you believe that he was going to try to put all of us on one ship? Horses and all?'

'That might have been just a bit crowded,' Ehlana

smiled. 'How many ships did he finally decide on?'

'I'm not sure. I still don't know for certain how many people are going. Your attendants are all absolutely convinced that you'll simply die without their company, my Queen. There are about forty or so who are making preparations for the trip.'

'You'd better weed them out, Ehlana,' Sparhawk suggested. 'I don't want to be saddled with the entire court.'

'I *will* need a few people, Sparhawk – if only for the sake of appearances.'

Talen came into the room. The gangly boy was wearing what he called his 'street clothes' – slightly mismatched, very ordinary and just this side of shabby. 'He's still out there,' he said, his eyes bright.

'Who?' Kalten asked.

'Krager. He's creeping around Chyrellos like a lost puppy looking for a home. Stragen's got people from the local thieves' community watching him. We haven't been able to figure out exactly what he's up to just yet. If Martel were still alive, I'd almost say he's doing the same sort of thing he used to do – letting himself be seen.'

'How does he look?'

'Worse.' Talen's voice cracked slightly. It was still hovering somewhere between soprano and baritone. 'The years aren't treating Krager very well. His eyes look like they've been poached in bacon grease. He looks absolutely miserable.'

'I think I can bear Krager's misery,' Sparhawk noted. 'He's beginning to make me just a little tired, though. He's been sort of hovering around the edge of my awareness for the last ten years or more – sort of like a hangnail or an ingrown toenail. He always seems to be working for the other side, but he's too insignificant to really worry about.'

'Stragen could ask one of the local thieves to cut his throat,' Talen offered.

Sparhawk considered it. 'Maybe not,' he decided. 'Krager's always been a good source of information. Tell Stragen that if the opportunity happens to come up, we might want to have a little chat with our old friend, though. The offer to braid his legs together usually makes Krager very talkative.'

Ulath stopped by about a half hour later. 'Did you finish that letter to Komier?' he asked Sparhawk.

'He has a draft copy, Sir Ulath,' Ehlana replied for her husband. 'It definitely needs some polish.'

'You don't have to polish things for Komier, your Majesty. He's used to strange letters. One of my Genidian brothers sent him a report written on human skin once.'

She stared at him. 'He did *what*?'

'There wasn't anything else handy to write on. A Genidian Knight just arrived with a message for me from Komier, though. The knight's going back to Emsat, and he can carry Sparhawk's letter if it's ready to go.'

'It's close enough,' Sparhawk said, folding the parchment and dribbling candle wax on it to seal it. 'What did Komier have to say?'

'It was good news for a change. All the Trolls have left Thalesia for some reason.'

'Where did they go?'

'Who knows? Who cares?'

'The people who live in the country they've gone to might be slightly interested,' Kalten suggested.

'That's their problem,' Ulath shrugged. 'It's funny, though. The Trolls don't really get along with each other. I couldn't even begin to guess at a reason why they'd all decide to pack up and leave at the same time. The discussions must have been very interesting. They usually kill each other on sight.'

* * *

'There's not much help I can give you, Sparhawk,' Dolmant said gravely when the two of them met privately later that day. 'The Church is fragmented in Daresia. They don't accept the authority of Chyrellos, so I can't order them to assist you.' Dolmant's face was careworn, and his white cassock made his complexion look sallow. In a very real sense, Dolmant ruled an empire that stretched from Thalesia to Cammoria, and the burdens of his office bore down on him heavily. The change they had all noticed in their friend in the past several years derived more likely from that than from any kind of inflated notion of his exalted station.

'You'll get more co-operation in Astel than either Edom or Daconia,' he continued. 'The doctrine of the Church of Astel is very close to ours – close enough that we even recognise Astellian ecclesiastical rank. Edom and Daconia broke away from the Astellian Church thousands of years ago and went their own way.' The Archprelate smiled ruefully. 'The sermons in those two kingdoms are generally little more than hysterical denunciations of the Church of Chyrellos – and of me personally. They're anti-hierarchical, much like the Rendors. If you should happen to go into those two kingdoms, you can expect the Church there to oppose you. The fact that you're a Church Knight will be held against you rather than the reverse. The children there are all taught that the Knights of the Church have horns and tails. They'll expect you to burn churches, murder clergymen and enslave the people.'

'I'll do what I can to stay away from those places, Sarathi,' Sparhawk assured him. 'Who's in charge in Astel?'

'The Archimandrite of Darsas is nominally the head of the Astellian Church. It's an obscure rank approximately the equivalent of our "patriarch". The Church of Astel's

127

organised along monastic lines. They don't have a secular clergy there.'

'Are there any other significant differences I should know about?'

'Some of the customs are different – liturgical variations primarily. I doubt that you'll be asked to conduct any services, so that shouldn't cause any problems. It's probably just as well. I heard you deliver a sermon once.'

Sparhawk smiled. 'We serve in different ways, Sarathi. Our Holy Mother didn't hire me to preach to people. How do I address the Archimandrite of Darsas – in case I meet him?'

'Call him "your Grace", the same as you would a patriarch. He's an imposing man with a huge beard, and there's nothing in Astel that he doesn't know about. His priests are everywhere. The people trust them implicitly, and they all submit weekly reports to the Archimandrite. The Church has enormous power there.'

'What a novel idea.'

'Don't mistreat me, Sparhawk. Things haven't been going very well for me lately.'

'Would you be willing to listen to an assessment, Dolmant?'

'Of me personally? Probably not.'

'I wasn't talking about that. You're too old to change, I expect. I'm talking about your policies in Rendor. Your basic idea was good enough, but you went at it the wrong way.'

'Be careful, Sparhawk. I've sent men to monasteries permanently for less than that.'

'Your policy of reconciliation with the Rendors was very sound. I spent ten years down there, and I know how they think. The ordinary people in Rendor would really like to be reconciled with the Church – if for no

128

other reason than to get rid of all the howling fanatics out in the desert. Your policy is good, but you sent the wrong people there to carry it out.'

'The priests I sent are all experts in doctrine, Sparhawk.'

'That's the problem. You sent doctrinaire fanatics down there. All they want to do is punish the Rendors for their heresy.'

'Heresy *is* a sort of problem, Sparhawk.'

'The heresy of the Rendors isn't theological, Dolmant. They worship the same God we do, and their body of religious belief is identical to ours. The disagreements between us are entirely in the field of Church government. The Church was corrupt when the Rendors broke away from us. The members of the Hierocracy were sending relatives to fill Church positions in Rendor, and those relatives were parasitic opportunists who were far more interested in lining their own purses than caring for the souls of the people. When you get right down to it, that's why the Rendors started murdering primates and priests – and they're doing it for exactly the same reason now. You'll never reconcile the Rendors to the Church if you try to punish them. They don't care who's governing our Holy Mother. They'll never see you personally, my friend, but they *will* see their local priest – probably every day. If he spends all his time calling them heretics and tearing the veils off their women, they'll kill him. It's as simple as that.'

Dolmant's face was troubled. 'Perhaps I *have* blundered,' he admitted. 'Of course if you tell anybody I said that, I'll deny it.'

'Naturally.'

'All right, what should I do about it?'

Sparhawk remembered something then. 'There's a Vicar in a poor church in Borrata,' he said. 'He's probably the closest thing to a saint I've ever seen, and I didn't even get his name. Berit knows what it is though. Disguise some investigators as beggars and send them down to Cammoria to observe him. He's exactly the kind of man you need.'

'Why not just send for *him*?'

'He'd be too tongue-tied to speak to you, Sarathi. He's what they had in mind when they coined the word "humble". Besides, he'd never leave his flock. If you order him to Chyrellos and then send him to Rendor, he'll probably die within six months. He's that kind of man.'

Dolmant's eyes suddenly filled with tears. 'You trouble me, Sparhawk,' he said. 'You trouble me. That's the ideal we all had when we took holy orders.' He sighed. 'How did we all get so far away from it?'

'You got too much involved in the world, Dolmant,' Sparhawk told him gently. 'The Church has to live in the world, but the world corrupts *her* much faster than she can redeem *it*.'

'What's the answer to that problem, Sparhawk?'

'I honestly don't know, Sarathi. Maybe there isn't any.'

'Sparhawk.' It was his daughter's voice, and it was somehow inside his head. He was passing through the nave of the Basilica, and he quickly knelt as if in prayer to cover what he was really doing.

'What is it, Aphrael?' he asked silently.

'You don't have to genuflect to me, Sparhawk.' Her voice was amused.

'I'm not. If they catch me walking through the corridors holding long conversations with somebody who isn't there, they'll lock me up in an asylum.'

'You look very reverential in that position, though. I'm touched.'

'Was there something significant, or are you just amusing yourself?'

'Sephrenia wants to talk with you again.'

'All right. I'm in the nave right now. Come down and meet me here. We'll go up to the cupola again.'

'I'll meet you up there.'

'There's only one stairway leading up there, Aphrael. We have to climb it.'

'*You* might have to, but I don't. I don't like going into the nave, Sparhawk. I always have to stop and talk with your God, and He's so tedious most of the time.'

Sparhawk's mind shuddered back from the implications of that.

The dried-out wooden stairs circling up to the top of the dome still shrieked their protest as Sparhawk mounted. It was a long climb, and he was winded when he reached the top.

'What took you so long?' Danae asked him. She wore a simple white smock. It was a little-girl sort of dress, so no one seemed to even notice that its cut was definitely Styric.

'You enjoy saying things like that to me, don't you?' Sparhawk accused.

'I'm only teasing, father,' she laughed.

'I hope no one saw you coming up here. I don't think the world's ready for a flying princess just yet.'

'No one saw me, Sparhawk. I've done this before, you know. Trust me.'

'Do I have any choice? Let's get to work. I've still got a lot left to do today if we're going to leave tomorrow morning.'

She nodded and sat cross-legged near one of the huge bells. She lifted her face again and raised that flute-like trill. Then her voice drifted off, and her face went blank.

'Where have you been?' Sephrenia asked, opening Danae's eyes to stare at her pupil.

He sighed. 'If you two don't stop that, I'm going to go into another line of work.'

131

'Has Aphrael been teasing you again?' she asked.

'Of course she has. Did you know that she can fly?'

'I've never seen her do it, but I'd assumed she could.'

'What did you want to see me about?'

'I've been hearing disturbing rumours. The northern Atans have been seeing some very large, shaggy creatures in the forests near their north coast.'

'So *that's* where they went.'

'Don't be cryptic, dear one.'

'Komier sent word to Ulath. It seems that the Trolls have all left Thalesia.'

'The Trolls!' she exclaimed. 'They wouldn't do that! Thalesia's their ancestral home!'

'Maybe you'd better go tell the Trolls about that. Komier swears that there's not a single one of them left in Thalesia.'

'Something very, very strange is going on here, Sparhawk.'

'Ambassador Oscagne said more or less the same thing. Can the Styrics there at Sarsos make any sense out of it yet?'

'No. Zalasta's at his wits' end.'

'Have you come up with any idea at all of who's behind it?'

'Sparhawk, we don't even know *what's* behind it. We can't even make a guess about the *species* of whatever it is.'

'We sort of keep coming back to the idea that it's the Troll-Gods again. *Something* had to have enough authority over the Trolls to command them to leave Thalesia, and that points directly at the Troll Gods. Are we absolutely *sure* that they haven't managed to get loose?'

'It's not a good idea to discount *any* possibility when you're dealing with Gods, Sparhawk. I don't know the spell Ghwerig used when he put them inside the Bhelliom, so I don't know if it can be broken.'

132

'Then it *is* possible.'

'That's what I just said, dear one. Have you seen that shadow – or the cloud – lately?'

'No.'

'Has Aphrael ever seen it?'

'No.'

'*She* could tell you, but I'd rather not have her exposed to whatever it is. Perhaps we can come up with a way to lure it out when you get here so that I can take a look at it. When are you leaving?'

'First thing tomorrow morning. Danae sort of told me that she can play with time the way she did when we were marching to Acie with Wargun's army. That would get us there faster, but can she do it as undetectably now as she did when she was Flute?'

The bell behind the motionless form of his daughter gave a deep, soft-toned sound. 'Why don't you ask *me*, Sparhawk?' Danae's voice hummed in the bell-sound. 'It's not as if I weren't here, you know.'

'How was I supposed to know that?' He waited. 'Well?' he asked the still-humming bell. 'Can you?'

'Well, of *course* I can, Sparhawk.' The Child Goddess sounded irritated. 'Don't you know *anything*?'

'That will do,' Sephrenia chided.

'He's such a lump.'

'Aphrael! I said that will do! You will *not* be disrespectful to your father.' A faint smile touched the lips of the apparently somnolent little princess. 'Even if he *is* a hopeless lump.'

'If you two want to discuss my failings, I'll go back downstairs so you can speak freely,' Sparhawk told them.

'No, that's all right, Sparhawk,' Aphrael said lightly. 'We're all friends, so we shouldn't have any secrets from each other.'

*   *   *

They left Chyrellos the following morning and rode south on the Arcian side of the Sarin river in bright morning sunshine with one hundred Church Knights in full armour riding escort. The grass along the riverbank was very green, and the blue sky was dotted with fluffy white clouds. After some discussion, Sparhawk and Ehlana had decided that the attendants she would need for the sake of appearances could be drawn for the most part from the ranks of the Church Knights. 'Stragen can coach them,' Sparhawk had told his wife. 'He's had a certain amount of experience, so he can make honest knights look like useless butterflies.'

It had been necessary, however, to include one lady-in-waiting, Baroness Melidere, a young woman of Ehlana's own age with honey-blonde hair, deep blue eyes and an apparently empty head. Ehlana also took along a personal maid, a doe-eyed girl named Alean. The two of them rode in the carriage with the Queen, Mirtai, Danae and Stragen, who, dressed in his elegant best, kept them amused with light banter. Sparhawk reasoned that between them, Stragen and Mirtai could provide his wife and daughter with a fairly significant defence if the occasion arose.

Patriarch Emban was going to be a problem. Sparhawk could see that after they had gone no more than a few miles. Emban was not comfortable on a horse, and he filled the air with complaints as he rode.

'That isn't going to work, you know,' Kalten observed about mid-morning. 'Churchman or not, if the knights have to listen to Emban feel sorry for himself all the way across the Daresian continent, he's likely to have some kind of an accident before we get to Matherion. I'm ready to drown him right now myself, and the river's very handy.'

Sparhawk thought about it. He looked at the queen's carriage. 'That landau's not quite big enough,' he told his friend. 'I think we need something grander. Six horses are more impressive than four anyway. See if you can find Bevier.'

When the olive-skinned Arcian rode forward, Sparhawk explained the situation. 'If we don't get Emban off that horse, it's going to take us a year to cross Daresia. Are you still on speaking terms with your cousin Lycien?'

'Of course. We're the best of friends.'

'Why don't you ride on ahead and have a chat with him? We need a large carriage – roomy enough for eight – six horses probably. We'll put Emban and Ambassador Oscagne in the carriage with my wife and her entourage. Ask your cousin to locate one for us.'

'That might be expensive, Sparhawk,' Bevier said dubiously.

'That's all right, Bevier. The Church will pay for it. After a week on horseback, Emban should be willing to sign for anything that doesn't wear a saddle. Oh, as long as you're going there anyway, have our ships moved up-river to Lycien's docks. Madel's not so attractive a city that any of us would enjoy a stay there all that much, and Lycien's docks are more conveniently arranged.'

'Will we need anything else, Sparhawk?' Bevier asked.

'Not that I can think of. Feel free to improvise, though. Add anything you can think of on your way to Madel. For once, we have a more or less unlimited budget at our disposal. The coffers of the Church are wide open to us.'

'I wouldn't tell that to Stragen or Talen, my friend,' Bevier laughed. 'I'll be at Lycien's house. I'll see you when you get there.' He wheeled his horse and rode south at a gallop.

'Why didn't you just have him pick up another carriage for Emban and Oscagne?' Kalten asked.

'Because I don't want to have to defend two when we get to Tamuli.'

'Oh. That makes sense – sort of.'

They arrived at the house of Sir Bevier's cousin the Marquis Lycien, late one afternoon, and met Bevier and his stout, florid-faced kinsman in the gravelled court in front of Lycien's opulent home. The Marquis bowed deeply to the Queen of Elenia and insisted that she accept his hospitality during her stay in Madel. Kalten dispersed the knights in Lycien's park-like grounds.

'Did you find a carriage?' Sparhawk asked Bevier.

Bevier nodded. 'It's large enough for our purposes,' he said a bit dubiously, 'but the cost of it may turn Patriarch Emban's hair white.'

'I wouldn't be too sure,' Sparhawk said. 'Let's ask him.' They crossed the gravelled court to where the Patriarch of Ucera stood beside his horse, clinging to his saddle-horn with a look of profound misery on his face.

'Pleasant little ride, wasn't it, your Grace?' Sparhawk asked the fat man brightly.

Emban groaned. 'I don't think I'll be able to walk for a week.'

'Of course we were only strolling,' Sparhawk continued. 'We'll have to move along much faster when we get to Tamuli.' He paused. 'May I speak frankly, your Grace?'

'You will anyway, Sparhawk,' Emban said sourly. 'Would you really pay any attention to me if I objected?'

'Probably not. You're slowing us down, you know.'

'Well, *excuse* me.'

'You're not really built for horseback riding, Patriarch Emban. Your talent's in your head, not your backside.'

Emban's eyes narrowed with hostility. 'Go on,' he said in an ominous tone of voice.

'Since we're in a hurry, we've decided to put wheels under you. Would you be more comfortable in a cushioned carriage, your Grace?'

'Sparhawk, I could kiss you!'

'I'm a married man, your Grace. My wife might misunderstand. For security reasons, one carriage is far better than two, so I've taken the liberty of locating one that's somewhat larger than the one Ehlana rode down from Chyrellos. You wouldn't mind riding with her, would you? We thought we'd put you and Ambassador Oscagne in the carriage with my queen and her attendants. Would that be satisfactory?'

'Did you want me to kiss the ground you're standing on, Sparhawk?'

'Oh, that won't be necessary, your Grace. All you really have to do is sign the authorisation for the carriage. This *is* urgent Church business, after all, so the purchase of the carriage is fully justified, wouldn't you say?'

'Where do I sign?' Emban's expression was eager.

'A carriage that large is expensive, your Grace,' Sparhawk warned him.

'I'd pawn the Basilica itself if it'd keep me out of that saddle.'

'You see?' Sparhawk said to Bevier as they walked away. 'That wasn't hard at all, was it?'

'How did you know he'd agree so quickly?'

'Timing, Bevier, timing. Later on, he might have objected to the price. You need to ask that sort of question while the man you're asking is still in pain.'

'You're a cruel fellow, Sparhawk,' Bevier laughed.

'All sorts of people have said that to me from time to time,' Sparhawk replied blandly.

'My people will finish loading the supplies for your voyage today, Sparhawk,' Marquis Lycien said as they rode

137

toward the riverside village and its wharves on the edge of his estate. 'You'll be able to sail with the morning tide.'

'You're a true friend, my Lord,' Sparhawk told him. 'You're always here when we need you.'

'You're exaggerating my benevolence, Sir Sparhawk,' Lycien laughed. 'I'm making a very handsome profit by outfitting your vessels.'

'I like to see friends get on in the world.'

Lycien looked back over his shoulder at the Queen of Elenia, who rode a grey palfrey some distance to the rear. 'You're the luckiest man in the world, Sparhawk,' he observed. 'Your wife is the most beautiful woman I've ever seen.'

'I'll tell her you said that, Marquis Lycien. I'm sure she'll be pleased.'

Ehlana and Emban had decided to accompany them as they rode down to the Marquis' enclave on the river, Ehlana to inspect the accommodations aboard ship, and Emban to have a look at the carriage he had just purchased.

The flotilla moored to Lycien's wharves consisted of a dozen large, well-fitted vessels, ships which made the merchantmen moored nearby look scruffy by comparison.

Lycien led the way through the village which had grown up around the wharves toward the river, which sparkled in the morning sun.

'Master Cluff!' The voice was not unlike a fog-horn.

Sparhawk turned in his saddle. 'Well strike me down if it isn't Captain Sorgi!' he said with genuine pleasure. He liked the blunt, silvery-haired sea captain with whom he had spent so many hours. He swung down from Faran's back and warmly clasped his friend's hand.

'I haven't seen you in a dog's age, Master Cluff,' Sorgi said expansively. 'Are you still running from those cousins?'

138

Sparhawk pulled a long face and sighed mournfully. It was just too good an opportunity to pass up. 'No,' he replied in a broken voice, 'not any more, I'm afraid. I made the mistake of staying in an ale-house in Apalia up in northern Pelosia for one last tankard. The cousins caught up with me there.'

'Were you able to escape?' Sorgi's face mirrored his concern.

'There were a dozen of them, Captain, and they were on me before I could even move. They clapped me in irons and took me to the estate of the ugly heiress I told you about.'

'They didn't force you to marry her, did they?' Sorgi asked, sounding shocked.

'I'm afraid so, my friend,' Sparhawk said in a tragic voice. 'That's my wife on that grey horse there.' He pointed at the radiant Queen of Elenia.

Captain Sorgi stared, his eyes growing wider and his mouth gaping open.

'Horrible, isn't it?' Sparhawk said with a broken-hearted catch in his voice.

CHAPTER 8

Baroness Melidere was a pretty girl with hair the colour of honey and eyes as blue as a summer sky. She did not have a brain in her head – at least that was what she wanted people to believe. In actuality, the baroness was probably more clever than most of the people in Ehlana's court, but she had learned early in life that people with limited intelligence feel threatened by pretty, clever young women, and she had perfected a vapid, empty-headed smile, a look of blank incomprehension and a silly giggle. She erected these defences as the situation required and kept her own counsel.

Queen Ehlana saw through the subterfuge and even encouraged it. Melidere was very observant and had excellent hearing. People tend not to pay much attention to brainless girls, and they say things in their presence they might not ordinarily say. Melidere always reported these conversational lapses back to the queen, and so Ehlana found the baroness useful to have around.

Melidere, however, drove Stragen absolutely wild. He knew with complete certainty that she could not be as stupid as she appeared, but he could never catch her off guard.

Alean, the queen's maid, was quite another matter. Her mind was very ordinary, but her nature was such that people automatically loved her. She was sweet, gentle and very loving. She had brown hair and enormous, soft brown eyes. She was shy and modest and seldom spoke. Kalten looked upon her as his natural prey, much as the wolf looks upon deer with a proprietary sense of ownership. Kalten was fond of maids.

They did not usually threaten him, and he could normally proceed with them without any particular fear of failure.

The ship in which they sailed from Madel that spring was well-appointed. It belonged to the Church and it had been built to convey high-ranking churchmen and their servants to various parts of Eosia.

There is a certain neat, cosy quality about ship cabins. They are uniformly constructed of dark-stained wood, the oily stain being a necessary protection for wood which is perpetually exposed to excessive humidity. The furniture is stationary, resisting all efforts to rearrange it, since it is customarily bolted to the floor to prevent its migration from one part of the cabin to another in rough weather. Since the ceiling of a ship's cabin is in reality the underside of the deck overhead where the sailors are working, the dark supporting beams are substantial.

In the particular vessel upon which the Queen of Elenia and her entourage sailed, there was a large cabin in the stern with a broad window running across the back of the ship. It was a sort of floating audience chamber, and it was ideally suited for gatherings. Because of the window at the back, the cabin was light and airy, and, since the vessel was moved by her sails, the wind always came from astern, and it efficiently carried the smell of the bilges forward for the crew to enjoy in their cramped quarters in the forecastle.

On the second day out, Sparhawk and Ehlana dressed themselves in plain, utilitarian garments and went up to what had come to be called 'the throne-room' from their private cabin just below. Alean was preparing Princess Danae's breakfast over a cunning little utensil which was part lamp and part stove. Alean prepared most of Danae's meals, since she accepted the child's dietary prejudices without question.

There was a polite knock, and then Kalten and Stragen entered. Kalten bore himself strangely, half crouched, twisted off to one side and quite obviously in pain.

'What happened to you?' Sparhawk asked him.

'I tried to sleep in a hammock,' Kalten groaned. 'Since we're at sea, I thought it was the thing to do. I think I've ruined myself, Sparhawk.'

Mirtai rose from her chair near the door. 'Stand still,' she peremptorily ordered the blond man.

'What are you doing?' he demanded suspiciously.

'Be quiet.' She ran one hand up his back, gently probing with her fingertips. 'Lie down on the floor,' she commanded, 'on your stomach.'

'Not *very* likely.'

'Do you want me to kick your feet out from under you?'

Grumbling, he painfully lowered himself to the deck. 'Is this going to hurt?' he asked.

'It won't hurt *me* a bit,' she assured him, removing her sandals. 'Try to relax.' Then she started to walk on him. There were crackling noises and loud pops. There were also gasps and cries of pain as Kalten writhed under her feet. She finally paused, thoughtfully probing at a stubborn spot between his shoulder blades with her toes. Then she rose up on her toes and came down quite firmly.

Kalten's shriek was strangled as his breath whooshed out, and the noise that came from his back was very loud, much like the sound which might come from a tree trunk being snapped in two. He lay face down, gasping and groaning.

'Don't be such a baby,' Mirtai told him heartlessly. 'Get up.'

'I can't. You've killed me.'

She picked him up by one arm and set him on his feet. 'Walk around,' she commanded him.

'*Walk?* I can't even breathe.'

She drew one of her daggers.

'All right. All right. Don't get excited. I'm walking.'

'Swing your arms back and forth.'

'Why?'

'Just do it, Kalten. You've got to loosen up those muscles.'

He walked back and forth, swinging his arms and gingerly turning his head back and forth. 'You know, I hate to admit it, but I do feel better – much better actually.'

'Naturally.' She put her dagger away.

'You didn't have to be so rough, though.'

'I can put you back into exactly the same condition as you were when you came in, if you'd like.'

'No. That's quite all right, Mirtai.' He said it very quickly and backed away from her. Then, always the opportunist, he sidled up to Alean. 'Don't you feel sorry for me?' he asked in an insinuating voice.

'Kalten!' Mirtai snapped. 'No!'

'I was only –'

She smacked him sharply on the nose with two fingers, much as one would do to persuade a puppy to give up the notion of chewing on a pair of shoes.

'That hurt,' he protested, putting his hand to his nose.

'It was meant to. Leave her alone.'

'Are you going to let her do that, Sparhawk?' Kalten appealed to his friend.

'Do as she says,' Sparhawk told him. 'Leave the girl alone.'

'Your morning's not going too well, is it, Sir Kalten?' Stragen noted.

Kalten went off to a corner to sulk.

The others drifted in, and they all sat down to the breakfast two crewmen brought from the galley. Princess Danae sat alone near the large window at the

143

stern where the salt-tinged breeze would keep the smell of pork sausage from her delicate nostrils.

After breakfast, Sparhawk and Kalten went up on deck for a breath of air and stood leaning on the port rail watching the south coast of Cammoria slide by. The day was particularly fine. The sun was very bright, and the sky very blue. There was a good following breeze, and their ship, her white sails spread wide, led the small flotilla across the white-cap-speckled sea.

'The captain says that we should pass Miruscum about noon,' Kalten said. 'We're making better time than we expected.'

'We've got a good breeze,' Sparhawk agreed. 'How's your back?'

'Sore. I've got bruises from my hips to my neck.'

'At least you're standing up straight.'

Kalten grunted sourly. 'Mirtai's very direct, isn't she? I still don't know exactly what to make of her. What I mean is, how are we supposed to treat her? She's obviously a woman.'

'You've noticed.'

'Very funny, Sparhawk. What I'm getting at is the fact that you can't really treat her like a woman. She's as big as Ulath, and she seems to expect us to accept her as a comrade in arms.'

'So?'

'It's unnatural.'

'Just treat her as a special case. That's what I do. It's easier than arguing with her. Are you in the mood for a bit of advice?'

'That depends on the advice.'

'Mirtai feels that it's her duty to protect the royal family, and she's extended that to include my wife's maid. I'd strongly recommend that you curb your instincts. We don't fully understand Mirtai, and so we don't know exactly how far she'll go. Even if Alean

144

seems to be encouraging you, I wouldn't pursue the matter. It could be very dangerous.'

'The girl likes me,' Kalten objected. 'I've been around long enough to know that.'

'You might be right, but I'm not sure if that'll make any difference to Mirtai. Do me a favour, Kalten. Just leave the girl alone.'

'But she's the only one on board ship,' Kalten protested.

'You'll live.' Sparhawk turned and saw Patriarch Emban and Ambassador Oscagne standing near the stern. They were an oddly matched pair. The Patriarch of Ucera had laid aside his cassock for the voyage and wore instead a brown jerkin over a plain robe. He was very nearly as wide as he was tall, and he had a florid face. Oscagne, on the other hand, was a slight man with fine bones and little flesh. His skin was a pallid bronze colour. Their minds, however, were very similar. They were both consummate politicians. Sparhawk and Kalten drifted back to join them.

'All power comes from the throne in Tamuli, your Grace,' Oscagne was explaining. 'Nothing is done there except at the express instruction of the emperor.'

'We delegate things in Eosia, your Excellency,' Emban told him. 'We pick a good man, tell him what we want done and leave the details up to him.'

'We've tried that, and it doesn't really work in our culture. Our religion is fairly superficial, and it doesn't encourage the kind of personal loyalty yours does.'

'Your emperor has to make *all* the decisions?' Emban asked a bit incredulously. 'How does he find the time?'

Oscagne smiled. 'No, no, your Grace. Day-to-day decisions are all taken care of by custom and tradition. We're great believers in custom and tradition. It's one of our more serious failings. Once a Tamul moves out

145

of those realms, he's obliged to improvise, and that's when he usually gets into trouble. His improvisations always seem to be guided by self-interest, for some reason. We've discovered that it's best to discourage these expeditions into free decision-making. By definition, the emperor is all-wise anyway, so it's probably best to leave these things in his hands.'

'A standard definition isn't always very accurate, your Excellency. "All-wise" means different things when it's applied to different people. We have one ourselves. We like to say that the Archprelate is guided by the voice of God. There have been a number of Archprelates in the past who didn't listen very well, though.'

'We've noticed the same sort of thing, your Grace. The definition "all wise" *does* seem to have a wide range of meaning. To be honest with you, my friend, we've had some frightfully stupid emperors from time to time. We're rather fortunate just now though. Emperor Sarabian is moderately accomplished.'

'What's he like?' Emban asked intently.

'He's an institution, unfortunately. He's as much at the mercy of custom and tradition as we are. He's obliged to speak in formulas, so it's almost impossible to get to know him.' The ambassador smiled. 'The visit of Queen Ehlana may just jerk him into humanity. He'll have to treat her as an equal – for political reasons – and he was raised to believe that he didn't have any equals. I hope your lovely blonde queen is gentle with him. I think I like him – or I would if I could get past all the formalities – and it would just be too bad if she happened to say something that stopped his heart.'

'Ehlana knows exactly what she's doing every minute of the day, your Excellency,' Emban assured him. 'You and I are babies compared to her. You don't have to tell her I said that, Sparhawk.'

146

'What's my silence worth to you, your Grace?' Sparhawk grinned.

Emban glowered at him for a moment. 'What are we likely to encounter in Astel, your Excellency?'

'Tears, probably,' Oscagne replied.

'I beg your pardon?'

'The Astels are an emotional people. They cry at the drop of a handkerchief. Their culture is much like that of the kingdom of Pelosia. They're tediously devout and invincibly backward. It's been demonstrated to them over and over again that serfdom is an archaic, inefficient institution, but they maintain it anyway – largely at the connivance of the serfs themselves. Astellian nobles don't exert themselves in any way, so they have no concept of the extent of human endurance. Their serfs take advantage of that outrageously. Astellian serfs have been known to collapse from sheer exhaustion at the very mention of such unpleasant words as "reaping" or "digging". The weepy nobles are tender-hearted, so the serfs get away with it almost every time. Western Astel's a silly place filled with silly people. That changes as one moves east.'

'One would hope so. I'm not certain just how much silliness I can –'

It was that same flicker of darkness at the very edge of Sparhawk's vision, and it was accompanied by that same chill. Patriarch Emban broke off, turning his head quickly to try to see it more clearly. 'What – ?'

'It'll pass,' Sparhawk told him tersely. 'Try to concentrate on it, your Grace, and you as well, if you don't mind, your Excellency.' They were seeing the shadow for the first time, and their initial reactions might be useful. Sparhawk watched them closely as they tried to turn their heads to look directly at the annoying darkness just beyond the range of sight. Then the shadow was gone.

'All right,' Sparhawk said crisply, 'Exactly what did you see?'

'I couldn't see anything,' Kalten told him. 'It was like having someone trying to sneak up behind me.' Although Kalten had seen the cloud several times, this was the first time he had encountered the shadow.

'What was it, Sir Sparhawk?' Ambassador Oscagne asked.

'I'll explain in a moment, your Excellency. Please try to remember exactly what you saw and felt.'

'It was something dark,' Oscagne replied, 'very dark. It seemed to be quite substantial, but somehow it was able to move just enough to stay where I couldn't quite see it. No matter how quickly I turned my head or moved my eyes, it was never where I could see it directly. It felt as if it were standing just behind my head.'

Emban nodded. 'And it made me feel cold.' He shuddered. 'I'm still cold, as a matter of fact.'

'It was unfriendly, too,' Kalten added. 'Not quite ready to attack, but very nearly.'

'Anything else?' Sparhawk asked them. 'Anything at all – no matter how small.'

'There was a peculiar odour,' Oscagne told him.

Sparhawk looked at him sharply. He had never noticed that. 'Could you describe it at all, your Excellency?'

'I seemed to catch the faintest smell of tainted meat – a haunch or a side that had been left hanging for perhaps a week too long.'

Kalten grunted. 'I caught that too, Sparhawk – just for a second, and it left a very bad taste in my mouth.'

Emban nodded vigorously. 'I'm an expert on flavours. It was definitely rotten meat.'

'We were sort of standing in a semi-circle,' Sparhawk

mused, 'and we all saw – or sensed – it right behind us. Did any of you see it behind anybody else?'

They all shook their heads.

'Would you please explain this, Sparhawk?' Emban said irritably.

'In just a moment, your Grace.' Sparhawk crossed the deck to a sailor who was splicing a loop into the bight of a rope. He spoke with the tar-smeared man for a few minutes and then returned.

'He saw it too,' he reported. 'Let's spread out and talk with the rest of the sailors on deck. I'm not being deliberately secretive, gentlemen, but let's get what information we can from the sailors before they forget the incident entirely. I'd like to know just how wide-spread this visitation was.'

It was about a half hour later when they gathered again near the aft companionway, and they had all begun to exhibit a kind of excitement.

'One of the sailors heard a kind of crackling noise – like a large fire,' Kalten reported.

'I talked to one fellow, and he thought there was a kind of reddish tinge to the shadow,' Oscagne added.

'No,' Emban disagreed. 'It was green. The sailor I talked with said that it was definitely green.'

'And I spoke with a man who'd just come up on deck, and he hadn't seen or felt a thing,' Sparhawk added.

'This is all very interesting, Sir Sparhawk,' Oscagne said, 'but could you *please* explain it to us?'

'Kalten already knows, your Excellency,' Sparhawk replied. 'It would appear that we've just been visited by the Troll-Gods.'

'Be careful, Sparhawk,' Emban warned, 'you're walking on the edge of heresy.'

'The Church Knights are permitted to do that, your Grace. Anyway, that shadow's followed me before, and Ehlana's seen it too. We'd assumed it was because we

149

were wearing the rings. The stones in the rings were fashioned from shards of the Bhelliom. The shadow seems to be a little less selective now.'

'That's all it is? Just a shadow?' Oscagne asked him.

Sparhawk shook his head. 'It can also show up as a very dark cloud, and everybody can see that.'

'But not the things that are concealed in it,' Kalten added.

'Such as what?' Oscagne asked.

Sparhawk gave Emban a quick sidelong glance. 'It would start an argument, your Excellency, and we don't really want to spend the morning in a theological debate, do we?'

'I'm not all *that* doctrinaire, Sparhawk,' Emban protested.

'What would be your immediate response if I told you that humans and Trolls are related, your Grace?'

'I'd have to investigate the condition of your soul.'

'Then I'd probably better not tell you the truth about our cousins, wouldn't you say? Anyway, Aphrael told us that the shadow – and later the cloud – were manifestations of the Troll-Gods.'

'Who's Aphrael?' Oscagne asked.

'We had a tutor in the Styric arts when we were novices, your Excellency,' Sparhawk explained. 'Aphrael is her Goddess. We thought that the cloud was somehow related to Azash, but we were wrong about that. The reddish colour and the heat that one sailor sensed was Khwaj, the God of Fire. The greenish colour and that rotten meat-smell was Ghnomb, the God of Eat.'

Kalten was frowning. 'I thought it was just one of those things you might expect from sailors,' he said, 'but one fellow told me that he had some rather overpowering thoughts about women while the shadow was lurking behind him. Don't the Trolls have a God of Mating?'

'I think so,' Sparhawk replied. 'Ulath would know.'

'This is all very interesting, Sir Sparhawk,' Oscagne said dubiously, 'but I don't quite see its relevance.'

'You've been encountering supernatural incidents that seem to be connected to the turmoil in Tamuli, your Excellency. There's almost exactly the same sort of disturbances cropping up in Lamorkand, and the same sort of unnatural events accompanying them. We were questioning a man who knew some things about it once, and the cloud engulfed him and killed him before he could talk. That strongly suggests some kind of connection. The shadow may have been present in Tamuli as well, but no one would have recognised it for what it really is.'

'Zalasta was right then,' Oscagne murmured. 'You *are* the man for this job.'

'The Troll-Gods are following you again, Sparhawk,' Kalten said. 'What is this strange fascination they seem to have with you? We can probably discount your looks – but then again, maybe not. They're used to Trolls, after all.'

Sparhawk looked meaningfully at the ship rail. 'How would you like to run alongside the ship for a while, Kalten?'

'No, that's all right, Sparhawk. I got all the exertion I need for the day when Mirtai decided to use me for a rug.'

The wind held, and the sky remained clear. They rounded the southern tip of Zemoch and sailed up the east coast in a northeasterly direction. Once, when Sparhawk and his daughter were standing in the bow, he decided to satisfy a growing curiosity.

'How long have we actually been at sea, Danae?' he asked her directly.

'Five days,' she replied.

'It seems like two weeks or more.'

'Thank you, father. Does that answer your question about how well I can manage time?'

'We certainly haven't eaten as much in five days as we would have in two weeks. Won't our cooks get suspicious?'

'Look behind us, father. Why do you suppose all those fish are gleefully jumping out of the water? And what are all those seagulls doing following us?'

'Maybe they're feeding.'

'Very perceptive, Sparhawk, but what could possibly be out there for that many of them to eat? Unless, of course, somebody's been throwing food to them off the aft deck.'

'When do you do that?'

'At night,' she shrugged. 'The fish are terribly grateful. I think they're right on the verge of worshipping me.' She laughed. 'I've never been worshipped by fish before, and I don't really speak their language very well. It's mostly bubbles. Can I have a pet whale?'

'No. You've already got a kitten.'

'I'll pout.'

'It makes you look silly, but go ahead if you feel like it.'

'*Why* can't I have a whale?'

'Because they can't be housebroken. They don't make good pets.'

'That's a ridiculous answer, Sparhawk.'

'It was a ridiculous request, Aphrael.'

The port of Salesha at the head of the Gulf of Daconia was an ugly city that reflected the culture which had prevailed in Zemoch for nineteen hundred years. The Zemochs appeared to be confused by what had happened in their capital six years before. No matter how often they were assured that Otha and Azash were no more, they still tended to start violently at sudden loud

152

noises, and they generally reacted to any sort of surprise by running away.

'I'd strongly advise that we spend the night on board our ships, your Majesty,' Stragen advised the queen after he had made a brief survey of the accommodations available in the city. 'I wouldn't kennel dogs in the finest house in Salesha.'

'That bad?' she asked.

'Worse, my Queen.'

And so they stayed on board and set out early the following morning.

The road they followed north was truly bad, and the carriage in which the queen and her entourage rode jolted and creaked as their column wound up into the low range of mountains lying between the coast and the town of Basne. After they had been travelling for no more than an hour, Talen rode forward. As the queen's page, it was one of the boy's duties to carry messages for her. Talen was not alone on his horse this time, however. Sparhawk's daughter rode behind him, her arms about his waist and her cheek resting against his back. 'She wants to ride with you,' Talen told Sparhawk. 'Your wife, Emban and the ambassador are talking politics. The princess kept yawning in their faces until the queen gave her permission to get out of the carriage.'

Sparhawk nodded. The suddenly-acquired timidity of the Zemochs made this part of the trip fairly safe. He reached over and lifted his daughter onto Faran's back in front of his saddle. 'I thought you liked politics,' he said to her after Talen had returned to his post beside the carriage.

'Oscagne's describing the organisation of the Tamul Empire,' she replied. 'I already know about that. He's not making too many mistakes.'

'Are you going to shrink the distance from here to Basne?'

'Unless you enjoy long, tedious journeys through boring terrain. Faran and the other horses appreciate my shortening things up a bit, don't you Faran?'

The big roan nickered enthusiastically.

'He's such a nice horse,' Danae said, leaning back against her father's armoured chest.

'Faran? He's a foul-tempered brute.'

'That's because you expect him to be that way, father. He's only trying to please you.' She rapped on his armour. 'I'm going to have to do something about this,' she said. 'How can you stand that awful smell?'

'You get used to it.' The Church Knights were all wearing full armour, and brightly-coloured pennons snapped from their lances. Sparhawk looked around to be sure no one was close enough to overhear them. 'Aphrael,' he said quietly, 'can you arrange things so that I can see real time?'

'Nobody can see time, Sparhawk.'

'You know what I mean. I want to see what's really going on, not the illusion you create to keep what you're doing a secret.'

'Why?'

'I like to know what's going on, that's all.'

'You won't like it,' she warned.

'I'm a Church Knight. I'm supposed to do things I don't like.'

'If you insist, father.'

He was not entirely certain what he had expected – some jerky, accelerated motion, perhaps, and the voices of his friends sounding like the twittering of birds as they condensed long conversations into little bursts of unintelligible babble. That was not what happened, however. Faran's gait became impossibly smooth. The big horse seemed almost to flow across the ground – or, more properly, the ground seemed to flow back beneath his hooves. Sparhawk swallowed hard and looked

154

around at his companions. Their faces seemed blank, wooden, and their eyes half-closed.

'They're sleeping just now,' Aphrael explained. 'They're all quite comfortable. They believe that they've had a good supper and that the sun's gone down. I fixed them a rather nice camp-site. Stop the horse, father. You can help me get rid of the extra food.'

'Can't you just make it vanish?'

'And waste it?' She sounded shocked. 'The birds and animals have to eat too, you know.'

'How long is it really going to take us to reach Basne?'

'Two days. We could go faster if there was an emergency, but there's nothing quite that serious going on just now.'

Sparhawk reined in, and he followed his little daughter back to where the pack animals stood patiently. 'You're keeping all of this in your head at the same time?' he asked her.

'It's not that difficult, Sparhawk. You just have to pay attention to details, that's all.'

'You sound like Kurik.'

'He'd have made an excellent God, actually. Attention to detail is the most important lesson we learn. Put that beef shoulder over near that tree with the broken-off top. There's a bear-cub back in the bushes who got separated from his mother. He's very hungry.'

'Do you keep track of every single thing that's happening around you?'

'Well *somebody* has to, Sparhawk.'

The Zemoch town of Basne lay in a pleasant valley where the main east-west road forded a small, sparkling river. It was a fairly important trading centre. Not even Azash had been able to curb the natural human instinct to do business. There was an encampment just outside of town.

Sparhawk had dropped back to return Princess Danae to her mother, and he was riding beside the carriage as they started down into the valley.

Mirtai seemed uncharacteristically nervous as the carriage moved down toward the encampment.

'It appears that your admirer has obeyed your summons, Mirtai,' Baroness Melidere observed brightly.

'Of course,' the giantess replied.

'It must be enormously satisfying to have such absolute control over a man.'

'I rather like it,' Mirtai admitted. 'How do I look? Be honest, Melidere. I haven't seen Kring for months, and I wouldn't want to disappoint him.'

'You're lovely, Mirtai.'

'You're not just saying that?'

'Of course not.'

'What do you think, Ehlana?' the Tamul woman appealed to her owner. Her tone was a bit uncertain.

'You're ravishing, Mirtai.'

'I'll know better when I see his face.' Mirtai paused. 'Maybe I *should* marry him,' she said. 'I think I'd feel much more secure if I had my brand on him.' She rose, opening the carriage door and leaning out to pull her tethered horse up from behind the carriage and then quite literally flowed onto his back. Mirtai never used a saddle. 'Well,' she sighed, 'I guess I'd better go down there and find out if he still loves me.' And she tapped her heels into her horse's flanks and galloped on down into the valley to meet the waiting Domi.

CHAPTER 9

The Peloi were nomadic herders from the marches of eastern Pelosia. They were superb horsemen and savage warriors. They spoke a somewhat archaic form of Elenic, and many of the words in their tongue had fallen out of use in the modern language. Among those words was 'Domi', a word filled with profoundest respect. It meant 'Chief' – sort of – although, as Sir Ulath had once said, it lost a great deal in translation.

The current Domi of the Peloi was named Kring. Kring was a lean man of slightly more than medium height. As was customary among the men of his people, he shaved his head, and there were savage-looking sabre scars on his scalp and face, an indication that the process of rising to a position of leadership among the Peloi involved a certain amount of rough-and-tumble competition. He wore black leather clothing, and a life-time spent on horseback had made him bandy-legged. He was a fiercely loyal friend, and he had worshipped Mirtai from the moment he had first seen her. Mirtai did not discourage him, although she refused to commit herself. They made an odd-looking couple, since the Atan woman towered more than a foot over her ardent suitor.

Peloi hospitality was generous, and the business of 'taking salt together' usually involved enormous amounts of roasted meat, during the consumption of which the men 'spoke of affairs', a phrase with many implications, ranging in subject matter from the weather to formal declarations of war.

After they had eaten, Kring described what he had

observed during the ride of the hundred Peloi across Zemoch. 'It never really was a kingdom, friend Sparhawk,' he said. 'Not the way we understand the word. There are too many different kinds of people living in Zemoch for them all to come together under one roof. The only thing that kept them united was their fear of Otha and Azash. Now that their emperor and their God aren't there any more, the Zemochs are just kind of drifting apart. There's not any sort of war or anything like that. It's just that they don't stay in touch with each other any more. They all have their own concerns, so they don't really have any reason to talk to each other.'

'Is there any kind of government at all?' Tynian asked the shaved-headed Domi.

'There's a sort of a framework, friend Tynian,' Kring replied. They were sitting in a large, open pavilion in the centre of the Peloi encampment feasting on roast ox. The sun was just going down and the shadows of the peaks lying to the west lay long across the pleasant valley. There were lights in the windows of Basne a half mile or so away. 'The departments of Otha's government have all moved to Gana Dorit,' Kring elaborated. 'Nobody will even go near the city of Zemoch any more. The bureaucrats in Gana Dorit spend their time writing directives, but their messengers usually just stop in the nearest village, tear up the directives, wait a suitable period of time, and then go back and tell their employers that all is going well. The bureaucrats are happy, the messengers don't have to travel very far, and the people go on about their business. Actually, it's not a bad form of government.'

'And their religion?' Sir Bevier asked intently. Bevier was a devout young knight, and he spent a great deal of his time talking and thinking about God. His companions liked him in spite of that.

'They don't speak very much about their beliefs,

friend Bevier,' Kring replied. 'It was their religion that got them into trouble in the first place, so they're a bit shy about discussing the matter openly. They grow their crops, tend their sheep and goats and let the Gods settle their own disputes. They're not a threat to anybody any more.'

'Except for the fact that a disintegrated nation is an open invitation to anyone nearby with anything even remotely resembling an army,' Ambassador Oscagne added.

'Why would anyone want to bother, your Excellency?' Stragen asked him. 'There's nothing in Zemoch of any value. The thieves there have to get honest jobs in order to make ends meet. Otha's gold appears to have been an illusion. It all vanished when Azash died.' He smiled sardonically. 'And you have no idea of how chagrined any number of people who'd supported the Primate of Cimmura were when that happened.'

Something rather peculiar happened to Kring's face. The savage horseman whose very name struck fear into the hearts of his neighbours went first pale, then bright red. Mirtai had emerged from the women's pavilion to which Peloi custom had relegated her and the others. Strangely, Queen Ehlana had not even objected, a fact which caused Sparhawk a certain nervousness. Mirtai had taken advantage of the accommodations within the pavilion to make herself 'presentable'. Kring, quite obviously, was impressed. 'You'll excuse me,' he said, rising quickly and moving directly toward the lode-star of his life.

'I think we're in the presence of a legend in the making,' Tynian noted. 'The Peloi will compose songs about Kring and Mirtai for the next hundred years at least.' He looked at the Tamul ambassador. 'Is Mirtai behaving at all the way other Atan women do, your Excellency? She obviously likes Kring's attentions, but she simply won't give him a definite answer.'

159

'The Atana's doing what's customary, Sir Tynian,' Oscagne replied. 'Atan women believe in long, leisurely courtships. They find being pursued entertaining, and most men turn their attention to other matters after the wedding. For this period of time in her life, she knows that she's the absolute centre of the Domi's attention. Women, I'm told, appreciate that sort of thing.'

'She wouldn't just be leading him on, would she?' Berit asked. 'I like the Domi, and I'd hate to see him get his heart broken.'

'Oh, no, Sir Berit. She's definitely interested. If she found his attentions annoying, she'd have killed him a long time ago.'

'Courtship among the Atans must be a very nervous business,' Kalten observed.

'Oh, yes,' Oscagne laughed. 'A man must be very careful. If he's too aggressive, the woman will kill him, and if he's not aggressive enough, she'll marry someone else.'

'That's very uncivilised,' Kalten said disapprovingly.

'Atan women seem to enjoy it, but then, women are more elemental than we are.'

They left Basne early the following morning and rode eastward toward Esos on the border between Zemoch and the kingdom of Astel. It was a peculiar journey for Sparhawk. It took three days, he was absolutely certain of that. He could clearly remember every minute of those three days and every mile they travelled. And yet his daughter periodically roused him when he was firmly convinced that he was sleeping in a tent, and he would be startled to find that he was dozing on Faran's back instead and that the position of the sun clearly indicated that what had appeared to be a full day's travel had taken less than six hours. Princess Danae woke her father for a very practical reason during what was in reality no more than a one-day ride. The addition of the Peloi had greatly increased the amount of stores that had to be carefully depleted each 'night', and Danae made her father help her dispose of the excess.

'What did you do with all the supplies when we were travelling with Wargun's army?' Sparhawk asked her on the second 'night' which actually consumed about a half hour during the early afternoon of that endless day.

'I did it the other way,' she shrugged.

'Other way?'

'I just made the excess go away.'

'Couldn't you do that this time too?'

'Of course, but then I couldn't leave it for the animals. Besides, this gives you and me the chance to talk when nobody's around to hear us. Pour that sack of grain under those bushes, Sparhawk. There's a covey of quail back in the grass. They haven't been eating very well lately, and the chicks are growing very fast right now.'

'Was there something you wanted to talk about?' he asked her, slitting open the grain sack with his dagger.

'Nothing special,' she said. 'I just like talking with you, and you're usually too busy.'

'And this gives you a chance to show off too, doesn't it?'

'I suppose it does, yes. It's not all that much fun being a Goddess if you can't show off just a little bit now and then.'

'I love you,' he laughed.

'Oh, that's *very* nice, Sparhawk!' she exclaimed happily. 'Right from the heart and without even thinking about it. Would you like to have me turn the grass lavender for you – just to show my appreciation.'

'I'll settle for a kiss. Lavender grass might confuse the horses.'

*   *   *

161

They reached Esos that evening. The Child Goddess so perfectly melded real and apparent time that they fitted together seamlessly. Sparhawk was a Church Knight, and he had been trained in the use of magic, but his imagination shuddered back from the kind of power possessed by this whimsical little divinity who, she had announced during the confrontation with Azash in the City of Zemoch, had willed herself into existence, and who had decided independently to be reborn as his daughter.

They set up for the night some distance from town, and after they had eaten, Talen and Stragen took Sparhawk aside. 'What's your feeling about a bit of reconnoitring?' Stragen asked the big Pandion.

'What did you have in mind?'

'Esos is a fair-sized town,' the blond Thalesian replied, 'and there's sure to be a certain amount of organisation among the thieves there. I thought the three of us might be able to pick up some useful information by getting in touch with their leader.'

'Would he know you?'

'I doubt it. Emsat's a long way away from here.'

'What makes you think he'd want to talk with you?'

'Courtesy, Sparhawk. Thieves and murderers are exquisitely courteous to each other. It's healthier that way.'

'If he doesn't know who you are, how will he know that he's supposed to be courteous toward you?'

'There are certain signals he'll recognise.'

'You people have a very complex society, don't you?'

'All societies are complex, Sparhawk. It's one of the burdens of civilisation.'

'Someday you'll have to teach me these signals.'

'No, I don't think so.'

'Why not?'

'Because you're not a thief. It's another of those complexities we were talking about. The point of all of this is that all we have to work with is the ambassador's rather generalised notion of what's going on. I think I'd like something a bit more specific, wouldn't you?'

'That I would, my friend.'

'Why don't we drift on into Esos and see what we can find out then?'

'Why don't we?'

The three of them changed into nondescript clothing and rode away from the encampment, circling around to the west to approach the town from that direction.

As they approached, Talen looked critically at the fortifications and the unguarded gate. 'They seem a little relaxed when you consider how close they are to the Zemoch border,' he observed.

'Zemoch doesn't pose much of a threat any more,' Stragen disagreed.

'Old customs die hard, Milord Stragen, and it hasn't been all *that* long since Otha was frothing at the frontier with Azash standing right behind him.'

'I doubt that these people found Azash to be all that impressive,' Sparhawk said. 'Otha's God didn't have any reason to come this way. He was looking west, because that's where Bhelliom was.'

'I suppose you're right,' Talen conceded.

Esos was not a very large town, perhaps about the size of the city of Lenda in central Elenia. There was a kind of archaic quality about it, though, since there had been a town on this spot since the dawn of time. The cobbled streets were narrow and crooked, and they wandered this way and that without any particular reason.

'How are we going to find the part of town where your colleagues stay?' Sparhawk asked Stragen. 'We can't just walk up to some burgher and ask him where we'll find the thieves, can we?'

163

'We'll take care of it,' Stragen smiled. 'Talen, go ask some pickpocket where the thieves' den is around here.'

'Right,' Talen grinned, slipping down from his horse.

'That could take him all night,' Sparhawk said.

'Not unless he's been struck blind,' Stragen replied as the boy moved off into a crowded byway. 'I've seen six pickpockets since we came into town, and I wasn't even looking very hard.' He pursed his lips. 'Their technique's a little different here. It probably has to do with the narrow streets.'

'What would that have to do with it?'

'People jostle each other in tight quarters,' Stragen shrugged. 'A pickpocket in Emsat or Cimmura could never get away with bumping into a client the way they do here. It's more efficient, I'll grant you, but it establishes bad work-habits.'

Talen returned after a few minutes. 'It's down by the river,' he reported.

'Inevitably,' Stragen said. 'Something seems to draw thieves to rivers. I've never been able to figure out why.'

Talen shrugged. 'It's probably so that we can swim for it in case things go wrong. We'd better walk. Mounted men attract too much attention. There's a stable down at the end of the street where we can leave the horses.'

They spoke briefly with the surly stableman and then proceeded on foot.

The thieves' den in Esos was in a shabby tavern at the rear of a narrow cul-de-sac. A crude sign depicting a bunch of grapes hung from a rusty hook just over the door, and a pair of burly loafers sprawled on the doorstep drinking ale from battered tankards.

'We're looking for a man named Djukta,' Talen told them.

164

'What was it about?' one of the loafers growled suspiciously.

'Business,' Stragen told him in a cold tone.

'Anybody could say that,' the unshaven man said, rising to his feet with a thick cudgel in his hand.

'This is always so tedious,' Stragen sighed to Sparhawk. Then his hand flashed to the hilt of his rapier, and the slim blade came whistling out of its sheath. 'Friend,' he said to the loafer, 'unless you want three feet of steel between your breakfast and your supper, you'll stand aside.' The needle-like point of the rapier touched the man's belly suggestively.

The other ruffian sidled off to one side, his hand reaching furtively toward the handle of his dagger.

'I wouldn't,' Sparhawk warned him in a dreadfully quiet voice. He pushed his cloak aside to reveal his mail-shirt and the hilt of his broadsword. 'I'm not entirely positive where your breakfast or your supper are located just now, neighbour, but I'll probably be able to pick them out when your guts are lying in the street.'

The fellow froze in his tracks, swallowing hard.

'The knife,' Sparhawk grated. 'Lose it.'

The dagger clattered to the cobblestones.

'I'm so happy that we could resolve this little problem without unpleasantness,' Stragen drawled. 'Now why don't we all go inside so you can introduce us to Djukta?'

The tavern had a low ceiling and the floor was covered with mouldy straw. It was lit by a few crude lamps that burned melted tallow.

Djukta was by far the hairiest man Sparhawk had ever seen. His arms and hands seemed to be covered with curly black fur. Great wads of hair protruded from the neck of his tunic; his ears and nostrils looked like bird's nests; and his beard began just under his lower eyelids.

'What's this?' he demanded, his voice issuing from somewhere behind his shaggy rug of a face.

'They made us let them come inside, Djukta,' one of the men from the doorway whined, pointing at Stragen's rapier.

Djukta's piggish eyes narrowed dangerously.

'Don't be tiresome,' Stragen told him, 'and pay attention. I've given you the recognition signal twice already, and you didn't even notice.'

'I noticed, but coming in here with a sword in your hand isn't the best way to get things off to a good start.'

'We were a little pressed for time. I think we're being followed.' Stragen sheathed his rapier.

'You're not from around here, are you?'

'No. We're from Eosia.'

'You're a long way from home.'

'That was sort of the idea. Things were getting unhealthy back there.'

'What line are you in?'

'We're vagabonds at heart, so we were seeking fame and fortune on the highways and byways of Pelosia. A high-ranking churchman suddenly fell ill and died while we were talking business with him, and the Church Knights decided to investigate the causes of his illness. My friends and I decided to find fresh scenery to look at right about then.'

'Are those Church Knights really as bad as they say?'

'Worse, probably. The three of us are all that's left of a band of thirty.'

'Are you planning to go into business around here?'

'We haven't decided yet. We thought we'd look things over first – and make sure that the knights aren't still following us.'

'Do you feel like telling us your names?'

'Not particularly. We're not sure we're going to stay,

166

and there's not much point in making up new names if we're not going to settle down.'

Djukta laughed. 'If you aren't sure you're going into business, what's the reason for this visit?'

'Courtesy, for the most part. It's terribly impolite not to pay a call on one's colleagues when one's passing through a town, and we thought it might save a bit of time if you could spare a few minutes to give us a run-down on local practices in the field of law-enforcement.'

'I've never been to Eosia, but I'd imagine that things like that are fairly standard. Highwaymen aren't held in high regard.'

'We're so misunderstood,' Stragen sighed. 'They have the usual sheriffs and the like, I suppose?'

'There are sheriffs right enough,' Djukta said, 'but they don't go out into the countryside very often in this part of Astel. The nobles out there more or less police their own estates. The sheriffs are usually involved in collecting taxes, and they aren't all that welcome when they ride out of town.'

'That's useful. All we'd really have to deal with would be poorly-trained serfs who fare better at catching chicken-thieves than at dealing with serious people. Is that more or less the way it is?'

Djukta nodded. 'The good part is that these serf-sheriffs won't go past the borders of their own estate.'

'That's a highwayman's dream,' Stragen grinned.

'Not entirely,' Djukta disagreed. 'It's not a good idea to make too much noise out there. The local sheriff wouldn't chase you, but he *would* send word to the Atan garrison up in Canae. A man can't run far enough or fast enough to get away from the Atans, and nobody's ever taught them how to take prisoners.'

'That could be a drawback,' Stragen conceded. 'Is there anything else we should know about?'

'Did you ever hear of Ayachin?'

'I can't say that I have.'

'That could get you into all kinds of trouble.'

'Who is he?'

Djukta turned his head. 'Akros,' he called, 'come here and tell our colleagues here about Ayachin.' He shrugged and spread his hands. 'I'm not too well-versed in ancient history,' he explained. 'Akros used to be a teacher before he got caught stealing from his employer. He may not be too coherent. He has a little problem with drink.'

Akros was a shabby-looking fellow with bloodshot eyes and a five-day growth of beard. 'What was it you wanted, Djukta?' he asked, swaying on his feet.

'Sort through what's left of your brain and tell our friends here what you can remember about Ayachin.'

The drunken pedagogue smiled, his bleary eyes coming alight. He slid into a chair and took a drink from his tankard. 'I'm only a little drunk,' he said, his speech slurred.

'That's true,' Djukta told Stragen. 'When he's really drunk, he can't even talk.'

'How much do you gentlemen know of the history of Astel?' Akros asked them.

'Not too much,' Stragen admitted.

'I'll touch the high spots then.' Akros leaned back in his chair. 'It was in the ninth century that one of the Archprelates in Chyrellos decided that the Elene faith ought to be re-united – under his domination, naturally.'

'Naturally,' Stragen smiled. 'It always seems to get down to that, doesn't it?'

Akros rubbed at his face. 'I'm a little shaky on this, so I might leave some things out. This was before the founding of the Church Knights, so this Archprelate forced the Kings of Eosia to provide him with armies, and they marched through Zemoch. That was before

168

Otha was born, so Zemoch wasn't much of a barrier. The Archprelate was interested in religious unity, but the noblemen in his army were more interested in conquest. They ravaged the kingdom of Astel until Ayachin came.'

Talen leaned forward, his eyes bright. It was the boy's one weakness. A good story could paralyse him.

Akros took another drink. 'There are all sorts of conflicting stories about who Ayachin really was,' he continued. 'Some say he was a prince, some that he was a baron, and there are even those who say he was only a serf. Anyway, whoever he was, he was a fervent patriot. He roused such noblemen as hadn't yet gone over to the invaders, and then he did something no one had ever dared do before. He armed the serfs. The campaign against the invaders lasted for years, and after a fairly large battle that he *seemed* to lose, Ayachin fled southward, luring the Eosian armies into the Astel marshes in the south of the kingdom. He'd made secret alliances with patriots in Edom, and there was a huge army lining the southern fringe of the marshes. Serfs who lived in the region guided Ayachin's armies through the bogs and quicksand, but the Eosians tried to just bull their way through, and most of them drowned, pulled under by all that muck. The few who reached the far side were slaughtered by the combined forces of Ayachin and his Edomish allies.

'He was a great national hero for a time, of course, but the nobles who had been outraged because he'd armed the serfs conspired against him, and he was eventually murdered.'

'Why do these stories always have to end that way?' Talen complained.

'Our young friend here is a literary critic,' Stragen said. 'He wants his stories to all have happy endings.'

'The ancient history is all well and good,' Djukta

growled, 'but the point of all this is that Ayachin's returned – or so the serfs say.'

'It's a part of the folk-lore of Astel,' Akros said. 'Serfs used to tell each other that someday a great crisis would arise, and that Ayachin would rise from the grave to lead them again.'

Stragen sighed. 'Can't anyone come up with a new story?'

'What's that?' Djukta asked him.

'Nothing, really. There's a similar story making the rounds in Eosia. Why would this concern us if we decided to go into business around here?'

'Part of that folk-lore Akros was telling you about is something that makes everybody's blood run cold. The serfs believe that when Ayachin returns, he's going to emancipate them. Now there's a hot-head out there stirring them up. We don't know his real name, but the serfs call him "Sabre". He's going around telling them that he's actually seen Ayachin. The serfs are secretly gathering weapons – or making them. They sneak out into the forests at night to listen to this "Sabre" make speeches. You should probably know that they're out there, since it might be dangerous if you happened upon them unexpectedly.' Djukta scratched at his shaggy beard. 'I don't normally feel this way, but I wish the government would catch this Sabre fellow and hang him or something. He's got the serfs all worked up about throwing off the oppressors, and he's not too specific about which oppressors he means. He could be talking about the Tamuls, but many of his followers think he's talking about the upper classes. Restless serfs are dangerous serfs. Nobody knows how many of them there really are, and if they begin to get wild ideas about equality and justice, God only knows where it might end.'

CHAPTER 10

'There are just too many similarities for it to be a coincidence,' Sparhawk was saying the following morning as they rode northeasterly along the Darsos road under a lowering sky. He and his companions had gathered around Ehlana's carriage to discuss Djukta's revelations. The air was close and muggy, and there was not a breath of air stirring.

'I'd almost have to agree,' Ambassador Oscagne replied. 'There's a certain pattern emerging here, if what you've told me about Lamorkand is at all accurate. Our empire is certainly not democratic, and I'd imagine that your western kingdoms are much the same; but we're not really such hard masters – either of us. I think we've become the symbols of the social injustices implicit in every culture. I'm not saying that people don't hate us. Everybody in the world loathes his government – no offence intended, your Majesty.' He smiled at Ehlana.

'I do what I can to keep my people from hating me too much, your Excellency,' she replied. Ehlana wore a pale blue velvet travelling cloak, and Sparhawk felt that she looked particularly pretty this morning.

'No one could possibly hate someone as lovely as you, your Majesty,' Oscagne smiled. 'The point though, is that the world seethes with discontent, and someone is playing on all those disparate resentments in an effort to bring down the established order – the empire here in Tamuli and the monarchies and the Church in Eosia. Somebody wants there to be a great deal of turmoil, and I don't think he's motivated by a hunger for social justice.'

171

'We'd go a long way toward understanding the situation if we could pinpoint just exactly what he *is* after,' Emban added.

'Opportunity,' Ulath suggested. 'If everything's all settled and the wealth and power have all been distributed, there's nothing left for the people coming up the ladder. The only way they can get their share is to turn everything upside down and shake it a few times.'

'That's a brutal political theory, Sir Ulath,' Oscagne said disapprovingly.

'It's a brutal world, your Excellency,' Ulath shrugged.

'I'd have to disagree,' Bevier stubbornly asserted.

'Go right ahead, my young friend,' Ulath smiled. 'I don't mind all that much when people disagree with me.'

'There *is* such a thing as genuine political progress. The people's lot is much better now than it was five hundred years ago.'

'Granted, but what's it going to be like next year?' Ulath leaned back in his saddle, his blue eyes speculative. 'Ambitious people need followers, and the best way to get people to follow you is to promise them that you're going to correct everything that's wrong with the world. The promises are all very stirring, but only babies expect leaders to actually keep them.'

'You're a cynic, Ulath.'

'I think that's the word people use, yes.'

The weather grew increasingly threatening as the morning progressed. A thick bank of purplish cloud marched steadily in from the west, and there were flickers of lightning along the horizon. 'It's going to rain, isn't it?' Tynian asked Khalad.

Khalad looked pointedly toward the cloud-bank. 'That's a fairly safe bet, Sir Knight,' the young man replied.

'How long until we start to get wet?'

'An hour or so – unless the wind picks up.'

'What do you think, Sparhawk?' Tynian asked. 'Should we look for some kind of shelter?'

There was a far-off rumble of thunder from the west.

'I think that answers that question,' Sparhawk decided. 'Men dressed in steel don't have any business being out in a thunderstorm.'

'Good point,' Tynian agreed. He looked around. 'The next question is where? I don't see any woods around.'

'We might have to set up the tents.'

'That's awfully tedious, Sparhawk.'

'So's being fried in your armour if you get struck by lightning.'

Kring came riding back toward the main column with a small, two-wheeled carriage following him. The man in the carriage was blond, plump and soft-looking. He wore clothing cut in a style which had gone out of fashion in the west forty years ago. 'This is the landowner Kotyk,' the Domi said to Sparhawk. 'He calls himself a baron. He wanted to meet you.'

'I am overwhelmed to meet the stalwarts of the Church, Sir Knights,' the plump man gushed.

'We are honoured, Baron Kotyk,' Sparhawk replied, inclining his head politely.

'My manor house is nearby,' Kotyk rushed on, 'and I do foresee unpleasant weather on the horizon. Might I offer my poor hospitality?'

'As I've told you so many times in the past, Sparhawk,' Bevier said mildly, 'you have but to put your trust in God. He will provide.'

Kotyk looked puzzled.

'A somewhat feeble attempt at humour, my Lord,' Sparhawk explained. 'My companions and I were just discussing our need for shelter. Your most generous offer solves a rather vexing problem for us.' Sparhawk was not familiar with local customs, but the Baron's ornate speech hinted at a somewhat stiff formality.

'I note that you have ladies in your company,' Kotyk observed, looking toward the carriage in which Ehlana rode. 'Their comfort must be our first concern. We can become better acquainted once we are safely under my roof.'

'We shall be guided by you, my Lord,' Sparhawk agreed. 'I pray you, lead us whither you will, and I shall inform the ladies of this fortuitous encounter.' If Kotyk wanted formal, Sparhawk would give him formal. He wheeled Faran and rode back along the column.

'Who's the fat fellow in the carriage, Sparhawk?' Ehlana asked.

'Speak not disparagingly of our host, light of my life.'

'Aren't you feeling well?'

'The fat fellow has just offered us shelter from that thunderstorm snapping at our heels. Treat him with gratitude if not respect.'

'What a nice man.'

'It might not be a bad idea for us to sort of keep your identity to ourselves. We don't know exactly what we're walking into. Why don't I just introduce you as an aristocrat of some kind, and –'

'A Margravine, I think,' she improvised. 'Margravine Ehlana of Cardos.'

'Why Cardos?'

'It's a nice district with mountains and a beautiful coastline. Absolutely perfect climate and industrious, law-abiding people.'

'You're not trying to sell it to him, Ehlana.'

'But I need to know the pertinent details so that I can gush suitably.'

Sparhawk sighed. 'All right, my Lady, practise gushing then, and come up with suitable stories for the others.' He looked at Emban. 'Are your morals flexible

174

enough to stand a bit of falsehood, your Grace?' he asked.

'That depends on what you want me to lie about, Sparhawk.'

'It won't exactly be a lie, your Grace,' Sparhawk smiled. 'If we demote my wife, you'll be the ranking member of our party. The presence of Ambassador Oscagne here suggests a high-level visit of some sort. I'll just tell Baron Kotyk that you're the Archprelate's personal emissary to the Imperial court, and that the Knights are *your* escort instead of the Queen's.'

'That doesn't stretch my conscience too far,' Emban grinned. 'Go ahead, Sparhawk. You lie, and I'll swear to it. Say whatever you have to. That storm is coming this way very fast.'

'Talen,' Sparhawk said to the boy, who was riding beside the carriage, 'sort of move up and down the column and let the knights know what we're doing. A misplaced "your Majesty" or two could expose us all as frauds.'

'Your husband shows some promise, Margravine Ehlana,' Stragen noted. 'Give me some time to train him a bit, and I'll make an excellent swindler of him. His instincts are good, but his technique's a little shaky.'

Baron Kotyk's manor house was a palatial residence in a park-like setting, and there was a fair-sized village at the foot of the hill upon which it stood. There were a number of large out-buildings standing to the rear of the main house. 'Fortunately, Sir Knights, I have ample room for even so large a party as yours,' the baron told them. 'The quarters for the bulk of your men may be a bit crude, though, I'm afraid. They're dormitories for the harvest crews.'

'We're Church Knights, my Lord Kotyk,' Sparhawk replied. 'We're accustomed to hardship.'

Kotyk sighed. 'We have no such institution here in

175

Astel,' he mourned. 'There are so many things lacking in our poor, backward country.' They approached the manor house by a long, white-gravelled drive lined on both sides by lofty elms and halted at the foot of the broad stone stairs leading up to an arched front door. The baron climbed heavily down from his carriage and handed his reins to one of the bearded serfs who had rushed from the house to meet them. 'I pray you, gentles all,' he said, 'stand not on ceremony. Let us enter ere the approaching storm descend upon us.'

Sparhawk could not be certain if the Baron's stilted speech was a characteristic of the country, a personal idiosyncrasy, or a nervous reaction to the rank of his visitors. He motioned to Kalten and Tynian. 'See to it that the knights and the Peloi are settled in,' he told them quietly. 'Then join us in the house. Khalad, go with them. Make sure that the serfs don't just leave the horses standing out in the rain.'

The door to the manor house swung wide, and three ladies dressed in antiquated gowns emerged. One was tall and angular. She had a wealth of dark hair and the lingering traces of youthful beauty. The years had not been kind to her, however. Her rigid, haughty face was lined, and she had a noticeable squint. The other two were both blonde, flabby, and their features clearly revealed a blood relationship to the baron. Behind them came a pale young man dressed all in black velvet. He seemed to have a permanent sneer stamped on his face. His dark hair was done in long curls that cascaded down his back in an artfully-arranged display.

After the briefest of introductions Kotyk led them all inside. The tall, dark-haired lady was the baron's wife, Astansia. The two blondes were, as Sparhawk had guessed, his sisters, Ermude the elder and Katina the younger. The pale young man was Baroness Astansia's brother, Elron, who she proudly advised them was a poet in a voice hovering on the verge of adoration. 'Do you think I could get away with pleading a sick head-ache?' Ehlana murmured to Sparhawk as they followed the baron and his family down a long, tapestry-lined corridor toward the centre of the house. 'This is going to be deadly, I'm afraid.'

'If I have to put up with it, so do you,' Sparhawk whispered. 'We need the baron's roof, so we'll have to endure his hospitality.'

She sighed. 'It might be a little more endurable if the whole place didn't reek of cooked cabbage.'

They were led into a 'sitting-room' that was only slightly smaller than the throne-room in Cimmura, a musty-smelling room filled with stiff, uncomfortable chairs and divans and carpeted in an unwholesome-looking mustard yellow.

'We are so isolated here,' Katina sighed to the Baron-ess Melidere, 'and so dreadfully out of fashion. My poor brother tries as best he can to keep abreast of what's happening in the west, but our remote location imprisons us and keeps visitors from our door. Ermude and I have tried over and over to persuade him to take a house in the capital where we can be near the centre of things, but *she* won't hear of it. The estate came to my brother by marriage, and his wife's so terribly pro-vincial. Would you believe that my poor sister and I are forced to have our gowns made up by *serfs*?'

Melidere put her palms to her cheeks in feigned shock. 'My goodness!' she exclaimed.

Katina reached for her handkerchief as tears of misery began to roll down her cheeks.

'Wouldn't your Atan be more comfortable with the serfs, Margravine?' Baroness Astansia was asking Ehlana, looking with some distaste at Mirtai.

'I rather doubt it, Baroness,' Ehlana replied, 'and even if she were, *I* wouldn't be. I have powerful enemies, my

177

Lady, and my husband is much involved in the affairs of Elenia. The queen relies heavily upon him, and so I must look to my own defences.'

'I'll admit that your Atan is imposing, Margravine,' Astansia sniffed, 'but she's still only a woman, after all.'

Ehlana smiled. 'You might tell that to the ten men she's already killed, Baroness,' she replied.

The baroness stared at her in horror.

'The Eosian continent has a thin veneer of civilisation, my Lady,' Stragen advised her, 'but underneath it all, we're really quite savage.'

'It's a tedious journey, Baron Kotyk,' Patriarch Emban said, 'but the Archprelate and the emperor have been in communication with each other since the collapse of Zemoch, and they both feel that the time has come to exchange personal envoys. Misunderstandings can arise in the absence of direct contact, and the world has seen enough of war for a while.'

'A wise decision, your Grace.' Kotyk was quite obviously overwhelmed by the presence of people of exalted station in his house.

'I have some small reputation in the capital, Sir Bevier,' Elron was saying in a lofty tone of voice. 'My poems are eagerly sought after by the intelligentsia. They're quite beyond the grasp of the unlettered, however. I'm particularly noted for my ability to convey colours. I *do* think that colour is the very soul of the real world. I've been working on my *Ode to Blue* for the past six months.'

'Astonishing perseverance,' Bevier murmured.

'I try to be as thorough as possible,' Elron declared. 'I've already composed two hundred and sixty-three stanzas, and there's no end in sight, I'm afraid.'

Bevier sighed. 'As a Knight of the Church, I have little time for literature,' he mourned. 'Because of my vocation, I must concentrate on military texts and

178

devotional works. Sir Sparhawk is more worldly than I, and his descriptions of people and places verge sometimes on the poetic.'

'I should be most interested,' Elron lied, his face revealing a professional's contempt for the efforts of amateurs. 'Does he touch at all on colour?'

'More with light, I believe,' Bevier replied, 'but then they're the same thing, aren't they? Colour doesn't exist without light. I remember that once he described a street in the city of Jiroch. The city lies on the coast of Rendor where the sun pounds the earth like a hammer. Very early in the morning, before the sun rises, and when the night is just beginning to fade, the sky has the colour of forged steel. It casts no shadows, and so everything seems etched by that sourceless grey. The buildings in Jiroch are all white, and the women go to the wells before the sun comes up to avoid the heat of the day. They wear hooded robes and veils all in black and they balance clay vessels on their shoulders. All untaught, they move with a grace beyond the capability of dancers. Their silent, beautiful procession marks each day's beginning as, like shadows, they greet the dawn in a ritual as old as time. Have you ever seen that peculiar light before the sun rises, Elron?'

'I seldom rise before noon,' the young man said stiffly.

'You should make an effort to see it sometime,' Bevier suggested mildly. 'An artist should be willing to make some sacrifices for his art, after all.'

'I trust you'll excuse me,' the young fellow with the dark curls said brusquely. He bowed slightly and then fled, a mortified expression replacing his supercilious sneer.

'That was cruel, Bevier,' Sparhawk chided, 'and you put words in my mouth. I'll admit that you have a certain flair for language though.'

'It had the desired effect, Sparhawk. If that conceited

179

young ass had patronised me about one more time, I'd have strangled him. Two hundred some odd verses in an ode to the colour blue? What a donkey!'

'The next time he bothers you about blue, describe Bhelliom to him.'

Bevier shuddered. 'Not me, Sparhawk. Just the thought of it makes my blood run cold.'

Sparhawk laughed and went over to the window to look at the rain slashing at the glass.

Danae came to his side and took his hand. 'Do we really have to stay here father?' she asked. 'These people turn my stomach.'

'We need some place to shelter us from the rain, Danae.'

'I can make it stop raining, if that's all you're worried about. If one of those disgusting women starts talking baby-talk to me one more time, I'm going to turn her into a toad.'

'I think I have a better idea.' Sparhawk bent and picked her up. 'Act sleepy,' he instructed.

Danae promptly went limp and dangled from his arms like a rag doll.

'You're overdoing it,' he told her. He crossed to the far side of the room, gently laid her on a divan and covered her with her travelling cloak. 'Don't snore,' he advised. 'You're not old enough to snore yet.'

She gave him an innocent little look. 'I wouldn't do that, Sparhawk. Find my cat and bring her to me.' Then her smile turned hard. 'Pay close attention to our host and his family, father. I think you should see what kind of people they *really* are.'

'What are you up to?'

'Nothing. I just think you should see what they're *really* like.'

'I can see quite enough already.'

'No, not really. They're trying to be polite, so they're

180

glossing over things. Let's take a look at the truth. For the rest of the evening, they'll tell you what they *really* think and feel.'

'I'd rather they didn't.'

'You're supposed to be brave, Sparhawk, and this horrid little family is typical of the gentry here in Astel. Once you understand them, you'll be able to see what's wrong with the kingdom. It might be useful.' Her eyes and face grew serious. 'There's something here, Sparhawk – something we absolutely have to know.'

'What?'

'I'm not sure. Pay attention, father. Somebody's going to tell you something important tonight. Now go find my cat.'

The supper they were offered was poorly prepared, and the conversation at the table was dreadful. Freed of constraint by Danae's spell, the baron and his family said things they might normally have concealed, and their spiteful, self-pitying vanity emerged all the more painfully under the influence of the inferior wine they all swilled like common tavern drunkards.

'I was not intended for this barbaric isolation,' Katina tearfully confided to poor Melidere. 'Surely God could not have meant for me to bloom unnoticed so far from the lights and gaiety of the capital. We were cruelly deceived before my brother's marriage to that dreadful woman. Her parents led us to believe that the estate would bring us wealth and position, but it scarcely provides enough to keep us in this hovel. There's no hope that we shall ever be able to afford a house in Darsas.' She buried her face in her hands. 'What shall become of me?' she wailed. 'The lights, the balls, the hordes of suitors flocking to my door, dazzled by my wit and beauty.'

'Oh, don't cry, Katina,' Ermude wailed. 'If you cry,

181

I shall surely cry too.' The sisters were so similar in appearance that Sparhawk had some difficulty telling them apart. Their plumpness was more like dough than flesh. Their colourless hair was limp and uninspired, and their complexions were bad. Neither of them was really very clean. 'I try so hard to protect my poor sister,' Ermude blubbered to the long-suffering Melidere, 'but this dreadful place is destroying her. There's no culture here. We live like beasts – like serfs. It's so meaningless. Life should have meaning, but what possible meaning can there be so far from the capital? That horrid woman won't permit our poor brother to sell this desolate waste so that we can take a proper residence in Darsas. We're trapped here – trapped, I tell you – and we shall live out our lives in this hideous isolation.' Then she too buried her face in her hands and wept.

Melidere sighed, rolling her eyes ceilingward.

'I have some influence with the governor of the district,' Baron Kotyk was telling patriarch Emban with pompous self-importance. 'He relies heavily on my judgement. We've been having a deuce of a time with the burghers in town – untitled rascals, every one of them – runaway serfs, if the truth were known. They complain bitterly at each new tax and try to shift the burden to *us*. We pay quite enough in taxes already, thank you, and *they're* the ones who are demanding all the services. What good does it do *me* if the streets in town are paved? It's the roads that are important. I've said that to his Excellency the governor over and over again.'

The baron was deep in his cups. His voice was slurred, and his head wobbled on his neck. 'All the burdens of the district are placed on *our* shoulders,' he declared, his eyes filling with self-pitying tears. 'I must support five hundred idle serfs – serfs so lazy that not even flogging can get any work out of them. It's all so unfair. I'm an aristocrat, but that doesn't count for anything any more.' The tears began to roll down his cheeks, and his nose started to run. 'No one seems to realise that the aristocracy is God's special gift to mankind. The burghers treat us no better than commoners. Considering our divine origins, such disrespect is the worst form of impiety. I'm sure your Grace agrees.' The Baron sniffed loudly.

Patriarch Emban's father had been a tavern-keeper in the city of Ucera, and Sparhawk was fairly sure that the fat little churchman most definitely did *not* agree.

Ehlana had been trapped by the baron's wife, and she was beginning to look a little desperate.

'The estate's *mine*, of course,' Astansia declared in a coldly haughty voice. 'My father was in his dotage when he married me off to that fat swine.' She sneered. 'Kotyk only had those piggish little eyes of his on the income from *my* estate. My father was so impressed with the idiot's title that he couldn't see him for what he really is, a titled opportunist with two fat, ugly sisters hanging from his coat-tails.' She sneered, and then the sneer slid from her face, and the inevitable tears filled her eyes. 'I can only find solace for my tragic state in religion, my beloved brother's art and in the satisfaction I take in making absolutely sure that those two harridans never see the lights of Darsas. They'll rot here – right up until the moment my pig of a husband eats and drinks himself to death. Then I shall turn them out with nothing but the clothes on their backs.' Her hard eyes became exultant. 'I can hardly wait,' she said fiercely. 'I *shall* have my revenge, and then my sainted brother and I can live here in perfect contentment.'

Princess Danae crawled up into her father's lap. 'Lovely people, aren't they?' she said quietly.

'Are you making all this up?' he asked accusingly.

183

'No, father, I can't do that. None of us can. People are what they are. We can't change them.'

'I thought you could do anything.'

'There *are* limits, Sparhawk.' Her dark eyes grew hard again. 'I am going to do *something*, though.'

'Oh?'

'Your Elene God owes me a couple of favours. I did something nice for Him once.'

'Why do you need *His* help?'

'These people are Elenes. They belong to Him. I can't do anything to them without His permission. That's the worst form of bad manners.'

'I'm an Elene, and you do things to me.'

'You're Anakha, Sparhawk. You don't belong to anybody.'

'That's depressing. I'm loose in the world with no God to guide me?'

'You don't need guidance. Advice sometimes, yes. Guidance, no.'

'Don't do anything exotic here,' he cautioned. 'We don't know exactly what we'll be dealing with when we get deeper into Tamuli. Let's not announce our presence until we have to.' Then his curiosity got the better of him. 'Nobody's said anything very relevant yet.'

'Then keep listening, Sparhawk. It *will* come.'

'Exactly what *were* you planning to ask God to do to these people?'

'Nothing,' she replied. 'Absolutely nothing at all. I won't ask Him to do a thing to change their circumstances. All I want Him to do is to make sure that they all live very, very long lives.'

He looked around the table at the petulant faces of their host's family. 'You're going to imprison them here?' he accused. 'Chain five people who loathe each other together for all eternity so that they can gradually tear each other to pieces?'

184

'Not quite eternity, Sparhawk,' the little girl corrected, '– though it's probably going to seem that way to them.'

'That's cruel.'

'No, Sparhawk. It's justice. These people richly deserve each other. I only want to be sure that they have a long time to enjoy each others' company.'

'What's your feeling about a breath of fresh air?' Stragen asked, leaning over Sparhawk's shoulder.

'It's raining out there.'

'I don't think you'll melt.'

'Maybe it's not a bad idea at that.' Sparhawk rose to his feet and carried his sleeping daughter back into the sitting room and the divan where Mmrr drowsed, purring absently and kneading one of the cushions with her needle-sharp claws. He covered them both and followed Stragen into the corridor. 'Are you feeling restless?' he asked the Thalesian.

'No, revolted. I've known some of the worst people in the world, my friend, and I'm no angel myself, but this little family –' He shuddered. 'Did you happen to lay in a store of poison while you were in Rendor?'

'I don't approve of poison.'

'A bit short-sighted there, old boy. Poison's a tidy way to deal with intolerable people.'

'Annias felt much the same way, as I recall.'

'I'd forgotten about that,' Stragen admitted. 'I imagine that prejudiced you slightly against a very practical solution to a sticky problem. Something really ought to be done about these monsters, though.'

'It's already been taken care of.'

'Oh? How?'

'I'm not at liberty to say.'

They stepped out onto the wide veranda that ran across the back of the house and stood leaning on the railing looking out into the muddy back yard.

'It doesn't show any signs of letting up, does it?' Stragen said. 'How long can it continue at this time of year?'

'You'll have to ask Khalad. He's the expert on the weather.'

'My Lords?'

Stragen and Sparhawk turned.

It was Elron, the baron's poetic brother-in-law. 'I came to assure you that my sister and I aren't responsible for Kotyk and his relatives,' he said.

'We were fairly sure that was the case, Elron,' Stragen murmured.

'All they had in the world was Kotyk's title. Their father gambled away their inheritance. It sickens me to have that clutch of out-at-the-elbows aristocrats lording it over us the way they do.'

'We've heard some rumours,' Stragen smoothly changed the subject. 'Some people in Esos were telling us that there was unrest among the serfs. We got some garbled account of a fellow called "Sabre" and another named Ayachin. We couldn't make any sense out of it.'

Elron looked around in an over-dramatically conspiratorial fashion. 'It is not wise to mention those names here in Astel, Milord Stragen,' he said in a hoarse whisper that probably could have been heard across the yard. 'The Tamuls have ears everywhere.'

'The serfs are unhappy with the Tamuls?' Stragen asked with some surprise. 'I'd have thought that they wouldn't have had so far to look for someone to hate.'

'The serfs are superstitious animals, Milord,' Elron sneered. 'They can be led anywhere with a combination of religion, folklore and strong drink. The *real* movement is directed at the yellow devils.' Elron's eyes narrowed. 'The honour of Astel demands that the Tamul yoke be thrown off. That's the real goal of the movement. Sabre is a patriot, a mysterious figure who

186

appears out of the night to inspire the men of Astel to rise up and smash the oppressor's chains. He's always masked, you know.'

'I hadn't heard that.'

'Oh, yes. It's necessary, of course. Actually, he's a well-known personage who very carefully conceals his real identity and opinions. By day he's an idle member of the gentry, but at night, he's a masked firebrand, igniting the patriotism of his countrymen.'

'You have certain opinions, I gather,' Stragen assumed.

Elron's expression grew cautious. 'I'm only a poet, Milord Stragen,' he said deprecatingly. 'My interest is in the drama of the situation – for the purposes of my art, you understand.'

'Oh, of course.'

'Where does this Ayachin come in?' Sparhawk asked. 'As I understand it, he's been dead for quite some time now.'

'There are strange things afoot in Astel, Sir Sparhawk,' Elron assured him. 'Things which have lain locked in the blood of all true Astels for generations. We know in our hearts that Ayachin is not dead. He can never die – not so long as tyranny is alive.'

'Just as a practical consideration, Elron,' Stragen said in his most urbane manner, 'this movement seems to rely rather heavily on the serfs for manpower. What's in it for them? Why should men who are bound to the soil have any concern at all about who runs the government?'

'They're sheep. They'll stampede in any direction you want them to. All you have to do is murmur the word "emancipation" and they'd follow you into the mouth of hell.'

'Then Sabre has no intention of actually freeing them?'

Elron laughed. 'My dear fellow, why would any

187

reasonable man want to do that? What's the point of liberating cattle?' He looked around furtively. 'I must return before I'm missed. Kotyk hates me, and he'd like nothing better than the chance to denounce me to the authorities. I'm obliged to smile and be polite to him and those two overfed sows he calls his sisters. I keep my own counsel, gentlemen, but when the day of our liberation comes, there will be changes here – as God is my judge. Social change is sometimes violent, and I can almost guarantee that Kotyk and his sisters will not live to see the dawn of the new day.' His eyes narrowed with a kind of self-important secretiveness. 'But I speak too much. I keep my own counsel, gentlemen. I keep my own counsel.' He swirled his black cloak around him and crept back into the house, his head high and his expression resolute.

'Fascinating young fellow,' Stragen observed. 'He makes my rapier itch for some reason.'

Sparhawk grunted his agreement and looked up at the rainy night. 'I hope this blows over by morning,' he said. 'I'd really like to get out of this sewer.'

CHAPTER 11

The following morning dawned blustery and unpromising. Sparhawk and his companions ate a hasty breakfast and made ready to depart. The baron and his family were not awake as yet, and none of his guests were in any mood for extended farewells. They rode out about an hour after sunrise and turned northeasterly on the Darsas road, moving at a distance-consuming canter. Although none of them mentioned it, they all wanted to get well out of the range of any possible pursuit before their hosts awakened.

About mid-morning, they reached the white stone pillar that marked the eastern border of the baron's estate and breathed a collective sigh of relief. The column slowed to a walk, and Sparhawk and the other knights dropped back to ride alongside the carriage.

Ehlana's maid, Alean, was crying, and the queen and Baroness Melidere were trying to comfort her. 'She's a very gentle child,' Melidere explained to Sparhawk. 'The horror of that sorry household has moved her to tears.'

'Did someone back there say something to you he shouldn't have?' Kalten asked the sobbing girl, his tone hard. Kalten's attitude toward Alean was strange. Once he had been persuaded not to press his attentions on her, he had become rather fiercely protective. 'If anybody insulted you, I'll go back and teach him better manners.'

'No, my Lord,' the girl replied disconsolately. 'It was nothing like that. It's just that they're all trapped in that awful place. They hate each other, but they'll have to

189

spend the rest of their lives together, and they'll go on cutting little pieces out of each other until they're all dead.'

'Someone once told me that there's a certain kind of justice at work in situations like that,' Sparhawk observed, not looking at his daughter. 'All right then, we all had the chance to talk with the members of our host's family individually. Did anyone pick up anything useful?'

'The serfs are right on the verge of open rebellion, my Lord,' Khalad said. 'I sort of drifted around the stable and other outbuildings and talked with them. The baroness' father was a kindly master, I guess, and the serfs loved him. After he died, though, Kotyk started to show his real nature. He's a brutal sort of man, and he's very fond of using the knout.'

'What's a knout?' Talen asked.

'It's a sort of scourge,' his half-brother replied bleakly.

'A whip?'

'It goes a little further than that. Serfs *are* lazy, Sparhawk. There's no question about that. And they've perfected the art of either pretending to be stupid or feigning illness or injury. It's always been a sort of game, I guess. The masters knew what the serfs were up to, and the serfs knew that they weren't really fooling anybody. Actually, I think they all enjoyed it. Then, a few years ago, the masters suddenly stopped playing. Instead of trying to coax the serfs to work, the gentry began to resort to the knout. They threw a thousand years of tradition out the window and turned vicious overnight. The serfs can't understand it. Kotyk's not the only noble who's been mistreating his serfs. They say it's been happening all over western Astel. Serfs tend to exaggerate things, but they all seem to be convinced that their masters have set out on a course of deliberate brutality designed to eradicate traditional rights and to reduce

190

the serfs to absolute slavery. A serf can't be sold, but a slave can. The one they call "Sabre" has been making quite an issue of that. If you tell a man that somebody's planning to sell his wife and children, you're going to get him just a little bit excited.'

'That doesn't match up too well with what Baron Kotyk was telling me,' Patriarch Emban put in. 'The baron drank more than was really good for him last night, and he let a number of things slip that he otherwise might not have. It's *his* position that Sabre's primary goal is to drive the Tamuls out of Astel. To be honest with you, Sparhawk, I was a bit sceptical about what that thief in Esos said about this Sabre fellow, but he certainly has the attention of the nobles. He's been making an issue of racial and religious differences between Elenes and Tamuls. Kotyk kept referring to the Tamuls as "godless yellow dogs".'

'We have Gods, your Grace,' Oscagne protested mildly. 'If you give me a few moments, I might even be able to remember some of their names.'

'Our friend Sabre's been busy,' Tynian said. 'He's saying one thing to the nobles and another to the serfs.'

'I think it's called talking out of both sides of your face at once,' Ulath noted.

'I believe the empire might want to give the discovery of Sabre's identity a certain priority,' Oscagne mused. 'It's embarrassingly predictable, but we brutal oppressors and godless yellow dogs always want to identify ring-leaders and troublemakers.'

'So that you can catch them and hang them?' Talen accused.

'Not necessarily, young man. When a natural talent rises to the surface, one shouldn't waste it. I'm sure we can find a use for this fellow's gifts.'

'But he hates your empire, your Excellency,' Ehlana pointed out.

'That's no real drawback, your Majesty,' Oscagne smiled. 'The fact that a man hates the empire doesn't automatically make him a criminal. Anyone with any common sense hates the empire. There are days when even the emperor himself hates it. The presence of revolutionaries is a fair indication that something's seriously wrong in a given province. The revolutionary's made it his business to pinpoint the problems, so it's easier in the long run to just let him go ahead and fix things. I've known quite a few revolutionaries who made very good provincial governors.'

'That's an interesting line of thought, your Excellency,' Ehlana said, 'but how do you persuade people who hate you to go to work for you?'

'You trick them, your Majesty. You just ask them if they think they can do any better. They inevitably think they can, so you just tell them to have a go at it. It usually takes them a few months to realise that they've been had. Being a provincial governor is the worst job in the world. *Everybody* hates you.'

'Where does this Ayachin fit in?' Bevier asked.

'I gather he's the rallying point,' Stragen replied. 'Sort of the way Drychtnath is in Lamorkand.'

'A figurehead?' Tynian suggested.

'Most probably. You wouldn't really expect a ninth-century hero to understand contemporary political reality.'

'He's sort of an enigma, though,' Ulath pointed out. 'The nobility believes he is one sort of man, and the serfs believe he's another. Sabre must have two different sets of speeches. Just exactly who *was* Ayachin anyway?'

'Kotyk told me that he was a minor nobleman who was very devoted to the Astellian Church,' Emban supplied. 'In the ninth century, there was a Church-inspired invasion from Eosia. Your thief in Esos was right about *that* part, at least. The Astels believe that our Holy

192

Mother in Chyrellos is heretical. Ayachin's supposed to have rallied the nobles and finally won a great victory in the Astel marshes.'

'The serfs have a different story,' Khalad told them. 'They believe that Ayachin was a serf disguised as a nobleman and that his real goal was the emancipation of his class. *They* say that the victory in the marshes was the work of the serfs, not the nobility. Later, when the nobles found out who Ayachin really was, they had him murdered.'

'He makes a perfect figurehead then,' Ehlana said. 'He was so ambiguous that he seems to offer something to everyone.'

Emban was frowning. 'The mistreatment of the serfs doesn't make any sense. Serfs aren't very industrious, but there are so many of them that all you have to do is pile on more people until you get the job done. If you maltreat them, all you really do is encourage them to turn on you. Even an idiot knows that. Sparhawk, is there some spell that might have induced the nobility to follow a course that's ultimately suicidal?'

'None that *I* know of,' Sparhawk replied. He looked around at the other knights, and they all shook their heads. Princess Danae nodded very slightly, however, indicating that there might very well be some way to do what Emban suggested. 'I wouldn't discount the possibility though, your Grace,' he added. 'Just because none of us know the spell doesn't mean that there isn't one. If someone wanted turmoil here in Astel, there's probably nothing that would have suited his purposes better than a serf uprising, and if all the nobles started knouting their serfs at about the same time, it would have been a perfect way to set one off.'

'And this Sabre fellow seems to be responsible,' Emban said. 'He's stirring the nobles against the godless yellow dogs – sorry, Oscagne – and at the same time

193

he's agitating the serfs against their masters. Was any-one able to pick up anything about him?'

'Elron was in his cups last night too,' Stragen said. 'He told Sparhawk and me that Sabre creeps around at night wearing a mask and making speeches.'

'You're not serious!' Bevier asked incredulously.

'Pathetic, isn't it? We're obviously dealing with a juv-enile mind here. Elron's quite overwhelmed by the melodrama of it all.'

'He would be,' Bevier sighed.

'It does sort of sound like the fabrication of a third-rate literary fellow, doesn't it?' Stragen smiled.

'That's Elron, all right,' Tynian said.

'You're flattering him,' Ulath grunted. 'He trapped me in a corner last night and recited some of his verse to me. "Third-rate" is a gross overstatement of his talent.'

Sparhawk was troubled. Aphrael had told him that someone at Kotyk's house would say something impor-tant, but, aside from the revelation of some fairly unsavoury personality defects, no one had directly told *him* anything of earth-shaking note. When he thought about it Aphrael had *not*, in fact, promised that what-ever was so important would be said to *him*. Quite poss-ibly, it had been revealed to one of the others. He brooded about it. The simplest way to resolve the ques-tion would have been to ask his daughter, but to do that would once more expose him to some offensive comments about his limited understanding, so he decided that he'd much prefer to work it out for himself.

Their map indicated that the journey to the capital at Darsas would take them ten days. It actually did not, of course.

'How do you deal with people who happen to see us when we're moving this way,' he asked Danae as they moved along at that accelerated pace later that day. He looked at his blank-faced uncomprehending friends. 'I've got a sort of an idea of how you convince the people who are travelling with us that we're just plodding along, but what about strangers?'

'We don't move this way when there are strangers around, Sparhawk,' she replied, 'but they wouldn't see us anyway. We're going too fast.'

'You're freezing time then, the same way Ghnomb did in Pelosia?'

'No, I'm actually doing just the opposite. Ghnomb froze time and made you plod along through an endless second. What I'm doing is –' She looked speculatively at her father. 'I'll explain it some other time,' she decided. 'We're moving in little spurts, a few miles at a time. Then we amble along for a while, and then we spurt ahead again. Making it all fit together is really very challenging. It gives me something to occupy my mind during these long, boring journeys.'

'Did that important thing you mentioned get said?' he asked her.

'Yes.'

'What was it?' He decided that a small bruise on his dignity wouldn't really hurt all that much.

'I don't know. I know that it was important and that somebody was going to say it, but I don't know the details.'

'Then you're *not* omniscient.'

'I never said that I was.'

'Could it have come in bits and pieces? A word or two to Emban, a couple to Stragen and me and quite a bit more to Khalad? And then we sort of had to put them all together to get the whole message?'

She thought about it. 'That's brilliant, father!' she exclaimed.

'Thank you.' Their speculations earlier had borne some fruit after all. Then he pushed it a bit further.

'Is someone here in Astel changing the attitudes of the people?'

'Yes, but that goes on all the time.'

'So when the nobility began to mistreat their serfs, it wasn't their own idea?'

'Of course not. Deliberate, calculated cruelty is very hard to maintain. You have to concentrate on it, and the Astels are too lazy for that. It was externally imposed.'

'Could a Styric magician have done it?'

'One by one, yes. A Styric could have selected one nobleman and turned him into a monster.' She thought a moment. 'Maybe two,' she amended. 'Three at the most. There are too many variables for a human to keep track of when you get past that.'

'Then it's a God – or Gods – that made them all start mistreating their serfs here a few years back?'

'I thought I just said that.'

He ignored that and went on. 'And the whole purpose of that was to make the serfs resentful and ready to listen to someone inciting them to revolution.'

'Your logic is blinding me, Sparhawk.'

'You can be a very offensive little girl when you set your mind to it, did you know that?'

'But you love me anyway, don't you? Get to the point, Sparhawk. It's almost time for me to wake the others.'

'And the sudden resentment directed at the Tamuls came from the same source, didn't it?'

'And probably at about the same time,' she agreed. 'It's easier to do it all at once. Going back into someone's mind over and over is so tedious.'

A sudden thought came to him. 'How many things can you think about at the same time?' he asked her.

'I've never counted – several thousand, I'd imagine. Of course there aren't really any limits. I guess if I really wanted to, I could think about everything all at once. I'll try it sometime and let you know.'

'That's really the difference between us, isn't it? You can think about more things at the same time than I can.'

'Well, that's *one* of the differences.'

'What's another?'

'You're a boy, and I'm a girl.'

'That's fairly obvious – and not very profound.'

'You're wrong Sparhawk. It's much, much more profound than you could ever imagine.'

After they crossed the river Antun, they entered a heavily forested region where rocky crags jutted up above the treetops here and there. The weather continued blustery and threatening, though it did not rain.

Kring's Peloi were very uncomfortable in the forest, and they rode huddled close to the Church Knights, their eyes a bit wild.

'We might want to remember that,' Ulath noted late that afternoon, jerking his chin in the direction of a pair of savage-looking, shaved-headed warriors following so closely behind Berit that their mounts were almost treading on his horse's hind hooves.

'What was that?' Kalten asked him.

'Don't take the Peloi into the woods.' Ulath paused and leaned back in his saddle. 'I knew a girl in Heid one summer who felt more or less the same way,' he reminisced. 'She was absolutely terrified of the woods. The young men of the town sort of gave up on her – even though she was a great beauty. Heid's a crowded little town, and there are always aunts and grandmothers and younger brothers underfoot in the houses. The young men have found that the woods offer the kind of privacy young people need from time to time, but this girl wouldn't go near the woods. Then I made an amazing discovery. The girl was afraid of the woods, but she was absolutely fearless where hay-barns were concerned. I tested the theory personally any number of times, and she never once showed the slightest bit of timidity about barns – or goat-sheds either, for that matter.'

'I really don't get the connection,' Kalten said. 'We were talking about the fact that the Peloi are afraid of the woods. If somebody attacks us here in this forest, we're not going to have time to stop and build a barn for them, are we?'

'No, I suppose you're right there.'

'All right, what *is* the connection then?'

'I don't think there is one, Kalten.'

'Why did you tell the story then?'

'Well, it's an awfully good story, don't you think?' Ulath sounded a bit injured.

Talen came galloping forward. 'I think you'd better come back to the carriage, Sir Knights,' he laughed, try-ing without much success to control his mirth.

'What's the trouble?' Sparhawk asked him.

'We've got company – well, not company exactly, but there's somebody watching us.'

Sparhawk and the others wheeled their mounts and rode back along the column to the carriage.

'You've *got* to see this, Sparhawk,' Stragen said, try-ing to stifle his laughter. 'Don't be too obvious when you look, but there's a man on horseback on top of that crag off to the left side of the road.'

Sparhawk leaned forward as if speaking to his wife and raised his eyes to look at the rocky crag jutting up from the forest floor.

The rider was about forty yards away, and he was outlined by the sunset behind him. He was making no attempt to conceal himself. He sat astride a black horse, and his clothing was all of the same hue. His inky cape streamed out from his shoulders in the stiff wind, and his broad-brimmed hat was crammed tightly down on his head. His face was covered with a bag-like black mask with two large, slightly off-centre eye holes in it.

'Isn't that the most ridiculous thing you've ever seen in your life?' Stragen laughed.

'Very impressive,' Ulath murmured. 'At least *he's* impressed.'

'I wish I had a crossbow,' Kalten said. 'Berit, do you think you could nick him a little with your long-bow?'

'It might be a little chancy in this wind, Kalten,' the young knight replied. 'It might deflect my arrow and kill him instead.'

'How long's he going to sit there?' Mirtai asked.

'Until he's sure that everybody in the column has seen him, I expect,' Stragen said. 'He went to a lot of trouble to deck himself out like that. What do you think, Sparhawk? Is that the fellow Elron told us about?'

'The mask certainly fits,' Sparhawk agreed. 'I wasn't expecting all the rest, though.'

'What's this?' Emban asked.

'Unless Sparhawk and I are mistaken, your Grace, we are privileged to be in the presence of a living legend. I think that's Sabre, the masked whatever-you-call-it, making his evening rounds.'

'What on earth is he doing?' Oscagne sounded baffled.

'I imagine that he's out wronging rights, depressing the oppressed and generally making an ass of himself, your Excellency. He looks as if he's having a lot of fun, though.'

The masked rider reared his horse dramatically, and his black cape swirled around him. Then he plunged down the far side of the crag and was gone.

'Wait,' Stragen urged before the others could move.

'For what?' Kalten asked.

'Listen.'

From beyond the crag came the brassy note of a horn that trailed off into a distinctly unmusical squawk.

'He *had* to have a horn,' Stragen explained. 'No performance like that would ever be complete without a horn.' He laughed delightedly. 'Maybe if he practises, he'll even learn to carry a tune with it.'

Darsas was an ancient city situated on the east bank of the Astel River. The bridge which approached it was a massive arch which had probably been in place for at least a thousand years, and most of the city's buildings showed a similar antiquity. The cobbled streets were narrow and twisting, following, quite probably, paths along which cows had gone to water aeons in the past. Although its antiquity seemed strange, there was still something profoundly familiar about Darsas. It was an almost prototypical Elene town, and Sparhawk felt as if his very bones were responding to its peculiar architecture. Ambassador Oscagne led them through the narrow streets and cluttered bazaars to an imposing square at the centre of the city. He pointed out a fairy-tale structure with a broad gate, and soaring towers bedecked with brightly-coloured pennons. 'The royal palace,' he told Sparhawk. 'I'll speak with Ambassador Fontan, our local man, and he'll take us to see King Alberen. I'll only be a moment.'

Sparhawk nodded. 'Kalten,' he called to his friend. 'Let's sort of form up the troops. A bit of ceremony might be in order here.'

When Oscagne emerged from the Tamul embassy, which was conveniently located in a building adjoining the palace, he was accompanied by an ancient-appearing Tamul whose head was totally hairless and whose face was as wrinkled as the skin of a very old apple. 'Prince Sparhawk,' Oscagne said quite formally, 'I have the honour to present his Excellency, Ambassador Fontan, his Imperial Majesty's representative here in the Kingdom of Astel.'

Sparhawk and Fontan exchanged polite bows.

'Have I your Highness' permission to present his Excellency to her Majesty, the Queen?' Oscagne asked.

'Tedious, isn't it Sparhawk?' Fontan asked in a voice as dry as dust. 'Oscagne's a good boy. He was my most promising pupil, but his fondness for ritual and formula overcomes him at times.'

'I'll borrow a sword and immolate myself at once, Fontan,' Oscagne bantered.

'I've seen you fumbling with a sword, Oscagne,' Fontan replied. 'If you're suicidally inclined, go molest a cobra instead. If you try to do it with a sword, you'll take all week.'

'I gather that I'm watching a reunion of sorts,' Sparhawk smiled.

'I always like to lower Oscagne's opinion of himself, Sparhawk,' Fontan replied. 'He's brilliant, of course, but sometimes he lacks humility. Now, why don't you introduce me to your wife? She's much prettier than you are, and the imperial messenger from Matherion rode three horses to death bringing me the emperor's instructions to be excruciatingly nice to her. We'll chat for a few moments, and then I'll take you to meet my dear, incompetent friend, the king. I'm sure he'll swoon at the unspeakable honour your queen's visit does him.'

Ehlana was delighted to meet the ambassador. Sparhawk knew that to be true because she said so herself. She invited the ancient Tamul, the real ruler of Astel, to join her in the carriage, and the entire party moved rather inexorably on to the palace gates.

The captain of the palace guard was nervous. When two hundred professional killers descend on one with implacable pace, one is almost always nervous. Ambassador Fontan put him at his ease, and three messengers were dispatched to advise the king of their arrival. Sparhawk decided not to ask the captain why he sent three. The poor man was having a bad enough day already. The party was escorted into the palace courtyard where they dismounted and turned their horses over to the stable hands. 'Behave yourself,' Sparhawk muttered to Faran as a slack-mouthed groom took the reins.

There seemed to be a great deal of activity going on in the palace. Windows kept popping open, and excited people stuck their heads out to gape.

'It's the steel clothing, I think,' Fontan observed to the queen. 'The appearance of your Majesty's escort on the doorstep may very well set a new fashion. A whole generation of tailors may have to learn black-smithing.' He shrugged. 'Oh, well,' he added. 'It's a useful trade. They can always shoe horses when business is slow.' He looked at his pupil, who had returned to the carriage. 'You should have sent word on ahead, Oscagne. Now we'll have to wait while everyone inside scurries around to make ready for us.'

After several minutes, a group of liveried trumpeters filed onto a balcony over the palace door and blew a shattering fanfare. The courtyard was enclosed by stone buildings, and the echoes from the trumpets were almost sufficient to unhorse the knights. Fontan climbed down from the carriage and offered Ehlana his arm with a graceful courtliness.

'Your Excellency is exquisitely courteous,' she murmured.

'Evidence of a misspent youth, my dear.'

'Your teacher's manner seems quite familiar, Ambassador Oscagne,' Stragen smiled.

'My imitation of him is only a poor shadow of my master's perfection, Milord.' Oscagne looked fondly at his wrinkled tutor. 'We all try to imitate him. His successes in the field of diplomacy are legendary. Don't be deceived, Stragen. When he's being urbane and ironically humorous, he's completely disarming you and gathering more information about you than you could ever imagine. Fontan can read a man's entire character in the twitch of one of his eyebrows.'

'I expect I'll be quite a challenge to him,' Stragen said, 'since I don't have any character to speak of.'

'You deceive yourself, Milord. You're not nearly as unprincipled as you'd like us to believe.'

A stout factotum in splendid scarlet livery escorted them into the palace and along a broad, well-lit corridor. Ambassador Oscagne walked just behind him, identifying the members of their party as they went.

The broad doors at the end of the corridor swung wide, and their liveried guide preceded them into a vast, ornate throne-room filled with excited courtiers. The factotum thunderously pounded on the floor with the butt of the staff which was his badge of office. 'My Lords and Ladies,' he boomed, 'I have the honour to present her Divine Majesty, Queen Ehlana of the Kingdom of Elenia!'

'Divine?' Kalten murmured to Sparhawk.

'It grows more evident as you get to know her better.'

The liveried herald continued his introductions, laboriously embellishing their individual titles as he presented them. Oscagne had quite obviously done his homework very thoroughly, and the herald dusted off seldom-used ornaments of rank in his introductory remarks. Kalten's nearly-forgotten baronetcy emerged. Bevier was exposed as a viscount, Tynian as a duke, and Ulath as an earl. Most surprising of all perhaps was the revelation that Berit, plain, earnest Berit, had been concealing the title of marquis in his luggage. Stragen was introduced as a baron. 'My father's title,' the blond thief explained to them in an apologetic whisper. 'Since

I killed him and my brothers, I suppose it technically belongs to me – spoils of war, you understand.'

'My goodness,' Baroness Melidere murmured, her blue eyes alight, 'I seem to be standing in the middle of a whole constellation of stars.' She seemed positively breathless.

'I wish she wouldn't do that,' Stragen complained.

'What's the problem?' Kalten asked him.

'She makes it seem as if the light in her eyes is the sun streaming in through the hole in the back of her head. I *know* she's far more clever than that. I *hate* dishonest people.'

'You?'

'Let it lie, Kalten.'

The throne-room of King Alberen of Astel was filled with an awed silence as the eminence of the visitors was revealed. King Alberen himself, an ineffectual-looking fellow whose royal robes looked a size or so too large for him, seemed to shrink with each new title. Alberen, it appeared, had weak eyes, and his myopic gaze gave him the fearful, timid look of a rabbit or some other such small helpless animal which all other creatures look upon as a food source. The splendour of his throne-room seemed to shrink him all the more, the wide expanses of crimson carpets and drapes, the massive gilt and crystal chandeliers and marble columns providing an heroic setting which he could never hope to fill.

Sparhawk's queen, regal and lovely, approached the throne on Ambassador Fontan's arm with her steel-plated entourage drawn up around her. King Alberen seemed a bit uncertain about the customary ceremonies. As the reigning monarch of Astel, he was entitled to remain seated upon his throne, but the fact that his entire court genuflected as Ehlana passed intimidated him, and he rose to his feet and even stepped down from the dais to greet her.

'Now has our life seen its crown,' Ehlana proclaimed in her most formal and oratorical style, 'for we have, as God most surely must have decreed since time's beginning, come at last into the presence of our dear brother of Astel, whom we have longed to meet since our earliest girlhood.'

'Is she speaking for all of us?' Talen whispered to Berit. 'I didn't really have a girlhood, you know.'

'She's using the royal plural,' Berit explained. 'The queen's more than one person. She's speaking for the entire kingdom.'

'We are honoured more than we can say, your Majesty,' Alberen faltered.

Ehlana quickly assessed her host's limitations and smoothly adopted a less formal tone. She abandoned ceremony and unleashed her charm on the poor fellow. At the end of five minutes they were chatting together as if they had known each other all their lives. At the end of ten, he'd have given her his crown had she asked for it.

After the obligatory exchanges, Sparhawk and the other members of Ehlana's entourage moved away from the throne to engage in that silly but necessary pastime known as 'circulating'. They talked about the weather mostly. The weather is a politically correct topic. Emban and Archimandrite Monsel, the head of the Church of Astel, exchanged theological platitudes without touching on those doctrinal differences which divided their two Churches. Monsel wore an elaborate mitre and intricately embroidered vestments. He also wore a full black beard that reached to his waist.

Sparhawk had discovered early in life that a scowl was his best defence in such situations, and he customarily intimidated whole rooms-full of people who might otherwise inflict conversational inanities upon him.

'Are you in some kind of distress, Prince Sparhawk?' It was Ambassador Fontan. 'Your face has a decidedly dyspeptic cast to it.'

'It's entirely tactical, your Excellency,' Sparhawk replied. 'When a military man doesn't want to be pestered, he digs a ditch and lines the bottom and sides with sharpened stakes. A scowl serves the same purpose in social situations.'

'You look bristly enough, my boy. Let's take a turn around the battlements and enjoy the view, the fresh air and the privacy. There are things you should know, and this may be my only chance to get you alone. King Alberen's court is full of inconsequential people who would all die for the chance to be able to manoeuvre conversations around to the point where they can assert that they know you personally. You have quite a reputation, you know.'

'Largely exaggerated, your Excellency.'

'You're too modest, my boy. Shall we go?'

They left the throne-room unobtrusively and climbed several flights of stairs until they came out on the windswept battlements.

Fontan looked down at the city spread below. 'Quaint, wouldn't you say?'

'Elene cities are always quaint, your Excellency,' Sparhawk replied. 'Elene architects haven't had a new idea in the last five millennia.'

'Matherion will open your eyes, Sparhawk. All right, then, Astel's right on the verge of flying apart. So's the rest of the world, but Astel's carrying it to extremes. I'm doing what I can to hold things together, but Alberen's so pliable that almost anyone can influence him. He'll literally sign anything anybody puts in front of him. You've heard about Ayachin, of course? And his running dog, Sabre?'

Sparhawk nodded.

206

'I've got every imperial agent in Astel out trying to identify Sabre, but we haven't had much luck so far. He's out there blithely dismantling a system the empire spent centuries creating. We don't really know very much about him.'

'He's an adolescent, your Excellency,' Sparhawk said. 'No matter what his age, he's profoundly juvenile.' He briefly described the incident in the forest.

'That's helpful,' Fontan said. 'None of my people have ever been able to infiltrate one of those famous meetings, so we had no idea of what sort of fellow we were dealing with. He's got the nobility completely in his grasp. I stopped Alberen just in time a few weeks ago when he was on the verge of signing a proclamation which would have criminalised a serf if he ran away. That would have brought the kingdom down around our ears, I'm afraid. That's always been the serf's final answer to an intolerable situation. If he can run away and stay away for a year and a day, he's free. If you take that away from the serfs, they'll revolt, and a serf rebellion is too hideous a notion to even contemplate.'

'It's quite deliberate, your Excellency,' Sparhawk advised him. 'Sabre's agitating the serfs as well. He *wants* a serf rebellion here in Astel. He's been using his influence over the nobility to persuade them to commit the exact blunders that will outrage the serfs all the more.'

'What's the man thinking of?' Fontan burst out. 'He'll drown Astel in blood.'

Sparhawk made an intuitive leap at the point. 'I don't think he really cares about Astel, your Excellency. Sabre's no more than a tool for someone who has his eye on a much bigger goal.'

'Oh? What's that?'

'I'm guessing, your Excellency, but I think there's

somebody out there who wants the whole world, and he'd sacrifice Astel and every living person in it to get what he wants.'

CHAPTER 12

'It's hard to put your finger on it, Prince Sparhawk,' Baroness Melidere said that evening after the extended royal family had retired to their oversized apartment for the night. At the queen's insistence, Melidere, Mirtai and Alean, her maid, had been provided with rooms in the apartment. Ehlana needed women around her for a number of reasons, some practical, some political and some very obscure. The ladies had removed their formal gowns, and, except for Mirtai, they wore soft pastel dressing gowns. Melidere was brushing Mirtai's wealth of blue-black hair, and the doe-eyed Alean was performing the same service for Ehlana.

'I'm not sure exactly how to describe it,' the honey-blonde baroness continued. 'It's a sort of generalised sadness. They all sigh a great deal.'

'I noticed that myself, Sparhawk,' Ehlana told her husband. 'Alberen hardly smiles at all, and I can make *anybody* smile.'

'Your presence alone is enough to make us all smile, my Queen,' Talen told her. Talen was the queen's page, and he was also a member of the extended family. The young thief was elegant tonight, dressed in a plum-coloured velvet doublet and knee-britches in the same shade and fabric. Knee-britches were just coming into fashion, and Ehlana had tried her very best to get Sparhawk into a pair of them. He had categorically refused, and his wife had been obliged to settle for coercing her page into the ridiculous-looking garments.

'The plan is to make you a knight, Talen,' Melidere told the boy pointedly, 'not a courtier.'

'Stragen says it's always a good idea to have something to fall back on, Baroness,' he shrugged, his voice cracking and warbling somewhere between soprano and baritone.

'He would,' the baroness sniffed. Melidere affected a strong disapproval of Stragen, but Sparhawk was not so sure about that.

Talen and Princess Danae sat on the floor rolling a ball back and forth between them. Mmrr was participating in the game enthusiastically.

'They all seem to secretly believe that the world's going to come to an end week after next,' the baroness went on, slowly drawing her brush through Mirtai's hair. 'They're all bright and brittle on the surface, but once you get beneath that, there's the blackest melancholy, and they all drink like fish. I couldn't prove this, but I really think they all believe they're going to die very soon.' She lifted Mirtai's hair speculatively. 'I think I'll braid a gold chain into it, dear,' she told the giantess.

'No, Melidere,' Mirtai said firmly. 'I'm not entitled to wear gold yet.'

'Every woman's entitled to wear gold, Mirtai,' Melidere laughed, 'provided that she can charm it out of some man.'

'Not among my people,' Mirtai disagreed. 'Gold is for adults. Children don't wear it.'

'You're hardly a child, Mirtai,'

'I am until I go through a certain ceremony. Silver, Melidere – or steel.'

'You can't make jewellery out of steel.'

'You can if you polish it enough.'

Melidere sighed. 'Fetch me the silver chains, Talen,' she said. At the moment, that was Talen's function. He fetched things. He didn't like it very much, but he did it – largely because Mirtai was bigger than he was.

There was a polite knock at the door, and Talen veered over to answer it.

Ambassador Oscagne entered. He bowed to Ehlana. 'I've spoken with Fontan, your Majesty,' he reported. 'He's sending to the garrison at Canae for two Atan legions to escort us to Matherion. I'm sure we'll all feel more secure with them around us.'

'What's a legion, your Excellency?' Talen asked, crossing the room to the jewellery cabinet.

'A thousand warriors,' Oscagne replied. He smiled at Ehlana. 'With two thousand Atans at your disposal, your Majesty could conquer Edom. Would you like to establish a toe-hold on the Daresian continent? It won't really be all that inconvenient. We Tamuls will administer it for you – for the usual fee, of course – and we'll send you glowing reports at the end of each year. The reports will be a tissue of lies, but we'll send them anyway.'

'Along with the profits?' She actually sounded interested.

'Oh no, your Majesty,' he laughed. 'For some reason, not one single kingdom in the whole empire ever shows a profit – except Tamul itself, of course.'

'Why would I want a kingdom that doesn't pay?'

'Prestige, your Majesty, and vanity. You'd have another title and another crown.'

'I don't really need another crown, your Excellency. I've only got one head. Why don't we just let the King of Edom keep his unprofitable kingdom?'

'Probably a wise decision, your Majesty,' he agreed. 'Edom's a tedious sort of place. They grow wheat there, and wheat-farmers are a stodgy group of people all obsessively interested in the weather.'

'How long is it likely to be until those legions arrive?' Sparhawk asked him.

'A week or so. They'll come on foot, so they'll make better time than they would on horseback.'

211

'Isn't it the other way around, your Excellency?' Melidere asked him. 'I thought horses moved much faster than men on foot.'

Mirtai laughed.

'Did I say something funny?' Melidere asked.

'When I was fourteen, a man down in Daconia insulted me,' the giantess told her. 'He was drunk. When he sobered up the next morning, he realised what he'd done and fled on horseback. It was about dawn. I caught up with him just before noon. His horse had died from exhaustion. I always felt sort of sorry for the horse. A trained warrior can run all day. A horse can't. A horse has to stop when he wants to eat, so he's not used to running for more than a few hours at a time. We eat while we're running, so we just keep on going.'

'What did you do to the fellow who insulted you?' Talen asked her.

'Do you really want to know?'

'Ah – no, Mirtai,' he replied. 'Now that you mention it, probably not.'

And so they had a week on their hands. Baroness Melidere devoted her time to breaking hearts. The young noblemen of King Alberen's court flocked around her. She flirted outrageously, made all sorts of promises – none of which she kept – and occasionally allowed herself to be kissed in dark corners by persistent suitors. She had a great deal of fun and gathered a great deal of information. A young man pursuing a pretty girl will often share secrets with her, secrets which he should probably keep to himself.

To the surprise of Sparhawk and his fellow knights, Sir Berit devastated the young ladies of the court quite nearly as much as the baroness did the young men.

'It's absolutely uncanny,' Kalten was saying one

212

evening. 'He doesn't really do anything at all. He doesn't talk to them; he doesn't smile at them; he doesn't do any of the things he's supposed to do. I don't know what it is, but every time he walks through a room, every young woman in the place starts to come all unravelled.'

'He *is* a very handsome young man, Kalten,' Ehlana pointed out.

'Berit? He doesn't even shave regularly yet.'

'What's that got to do with it? He's tall, he's a knight, he has broad shoulders and good manners. He's also got the deepest blue eyes I've ever seen – and the longest eyelashes.'

'But he's only a boy.'

'Not any more. You haven't really looked at him lately. Besides, the young ladies who sigh and cry into their pillows over him are quite young themselves.'

'What's really so irritating is the fact that he doesn't even know what effect he has on all those poor girls,' Tynian observed. 'They're doing everything but tearing their clothes off to get his attention, and he hasn't got the faintest notion of what's going on.'

'That's part of his charm, Sir Knight,' Ehlana smiled. 'If it weren't for that innocence of his, they wouldn't find him nearly so attractive. Sir Bevier here has much the same quality. The difference though, is that Bevier *knows* that he's an extraordinarily handsome young man. He chooses not to do anything about it because of his religious convictions. Berit doesn't even know.'

'Maybe one of us should take him aside and tell him,' Ulath suggested.

'Never mind,' Mirtai told him. 'He's fine just the way he is. Leave him alone.'

'Mirtai's right,' Ehlana said. 'Don't tamper with him, gentlemen. We'd like to keep him innocent for just a while longer.' A hint of mischief touched her lips. 'Sir Bevier, on the other hand, is quite another matter. It's time for us to find him a wife. He'll make some girl an excellent husband.'

Bevier smiled faintly. 'I'm already married, your Majesty – to the Church.'

'Betrothed perhaps, Bevier, but not yet married. Don't start buying ecclesiastical garb just yet, Sir Knight. I haven't entirely given up on you.'

'Wouldn't it be easier to start closer to home, your Majesty?' he suggested. 'If you feel the urge to marry someone off, Sir Kalten is readily at hand.'

'Kalten?' she asked incredulously. 'Don't be absurd, Bevier. I wouldn't do that to *any* woman.'

'Your *Majesty!*' Kalten protested.

'I love you dearly, Kalten,' she smiled at the blond Pandion, 'but you're just not husband material. I couldn't *give* you away. In good conscience I couldn't even *order* anyone to marry you. Tynian is remotely possible, but God intended you and Ulath to be bachelors.'

'Me?' Ulath said mildly.

'Yes,' she said, 'you.'

The door opened, and Stragen and Talen entered. They were both dressed in the plain clothing they usually wore when making one of their sorties into the streets.

'Any luck?' Sparhawk asked them.

'We found him,' Stragen replied, handing his cloak to Alean. 'He's not really my sort. He's a pickpocket by profession, and pickpockets don't really make good leaders. There's something fundamentally lacking in their character.'

'Stragen!' Talen protested.

'You're not really a pickpocket, my young friend,' Stragen told him. 'That's only an interim occupation while you're waiting to grow up. Anyway, the local chief's named Kondrak. He could see that we all have a mutual interest in stable governments, I'll give him that. Looting houses when there's turmoil in the streets is a fast way to make a lot of money, but over the long run, a good thief can accumulate more in times of domestic tranquillity. Of course Kondrak can't make any kind of overall decision on his own. He'll have to consult with his counterparts in other cities in the empire.'

'That shouldn't take more than a year or so,' Sparhawk noted drily.

'Hardly,' Stragen disagreed. 'Thieves move much more rapidly than honest men. Kondrak's going to send out word of what we're trying to accomplish. He'll put it in the best possible light, so there's a very good chance that the thieves of all the kingdoms in the empire will co-operate.'

'How will we know their decision?' Tynian asked him.

'I'll make courtesy calls each time we come to a fair-sized city,' Stragen shrugged. 'Sooner or later I'll get an official reply. It shouldn't take all that long. We'll certainly have a final decision by the time we reach Matherion.' He looked speculatively at Ehlana. 'Your Majesty's learned a great deal about the subterranean government in the past few years,' he noted. 'Do you suppose we could put that information on the level of a state secret? We're perfectly willing to co-operate and even assist on occasion, but we'd be much happier if the other monarchs of the world didn't know too much about the way we operate. Some crusader might decide to smash the secret government, and that would inconvenience us a bit.'

'What's it worth to you, Milord Stragen?' she teased him.

His eyes grew very serious. 'It's a decision you'll have to make for yourself, Ehlana,' he told her, cutting across

215

rank and customary courtesies. 'I've tried to assist you whenever I could because I'm genuinely fond of you. If you make a little conversational slip, though, and other monarchs find out things they shouldn't know, I won't be able to do that any more.'

'You'd abandon me, Milord Stragen?'

'Never, my Queen, but my colleagues would have me killed, and I wouldn't really be of much use to you in that condition, now would I?'

Archimandrite Monsel was a large, impressive man with piercing black eyes and an imposing black beard. It was a forceful beard, an assertive beard, a beard impossible to overlook, and the Archimandrite used it like a battering ram. It preceded him by a yard wherever he went. It bristled when he was irritated – which was often – and in damp weather it knotted up into snarls like half a mile of cheap fishing line. The beard waggled when Monsel talked, emphasising points all on its own. Patriarch Emban was absolutely fascinated by the Archimandrite's beard. 'It's like talking to an animated hedge,' he observed to Sparhawk as the two of them walked through the corridors of the palace toward a private audience with the Astellian ecclesiaste.

'Are there any topics I should avoid, your Grace?' Sparhawk asked. 'I'm not familiar with the Church of Astel, and I don't want to start any theological debates.'

'Our disagreements with the Astels are in the field of Church government, Sparhawk. Our purely theological differences are very minor. We have a secular clergy, but their Church is monastically organised. Our priests are just priests; theirs are also monks. I'll grant you that it's a fine distinction, but it's a distinction nonetheless. They also have many, many more priests and monks than we do – probably about a tenth of the population.'

'That many?'

'Oh, yes. Every noble mansion in Astel has its own private chapel and its own priest, and the priest "assists" in making decisions.'

'Where do they find so many men willing to enter the priesthood?'

'From the ranks of the serfs. Being a clergyman has its drawbacks, but it's better than being a serf.'

'I suppose the Church *would* be preferable.'

'Much. Monsel will respect you, because you're a member of a religious order. Oh, incidentally, since you're the interim preceptor of the Pandion Knights, you're technically a patriarch. Don't be surprised if he addresses you as "your Grace".'

They were admitted into Monsel's chambers by a long-bearded monk. Sparhawk had noticed that all Astellian clergymen wore beards. The room was small and panelled in dark wood. The carpet was a deep maroon, and the heavy drapes at the windows were black. There were books and scrolls and dog-eared sheets of parchment everywhere.

'Ah, Emban,' Monsel said. 'What have you been up to?'

'Mischief, Monsel. I've been out proselytising among the heathens.'

'Really? Where did you find any here? I thought most heathens lived in the Basilica in Chyrellos. Sit down, gentlemen. I'll send for some wine and we can debate theology.'

'You've met Sparhawk?' Emban asked as they all took chairs before an open window where the breeze billowed the black drapes.

'Briefly,' Monsel replied. 'How are you today, your Highness?'

'Well. And you, your Grace?'

'Curious, more than anything. Why are we engaging in private consultations?'

'We're all clergymen, your Grace,' Emban pointed out. 'Sparhawk wears a cassock made of steel most of the time, but he *is* of the clergy. We've come to discuss something that probably concerns you as much as it does us. I think I know you well enough to know that you've got a practical side that's not going to get sidetracked by the fact that you think we genuflect wrong.'

'What's this?' Sparhawk asked.

'We kneel on our right knee,' Emban shrugged. 'These poor, benighted heathens kneel on the left.'

'Shocking,' Sparhawk murmured. 'Do you think we should come here in force and compel them to do it right?'

'You see?' Emban said to the Archimandrite. 'That's exactly what I was talking about. You should fall to your knees and thank God that you're not saddled with Church Knights, Monsel. I think most of them secretly worship Styric Gods.'

'Only the Younger Gods, your Grace,' Sparhawk said mildly. 'We've had our differences with the Elder Gods.'

'He says it so casually,' Monsel shuddered. 'If you think we've exhausted the conversational potential of genuflectory variation, Emban, why don't you get to the point?'

'This is in strictest confidence, your Grace, but our mission here to Tamuli's not entirely what it seems. It was Queen Ehlana's idea, of course. She's not the sort to go *anywhere* just because somebody tells her to – but all of this elaborate fol-de-rol was just a subterfuge to hide our real purpose, which was to put Sparhawk on the Daresian Continent. The world's coming apart at the seams, so we've decided to let him fix it.'

'I thought that was God's job.'

'God's busy just now, and He's got complete confidence in Sparhawk. All sorts of Gods feel that way about him, I understand.'

Monsel's eyes widened, and his beard bristled.

'Relax, Monsel,' Emban told him. 'We of the Church are not required to believe in other Gods. All we have to do is make a few allowances for their speculative existence.'

'Oh, that's different. If this is speculation, I suppose it's all right.'

'There's one thing that *isn't* speculation, your Grace,' Sparhawk said. 'You've got trouble here in Astel.'

'You've noticed. Your Highness is very perceptive.'

'You may not have been advised, since the Tamuls are trying to keep it on a low key, but very similar things are afoot in many other Daresian kingdoms, and we're beginning to encounter the same sort of problem in Eosia.'

'I think the Tamuls sometimes keep secrets just for the fun of it,' Monsel grunted.

'I have a friend who says the same thing about our Eosian Church,' Sparhawk said cautiously. They had not yet fully explored the Archimandrite's political opinions. A wrong word or two here would not only preclude any possibility of obtaining his help, but might even compromise their mission.

'Knowledge is power,' Emban said rather sententiously, 'and only a fool shares power if he doesn't have to. Let me be blunt, Monsel. What's your opinion of the Tamuls?'

'I don't like them.' Monsel's response was to the point. 'They're heathens, they're members of an alien race, and you can't tell what they're thinking.'

Sparhawk's heart sank.

'I have to admit, though, that when they absorbed Astel into their empire, it was the best thing that ever happened to us. Whether we like them or not is beside the point. Their passion for order and stability has averted war time and time again in my own lifetime.

There have been other empires in ages past, and their time of ascendancy was a time of unmitigated horror and suffering. I think we'll candidly have to admit that the Tamuls are history's finest imperialists. They don't interfere with local customs or religions. They don't disrupt the social structure, and they function *through* the established governments. Their taxes, however much we complain about them, are really minimal. They build good roads and encourage trade. Aside from that, they generally leave us alone. About all they really insist upon is that we don't go to war with each other. I can live with that – although some of my predecessors felt dreadfully abused because the Tamuls wouldn't let them convert their neighbours by the sword.'

Sparhawk breathed a little easier.

'But I'm straying from the point here,' Monsel said. 'You were suggesting a world-wide conspiracy of some kind, I think.'

'Were we suggesting that, Sparhawk?' Emban asked.

'I suppose we were, your Grace.'

'Do you have anything concrete upon which to base this theory, Sir Sparhawk?' Monsel asked.

'Logic is about all, your Grace.'

'I'll listen to logic – as long as she doesn't contradict my beliefs.'

'If a series of events happens in one place and it's identical to a series of events taking place in another, we're justified in considering the possibility of a common source, wouldn't you say?'

'On an interim basis, perhaps.'

'It's about all we have to work with at the moment, your Grace. The same sort of thing could happen at the same time in two different places and still be a coincidence, but when you get up to five or ten different occurrences, coincidence sort of goes out the window. This current upheaval involving Ayachin and the one they call Sabre here in Astel is almost exactly duplicated in the kingdom of Lamorkand in Eosia, and Ambassador Oscagne assures us that the same sort of thing's erupting in other Daresian kingdoms as well. It's always the same. First there are the rumours that some towering hero of antiquity has somehow returned. Then some firebrand emerges to keep things stirred up. Here in Astel, you've got the wild stories about Ayachin. In Lamorkand, they talk about Drychtnath. Here you have a man named Sabre, and in Lamorkand they've got one named Gerrich. I'm fairly sure we'll find the same sort of thing in Edom, Daconia, Arjuna and Cynesga. Oscagne tells us that *their* national heroes are putting in an appearance as well.' Sparhawk rather carefully avoided mentioning Krager. He was still not entirely certain where Monsel's sympathies lay.

'You build a good case, Sparhawk,' Monsel conceded. 'But couldn't this master plot be directed at the Tamuls? They aren't widely loved, you know.'

'I think your Grace is overlooking Lamorkand,' Emban said. 'There aren't any Tamuls there. I'm guessing, but I'd say that the master plot – if that's what we want to call it – is directed at the *Church* in Eosia as opposed to the empire here.'

'Organised anarchy perhaps?'

'I believe that's a contradiction in terms, your Grace,' Sparhawk pointed out. 'I'm not sure that we're far enough along to deal with causes yet, though. Right now we're trying to sort through effects. If we're correct in assuming that this plot is all coming from the same person, then what we're seeing is someone who's got a basic plan with common elements which he modifies to fit each particular culture. What we really want to do is to identify this Sabre fellow.'

'So that you can have him killed?' Monsel's tone was accusing.

'No, your Grace, that wouldn't be practical. If we kill him, he'll be replaced by someone else – somebody we don't know. I want to know *who* he is, and *what* he is and everything I can possibly find out about him. I want to know how he thinks, what drives him and what his personal motivations are. If I know all of that, I can neutralise him *without* killing him. To be completely honest with you, I don't really care about Sabre. I want the one who's behind him.'

Monsel seemed shaken. 'This is a dreadful man, Emban,' he said in a hushed tone.

'Implacable is the word, I think.'

'If we can believe Oscagne – and I think we can – someone's using the arcane arts in this business,' Sparhawk told them. 'That's why the Church Knights were created originally. It's *our* business to deal with magic. Our Elene religion can't cope with it because there's no place in our faith for it. We had to go outside the faith – to the Styrics – to learn how to counteract magic. It opened some doors we might have preferred had been left closed, but that's the price we had to pay. *Somebody* – or some*thing* – on the other side's using magic of a very high order. I'm here to stop him – to kill him if need be. Once he's gone, the Atans can deal with Sabre. I know an Atan, and if her people are at all like her, I know we can count on them to be thorough.'

'You trouble me, Sparhawk,' Monsel admitted. 'Your devotion to your duty's almost inhuman, and your resolve goes even beyond that. You shame me, Sparhawk.' He sighed and sat tugging at his beard, his eyes lost in thought. Finally, he straightened. 'All right, Emban, can we suspend the rules?'

'I didn't quite follow that.'

'I wasn't going to tell you this,' the Archimandrite said, 'first of all because it'll probably raise your doctrinal hackles, but more importantly because I didn't really want to share it with you. This implacable Sparhawk of yours has convinced me otherwise. If I don't tell you what I know, he'll dismantle Astel and everyone in it to get the information, won't you, Sparhawk?'

'I'd really hate that, your Grace.'

'But you'd do it anyway, wouldn't you?'

'If I had to.'

Monsel shuddered. 'You're both churchmen, so I'm going to invoke the rule of clerical confidentiality. You haven't changed the requirements of *that* in Chyrellos yet, have you, Emban?'

'Not unless Sarathi did it since I've been gone. At any rate, you have our word that neither of us will reveal anything you tell us.'

'Except to another clergyman,' Monsel amended. 'I'll go that far.'

'All right,' Emban agreed.

Monsel leaned back in his chair, stroking his beard. 'The Tamuls have no real conception of how powerful the Church is in the Elene kingdoms here in Western Daresia,' he began. 'In the first place, their religion's hardly more than a set of ceremonies. Tamuls don't even think about religion, so they can't understand the depth of the faith in the hearts of the devout – and the serfs of Astel are quite likely the most devout people on earth. They take all of their problems to their priests – and not only their own problems, but their neighbours' as well. The serfs are everywhere and they see everything, and they tell their priests.'

'I think it was called tale-bearing when I was in the seminary,' Emban noted.

'We had a worse name for it during our novitiate,' Sparhawk added. 'All sorts of unpleasant accidents used to happen on the training-field because of it.'

'Nobody likes a snitch,' Monsel agreed, 'but like it or not, the Astellian clergy knows everything that happens in the kingdom – literally everything. We're sworn to keep these secrets, of course, but we feel that our primary responsibility is to the spiritual health of our flock. Since a large proportion of our priests were originally serfs, they simply don't have the theological training to deal with complex spiritual problems. We've devised a way to provide them with the advice they need. The serf-priests do not reveal the names of those who have come to them, but they *do* take serious matters to their superiors, and their superiors bring those matters to *me*.'

'I have no real difficulty with that,' Emban said. 'As long as the names are kept secret, the confidentiality hasn't been violated.'

'We'll get on well together, Emban.' Monsel smiled briefly. 'The serfs look upon Sabre as a liberator.'

'So we gathered,' Sparhawk told him. 'There seems to be a certain lack of consistency in his speeches, though. He tells the nobles that Ayachin wants to throw off the Tamul yoke, and then he tells the serfs that Ayachin's real goal is the abolition of serfdom. Moreover, he's persuaded the nobles to become very brutal in their dealings with the serfs. That's not only disgusting, it's irrational. The nobles should be trying to *enlist* the serfs, not alienate them. Viewed realistically, Sabre's no more than an agitator, and he's not even particularly subtle. He's a political adolescent.'

'That's going a little far, Sparhawk,' Emban protested. 'How do you account for his success then? An idiot like that could never persuade the Astels to accept his word.'

'They're not accepting *his* word. They're accepting Ayachin's.'

'Have you taken leave of your senses, Sparhawk?'

'No, your Grace. I mentioned before that someone on the other side's been using magic. *This* is what I was talking about. The people here have actually been seeing Ayachin himself.'

'That's absurd!' Monsel seemed profoundly disturbed.

Sparhawk sighed. 'For the sake of your Grace's theological comfort, let's call it some kind of hallucination – a mass illusion created by a clever charlatan, or some accomplice dressed in archaic clothing who appears suddenly in some spectacular fashion. Whatever its source, if what's happening here is anything like what's happening in Lamorkand, your people are absolutely convinced that Ayachin's returned from the grave. Sabre probably makes a speech – a rambling collection of disconnected platitudes – and then this hallucination appears in a flash of light and a clap of thunder and confirms all his pronouncements. That's a guess, of course, but it's probably not too far off the mark.'

'It's an elaborate hoax then?'

'If that's what you want to believe, your Grace.'

'But you *don't* believe it's a hoax, do you Sparhawk?'

'I've been trained not to actively disbelieve things, your Grace. Whether the apparition of Ayachin is real or some trick is beside the point. It's what the people believe that's important, and I'm sure *they* believe that Ayachin's returned and that Sabre speaks for him. That's what makes Sabre so dangerous. With the apparition to support him, he can make people believe anything. That's why I have to find out everything about him that I can. I have to be able to know what he's going to do so that I can counter him.'

'I'm going to behave as if I believe what you've just told me, Sparhawk,' Monsel said in a troubled voice. 'I really think you need some spiritual help, though.' His face grew grave. 'We know who Sabre is,' he said finally. 'We've known for over a year now. At first we believed as you do – that he was no more than a disturbed fanatic with a taste for melodrama. We expected the Tamuls to deal with him, so we didn't think we had to do anything ourselves. I've had some second thoughts on that score of late, though. On the condition that neither of you will reveal anything I say except to another clergyman, I'll tell you who he is. Do I have your word on that condition?'

'You have, your Grace,' Emban swore.

'And you, Sparhawk?'

'Of course.'

'Very well, then. Sabre's the younger brother-in-law of a minor nobleman who has an estate a few leagues to the east of Esos.'

It all fell into place in Sparhawk's mind with a loud clank.

'The nobleman is a Baron Kotyk, a silly, ineffectual ass,' Monsel told them. 'And you were quite right, Sparhawk. Sabre's a melodramatic adolescent named Elron.'

CHAPTER 13

'That's impossible!' Sparhawk exclaimed.

Monsel was taken aback by his sudden vehemence. 'We have more than ample evidence, Sir Sparhawk. The serf who reported the fact has known him since childhood. You've met Elron, I gather.'

'We took shelter from a storm in Baron Kotyk's house,' Emban explained. 'Elron *could* be Sabre, you know, Sparhawk. He's certainly got the right kind of mentality. Why are you so certain he's not the one?'

'He couldn't have caught up with us,' Sparhawk said lamely.

Monsel looked baffled.

'We saw Sabre in the woods on our way here,' Emban told him. 'It was the sort of thing you'd expect – a masked man in black on a black horse outlined against the sky – silliest thing I ever saw. We weren't really moving all that fast, Sparhawk. Elron could have caught up with us quite easily.'

Sparhawk could not tell him that they *had*, in fact, been moving far too rapidly for anyone to have caught them – not with Aphrael tampering with time and distance the way she had been. He choked back his objections. 'It just surprised me, that's all,' he lied. 'Stragen and I spoke with Elron the night we were there. I can't believe he'd be out stirring up the serfs. He had nothing but contempt for them.'

'A pose, perhaps?' Monsel suggested. 'Something to conceal his real feelings?'

'I don't think he's capable of that, your Grace. He was too ingenuous for that kind of subtlety.'

'Don't be too quick to make judgements, Sparhawk,' Emban told him. 'If there's magic involved, it wouldn't make any difference *what* kind of man Sabre is, would it? Isn't there some way he could be rather tightly controlled?'

'Several, actually,' Sparhawk admitted.

'I'm a little surprised you didn't consider that yourself. You're the expert on magic. Elron's personal beliefs are probably beside the point. When he's speaking as Sabre, it's the man behind him – our real adversary – who's talking.'

'I should have thought of that.' Sparhawk was angry with himself for having overlooked the obvious – and the equally obvious explanation for Elron's ability to overtake them. Another God could certainly compress time and distance the same way Aphrael could. 'Just how widespread is this contempt for the serfs, your Grace?' he asked Monsel.

'Unfortunately, it's almost universal, Prince Sparhawk,' Monsel sighed. 'The serfs are uneducated and superstitious, but they're not nearly as stupid as the nobility would like to believe. The reports I've received tell me that Sabre spends almost as much time denouncing the serfs as he does the Tamuls when he's speaking to the nobility. "Lazy" is about the kindest thing he says about them. He's managed to half-persuade the gentry that the serfs are in league with the Tamuls in some vast, dark plot with its ultimate goal being the emancipation of the serfs and the redistribution of the land. The nobles are responding predictably. First they were goaded into hating the Tamuls, and then they were led to believe that the serfs are in league with the Tamuls and that their estates and positions are threatened by that alliance. They don't dare confront the Tamuls directly because of the Atans, so they're venting their hostility on their own serfs. There have been incidents of unprovoked savagery upon a class of people who will march *en masse* into heaven at the final judgement. The Church is doing what she can, but there's only so far we can go in restraining the gentry.'

'You need some Church Knights, your Grace,' Sparhawk said in a bleak tone of voice. 'We're very good in the field of justice. If you take a nobleman's knout away from him and apply it to his own back a few times, he tends to see the light very quickly.'

'I wish that were possible here in Astel, Sir Sparhawk,' Monsel replied sadly. 'Unfortunately –'

It was the same chill, and that same annoying flicker at the edge of the eye. Monsel broke off and looked around quickly, trying to see what could not really be seen. 'What –?' he started.

'It's a visitation, your Grace,' Emban told him, his voice tense. 'Don't dislocate your neck trying to catch a glimpse of it.' He raised his voice slightly. 'Awfully good to see you again, old boy,' he said. 'We were beginning to think you'd forgotten about us. Was there something you wanted in particular? Or were you just yearning for our company? We're flattered, of course, but we're a little busy at the moment. Why don't you run along and play now? We can chat some other time.'

The chill quite suddenly turned hot, and the flicker darkened.

'Are you insane, Emban?' Sparhawk choked.

'I don't think so,' the fat little Patriarch said. 'Your flickering friend – or friends – are irritating me, that's all.'

The shadow vanished, and the air around them returned to normal.

'What was that all about?' Monsel demanded.

'The Patriarch of Ucera just insulted a God – several Gods, probably,' Sparhawk replied through clenched teeth. 'For a moment there, we all hovered on the brink of obliteration. Please don't do that again, Emban – at least not without consulting me first.' He suddenly laughed a bit sheepishly. 'Now I know exactly how Sephrenia felt on any number of occasions. I'll have to apologise to her the next time I see her.'

Emban was grinning with delight. 'I sort of caught them off balance there, didn't I?'

'Don't do it again, your Grace,' Sparhawk pleaded. 'I've seen what Gods can do to people, and I don't want to be around if you *really* insult them.'

'Our God protects me.'

'Annias was praying to our God when Azash wrung him out like a wet rag, your Grace. It didn't do him all that much good, as I recall.'

'That was really stupid, you know,' Emban said then.

'I'm glad you realise that.'

'Not me, Sparhawk. I'm talking about our adversary. Why did it reveal itself at this particular moment? It should have kept its flamboyant demonstration to itself and just listened. It could have found out what our plans are. Not only that, it revealed itself to Monsel. Until it appeared, he only had our word for the fact of its existence. Now he's seen it for himself.'

'Will someone *please* explain this?' Monsel burst out.

'It was the Troll-Gods, your Grace,' Sparhawk told him.

'That's absurd. There's no such thing as a Troll, so how can they have Gods?'

'This may take longer than I'd thought,' Sparhawk muttered half to himself. 'As a matter of fact, your Grace, there *are* Trolls.'

'Have you ever seen one?' Monsel challenged.

'Only one, your Grace. His name was Ghwerig. He was dwarfed, so he was only about seven feet tall. He was still very difficult to kill.'

'You killed him?' Monsel gasped.

'He had something I wanted,' Sparhawk shrugged. 'Ulath's seen a lot more of them than I have, your Grace. He can tell you all about them. He even speaks their language. I did for a while myself, but I've probably forgotten by now. Anyway, they have a language, which means that they're semi-human, and that means that they have Gods, doesn't it?'

Monsel looked helplessly at Emban.

'Don't ask *me*, my friend,' the fat Patriarch said. 'That's a long way out of *my* theological depth.'

'For the time being, you'll have to take my word for it,' Sparhawk told them. 'There *are* Trolls, and they *do* have Gods – five of them – and they aren't very nice. That shadow Patriarch Emban just so casually dismissed was them – or something very much like them – and that's what we're up against. That's what's trying to bring down the empire and the Church – both our churches, probably. I'm sorry I have to put it to you so abruptly, Archimandrite Monsel, but you have to know what you're dealing with. Otherwise, you'll be totally defenceless. You don't have to believe what I just told you, but you'd better behave as if you did, because if you don't, your Church doesn't have a chance of surviving.'

The Atans arrived a few days later. A hush fell over the city of Darsas as the citizens scurried for cover. No man is so entirely guiltless in his own soul that the sudden appearance of a few thousand police does not give him a qualm or two. The Atans were superbly conditioned giants. The two thousand warriors of both sexes ran in perfect unison as they entered the city four abreast. They wore short leather kirtles, burnished steel breastplates and black half-boots. Their bare limbs gleamed golden in the morning sun as they ran, and their faces were stern and unbending. Though they were obviously

231

soldiers, there was no uniformity in their weapons. They carried a random collection of swords, short spears and axes, as well as other implements for which Sparhawk had no names. They all had several sheathed daggers strapped tightly to their arms and legs. They wore no helmets, but had slender gold circlets about their heads instead.

'Lord,' Kalten breathed to Sparhawk as the two of them stood on the palace battlements to watch the arrival of their escort, 'I'd really hate to come up against that lot on a battlefield. Just looking at them makes my blood cold.'

'I believe that's the idea, Kalten,' Sparhawk said. 'Mirtai's impressive all by herself, but when you see a couple of thousand of them like this, you begin to understand how the Tamuls were able to conquer a continent without any particular difficulty. I'd imagine that whole armies simply capitulated when they saw them coming.'

The Atans entered the square in front of the palace and formed up before the residence of the Tamul Ambassador. A huge man went to Ambassador Fontan's door, his pace quite clearly indicating that if the door were not opened for him, he would walk right through it.

'Why don't we go down?' Sparhawk suggested. 'I expect that Fontan will be bringing that fellow to call in a few moments. Watch what you say, Kalten. Those people strike me as a singularly humourless group. I'm sure they'd miss the point of almost any joke.'

'Really,' Kalten breathed his agreement.

The party accompanying the Queen of Elenia gathered in her Majesty's private quarters and stood about rather nervously awaiting the arrival of the Tamul Ambassador and his general. Sparhawk watched Mirtai rather closely to see what her reaction might be upon being re-united with her people after so many years.

She wore clothing he had not seen her wear before, clothing which closely resembled that worn by her countrymen. In place of the steel breastplate, however, she wore a tight-fitting, sleeveless black leather jerkin, and the band about her brow was of silver rather than gold. Her face was serene, seeming to show neither anticipation nor nervous apprehension. She merely waited.

Then Fontan and Oscagne arrived with the tallest man Sparhawk had ever seen. They introduced him as Atan Engessa. The word 'Atan' appeared to be not only the name of the people, but some kind of title as well. Engessa was well over seven feet tall, and the room seemed to shrink as he entered. His age, probably because of his race, was indeterminate. He was lean and muscular, and his expression sternly unyielding. His face showed no evidence that he had ever smiled.

Immediately upon his entrance into the room, he went directly to Mirtai, as if none of the rest of them were even in the room. He touched the fingertips of both hands to his steel-armoured chest and inclined his head to her. 'Atana Mirtai,' he greeted her respectfully.

'Atan Engessa,' she replied, duplicating his gesture of greeting. Then they spoke to each other at some length in the Tamul tongue.

'What are they saying?' Ehlana asked Oscagne, who had crossed to where they all stood.

'It's a ritual of greeting, your Majesty,' Oscagne replied. 'There are a great many formalities involved when Atans meet. The rituals help to hold down the bloodshed, I believe. At the moment, Engessa's questioning Mirtai concerning her status as a child – the silver headband, you understand. It's an indication that she hasn't yet gone through the Rite of Passage.' He stopped and listened for a moment as Mirtai spoke. 'She's explaining that she's been separated from humans since childhood and hasn't had the opportunity to participate in the ritual as yet.'

'Separated from humans?' Ehlana objected. 'What does she think *we* are?'

'Atans believe that *they* are the only humans in the world. I'm not sure exactly what they consider us to be.' The ambassador blinked. 'Has she really killed that many people?' he asked with some surprise.

'Ten?' Sparhawk asked.

'She said thirty-four.'

'That's impossible!' Ehlana exclaimed. 'She's been a member of my court for the past seven years. I'd have known if she'd killed anyone while she was in my service.'

'Not if she did it at night, you wouldn't, my Queen,' Sparhawk disagreed. 'She locks us in our rooms every night. She *says* that it's for our own protection, but maybe it's really so that she can go out looking for entertainment. Maybe we should change the procedure when we get home. Let's start locking *her* up for the night instead of the other way around.'

'She'll just kick the door down, Sparhawk.'

'That's true, I suppose. We could always chain her to the wall at night I guess.'

'*Sparhawk!*' Ehlana exclaimed.

'We can talk about it later. Here comes Fontan and General Engessa.'

'*Atan* Engessa, Sparhawk,' Oscagne corrected. 'Engessa wouldn't even recognise the title of general. He's a warrior – an "Atan". That's all the title he seems to need. If you call him "General", you'll insult him, and that's not a good idea.'

Engessa had a deep, quiet voice, and he spoke the Elenic language haltingly and with an exotic accent. He carefully repeated each of their names when Fontan introduced them, obviously committing them to memory. He accepted Ehlana's status without question, although the concept of a queen must have been alien to him. He recognised Sparhawk and the other knights as warriors, and respected them as such. The status of Patriarch Emban, Talen, Stragen and Baroness Melidere obviously baffled him. He greeted Kring, however, with the customary Peloi salute. 'Atana Mirtai advises me that you seek marriage with her,' he said.

'That's right,' Kring replied a bit pugnaciously. 'Have you any objections?'

'That depends. How many have you killed?'

'More than I can conveniently count.'

'That could mean two things. Either you have slain many, or you have a poor head for figures.'

'I can count past two hundred,' Kring declared.

'A respectable number. You are Domi among your people?'

'I am.'

'Who cut your head?' Engessa pointed at the scars on Kring's scalp and face.

'A friend. We were discussing each others' qualifications for leadership.'

'Why did you let him cut you?'

'I was busy. I had my sabre in his belly at the time, and I was probing around for various things inside him.'

'Your scars are honourable then. I respect them. Was he a good friend?'

Kring nodded. 'The best. We were like brothers.'

'You spared him the inconvenience of growing old.'

'I did that, all right. He never got a day older.'

'I take no exception to your suit of Atana Mirtai,' Engessa told him. 'She is a child with no family. As the first adult Atan she has met, it is my responsibility to serve as her father. Have you an Oma?'

'Sparhawk serves as my Oma.'

235

'Send him to me, and he and I will discuss the matter. May I call you friend, Domi?'

'I would be honoured, Atan. May I also call you friend?'

'I also would be honoured, friend Kring. Hopefully, your Oma and I will be able to arrange the day when you and Atana Mirtai will be branded.'

'May God speed the day, friend Engessa.'

'I feel as if I've just witnessed something from the dark ages,' Kalten whispered to Sparhawk. 'What do you think would have happened if they'd taken a dislike to each other?'

'It probably would have been messy.'

'When do you want to leave, Ehlana, Queen of Elenia?' Engessa asked.

Ehlana looked at her friends questioningly. 'Tomorrow?' she suggested.

'You should not ask, Ehlana-Queen,' Engessa reprimanded her firmly. 'Command. If any object, have Sparhawk-Champion kill them.'

'We've been trying to cut back on that, Atan Engessa,' she said. 'It's always so hard on the carpeting.'

'Ah,' he said. 'I knew there was a reason. Tomorrow then?'

'Tomorrow, Engessa.'

'I will await you at first light, Ehlana-Queen.' And he turned on his heel and marched from the room.

'Abrupt sort of fellow, isn't he?' Stragen noted.

'He doesn't waste any words,' Tynian agreed.

'A word with you, Sparhawk?' Kring said.

'Of course.'

'You *will* serve as my Oma, won't you?'

'Of course.'

'Don't pledge *too* many horses.' Kring frowned. 'What did he mean when he was talking about branding?'

Sparhawk suddenly remembered. 'It's an Atan

wedding custom. During the ceremony the happy couple is branded. Each wears the mark of the other.'

'Branded?'

'So I understand.'

'What if a couple doesn't get along?'

'I imagine they cross out the brand.'

'How do you cross out a brand?'

'Probably with a hot iron. Are you still bent on marriage, Kring?'

'Find out where the brand goes, Sparhawk. I'll know better once I have that information.'

'I gather there are places where you'd rather not be branded?'

'Oh, yes. There are *definitely* places, Sparhawk.'

They left Darsas at first light the following morning and rode eastward toward Pela on the steppes of central Astel. The Atans enclosed the column, loping easily to match the speed of the horses. Sparhawk's concerns about the safety of his queen diminished noticeably. Mirtai had very briefly – even peremptorily – advised her owner that she would travel with her countrymen. She did not precisely ask. A rather peculiar change had come over the golden giantess. That wary tension which had always characterised her seemed to have vanished. 'I can't exactly put my finger on it,' Ehlana confessed about mid-morning when they were discussing it. 'She just doesn't seem quite the same.'

'She isn't, your Majesty,' Stragen told her. 'She's come home, that's all. Not only that, the presence of adults allows her to take her natural place in her own society. She's still a child – in her own eyes at least. She's never talked about her childhood, but I gather it wasn't a time filled with happiness and security. Something happened to her parents, and she was sold into slavery.'

'All of her people are slaves, Milord Stragen,' Melidere objected.

'There are different kinds of slavery, Baroness. The slavery of the Atan race by the Tamuls is institutionalised. Mirtai's is personal. She was taken as a child, enslaved and then forced to take her own steps to protect herself. Now that she's back among the Atans, she's able to recapture some sense of her childhood.' He made a wry face. 'I never had that opportunity, of course. I was born into a different kind of slavery, and killing my father didn't really liberate me.'

'You concern yourself overmuch about that, Milord Stragen,' Melidere told him. 'You really shouldn't make the issue of your unauthorised conception the central fact of your whole existence, you know. There are much more important things in life.'

Stragen looked at her sharply, then laughed, his expression a bit sheepish. 'Do I really seem so self-pitying to you, Baroness?'

'No, not really, but you always insist on bringing it up. Don't worry at it so much, Milord. It doesn't make any difference to the rest of us, so why brood about it?'

'You, see, Sparhawk,' Stragen said. 'That's exactly what I meant about this girl. She's the most dishonest person I've ever known.'

'*Milord Stragen!*' Melidere protested.

'But you are, my dear Baroness,' Stragen grinned. 'You don't lie with your mouth, you lie with your entire person. You pose as someone whose head is filled with air, and then you puncture a façade I've spent a lifetime building with one single observation. "Unauthorised conception" indeed. You've managed to trivialise the central tragedy of my entire life.'

'Can you ever forgive me?' Her eyes were wide and dishonestly innocent.

'I give up,' he said, throwing his hands in the air in

238

mock surrender. 'Where was I? Oh yes, Mirtai's apparent change of personality. I think the Rite of Passage among the Atans is very significant to them, and that's another reason our beloved little giantess is reverting to the social equivalent of baby-talk. Engessa's obviously going to put her through the rite when we reach her homeland, so she's enjoying the last few days of childhood to the hilt.'

'Can I ride with you, Father?' Danae asked.

'If you wish.'

The little princess rose from her seat in the carriage, handed Rollo to Alean and Mmrr to Baroness Melidere and held out her hands to Sparhawk.

He lifted her to her usual seat in front of his saddle.

'Take me for a ride, Father,' she coaxed in her most little-girl tone.

'We'll be back in a bit,' Sparhawk told his wife and cantered away from the carriage.

'Stragen can be so tedious at times,' Danae said tartly. 'I'm glad Melidere's the one who's going to have to modify him.'

'What?' Sparhawk was startled.

'Where are your eyes, father?'

'I wasn't actually looking. Do they *really* feel that way about each other?'

'*She* does. She'll let him know how *he* feels when she's ready. What happened in Darsas?'

Sparhawk wrestled with his conscience a bit at that point. 'Would you say that you're a religious personage?' he asked carefully.

'That's a novel way to put it.'

'Just answer the question, Danae. Are you or are you not affiliated with a religion?'

'Well, of *course* I am, Sparhawk. I'm the *focus* of a religion.'

239

'Then in a general sort of way, you could be defined as a clergyman – uh – person?'

'What are you getting at, Sparhawk?'

'Just say yes, Danae. I'm tiptoeing around the edges of violating an oath, and I need a technical excuse for it.'

'I give up. Yes, technically you could call me a church personage – it's a different church, of course, but the definition still fits.'

'Thank you. I swore not to reveal this except to another clergyman – personage. You're a clergyperson, so I can tell you.'

'That's sheer sophistry, Sparhawk.'

'I know, but it gets me off the hook. Baron Kotyk's brother-in-law, Elron, is Sabre.' He gave her a suspicious look. 'Have you been tampering again?'

'Me?'

'You're starting to stretch the potentials of coincidence a bit, Danae,' he said. 'You knew what I just told you all along, didn't you?'

'Not the details, no. What you call "omniscience" is a human concept. It was dreamed up to make people think that they couldn't get away with anything. I get hints – little flashes of things, that's all. I knew there was something significant in Kotyk's house, and I knew that if you and the others listened carefully, you'd hear about it.'

'It's like intuition then?'

'That's a very good word for it, Sparhawk. Ours is a little more developed than yours, and we pay close attention to it. You humans tend to ignore it – particularly you men. Something else happened in Darsas, didn't it?'

He nodded. 'That shadow put in another appearance. Emban and I were talking with Archimandrite Monsel, and we were visited.'

240

'Whoever's behind this is very stupid, then.'

'The Troll-Gods? Isn't that part of the definition of them?'

'We're not absolutely *certain* it's the Troll-Gods, Sparhawk.'

'Wouldn't *you* know? I mean, isn't there some way you can identify who's opposing you?'

She shook her head. 'I'm afraid not, Sparhawk. We can conceal ourselves from each other. The stupidity of that appearance in Darsas certainly suggests the Troll-Gods, though. We haven't been able to make them understand why the sun comes up in the east as yet. They know it's going to come up every morning, but they're never sure just exactly where.'

'You're exaggerating.'

'Of course I am.' She frowned. 'Let's not set our feet in stone on the idea that we're dealing with the Troll-Gods just yet, though. There are some very subtle differences – of course that may be the result of their encounter with you in the Temple of Azash. You frightened them very much, you know. I'd be more inclined to suspect an alliance between them and somebody else. I think the Troll-Gods would be more direct. If there *is* somebody else involved, he's just a bit childish. He hasn't been out in the world. He surrounded himself with people who aren't bright, and he's judging all humans by *his* worshippers. That appearance at Darsas was really a blunder, you know. He didn't have to do it, and all he really did was to confirm what you'd already told that clergyman – you *did* tell him what's happening, didn't you?'

Sparhawk nodded.

'We really need to get to Sarsos and talk with Sephrenia.'

'You're going to speed up the journey again then?'

'I think I'd better. I'm not entirely sure what the ones

on the other side are doing yet, but they're starting to move faster for some reason, so we'd better see what we can do to keep up. Take me back to the carriage, Sparhawk. Stragen's probably finished showing off his education by now, and the smell of your armour's beginning to make me nauseous.'

Although there was a community of interest between the three disparate segments of the force escorting the Queen of Elenia, Sparhawk, Engessa and Kring decided to make some effort to keep the Peloi, the Church Knights and the Atans more or less separate from each other. Cultural differences obviously made a general mingling unwise. The possibilities for misunderstandings were simply too numerous to be ignored. Each leader stressed the need for the strictest of courtesy and formality to his forces, and the end result was a tense and exaggerated stiffness. In a very real sense, the Atans, the Peloi and the knights were allies rather than comrades. The fact that very few of the Atans spoke Elenic added to the distance between the component parts of the small army moving out onto the treeless expanse of the steppes.

They encountered the eastern Peloi some distance from the town of Pela in central Astel. Kring's ancestors had migrated from this vast grassland some three thousand years earlier, but despite the separation of time and distance, the two branches of the Peloi family were remarkably similar in matters of dress and custom. The only really significant difference seemed to be the marked preference of the eastern Peloi for the javelin as opposed to the sabre favoured by Kring's people. After a ritual exchange of greetings and a somewhat extended ceremony during which Kring and his eastern cousin sat cross-legged on the turf 'taking salt together and talking of affairs' while two armies warily faced each other across three hundred yards of open grass. The decision not to go to war with each other today was apparently reached, and Kring led his new-found friend and kinsman to the carriage to introduce him all around. The Domi of the eastern Peloi was named Tikume. He was somewhat taller than Kring, but his head was also shaved, a custom among those horsemen dating back to antiquity.

Tikume greeted them all politely. 'It is passing strange to see Peloi allied with foreigners,' he noted. 'Domi Kring has told me of the conditions which prevail in Eosia, but I had not fully realised that they had led to such peculiar arrangements. Of course he and I have not spoken together for more than ten years.'

'You've met before, Domi Tikume?' Patriarch Emban asked with a certain surprise.

'Yes, your Grace,' Kring replied. 'Domi Tikume journeyed to Pelosia with the King of Astel some years back. He made a point of looking me up.'

'King Alberen's father was much wiser than his son,' Tikume explained, 'and he read a great deal. He saw many similarities between Pelosia and Astel, so he paid a state visit to King Soros. He invited me to go along.' His expression became one of distaste. 'I might have declined if I'd known he was going to travel by boat. I was sick every day for two months. Domi Kring and I got on well together. He was kind enough to take me with him to the marshes to hunt ears.'

'Did he share the profits with you, Domi Tikume?' Ehlana asked him.

'What was that, Queen Ehlana?' Tikume looked baffled.

Kring, however, laughed nervously and flushed just a bit.

Then Mirtai strode up to the carriage.

'Is this the one?' Tikume asked Kring.

Kring nodded happily. 'Isn't she stupendous?'

'Magnificent,' Tikume agreed fervently, his tone almost reverential. Then he dropped to one knee. 'Doma,' he greeted her, clasping both hands in front of his face.

Mirtai looked inquiringly at Kring.

'It's a Peloi word, beloved,' he explained. 'It means "Domi's mate".'

'That hasn't been decided yet, Kring,' she pointed out.

'Can there be any doubt, beloved?' he replied.

Tikume was still down on one knee. 'You shall enter our camp with all honours, Doma Mirtai,' he declared, 'for among our people, you are a queen. All shall kneel to you, and all shall give way to you. Poems and songs shall be composed in your honour, and rich gifts shall be bestowed upon you.'

'*Well*, now,' Mirtai said.

'Your beauty is clearly divine, Doma Mirtai,' Tikume continued, warming to his subject. 'Your very presence brightens a drab world and puts the sun to shame. I am awed at the wisdom of my brother Kring in having selected you as his mate. Come straightaway to our camp, divine one, so that my people may adore you.'

'My goodness,' Ehlana breathed. 'Nobody's ever said anything like that to *me*.'

'We just didn't want to embarrass you, my Queen,' Stragen told her blandly. 'We *feel* that way about you of course, but we didn't want to be too obvious about it.'

'Well said,' Ulath approved.

Mirtai looked at Kring with a new interest. 'Why didn't you tell me about this, Kring?' she asked him.

'I thought you knew, beloved.'

'I didn't,' she replied. Her lower lip pushed forward slightly in a thoughtful kind of pout. 'But I do now,' she added. 'Have you chosen an Oma as yet?'

'Sparhawk serves me in that capacity, beloved.'

'Why don't you go have a talk with Atan Engessa, Sparhawk?' she suggested. 'Tell him for me that I do not look upon Domi Kring's suit with disfavour.'

'That's a *very* good idea, Mirtai,' Sparhawk replied. 'I'm surprised I didn't think of it myself.'

CHAPTER 14

The town of Pela in central Astel was a major trading centre where merchants and cattle-buyers came from all parts of the empire to do business with the Peloi herders. It was a shabby-looking, unfinished sort of place. Many of its buildings were no more than ornate fronts with large tents erected behind them. No attempt had ever been made to pave its rutted streets, and the passage of strings of wagons and herds of cattle raised a cloud of dust that entirely obscured the town most of the time. Beyond the poorly-defined outskirts lay an ocean of tents, the portable homes of the nomadic Peloi.

Tikume led them through the town and on out to a hill-top where a number of brightly-striped pavilions encircled a large open area. A canopy held aloft by poles shaded a place of honour at the very top of the hill, and the ground beneath that canopy was carpeted and strewn with cushions and furs.

Mirtai was the absolute centre of attention. Her rather scanty marching clothes had been covered with a purple robe that reached to the ground, an indication of her near-royal status. Kring and Tikume formally escorted her to the ceremonial centre of the camp and introduced her to Tikume's wife, Vida, a sharp-faced woman who also wore a purple robe and looked at Mirtai with undisguised hostility.

Sparhawk and the rest joined the Peloi leaders in the shade as honoured guests.

The face of Tikume's wife grew darker and darker as Peloi warriors vied with each other to heap extravagant compliments upon Mirtai as they were presented to Kring and his purported bride-to-be. There were gifts and a number of songs praising the beauty of the golden giantess.

'How did they find time to make up songs about her?' Talen quietly asked Stragen.

'I'd imagine that the songs have been around for a long time,' Stragen replied. 'They've substituted Mirtai's name, that's all. I expect there'll be poems as well. I know a third-rate poet in Emsat who makes a fairly good living writing poems and love-letters for young nobles too lazy or uninspired to compose their own. There's a whole body of literature with blank spaces in it that serves in such situations.'

'They just fill in the blanks with the girl's name?' Talen demanded incredulously.

'It wouldn't really make much sense to fill them in with some other girl's name, would it?'

'That's dishonest!' Talen exclaimed.

'What a novel attitude, Talen,' Patriarch Emban laughed, 'particularly coming from you.'

'You aren't supposed to cheat when you're telling a girl how you feel about her,' Talen insisted. Talen had begun to notice girls. They had been there all along, of course, but he had not noticed them before, and he had some rather surprisingly strong convictions. It is to the credit of his friends that not one of them laughed at his peculiar expression of integrity. Baroness Melidere, however, impulsively embraced him.

'What was that all about?' he asked her a little suspiciously.

'Oh, nothing,' she replied, touching a gentle hand to his cheek. 'When was the last time you shaved?' she asked him.

'Last week sometime, I think – or maybe the week before.'

'You're due again, I'd say. You're definitely growing up, Talen.'

The boy flushed slightly.

Princess Danae gave Sparhawk a sly little smirk.

After the gifts and the poems and songs came the demonstrations of prowess. Kring's tribesmen demonstrated their proficiency with their sabres. Tikume's men did much the same with their javelins, which they either cast or used as short lances. Sir Berit unhorsed an equally youthful Cyrinic Knight, and two blond-braided Genidians engaged in a fearsomely realistic mock axe-fight.

'It's all relatively standard, of course, Emban,' Ambassador Oscagne said to the Patriarch of Ucera. The friendship of the two men had progressed to the point where they had begun to discard titles. 'Warrior cultures almost totally circumscribe their lives with ceremonies.'

Emban smiled. 'I've noticed that, Oscagne. Our Church Knights are the most courteous and ceremonial men I know.'

'Prudence, your Grace,' Ulath explained cryptically.

'You'll get used to that in time, your Excellency,' Tynian assured the ambassador. 'Sir Ulath hates to waste words.'

'I wasn't being mysterious, Tynian,' Ulath told him. 'I was only pointing out that you almost have to be polite to a man who's holding an axe.'

Atan Engessa rose and bowed a bit stiffly to Ehlana. 'May I test your slave, Ehlana-Queen?' he asked.

'How exactly do you mean, Atan Engessa?' she asked warily.

'She approaches the time of the Rite of Passage. We must decide if she is ready. I will not harm her. These others are demonstrating their skill. Atana Mirtai and I will participate. It will be a good time for the test.'

'As you think best, Atan,' Ehlana consented, 'as long as the Atana does not object.'

248

'If she is truly Atan, she will not object, Ehlana-Queen.' He turned abruptly and crossed to where Mirtai sat with the Peloi.

'Mirtai's certainly the centre of things today,' Melidere observed.

'I think it's very nice,' Ehlana said. 'She keeps herself in the background most of the time. She's entitled to a bit of attention.'

'It's political, you realise,' Stragen told her. 'Tikume's people are showering Mirtai with attention for Kring's benefit.'

'I know, Stragen, but it's nice all the same.' She looked speculatively at her golden slave. 'Sparhawk, I'd take it as a personal favour if you'd actively pursue the marriage-negotiations with Atan Engessa. Mirtai deserves some happiness.'

'I'll see what I can arrange for her, my Queen.'

Mirtai readily agreed to Engessa's proposed test. She rose gracefully to her feet, unfastened the neck of her purple robe and let it fall.

The Peloi gasped. Their women-folk were customarily dressed in far more concealing garments. The sneer on the face of Tikume's wife Vida, however, was a bit wan. Mirtai was significantly female. She was also fully armed, and that also shocked the Peloi. She and Engessa moved to the area in front of the canopy, curtly inclined their heads to each other and drew their swords.

Sparhawk thought he knew the differences between contest and combat, but what followed blurred that boundary for him. Mirtai and Engessa seemed to be fully intent on killing each other. Their swordsmanship was superb, but their manner of fencing involved a great deal more physical contact than did western-style fighting.

'It looks like a wrestling-match with swords,' Kalten observed to Ulath.

'Yes,' Ulath agreed. 'I wonder if a man could do that in an axe-fight. If you could kick somebody in the face the way she just did and then follow up with an axe-stroke, you could win a lot of fights in a hurry.'

'I *knew* she was going to do that to him,' Kalten chuckled as Engessa landed flat on his back in the dust. 'She did it to me once.'

Engessa, however, did not lie gasping on the ground as Kalten had. He rolled away from Mirtai instead and came to his feet with his sword still in his hand. He raised his blade in a kind of salute and then immediately attacked again.

The 'test' continued for several more minutes until a watching Atan sharply banged his fist on his breastplate to signal the end of the match. The man who had signalled was much older than his compatriots, or so it seemed. His hair was white. Nothing else about him seemed any different, however.

Mirtai and Engessa bowed formally to each other, and he returned her to her place where she once again drew on her robe and sank down onto a cushion. Vida no longer sneered.

'She is fit,' Engessa reported to Ehlana. He reached up under his breastplate and tenderly touched a sore-spot. 'More than fit,' he added. 'She is a skilled and dangerous opponent. I am proud to be the one she will call father. She will add lustre to my name.'

'*We* rather like her, Atan Engessa,' Ehlana smiled. 'I'm so glad you agree with us.' She let the full impact of that devastating smile wash over the stern-faced Atan, and hesitantly, almost as if it were in spite of himself, he smiled back.

'I think he lost two fights today,' Talen whispered to Sparhawk.

'So it would seem,' Sparhawk replied.

*   *   *

'We can never catch up with them, friend Sparhawk,' Tikume said that evening as they all relaxed on carpets near a flaring campfire. 'These steppes are open grasslands with only a few groves of trees. There isn't really any place to hide, and you can't ride a horse through tall grass without leaving a trail a blind man could follow. They come out of nowhere, kill the herders and run off the cattle. I followed one of those groups of raiders myself. They'd stolen a hundred cattle, and they left a broad trail through the grass. After a few miles, the trail just ended. There was no sign that they'd dispersed. They just vanished. It was as if something had reached down and carried them off into the sky.'

'Have there been any other disturbances, Domi?' Tynian asked carefully. 'What I'm trying to say is, has there been unrest of any kind among your people? Wild stories? Rumours? That sort of thing?'

'No, friend Tynian.' Tikume smiled. 'We are an open-faced people. We do not conceal our emotions from each other. I'd know if there were something afoot. I've heard about what's been happening over around Darsas, so I know why you ask. Nothing like that is happening here. We don't worship our heroes the way they do, we just try to be like them. Someone's stealing our cattle and killing our herdsmen.' He looked a bit accusingly at Oscagne. 'I would not insult you for all the world, your Honour,' he said, 'but you might suggest to the emperor that he would be wise to have some of his Atans look into it. If we have to deal with it ourselves, our neighbours won't like it very much. We of the Peloi tend to be a bit indiscriminate when someone steals our cattle.'

'I'll bring the matter to his Imperial Majesty's attention,' Oscagne promised.

'Soon, friend Oscagne,' Tikume recommended. 'Very soon.'

*   *   *

'She's a highly-skilled warrior, Sparhawk-Knight,' Engessa was saying the following morning as the two sat by a small fire.

'Granted,' Sparhawk replied, 'but by your own traditions, she's still a child.'

'That's why it's my place to negotiate for her,' Engessa pointed out. 'If she were adult, she would do it herself. Children sometimes do not know their own worth.'

'But a child cannot be as valuable as an adult.'

'That's not always entirely true, Sparhawk-Knight. The younger a woman, the greater her price.'

'Oh, this is absurd,' Ehlana broke in. The negotiations were of a delicate nature and would normally have taken place in private. 'Normally', however, did not always apply to Sparhawk's wife. 'Your offer's completely unacceptable, Sparhawk.'

'Whose side are you on, dear?' he asked her mildly.

'Mirtai's my friend. I won't permit you to insult her. Ten horses indeed! I could get that much for Talen.'

'Were you planning to sell him too?'

'I was just illustrating a point.'

Sir Tynian had also stopped by. Of all of their group, he was closest to Kring, and he keenly felt the responsibilities of friendship. 'What sort of offer would your Majesty consider properly respectful?' he asked Ehlana.

'Not a horse less than sixty,' she declared adamantly.

'*Sixty!*' Tynian exclaimed. 'You'll impoverish him! What kind of a life will Mirtai have if you marry her off to a pauper?'

'Kring's hardly a pauper, Sir Knight,' she retorted. 'He still has all that gold King Soros paid him for those Zemoch ears.'

'But that's not *his* gold, your Majesty,' Tynian pointed out. 'It belongs to his people.'

Sparhawk smiled and motioned with his head to Engessa. Unobtrusively, the two stepped away from the fire. 'I'd guess that they'll settle on thirty, Atan Engessa,' he tentatively suggested.

'Most probably,' Engessa agreed.

'It seems like a fair number to me. Doesn't it to you?' It hovered sort of on the verge of an offer.

'It's more or less what I had in mind, Sparhawk-Knight.'

'Me too. Done then?'

'Done.' The two of them clasped hands. 'Should we tell them?' the Atan asked, the faintest hint of a smile touching his face.

'They're having a lot of fun,' Sparhawk grinned. 'Why don't we let them play it out? We can find out how close our guess was. Besides, these negotiations are very important to Kring and Mirtai. If we were to agree in just a few minutes, it might make them feel cheapened.'

'You have been much in the world, Sparhawk-Knight,' Engessa observed. 'You know well the hearts of men – and of women.'

'No man ever truly knows the heart of a woman, Engessa-Atan,' Sparhawk replied ruefully.

The negotiations between Tynian and Ehlana had reached the tragic stage, each of them accusing the other of ripping out hearts and similar extravagances. Ehlana's performance was masterful. The Queen of Elenia had a strong flair for histrionics, and she was a highly skilled orator. She extemporised at length upon Sir Tynian's disgraceful niggardliness, her voice rising and falling in majestic cadences. Tynian, on the other hand, was coolly rational, although he too became emotional at times.

Kring and Mirtai sat holding hands not far away, their eyes filled with concern as they hung breathlessly on every word. Tikume's Peloi encircled the haggling pair, straining to hear.

It went on for hours, and it was nearly sunset when

Ehlana and Tynian finally reached a grudging agreement – thirty horses – and concluded the bargain by spitting in their hands and smacking their palms together. Sparhawk and Engessa formalised the agreement in the same fashion, and a tumultuous cheer went up from the rapt Peloi. It had been a highly entertaining day all round, and that evening's celebration was loud and long.

'I'm exhausted,' Ehlana confessed to her husband after they had retired to their tent for the night.

'Poor dear,' Sparhawk commiserated.

'I had to step in, though. You were just being too meek, Sparhawk. You'd have given her away. It's a good thing I was there. You'd never have managed to reach that kind of agreement.'

'I was on the other side, Ehlana, remember?'

'That's what I don't understand, Sparhawk. How *could* you treat poor Mirtai so disgracefully?'

'Rules of the game, love. I was representing Kring.'

'I'm still very disappointed in you, Sparhawk.'

'Well, fortunately, you and Tynian were there to get it all done properly. Engessa and I couldn't have done half so well.'

'It *did* turn out rather well, didn't it – even though it took us all day.'

'You were brilliant, my love, absolutely brilliant.'

'I've been in some very shabby places in my life, Sparhawk,' Stragen said the next morning, 'but Pela's the absolute worst. It's been abandoned several times, did you know that? Maybe abandoned isn't the right word. "Moved" is probably closer to the truth. Pela exists wherever the Peloi establish their summer encampment.'

'I'd imagine that sends the map-makers into hysterics.'

254

'More than likely. It's a temporary town, but it absolutely reeks of money. It takes a great deal of ready cash to buy a cattle-herd.'

'Were you able to make contact with the local thieves?'

'They contacted us actually,' Talen grinned. 'A boy no more than eight lifted Stragen's purse. He's very good – except that he doesn't run very well. I caught him within fifty yards. After we'd explained who we were, he was very happy to take us to see the man in charge.'

'Has the thieves' council made any decision as yet?' Sparhawk asked Stragen.

'They're still mulling it over,' Stragen replied. 'They're a bit conservative here in Daresia. The notion of co-operating with the authorities strikes them as immoral for some reason. I sort of expect an answer when we get to Sarsos. The thieves of Sarsos carry a great deal of weight in the empire. Did anything meaningful happen while we were gone?'

'Kring and Mirtai got betrothed.'

'That was quick. I'll have to congratulate them.'

'Why don't you two get some sleep,' Sparhawk suggested. 'We'll be leaving for Sarsos tomorrow. Tikume's going to ride along with us to the edge of the steppes. I think he'd like to go a bit farther, but the Styrics at Sarsos make him nervous.' He rose to his feet. 'Get some sleep,' he told them. 'I want to go have a talk with Oscagne.'

The Peloi encampment was quiet. It was early summer now, and the midday heat kept the nomads inside their tents. Sparhawk walked across the hard-packed earth toward the tent shared by Ambassador Oscagne and Patriarch Emban. His chain-mail jingled as he walked. Since they were in a secure encampment, the knights had decided to forego the discomfort of their formal armour.

He found them sitting beneath a canopy at the side of their tent eating a melon.

'Well-met, Sir Knight,' Oscagne said as the Pandion approached.

'That's an archaic form of greeting, Oscagne,' Emban told him.

'I'm an archaic sort of fellow, Emban.'

'I was curious about something,' Sparhawk said, joining them on the shaded carpet.

'It's a characteristic of the young, I suppose,' Oscagne smiled.

Sparhawk let that pass. 'This part of Astel seems quite different from what we ran into farther west,' he observed.

'Yes,' Oscagne agreed. 'Astel's the melting-pot that gave rise to all Elene cultures – both here in Daresia and in Eosia as well.'

'We might want to argue about that some day,' Emban murmured.

'Daresia's older, that's all,' Oscagne shrugged. 'That doesn't necessarily mean that it's better. Anyway, what you've seen of Astel so far is very much like what you'd encounter in the Elene Kingdom of Pelosia, wouldn't you say?'

'There are similarities, yes,' Sparhawk replied.

'The similarities will stop when we reach the edge of the steppes. The western two-thirds of Astel are Elene. From the edge of the steppes to the Atan border, Astel's Styric.'

'How did that happen?' Emban asked. 'The Styrics in Eosia are widely dispersed. They live in their own villages and follow their own laws and customs.'

'How cosmopolitan are you feeling today, Emban?'

'You're planning to insult my provincialism, I take it.'

'Not too much, I hope. Your prototypical Elene is a

bigot.' Oscagne held up one hand. 'Let me finish before you explode. Bigotry's a form of egotism, and I think you'll have to concede that Elenes have a very high opinion of themselves. They seem to feel that God smiles particularly for them.'

'Doesn't He?' Emban feigned surprise.

'Stop that. For reasons only God can understand, the Styrics particularly irritate the Elenes.'

'I have no trouble understanding it,' Emban shrugged. 'It's their superior attitude. They treat us as if we were children.'

'From their perspective, we are, your Grace,' Sparhawk told him. 'Styrics have been civilised for forty thousand years. We got started somewhat later.'

'For whatever the reason,' Oscagne continued, 'the initial impulse of the Elenes has been to drive the Styrics out – or to kill them. That's why the Styrics migrated to Eosia much earlier than you Elenes did. They were driven into the wilderness by Elene prejudice. Eosia was not the only wilderness, however. There's another that exists along the Atan border, and many Styrics fled there in antiquity. After the Empire was formed, we Tamuls asked the Elenes to stop molesting the Styrics living around Sarsos.'

'Asked?'

'We were quite firm – and we *did* have all those Atans with nothing else to do. We've agreed to let the Elene clergy deliver thunderous denunciations from the pulpit, but we garrison enough Atans around Sarsos to keep the two peoples separate. It's quieter that way, and we Tamuls are extraordinarily fond of quiet. I think you gentlemen are in for a surprise when we reach Sarsos. It's the only truly Styric city in the entire world. It's an astonishing place. God seems to smile in a very special way there.'

'You keep talking about God, Oscagne,' Emban

noted. 'I thought a preoccupation with God was an Elene conceit.'

'You're more cosmopolitan than I thought, your Grace.'

'Just exactly what do you mean when you use the word God, your Excellency?'

'We use the term generically. Our Tamul religion isn't very profound. We tend to think that a man's relationship with his God – or Gods – is his own affair.'

'That's heresy, you know. It would put the Church out of business.'

'That's all right, Emban,' Oscagne smiled. 'Heresy's encouraged in the Tamul Empire. It gives us something to talk about on long, rainy afternoons.'

They rode out with a huge Peloi escort the following morning. The party moving northeasterly looked not so much like an army on the march as it did a migration. Kring and Tikume rode more or less by themselves for the next several days, renewing their blood-ties and discussing an exchange of breeding-stock.

Sparhawk attempted an experiment during the ride from Pela to the edge of the steppes, but try though he might, he could not detect any traces of Aphrael's tampering with time and distance. The Child Goddess was simply too skilled, and her manipulations too seamless for him to detect them.

Once, when she had joined him on Faran's back, he raised an issue that had been troubling him. 'I'm not trying to pry, but it seems that it's been about fifty days since we landed at Salesha. How long has it really been?'

'Quite a bit less than that, Sparhawk,' she replied. 'Half that long at most.'

'I was sort of looking for an exact answer, Danae.'

'I'm not very good with numbers, father. I know the

difference between a few and a lot, and that's all that's really important, isn't it?'

'It's a bit imprecise, wouldn't you say?'

'Is precision all that important to you, Sparhawk?'

'You can't begin to think logically without precision, Danae.'

'Don't think logically then. Try being intuitive for a change. You might even find that you like it.'

'How long, Danae?' he insisted.

'Three weeks,' she shrugged.

'That's a little better.'

'Well – more or less.'

The edge of the steppes was marked by a dense forest of pale-trunked birches, and Tikume and his tribesmen turned back there. Since it was late in the day, the royal escort made camp on the edge of the forest so that they might follow the shaded road leading off through the trees in the full light of day.

After they had settled down and the cooking fires were going, Sparhawk took Kring and they went looking for Engessa. 'We have a peculiar situation here, gentlemen,' he told them as they walked together near the edge of the forest.

'How so, Sparhawk-Knight?' Engessa asked.

'We've got three different kinds of warrior in this group, and I'd imagine there are three different approaches to engagement. We should probably discuss the differences so that we won't be working at cross-purposes if trouble arises. The standard approach of the Church Knights is based on our equipment. We wear armour, and we ride large horses. Whenever there's trouble, we usually just smash the centre of an opposing army.'

'We prefer to peel an enemy like an apple,' Kring said. 'We ride around his force very fast and slice off bits and pieces as we go.'

'We fight on foot,' Engessa supplied. 'We're trained to be self-sufficient, so we just rush the enemy and engage him hand-to-hand.'

'Does that work very well?' Kring asked him.

'It always has,' Engessa shrugged.

'If we happen to run into any kind of trouble, it probably wouldn't be a good idea for us all to dash right in,' Sparhawk mused. 'We'd be stumbling all over each other. See what you think of this. If a force of any significant size tries to attack us, Kring and his men circle around behind them, I form up the knights and charge the centre and Atan Engessa spreads his force out along a broad front. The enemy will sort of fold in behind the knights after we bash a hole in their centre. They always do for some reason. Kring's attacks along the rear and the flanks will add to their confusion. They'll be disorganised and most of them will be cut off from their leaders in one way or another. That would be a good time for Engessa to attack. The best soldiers in the world don't function too well when nobody's close enough to give orders.'

'It's a workable tactic,' Engessa conceded. 'It's a bit surprising to find that other people in the world know how to plan battles too.'

'The story of man has been pretty much the story of one long battle, Atan Engessa,' Sparhawk told him. 'We're all experienced at it, so we devise tactics that take advantage of our strengths. Do we want to do it the way I suggested?'

Kring and Engessa looked at each other. 'Almost any plan will work,' Kring shrugged, 'as long as we all know what we're doing.'

'How will we know when you're ready for us to attack?' Engessa asked Sparhawk.

'My friend Ulath has a horn,' Sparhawk replied. 'When he blows it once, my knights will charge. When he blows it twice, Kring's men will start peeling off the rear elements. When we've got the enemy's full attention, I'll have Ulath blow three times. That's when you'll want to charge.'

Engessa's eyes were alight. 'It's the sort of strategy that doesn't leave very many survivors among the enemy, Sparhawk-Knight,' he said.

'That was sort of the idea, Engessa-Atan.'

The birch forest lay on a long, gradual slope rising from the steppes of central Astel to the rugged foothills on the Atan border. The road was broad and well-maintained, though it tended to wander a great deal. Engessa's unmounted Atans ranged out about a mile on each side of the road, and for the first three days they reported no sightings of men, although they did encounter large herds of deer. Summer had not yet dried the lingering dampness from the forest floor, and the air in the sun-dappled shade was cool and moist, still smelling of new growth and renewal.

Since the trees obstructed their vision, they rode cautiously. They set up their nighttime encampments while the sun was still above the horizon, and erected certain rudimentary fortifications to prevent surprises after dark.

On the morning of their fourth day in the forest, Sparhawk rose early and walked through the first steel-grey light of dawn to the line where the horses were picketed. He found Khalad there. Kurik's eldest son had snubbed Faran's head up close to a birch tree and was carefully inspecting the big roan's hooves. 'I was just going to do that,' Sparhawk said quietly. 'He seemed to be favouring his left forehoof yesterday.'

'Stone bruise,' Khalad said shortly. 'You know, Sparhawk, you might want to give some thought to putting him out to pasture when we get back home. He's not a colt any more, you know.'

261

'Neither am I, when you get right down to it. Sleeping on the ground's not nearly as much fun as it used to be.'

'You're just getting soft.'

'Thanks. Is this weather going to hold?'

'As nearly as I can tell, yes.' Khalad lowered Faran's hoof to the ground and took hold of the snubbing rope. 'No biting,' he cautioned the horse. 'If you bite me, I'll kick you in the ribs.'

Faran's long face took on an injured expression.

'He's an evil-tempered brute,' Khalad noted, 'but he's far and away the smartest horse I've ever come across. You should put him to stud. It might be interesting to train intelligent colts for a change. Most horses aren't really very bright.'

'I thought horses were among the cleverest of animals.'

'That's a myth, Sparhawk. If you want a smart animal, get yourself a pig. I've never yet been able to build a pen that a pig couldn't think his way out of.'

'They're built a little close to the ground for riding. Let's go see how breakfast's coming.'

'Who's cooking this morning?'

'Kalten, I think. Ulath would know.'

'Kalten? Maybe I'll stay here and eat with the horses.'

'I'm not sure that a bucketful of raw oats would taste all that good.'

'I'd put it up against Kalten's cooking any day, my Lord.'

They rode out shortly after the sun rose, and proceeded through the cool, sun-speckled forest. The birds seemed to be everywhere, and they sang enthusiastically. Sparhawk smiled as he remembered how Sephrenia had once punctured his illusion that bird-song was an expression of a love for music. 'Actually they're warning other birds to stay away, dear one,' she had said. 'They're claiming possession of nesting-sites. It sounds very pretty, but all they're really saying is, "My tree. My tree. My tree".'

Mirtai came back along the road late that morning running with an effortless stride. 'Sparhawk,' she said quietly when she reached the carriage, 'Atan Engessa's scouts report that there are people up ahead.'

'How many?' he asked, his tone suddenly all business.

'We can't be certain. The scouts didn't want to be seen. There are soldiers of some kind out there, and they seem to be waiting for us.'

'Berit,' Sparhawk said to the young knight, 'why don't you ride on ahead and ask Kalten and the others to join us? Don't run. Try to make it look casual.'

'Right.' Berit rode forward at a trot.

'Mirtai,' the big knight said, trying to keep his voice calm, 'is there any kind of defensible position nearby?'

'I was just coming to that,' she replied. 'There's a kind of hill about a quarter of a mile ahead. It sort of juts up from the floor of the forest – boulders mostly. They're covered over with moss.'

'Could we get the carriage up there?'

She shook her head.

'You get to walk then, my Queen,' he said to his wife.

'We don't *know* that they're hostile, Sparhawk,' Ehlana objected.

'That's true,' he conceded, 'but we don't know that they aren't either, and that's far more important.'

Kalten and the others came back along the column with Kring and Engessa.

'Are they doing anything at all, Atan Engessa?' Sparhawk asked.

'Just watching, Sparhawk-Knight. There are more of them than we thought at first – a thousand at least – probably a lot more.'

'It's going to be tricky with all these trees,' Kalten pointed out.

'I know,' Sparhawk grunted. 'Khalad, how close is it to noon?'

'About another hour, my Lord,' Khalad replied from the carriage driver's seat.

'Close enough then. There's a hill just up ahead. We'll ride on to it and make some show of stopping for our midday meal. Our friends here in the carriage will sort of stroll up to the top. The rest of us will spread out around the base of the hill. We'll build fires and rattle pots and pans together. Ehlana, be silly. I want you and the baroness to do a lot of laughing up there on that hilltop. Stragen, take some men and erect a pavilion of some kind up there. Try to make it look festive. Move some rocks out of your way and sort of pile them up around the hilltop.

'A siege again, Sparhawk?' Ulath said disapprovingly.

'Have you got a better idea?'

'Not really, but you know how I feel about sieges.'

'Nobody said you had to *like* it, Ulath,' Tynian told him.

'Spread the word,' Sparhawk told them, 'and let's try to make it all look very casual.'

They were tense as they proceeded along the road at a leisurely-appearing pace. When they rounded a bend and Sparhawk saw the hill, he immediately approved of its strategic potential. It was one of those rock-piles that inexplicably rear up out of forests the world over. It was a conical heap of rounded boulders perhaps forty feet high, green with moss and totally devoid of trees or brush. It stood about two hundred yards to the left of the road. Talen rode to its base, dismounted, scampered up to the top and looked around. 'It's perfect, my Queen,' he shouted back down. 'You can see for miles up here. It's just what you were looking for.'

'That's a nice touch,' Bevier noted, 'assuming that our friends out there speak Elenic, of course.'

Stragen came forward from the line of pack-horses carrying a lute. 'A little finishing touch, my Queen,' he smiled to Ehlana.

'Do you play, Milord?' she asked him.

'Any gentleman plays, your Majesty.'

'Sparhawk doesn't.'

'We're still working on a definition of Sparhawk, Queen Ehlana,' Stragen replied lightly. 'We're not altogether certain that "gentleman" really fits him – no offence intended of course, old boy,' he hastily assured the black-armoured Pandion.

'A suggestion, Sparhawk?' Tynian said.

'Go ahead.'

'We don't know anything about those people out there, but they don't know anything about us either – or at the most, very, very little.'

'That's probably true.'

'Just because they're watching doesn't mean they're planning an immediate attack – if they're even planning to attack at all. If they are, they could just sit and wait until we're back on the road again.'

'All right.'

'But we're travelling with some giddy noblewomen – begging your Majesty's pardon – and noblewomen don't really need reasons for the things they do.'

'Your popularity isn't growing in certain quarters, Sir Tynian,' Ehlana said ominously.

'I'm crushed, but couldn't your Majesty decide – on a whim – that you absolutely adore this place and that you're bored with riding in a carriage? Under those circumstances, wouldn't it be natural for you to order a halt for the day?'

'It's not bad, Sparhawk,' Kalten said. 'While we're all lunching, we can sort of unobtrusively fortify that hill a little better. Then, after a few hours, when it's obvious that we aren't going any further today, we can set up the usual evening camp – field fortifications and the like. We're not on any specific timetable, so a half a day lost isn't going to put us behind any sort of schedule. The queen's safety's a lot more important than speed right now, wouldn't you say?'

'You know how I'm going to answer that, Kalten.'

'I was sure I could count on you.'

'It's good, Sparhawk-Knight,' Engessa approved. 'Give my scouts one whole night to work with, and we'll not only know how many are out there, but their names as well.'

'Break a wheel,' Ulath added.

'What was that, Sir Knight?' Ambassador Oscagne asked, looking perplexed.

'That would give us another excuse for stopping,' the Thalesian replied. 'If the carriage broke down, we'd *have* to stop.'

'Can you fix a wheel, Sir Ulath?'

'No, but we can rig some kind of a skid to get us by until we can find a blacksmith.'

'Wouldn't a skid make the carriage jolt and bump around a great deal?' Patriarch Emban asked with a pained look.

'Probably,' Ulath shrugged.

'I'm almost certain we can find some other reason to stop, Sir Knight. Have you any idea of how uncomfortable that would be?'

'I didn't really give it much thought, your Grace,' Ulath replied blandly. 'But then, I won't be riding in the carriage, so it wouldn't bother *me* in the slightest.'

CHAPTER 15

The addition of a dozen female Atans added to the subterfuge of a courtly gathering on the hilltop, although it
was difficult to persuade the Atan girls that their faces
would not break if they smiled or that the Gods had
issued no commandment against laughing. Berit and a
number of other youthful knights entertained the ladies
while casually clearing inconvenient – and not a few
convenient – bushel-basket sized rocks from the kind of
natural amphitheatre at the top of the hill. The back-side
of the pile of boulders was more precipitous than the
front, and the rim of the hilltop on that side formed a
naturally defensible wall. The young knights piled up
enough rock to form a crude kind of breastwork around
the other three sides. It was all very casual, but within
an hour some fairly substantial fortifications had been
erected.

There were many cooking-fires around the base of the
hill, and their smoke laid a kind of blue haze out among
the white tree trunks. There was a great deal of clanking
and rattling and shouting back and forth as the oddly-
assorted force made some show of preparing a meal.
Engessa's Atans gathered up large piles of firewood –
mostly in ten-foot lengths – and all of the cooks stated
a loud preference for wood chips for their fires rather
than chunks. It was therefore necessary to chop at the
ends of the birch logs, and there were soon neat piles of
sharpened ten-foot poles spaced out at regular intervals
around the hill, ready for use either as firewood or a
palisade that could be erected in a few minutes. The
knights and the Peloi tethered their horses nearby and

lounged around the foot of the hill while the Atans were evenly dispersed a bit further out under the trees. Sparhawk stood at the top of the hill surveying the progress of the work below. The ladies were gathered under a broad canopy erected on poles in the centre of the depressed basin on the hilltop. Stragen was strumming his lute and singing to them in his deep rich voice.

'How's it going down there?' Talen asked, coming up to where Sparhawk stood.

'It's about as secure as Khalad can make it without being obvious about it,' Sparhawk replied.

'He's awfully good, isn't he?' Talen said with a certain pride.

'Your brother? Oh, yes. Your father trained him very well.'

'It might have been nice to grow up with my brothers.' Talen sounded a bit wistful. He shrugged. 'But then . . .' He peered out at the forest. 'Any word from Engessa?'

'Our friends are still out there.'

'They're going to attack, aren't they?'

'Probably. You don't gather that many armed men in one place without having something military in mind.'

'I like your plan here, Sparhawk, but I think it's got a hole in it.'

'Oh?'

'Once they finally realise that we aren't going to move from this spot, they might decide to wait and then come at us after dark. Fighting at night's a lot different from doing it in the daytime, isn't it?'

'Usually, yes, but we'll cheat.'

Talen gave him a quizzical look.

'There are a couple of spells that brighten things up when you need to see.'

'I keep forgetting about that.'

'You might as well get used to it, Talen,' Sparhawk

told him with a faint smile. 'When we get back home, you're going to start your novitiate.'

'When did we decide that?'

'Just now. You're old enough, and if you keep on growing the way you have been lately, you'll be big enough.'

'Is magic hard to learn?'

'You have to pay attention. It's all done in Styric, and Styric's a tricky language. If you use the wrong word, all sorts of things can go wrong.'

'Thanks, Sparhawk. That's all I need – something else to worry about.'

'We'll talk with Sephrenia when we get to Sarsos. Maybe she'll agree to train you. Flute likes you, so she'll forgive you if you make any mistakes.'

'What's Flute got to do with it?'

'If Sephrenia trains you, you'll be submitting your requests to Aphrael.'

'Requests?'

'That's what magic is, Talen. You ask a God to do something for you.'

'Praying?' the boy asked incredulously.

'Sort of.'

'Does Emban know that you're praying to a Styric Goddess?'

'More than likely. The Church chooses to ignore the fact, though – for practical reasons.'

'She's a hypocrite then.'

'I wouldn't mention that to Emban, if I were you.'

'Let me get this straight. If I get to be a Church Knight, I'll be worshipping Flute?'

'Praying to her, Talen. I didn't say anything about worshipping.'

'Praying, worshipping, what's the difference?'

'Sephrenia will explain it.'

'She's in Sarsos, you say?'

'I didn't say that.' Sparhawk silently cursed his careless tongue.

'Yes, as a matter of fact you did.'

'All right, but keep it to yourself.'

'That's why we came overland, isn't it?'

'One of the reasons, yes. Haven't you got something else to do?'

'Not really, no.'

'Go find something – because if you don't, I will.'

'You don't have to get all huffy.'

Sparhawk gave him a steady stare.

'All right, all right, don't get excited. I'll go entertain Danae and her cat.'

Sparhawk stood watching the boy as he returned to the festivities under the canopy. It was obviously time to start being a little careful around Talen. He was dangerously intelligent, and a slip of the tongue might give away things that were supposed to be kept private. The discussion had raised an issue, however. Sparhawk went back to the group gathered on the hilltop and took Berit aside. 'Go tell the knights that if those people out there decide to wait until after dark to attack, *I'll* take care of giving us light to work by. If we all try to do it at the same time, we might confuse things.'

Berit nodded.

Sparhawk considered it further. 'And I'll go talk with Kring and Engessa,' he added. 'We don't want the Atans and the Peloi going into a panic if the sky suddenly lights up along about midnight tonight.'

'Is that what you're going to do?' Berit asked.

'It usually works out about the best in cases like this. One big light's easier to control than several hundred little ones – and it disrupts the enemy's concentration a lot more.'

Berit grinned. 'It *would* be a little startling to be

creeping through the bushes and have the sun come back up again, wouldn't it?'

'A lot of battles have been averted by lighting up the night, Berit, and a battle averted is sometimes even better than one you win.'

'I'll remember that, Sparhawk.'

The afternoon wore on, and the party on the hilltop became a little strained. There were only so many things to laugh at, and only so many jokes to tell. The warriors around the base of the hill either spent their time attending to equipment or pretending to sleep.

Sparhawk met with the others about mid-afternoon out near the road.

'If they don't know by now that we aren't going any farther today, they aren't very bright,' Kalten noted.

'We *do* look a bit settled in, don't we?' Ulath agreed.

'A suggestion, Sparhawk?' Tynian offered.

'Why do you always say that?'

'Habit, I suppose. I was taught to be polite to my elders. Even the best of spells isn't going to give us the same kind of light we'll have before the sun goes down. We know they're out there, we're in position and we're rested. Why don't we push things a bit? If we can force them to attack now, we can fight them in daylight.'

'How are you going to make somebody attack when he doesn't want to?' Patriarch Emban asked.

'We start making obvious preparations, your Grace,' Tynian replied. 'It's logical to start on the field fortifications about now anyway. Let's put up the palisade around the foot of the hill, and start digging ditches.'

'And cutting trees,' Ulath added. 'We could clear away some avenues leading out into the woods and pile all the tree trunks up where they'll hinder anybody trying to come through the forest. If they're going to

271

attack, let's make them attack across open ground.'

It took a surprisingly short time. The logs for the fence around the base of the hill were already sharpened and stacked in neat piles where they were handy. Digging them in was an easy matter. The birch trees in the forest were all no more than ten inches thick at the base, and they fell quickly to the axes of the warriors and were dragged into the surrounding forest to form large, jumbled piles which would be virtually impossible to penetrate, even for men on foot.

Sparhawk and the others went back up to the hilltop to survey their preparations. 'Why don't they attack us now, before we're ready?' Emban tensely asked the knights.

'Because it takes time to organise an attack, your Grace,' Bevier explained. 'The scouts have to run back and tell the generals what we're doing; the generals have to sneak through the woods to have a look for themselves; and then they all have to get together and argue about what they're going to do. They were planning an ambush. They aren't really ready to attack fortified positions. The business of adjusting one's thinking to a different tactical situation is what takes the longest.'

'How long?'

'It depends entirely on the personality of the man in charge. If his mind was really set on an ambush, it could take him as long as a week.'

'He's dead then, Bevier-Knight,' Engessa told the Cyrinic tersely. 'As soon as we saw the warriors in the woods I dispatched a dozen of my people to the garrison at Sarsos. If our enemy takes more than two days to make up his mind, he'll have five thousand Atans climbing his back.'

'Sound thinking, Atan Engessa,' Tynian approved. He pondered it. 'A thought, Sparhawk. If our friend out there gets all caught up in indecision, we can just

272

continue to strengthen our defences around this hill – ditches, sharpened stakes, the usual encumbrances. Each improvement we add will make him think things over that much longer – which will give us time to add more fortifications, which will make him think all the more. If we can keep him thinking for two days, the Atans from Sarsos will come up behind him and wipe out his force before he ever gets around to using it.'

'Good point,' Sparhawk agreed. 'Let's get to it.'

'I thought that being a military person just involved banging on people with axes and swords,' Emban conceded.

'There's a lot of that involved too, your Grace,' Ulath smiled, 'but it doesn't hurt to outsmart your enemy a little too.' He looked at Bevier. 'Engines?' he asked.

Bevier blinked. Ulath's cryptic questions always took him by surprise for some reason.

'As long as we have some time on our hands, we could erect some catapults on the hilltop. Attacking through a rain of boulders is always sort of distracting. Getting hit on the head with a fifty pound rock always seems to break a man's concentration for some reason. If we're going to set up for a siege, we might as well do it right.' He looked around at them. 'I still don't like sieges though,' he added. 'I want everybody to understand that.'

The warriors set to work, and the ladies and the young men attending them renewed their festivities, although their hilarity was even more forced now.

Sparhawk and Kalten were re-enforcing the breastworks atop the hill. Since his wife and daughter were going to be inside those fortifications, their strength was a matter of more than passing interest to the prince consort.

273

The party under the pavilion had begun to show gaps, and Stragen was increasingly obliged to fill them with his lute.

'He's going to wear out his fingers,' Kalten grunted, lifting another large rock into place.

'Stragen enjoys attention,' Sparhawk shrugged. 'He'll keep playing until the blood runs out from under his fingernails if there's anybody around to listen.'

Stragen's lute took up a very old air, and he began to sing again. Sparhawk didn't really have much of an ear for music, but he had to admit that the Thalesian thief had a beautiful voice.

And then Baroness Melidere joined in. Her voice was a rich contralto that blended smoothly with Stragen's baritone. Their duet was perfectly balanced, smooth and rich with the dark tones of their deeper voices. Sparhawk smiled to himself. The baroness was continuing her campaign. Once Aphrael had alerted him to the blonde girl's designs on Stragen, Sparhawk could see dozens of artful little ploys she was using to keep her intended victim's attention. He almost felt sorry for Stragen, but he concluded that Melidere would be good for him. The pair concluded their duet to loud applause. Sparhawk glanced toward the pavilion and saw Melidere lay one lingering hand almost caressingly on Stragen's wrist. Sparhawk knew just how potent those accidental-seeming contacts were. Lillas had explained it to him once, and Lillas had been the world's champion seductress – as probably half the men in Jiroch could have sworn to.

Then Stragen turned to another traditional air, and a new voice lifted in song. Kalten dropped the rock he had been lifting. It fell onto his foot, but he did not even wince. The voice was that of an angel, high, sweet, and as clear as glass. It soared effortlessly toward the upper reaches of the soprano range. It was a lyric voice, uncontaminated by the subtle variations of the coloratura, and it seemed as untaught as bird-song.

It was Ehlana's maid, Alean. The doe-eyed girl, always so quiet and unassuming, stood in the centre of the Pavilion, her face luminous as she sang.

Sparhawk heard Kalten snuffle, and he was astonished to see great tears streaming down his friend's face as the blond Pandion wept unashamed.

Perhaps his recent conversation with the Child Goddess had alerted Sparhawk to the potentials of intuition, and he suddenly knew, without knowing exactly *how* he knew, that *two* campaigns were in progress – and, moreover, that the one being waged by Baroness Melidere was the more overt and blatant. He carefully concealed a smile behind his hand.

'Lord, that girl's got a beautiful voice!' Kalten said in stunned admiration as Alean concluded her song. 'God!' he said then, doubling over to clutch at the foot he had unwittingly injured five minutes earlier.

The work progressed until sunset, and then the combined army pulled back behind the reinforced palisade and waited. Sir Bevier and his Cyrinic Knights retired to the hilltop, where they completed the construction of their catapults. Then they amused themselves by lobbing large rocks into the forest seemingly at random.

'What are they shooting at, Sparhawk?' Ehlana asked after supper.

'The trees,' he shrugged.

'The trees aren't threatening us.'

'No, but there are probably people hiding among them. The boulders falling out of the sky should make them a little jumpy.' He smiled. 'Actually, Bevier's men are testing the range of the engines, dear. If our friends in the forest decide to attack down those avenues we've provided for them, Bevier wants to know exactly when to start shooting.'

'There's a great deal more involved in being a soldier than just keeping your equipment clean, isn't there?'

'I'm glad you appreciate that, my Queen.'

'Shall we go to bed then?'

'Sorry, Ehlana,' he replied, 'but I won't be sleeping tonight. If our friend out there makes up his mind and attacks, there are some things I'll have to do rather quickly.' He looked around. 'Where's Danae?'

'She and Talen are over there watching Bevier's people throw rocks at the trees.'

'I'll go get her. You'll probably want to keep her close to you tonight.' He crossed the basin to where Bevier was directing the activities of his knights. 'Bed-time,' he told his daughter, lifting her into his arms.

She pouted a little at that, but raised no other objections. When Sparhawk was about half-way back to his wife's tent, he slowed. 'How much of a stickler are you for formality, Aphrael?' he asked.

'A few genuflections are nice, father,' she replied, 'but I can live without them – in an emergency.'

'Good. If the attack comes tonight, we're going to need some light to see them by.'

'How much light?'

'Sort of noonish would be good.'

'I can't do that, Sparhawk. Do you have any idea of how much trouble I'd get into if I made the sun rise when it wasn't supposed to?'

'I wasn't really suggesting that. I just want enough light so that people can't sneak up on us through the shadows. The spell's a fairly long one with a lot of formalities involved and many, many specifics. I may be a little pressed for time, so would you be terribly offended if I just asked you for light and left the details up to you?'

'It's highly irregular, Sparhawk,' she chided him primly.

'I know, but just this once maybe?'

'Oh, I *guess* so, but let's not make a habit of it. I *do* have a reputation to maintain, after all.'

'I love you,' he laughed.

'Oh, if that's the case, it's perfectly all right then. We can bend all sorts of rules for people who really love us. Just ask for light, Sparhawk. I'll see to it that you get lots and lots of light.'

The attack came shortly before midnight. It began with a rain of arrows lofting in out of the darkness, followed quickly by attacks on the Atan pickets. That last proved to be what might best be described as a tactical blunder. The Atans were the finest foot-soldiers in the world, and they welcomed hand-to-hand combat.

Sparhawk could not clearly see the attacking force from his vantage-point on the hilltop, but he firmly controlled his curiosity and held off on illuminating the battlefield until such time as the opposing force was more fully engaged. As they had anticipated, their enemies used the cover of these first probing moves to attack the log-jams designed to impede their progress through the belts of trees set off by Sir Ulath's avenues radiating out from the base of the hill like the spokes of a huge wheel. As it turned out, Bevier's Cyrinics had not been lobbing rocks out into the forest entirely for the fun of it. They had rather precisely pin-pointed the range of those jumbles of fallen trees with their catapults, and they hurled basketfuls of fist-sized rocks into the air to rain down on the men attempting to tear down the barricades or to widen the narrow gaps which had been deliberately left to permit the Peloi to ride out in search of entertainment. A two-pound rock falling out of the sky will not crush a man, but it will break his bones, and after ten minutes or so, the men out in the woods withdrew.

'I confess it to you, Sparhawk-Knight,' Engessa said gravely, 'I had thought your elaborate preparations a bit silly. Atans do not fight so. Your approach does have certain advantages, though.'

'Our societies are different, Atan Engessa. Your people live and fight in the wilderness where enemies are encountered singly or in small groups. Our wilderness has been tamed, so our enemies come at us in large numbers. We build forts to live in, and over the centuries we've devised many means to defend those forts.'

'When will you make the light come?'

'At a time when it's most inconvenient for our enemy. I want him to commit a large part of his force and to have them fully engaged before I sweep away the darkness. He won't expect that, and it takes time to get orders through to men who are already fighting. We should be able to eliminate a sizeable part of his army before he can pull them back. Defensive warfare has certain advantages if you make the proper preparations.'

'Ulath-Knight does not like it.'

'Ulath doesn't have the patience for it. Bevier's the expert on defence. He'd be perfectly willing to wait for ten years if need be for the enemy to come to him on *his* terms.'

'What will the enemy do next? We Atans are not accustomed to interrupted fights.'

'He'll draw back and shoot arrows at us while he thinks things over. Then he'll probably try a direct assault down one of those avenues.'

'Why only one? Why not attack from all directions at once?'

'Because he doesn't know how much we can hurt him yet. He'll have to find that out first. He'll learn in time, but it's going to cost him a great deal to get his education. After we've killed about half of his soldiers, he'll do one of two things. He'll either go away, or he'll throw everything he's got at us from all sides at once.'

'And then?'

'Then we'll kill the rest of his soldiers and be on our way,' Sparhawk shrugged. 'Assuming that everything goes the way we've planned, of course.'

At two hundred paces and with only starlight to see by, the figures were hardly more than shadows. They marched out into the centre of one of Ulath's corridors and halted while others filed out to join them and to form up into a kind of massed formation.

'I can't believe that!' Kalten exclaimed, gaping at the shadowy soldiers at the end of the corridor.

'Is something wrong, Sir Kalten?' Emban's voice was a little shrill.

'Not in the least, your Grace,' Kalten replied gaily. 'It's just that we're dealing with an idiot.' He turned his head slightly. 'Bevier,' he called, 'he's forming up his troops on the *road* to march them into place.'

'You're not serious!'

'May all of my toenails fall out if I'm not.'

Bevier barked a number of commands, and his knights swung the catapults around to bring them to bear on the unseen avenue leading toward the road. 'Give the word, Sparhawk,' the young Cyrinic called.

'We're going on down now,' Sparhawk called back. 'You can start as soon as we reach the bottom. We'll wait so that you can pound them for a while, and then we'll charge. We'd take it as a kindness if you'd stop about then.'

Bevier grinned at him.

'Look after my wife while I'm gone.'

'Naturally.'

Sparhawk and the other warriors began to climb down the hill. 'I'll break my men into two groups, friend Sparhawk,' Kring said. 'We'll circle around and come up onto the road about a half mile behind them on either side. We'll wait for your signal there.'

'Don't kill all of them.' Engessa cautioned. 'My Atans grow sulky if there's fighting and they aren't allowed to participate.'

They reached the bottom of the hill, and Bevier's catapults began to thud, launching large rocks this time. There were sounds from off in the direction of the road indicating that the Cyrinic Knights had found the proper range.

'Luck, Sparhawk,' Kring said tersely and melted off into the shadows.

'Be careful, Sir Knights,' Khalad cautioned them. 'Those tree-stumps out there are dangerous in the dark.'

'It won't be dark when we charge, Khalad,' Sparhawk assured him. 'I've made some arrangements.'

Engessa slipped quietly through an opening in the palisade to join his warriors out in the forest.

'Is it just my imagination, or does it seem to the rest of you that we're dealing with someone who's not really very sophisticated?' Tynian said. 'He doesn't seem to have any conception of modern warfare or modern technology.'

'I think the word you're groping for is "stupid", Tynian,' Kalten chuckled.

'I'm not so sure,' Tynian frowned. 'It was too dark for me to make out very much from the hilltop, but it looked almost as if he were forming up his troops into a phalanx. Nobody's done that in the west for over a thousand years.'

'It wouldn't be very effective against mounted knights, would it?' Kalten asked.

280

'I'm not so sure. It would depend on how long his spears are and the size of those overlapping shields. He could give us trouble.'

'Berit,' Sparhawk said, 'go back up the hill and tell Bevier to shift his catapults a bit. I'd like the enemy formation broken up.'

'Right.' The young knight turned and scrambled back on up the hill.

'If he *is* using a phalanx formation,' Tynian continued, 'it means that he's never come up against mounted troops before and that he's used to fighting in open country.'

Bevier's catapults began to hurl boulders at the shadowy formation at the far end of the cleared avenue.

'Let's get started,' Sparhawk decided. 'I was going to wait a while, but let's see what we're up against.' He hauled himself up onto Faran's back and led the knights to a position outside the palisade. Then he drew in a deep breath. 'We could use a bit of light now, Divine One.' He cast the thought out without even bothering to frame it in Styric.

'That's *really* improper, Sparhawk,' Aphrael's voice in his ear was tart. 'You know I'm not supposed to respond to prayers in Elenic.'

'You know both languages. What difference does it make?'

'It's a question of style, Sparhawk.'

'I'll try to do better next time.'

'I'd really appreciate it. How's this?'

It began as a kind of pulsating lavender glow along the northern horizon. Then long streaks of pure, multi-coloured light spread upward in seething, curtain-like sheets, wavering, undulating like a vast curtain shimmering against the night sky.

'What is it?' Khalad exclaimed.

'The northern lights,' Ulath grunted. 'I've never seen

281

them this far south – or quite so bright. I'm impressed, Sparhawk.'

The shimmering curtain of light, rising and falling, crept up and up into the darkness, erasing the stars and filling the night with rainbow light.

A huge groan of consternation and awe rose from the army massing near the road. Sparhawk looked intently down the stump-dotted avenue. The soldiers facing them wore antique armour – breastplates, horse-hair crested helmets and large, round shields. They wore short swords and carried twelve-foot spears. Their front rank had evidently been formed with overlapping shields and advanced spears. Bevier's catapults, how-ever, had broken those tightly-packed ranks, and the rain of boulders continued to smash down among men so jammed together they could not flee.

Sparhawk watched grimly for a few moments. 'All right, Ulath,' he said at last, 'sing the Ogre's song for them.'

Ulath grinned and lifted his curled Ogre-horn to his lips and blew a single, deep-toned blast.

The massed foot-troops, their ranks broken by the catapults and their minds filled with wonder and dismay by the sudden brilliant light covering half the sky, were in no way prepared to meet the awesome charge of the armoured knights and their massive horses. There was a resounding crash, and the front ranks of the massed foot-soldiers fell beneath the churning hooves of the war-horses. The knights discarded their lances, drew their swords and axes and fell to work, carving great swathes through the tightly-packed ranks.

'Ulath!' Sparhawk bellowed. 'Turn loose the Peloi!'

Sir Ulath blew his Ogre-horn again – twice this time.

The Peloi war-cries were shrill and ululating. Sparhawk glanced quickly along the road. The warriors Kring's Peloi were attacking were not the same as the ones facing the knights. Sparhawk had led a charge against infantry, men in breastplates and horse-hair crested helmets who fought on foot. Kring was attacking mounted men, men wearing flowing robes and cloth head-coverings, all armed with curved swords much like the Peloi sabres. Quite obviously, the attacking force was comprised of two different elements. There would be time later to ponder those differences. Right now, they were all very busy.

Sparhawk swung his heavy broadsword rhythmically in huge overhead strokes that sheared down into the sea of horsehair-crested helmets surrounding him. He continued for several minutes until the sounds from along the road indicated that the Peloi were fully engaged. 'Sir Ulath!' he roared. 'Ask the Atans to join us!'

The Ogre-horn sang again – and again – and yet once again.

Sounds of fighting erupted back among the trees. Enemy soldiers who had fled the charge of the knights and the slashing attack of the Peloi found no sanctuary in the woods. Engessa's Atans, silent and deadly, moved through the eerie, multi-coloured light streaming down from the pulsating sky, seeking and destroying.

'Sparhawk!' Kalten shouted. 'Look!'

Sparhawk jerked his head around, and his heart froze.

'I thought that thing was dead!' Kalten exclaimed.

The figure was robed and hooded all in black, and it was astride a gaunt horse. A kind of greenish nimbus surrounded it, and waves of implacable hatred seemed to shimmer out from it. Sparhawk looked a bit more closely and then let out his breath relieved. 'It's not a Seeker,' he told Kalten. 'It's got human hands. It's probably the one we've been fighting, though.'

Then another man in black rode out from farther back in the trees. This one wore exaggeratedly dramatic clothing. He had on a black, wide-brimmed hat and wore a black bag with ragged eye-holes over his head.

'Has this all been some sort of joke?' Tynian demanded. 'Is that who I think it is?'

'I'd guess that it's the one in the robe who's been in charge,' Ulath said. 'I doubt that Sabre could successfully herd goats.'

'Savour thine empty victory, Anakha,' the hooded figure called in a hollow, strangely metallic voice. 'I did but test thee that I might discern thy strength – and thy weaknesses. Go thy ways now. I have learned what I needed to learn. I will trouble thee no further – for now. But mistake me not, oh man without destiny, we will meet anon, and in our next meeting shall I try thee more significantly.' Then Sabre and his hooded companion wavered and vanished.

The wailing and groaning of the wounded enemies all around them suddenly broke off. Sparhawk looked around quickly. The strangely-armoured foot troops he and his friends had been fighting were all gone. Only the dead remained. Back along the road in either direction, Kring's Peloi were reining in their horses in amazement. The troops they had engaged had vanished as well, and startled exclamations from back among the trees indicated that the Atans had also been bereft of enemies.

'What's going on here?' Kalten exclaimed.

'I'm not sure,' Sparhawk replied, 'but I *am* sure that I don't like it very much.' He swung down from his saddle and turned one of the fallen enemies over with his foot.

The body was little more than a dried husk, browned, withered and totally desiccated. It looked very much like the body of a man who had been dead for several centuries at least.

*   *   *

284

'We've encountered it once before, your Grace,' Tynian was explaining to Patriarch Emban. It was nearly morning, and they were gathered once again atop the rocky hill. 'Last time it was antique Lamorks. I don't know what kind of antiques these were.' He looked at the two mummified corpses the Atans had brought up the hill.

'This one is a Cynesgan,' Ambassador Oscagne said, pointing at one of the dead men.

'Looks almost like a Rendor, doesn't he?' Talen observed.

'There would be certain similarities,' Oscagne agreed. 'Cynesga is a desert, much like Rendor, and there are only so many kinds of clothing suitable for such a climate.'

The dead man in question was garbed in a flowing, loose-fitting robe, and his head was covered with a sort of cloth binding that flowed down to protect the back of his neck.

'They aren't very good fighters,' Kring told them. 'They all sort of went to pieces when we charged them.'

'What about the other one, your Excellency?' Tynian asked. 'These ones in armour were *very* good fighters.'

The Tamul Ambassador's eyes grew troubled. 'That one's a figment of someone's imagination,' he declared.

'I don't really think so, your Excellency,' Sir Bevier disagreed. 'The men we encountered back in Eosia had been drawn from the past. They were fairly exotic, I'll grant you, but they *had* been living men once. Everything we've seen here tells us that we've run into the same thing again. This fellow's most definitely *not* an imaginary soldier. He *did* live once, and what he's wearing was his customary garb.'

'It's impossible,' Oscagne declared adamantly.

'Just for the sake of speculation, Oscagne,' Emban

said, 'let's shelve the word "impossible" for the time being. Who would you say he was if he *weren't* impossible?'

'It's a very old legend,' Oscagne said, his face still troubled. 'We're told that once, a long, long time ago, there were people in Cynesga who pre-dated the current inhabitants. The legend calls them the Cyrgai. Modern Cynesgans are supposed to be their degenerate descendants.'

'They look as if they come from two different parts of the world,' Kalten noted.

'Cyrga, the city of the Cyrgai, was supposed to lie in the central highlands of Cynesga,' Oscagne told him. 'It's higher than the surrounding desert, and the legend says there was a large, spring-fed lake there. The stories say that the climate there was markedly different from that of the desert. The Cyrgai wouldn't have needed protection from the sun the way their bastard offspring would have. I'd imagine that there were indications of rank and status involved as well. Given the nature of the Cyrgai, they'd have definitely wanted to keep their inferiors from wearing the Cyrgai costume.'

'They lived at the same time then?' Tynian asked.

'The legends are a little vague on that score, Sir Tynian. Evidently there *was* a period when the Cyrgai and the Cynesgans co-existed. The Cyrgai would certainly have been dominant, though.' He made a face. 'Why am I talking this way about a myth?' he said plaintively.

'This is a fairly substantial myth, Oscagne,' Emban said, nudging the mummified Cyrgai with his foot. 'I gather that these fellows had something of a reputation?'

'Oh, yes,' Oscagne said with distaste. 'They had a hideous culture – all cruelty and militarism. They held themselves aloof from other peoples in order to avoid what they called contamination. They were said to be

obsessively concerned with racial purity, and they w
militantly opposed to any new ideas.'

'That's a futile sort of obsession,' Tynian noted. 'Any time you engage in trade, you're going to encounter new ideas.'

'The legends tell us they understood that, Sir Knight. Trade was forbidden.'

'No commerce at all?' Kalten asked incredulously.

Oscagne shook his head. 'They were supposed to be totally self-sufficient. They even went so far as to forbid the possession of gold or silver in their society.'

'Monstrous!' Stragen exclaimed. 'They had no money at all?'

'Iron bars, we're told – heavy ones, I guess. It tended to discourage trade. They lived only for war. All the men were in the army, and all the women spent their time having babies. When they grew too old to either fight or bear children, they were expected to kill themselves. The legends say that they were the finest soldiers the world has ever known.'

'The legends are exaggerated, Oscagne,' Engessa told him. 'I killed five of them myself. They spent a great deal of time flexing their muscles and posing with their weapons when they should have been paying attention to business.'

'The ancients were very formal, Atan Engessa,' Oscagne murmured.

'Who was the fellow in the robe?' Kalten asked. 'The one who seemed to be trying to pass himself off as a Seeker?'

'I'd guess that he holds a position somewhat akin to Gerrich in Lamorkand and to Sabre in Western Astel,' Sparhawk surmised. 'I was a little surprised to see Sabre here,' he added. He had to step rather carefully here. Both he and Emban were sworn to secrecy on the matter of Sabre's real identity.

courtesy, no doubt,' Stragen murmured.
 that he was here sort of confirms our guess
 these assorted upheavals and disturbances are
 together. There's somebody in back of all this –
somebody we haven't seen or even heard of yet. We're
going to have to catch one of these intermediaries of his
and wring some information out of him sooner or later.'
The blond thief looked around. 'What now?' he asked.

'How long did you say it would be until the Atans
arrive from Sarsos, Engessa?' Sparhawk asked the
towering Atan.

'They should arrive sometime the day after tomorrow,
Sparhawk-Knight.' The Atan glanced toward the east.
'Tomorrow, that is,' he corrected, 'since it's already
starting to get light.'

'We'll care for our wounded and wait for them then,'
Sparhawk decided. 'I like lots of friendly faces around
me in times like this.'

'One question, Sparhawk-Knight,' Engessa said.
'Who is Anakha?'

'That's Sparhawk,' Ulath told him. 'The Styrics call
him that. It means "without destiny".'

'All men have a destiny, Ulath-Knight.'

'Not Sparhawk, apparently, and you have no idea
how nervous that makes the Gods.'

As Engessa had calculated, the Sarsos garrison arrived
about noon the following day, and the hugely increased
escort of the Queen of Elenia marched easterly. Two
days later, they crested a hill and gazed down at a
marble city situated in a broad green field backed by a
dark forest stretching to the horizon.

Sparhawk had been sensing a familiar presence since
early that morning, and he had ridden on ahead eagerly.

Sephrenia was sitting on her white palfrey beside the
road. She was a small, beautiful woman with black hair,

snowy skin and deep blue eyes. She wore a white robe of a somewhat finer weave than the homespun she had normally worn in Eosia.

'Hello, little mother,' he smiled, saying it as if they had been apart for no more than a week. 'You've been well, I trust?' He removed his helmet.

'Tolerable, Sparhawk.' Her voice was rich and had that familiar lilt.

'Will you permit me to greet you?' he asked in that formal manner all Pandions used when meeting her after a separation.

'Of course, dear one.'

Sparhawk dismounted, took her wrists and turned her hands over. Then he kissed her palms in the ritual Styric greeting. 'And will you bless me, little mother?' he asked.

She fondly placed her hands on his temples and spoke her benediction in Styric. 'Help me down, Sparhawk,' she commanded.

He reached out and put his hands about her almost child-like waist. Then he lifted her easily from her saddle. Before he could set her down, however, she put her arms about his neck and kissed him full on the lips, something she had almost never done before. 'I've missed you, my dear one,' she breathed. 'You cannot believe how I've missed you.'

PART THREE

Atan

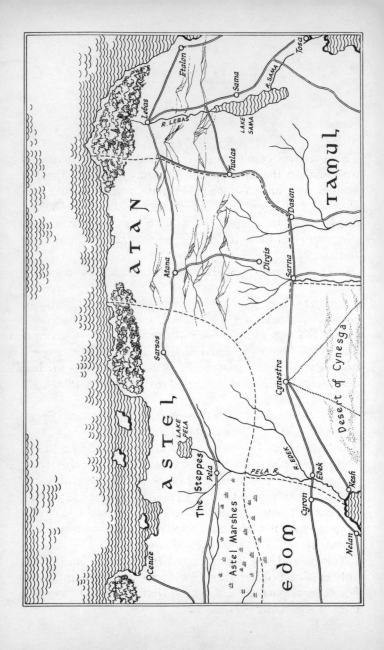

CHAPTER 16

The carriage came around a bend in the road and approached the spot where Sparhawk and Sephrenia waited. Ehlana was talking animatedly to Oscagne and Emban, but she broke off suddenly, her eyes wide. *'Sephrenia?'* she gasped. *'It is! It's Sephrenia!'* Royal dignity went out the window as she scrambled down from the carriage.

'Brace yourself,' Sparhawk cautioned with a gentle smile.

Ehlana ran to them, threw her arms around Sephrenia's neck and kissed her, weeping for joy.

The queen's tears were not the only ones shed that afternoon. Even the hard-bitten Church Knights were misty-eyed for the most part. Kalten went even further and wept openly as he knelt to receive Sephrenia's blessing.

'The Styric woman has a special significance, Sparhawk-Knight?' Engessa asked curiously.

'A very special significance, Atan Engessa,' Sparhawk replied, watching his friends clustered around the small woman. 'She touches our hearts in a profound way. We'd probably take the world apart if she asked us to.'

'That's a very great authority, Sparhawk-Knight.' Engessa said it with some approval. Engessa respected authority.

'It is indeed, my friend,' Sparhawk agreed, 'and that's only the least of her gifts. She's wise and beautiful, and I'm at least partially convinced that she could stop the tides if she really wanted to.'

'She is quite small, though,' Engessa noted.

'Not really. In our eyes she's at least a hundred feet tall – maybe even two hundred.'

'The Styrics are a strange people with strange powers, but I had not heard of this ability to alter their size before.' Engessa was a profoundly literal man, and hyperbole was beyond his grasp. 'Two hundred, you say?'

'At least, Atan.'

Sephrenia was completely caught up in the out-pouring of affection, and so Sparhawk was able to observe her rather closely. She had changed. She seemed more open, for one thing. No Styric could ever completely lower his defences among Elenes. Thousands of years of prejudice and oppression had taught them to be wary – even of those Elenes they loved the most. Sephrenia's defensive shell, a shell she had kept in place around her for so long that she had probably not even known it was there, was gone now. The doors were all open.

There was something more, however. Her face had been luminous before, but now it was radiant. A kind of regretful longing had always seemed to hover in her eyes, and it was gone now. For the first time in all the years Sparhawk had known her, Sephrenia seemed complete and totally happy.

'Will this go on for long, Sparhawk-Knight?' Engessa asked politely. 'Sarsos is close at hand, but . . .' He left the suggestion hanging.

'I'll talk with them, Atan. I *might* be able to persuade them that they can continue this later.' Sparhawk walked toward the excited group near the carriage. 'Atan Engessa just made an interesting suggestion,' he said to them. 'It's a novel idea, of course, but he pointed out that we could probably do all of this inside the walls of Sarsos – since it's so close anyway.'

'I see *that* hasn't changed,' Sephrenia observed to Ehlana. 'Does he still make these clumsy attempts at humour every chance he gets?'

'I've been working on that, little mother,' Ehlana smiled.

'The question I was really asking was whether or not you ladies would like to ride on into the city, or would you like to have us set up camp for the night.'

'Spoil-sport,' Ehlana accused.

'We really should go on down,' Sephrenia told them. 'Vanion's waiting, and you know how cross he gets when people aren't punctual.'

'Vanion?' Emban exclaimed. 'I thought he'd be dead by now.'

'Hardly. He's quite vigorous, actually. *Very* vigorous at times. He'd have come with me to meet you, but he sprained his ankle yesterday. He's being terribly brave about it, but it hurts him more than he's willing to admit.'

Stragen stepped up and effortlessly lifted her up into the carriage. 'What should we expect in Sarsos, dear sister?' he asked her in his flawless Styric.

Ehlana gave him a startled look. 'You've been hiding things from me, Milord Stragen. I didn't know you spoke Styric.'

'I always meant to mention it to you, your Majesty, but it kept slipping my mind.'

'I think you'd better be prepared for some surprises, Stragen,' Sephrenia told him. 'All of you should.'

'What sort of surprises?' Stragen asked. 'Remember that I'm a thief, Sephrenia, and surprises are very bad for thieves. Our veins tend to come untied when we're startled.'

'I think you'd all better discard your preconceptions about Styrics,' Sephrenia advised. 'We aren't obliged to be simple and rustic here in Sarsos, so you'll find an altogether different kind of Styric in those streets.' She seated herself in the carriage and held out her arms to Danae. The little princess climbed up into her lap and kissed her. It seemed very innocuous and perfectly natural, but Sparhawk was privately surprised that they were not surrounded by a halo of blazing light.

Then Sephrenia looked at Emban. 'Oh, dear,' she said. 'I hadn't really counted on your being here, your Grace. How firmly fixed are your prejudices?'

'I like *you*, Sephrenia,' the little fat man replied. 'I resent the Styrics' stubborn refusal to accept the true faith, but I'm not really a howling bigot.'

'Are you open to a suggestion, my friend?' Oscagne asked.

'I'll listen.'

'I'd recommend that you look upon your visit to Sarsos as a holiday, and put your theology on a shelf someplace. Look all you want, but let the things you don't like pass without comment. The empire would really appreciate your co-operation in this, Emban. Please don't stir up the Styrics. They're a very prickly people with capabilities we don't entirely understand. Let's not precipitate avoidable explosions.'

Emban opened his mouth as if to retort, but then his eyes grew troubled, and he apparently decided against it.

Sparhawk conferred briefly with Oscagne and Sephrenia and decided that the bulk of the Church Knights should set up camp with the Peloi outside the city. It was a precaution designed to avert incidents. Engessa sent his Atans to their garrison just north of the city wall, and the party surrounding Ehlana's carriage entered through an unguarded gate.

'What's the trouble, Khalad?' Sephrenia asked Sparhawk's squire. The young man was looking around, frowning.

'It's really none of my business, Lady Sephrenia,' he said, 'but are marble buildings really a good idea this far north? Aren't they awfully cold in the winter time?'

'He's so much like his father,' she smiled. 'I think you've exposed one of our vanities, Khalad. Actually, the buildings are made of brick. The marble's just a sheathing to make our city impressive.'

'Even brick isn't too good at keeping out the cold, Lady Sephrenia.'

'It is when you make double walls and fill the space between those walls with a foot of plaster.'

'That would take a lot of time and effort.'

'You'd be amazed at the amount of time and effort people will waste for the sake of vanity, Khalad, and we can always cheat a little, if we have to. Our Gods are fond of marble buildings, and we like to make them feel at home.'

'Wood's still more practical,' he said stubbornly.

'I'm sure it is, Khalad, but it's so commonplace. We like to be different.'

'It's different, all right.'

Sarsos even smelled different. A faint miasma hung over every Elene city in the world, an unpleasant blend of sooty smoke, rotting garbage and the effluvium from poorly-constructed and infrequently drained cesspools. Sarsos, on the other hand, smelled of trees and roses. It was summer, and there were small parks and rose bushes everywhere. Ehlana's expression grew speculative. With a peculiar flash of insight, Sparhawk foresaw a vast programme of public works looming on the horizon for the capital of Elenia.

The architecture and layout of the city was subtle and highly sophisticated. The streets were broad and, except where the inhabitants had decided otherwise for aesthetic reasons, they were straight. The buildings were all sheathed in marble, and they were fronted by graceful white pillars. This was most definitely *not* an Elene city.

The citizens looked strangely un-Styric. Their kinsmen to the west all wore robes of lumpy white homespun. The garb was so universal as to be a kind of identifying badge. The Styrics of Sarsos, however, wore silks and linens. White still appeared to be the preferred colour, but there were other hues as well, blue and green and yellow, and not a few garments were a brilliant scarlet. Styric women in the west were very seldom seen, but they were much more in evidence here. They also wore colourful clothing and flowers in their hair.

More than anything, however, there was a marked difference in attitude. The Styrics of the west were timid, sometimes as fearful as deer. They were meek – a meekness designed to soften Elene aggressiveness, but that very attitude quite often inflamed the Elenes all the more. The Styrics of Sarsos, on the other hand, were definitely not meek. They did not keep their eyes lowered or speak in soft, hesitant voices. They were assertive. They argued on street corners. They laughed out loud. They walked along the broad avenues of their city with their heads held high as if they were actually proud to be Styric. The one thing that bespoke the difference more than anything else, however, was the fact that the children played in the parks without any signs of fear.

Emban's face had grown rigid, and his nostrils were pinched-in with anger. Sparhawk knew exactly why the Patriarch of Ucera was showing so much resentment. Candour compelled him to privately admit that he shared it. All Elenes believed that Styrics were an inferior race, and despite their indoctrination, the Church Knights still shared that belief at the deepest level of their minds. Sparhawk felt the thoughts rising in him unbidden. How dare these puffed-up, loud-mouthed Styrics have a more beautiful city than any the Elenes could construct? How dare they be prosperous? How dare they be happy? How dare they strut through these streets behaving for all the world as if they were every bit as good as Elenes?

Then he saw Danae looking at him sadly, and he pulled his thoughts and unspoken resentments up short. He took hold of those unattractive emotions firmly and looked at them. He didn't like what he saw very much. So long as Styrics were meek and submissive and lived in misery in rude hovels, he was more than willing to leap to their defence, but when they brazenly looked him squarely in the eye with unbowed heads and challenging expressions, he found himself wanting to teach them lessons.

'Difficult, isn't it, Sparhawk?' Stragen said wryly. 'My bastardy has always made me feel a certain kinship with the downtrodden and despised. I found the towering humility of our Styric brethren so inspiring that I even went out of my way to learn their language. I'll admit that the people here set my teeth on edge, though. They all seem so disgustingly self-satisfied.'

'Stragen, sometimes you're so civilised you make me sick.'

'My, aren't *we* touchy today?'

'Sorry. I just found something in myself that I don't like. It's making me grouchy.'

Stragen sighed. 'We should probably never look into our own hearts, Sparhawk. I don't think anybody likes everything he finds there.'

Sparhawk was not the only one having trouble with the City of Sarsos and its inhabitants. Sir Bevier's face reflected the fact that he was feeling an even greater resentment than the others. His expression was shocked, even outraged.

'Heard a story once,' Sir Ulath said to him in that

disarmingly reminiscent fashion that always signalled louder than words that Ulath was about to make a point. That was one of Sir Ulath's characteristics. He almost never spoke *unless* he was trying to make a point. 'It seems that there was a Deiran, an Arcian and a Thalesian. It was a long time ago, and they were all speaking in their native dialects. Anyway, they got to arguing about which of their modes of speech was God's own. They finally agreed to go to Chyrellos and ask the Archprelate to put the question directly to God himself.'

'And?' Bevier asked him.

'Well, sir, everybody knows that God always answers the Archprelate's questions, so the word finally came back and settled their argument once and for all.'

'Well?'

'Well what?'

'What *is* God's native dialect?'

'Why, Thalesian, of course. Everybody knows that, Bevier.' Ulath was the kind of man who could say that with a perfectly straight face. 'It only stands to reason, though. God was a Genidian Knight before he decided to take the universe in hand. I'll bet you didn't know that, did you?'

Bevier stared at him for a moment, and then began to laugh a bit sheepishly.

Ulath looked at Sparhawk, and one of his eyelids closed in a slow, deliberate wink. Once again Sparhawk felt obliged to reassess his Thalesian friend.

Sephrenia had a house here in Sarsos, and that was another surprise. There had always been a kind of possessionless transience about her. The house was quite large, and it was set apart in a kind of park where tall old trees shaded gently-sloping lawns and gardens and sparkling fountains. Like all the other buildings in Sarsos, Sephrenia's house was constructed of marble, and it looked very familiar.

'You cheated, little mother,' Kalten accused her as he helped her down from the carriage.

'I beg your pardon?'

'You imitated the temple of Aphrael on the island we all saw in that dream. Even the colonnade along the front is the same.'

'I suppose you're right, dear one, but it's sort of expected here. All the members of the Council of Styricum boast about their own Gods. It's expected. Our Gods would feel slighted if we didn't.'

'You're a member of the council here?' He sounded a bit surprised.

'Of course. I *am* the high priestess of Aphrael, after all.'

'It seems a little odd to find somebody from Eosia on the ruling council of a city in Daresia.'

'What makes you think I came from Eosia?'

'You *didn't*?'

'Of course not – and the council here in Sarsos isn't just the local government. We make the decisions for *all* Styrics, no matter where they are. Shall we go inside? Vanion's waiting.' She led them up the marble stairs to a broad, intricately engraved bronze door, and they went on into the house.

The building was constructed around an interior courtyard, a lush garden with a marble fountain in the centre. Vanion half-lay on a divan-like chair near the fountain with his right leg propped up on a number of cushions. His ankle was swathed in bandages, and he had a disgusted expression in his face. His hair and beard were silvery now, and he looked very distinguished. His face was unlined, however. The cares that had weighed him down had been lifted, but that would hardly account for the startling change in him. Even the effects of the dreadful weight of the swords he had forced Sephrenia to give him had somehow been erased.

301

His face looked younger than Sparhawk had ever seen it. He lowered the scroll he had been reading. 'Sparhawk,' he said irritably, 'where have you been?'

'I'm glad to see you too, my Lord,' Sparhawk replied.

Vanion looked at him sharply and then laughed, his face a bit sheepish. 'I guess that *was* a little ungracious, wasn't it?'

'Crotchety, my Lord,' Ehlana told him. 'Definitely crotchety.' Then she cast dignity aside, ran to him and threw her arms about his neck. 'We are displeased with you, my Lord Vanion,' she said in her most imperious manner. Then she kissed him soundly. 'You have deprived us of your counsel and your company in our hour of need.' She kissed him again. 'It was churlish of you in the extreme to absent yourself from our side without our permission.' She kissed him yet again.

'Am I being reprimanded or re-united with my Queen?' he asked, looking a bit confused.

'A little of each, my Lord,' she shrugged. 'I thought I'd save some time and take care of everything all at once. I'm really very, very glad to see you again, Vanion, but I was most unhappy when you crept away from Cimmura like a thief in the night.'

'We don't really do that, you know,' Stragen noted clinically. 'After you've stolen something, the idea is to look ordinary, and creeping attracts attention.'

'Stragen,' she said, 'hush.'

'I took him away from Cimmura for his health,' Sephrenia told her. 'He was dying there. I had a certain personal interest in keeping him alive, so I took him to a place where I could nurse him back to health. I badgered Aphrael unmercifully for a couple of years, and she finally gave in. I can make a serious pest of myself when I want something, and I *really* wanted Vanion.' She made no attempt to conceal her feelings now. The years of unspoken love between her and the Pandion Preceptor were out in the open. She also made no effort to conceal what was quite obviously in both the Styric and the Elene cultures a scandalous arrangement. She and Vanion were openly living in sin, and neither of them showed the slightest bit of remorse about it.

'How's the ankle, dear one?' she asked him.

'It's swelling up again.'

'Didn't I tell you to soak it in ice when it did that?'

'I didn't have any ice.'

'*Make* some, Vanion. You know the spell.'

'The ice I make doesn't seem as cold as yours, Sephrenia.' His voice was plaintive.

'Men!' she cried in seeming exasperation. 'They're all such babies!' She bustled away in search of a basin.

'You followed that, didn't you, Sparhawk?' Vanion said.

'Of course, my Lord. It was very smooth, if I may say so.'

'Thank you.'

'What was that all about?' Kalten asked.

'You'd never understand, Kalten,' Sparhawk replied.

'Not in a million years,' Vanion added.

'How did you sprain your ankle, Lord Vanion?' Berit asked.

'I was proving a point. I advised the Council of Styricum that the young men of Sarsos were in extremely poor physical condition. I had to demonstrate by outrunning the whole bloody town. I was doing fairly well until I stepped in that rabbit-hole.'

'That's a real shame, Lord Vanion,' Kalten said. 'As far as I know, that's the first contest you ever lost.'

'Who said I lost? I was far enough ahead and close enough to the finish line that I was able to hobble on and win. The Council's going to at least *think* about some military training for the young men.' He glanced at

303

Sparhawk's squire. 'Hello, Khalad,' he said. 'How are your mothers?'

'Quite well, my Lord. We stopped by to see them when we were taking the queen to Chyrellos so that she could turn the Archprelate over her knee and spank him.'

'Khalad!' Ehlana protested.

'Wasn't I supposed to say that, your Majesty? We all thought that's what you had in mind when we left Cimmura.'

'Well – sort of, I guess – but you're not supposed to come right out and say it like that.'

'Oh, I didn't know that. I thought it was sort of a good idea, myself. Our Holy Mother needs to have something to worry about now and then. It keeps her out of mischief.'

'Astonishing, Khalad,' Patriarch Emban murmured dryly. 'You've managed to insult both Church and State in under a minute.'

'What's been going on in Eosia since I left?' Vanion demanded.

'It was just a small misunderstanding between Sarathi and me, my Lord Vanion,' Ehlana replied. 'Khalad was exaggerating. He does that quite often – when he's not busy insulting the Church and State at the same time.'

'We may just have another Sparhawk coming up here,' Vanion grinned.

'God defend the Church,' Emban said.

'And the crown,' Ehlana added.

Princess Danae pushed her way through to Vanion. She was carrying Mmrr, her hand wrapped around the kitten's middle. Mmrr, had a resigned expression on her furry face, and her legs dangled ungracefully. 'Hello, Vanion,' Danae said, climbing up into his lap and giving him an offhand sort of kiss.

'You've grown, Princess,' he smiled.

'Did you expect me to shrink?'

'*Danae!*' Ehlana scolded.

'Oh, mother, Vanion and I are old friends. He used to hold me when I was a baby.'

Sparhawk looked carefully at his friend, trying to decide whether or not Vanion knew about the little princess. Vanion's face, however, revealed nothing. 'I've missed you, Princess,' he said to her.

'I know. Everybody misses me when I'm not around. Have you met Mmrr yet? She's my cat. Talen gave her to me. Wasn't that nice of him?'

'Very nice, Danae.'

'I thought so myself. Father's going to put him in training when we get home. It's probably just as well to get that all done while I'm still a little girl.'

'Oh? Why's that, Princess?'

'Because I'm going to marry him when I grow up, and I'd like to have all that training nonsense out of the way. Would you like to hold my cat?'

Talen blushed and laughed a bit nervously, trying to pass off Danae's announcement as some sort of little-girl whim. His eyes looked a bit wild, however.

'You should never warn them like that, Princess,' Baroness Melidere advised. 'You're supposed to wait and tell them at the last possible minute.'

'Oh. Is that the way it's done?' Danae looked at Talen. 'Why don't you forget what I just said then?' she suggested. 'I'm not going to do anything about it for the next ten or twelve years anyway.' She paused. 'Or eight, maybe. There's no real point in wasting time, is there?'

Talen was staring at her with the first faint hints of terror in his eyes.

'She's only teasing you, Talen,' Kalten assured the boy. 'And even if she isn't, I'm sure she'll change her mind before she gets to the dangerous age.'

'Never happen, Kalten,' Danae told him in a voice like steel.

That evening, after arrangements had been made and the crowd had been mostly dispersed to nearby houses, Sparhawk sat in the cool garden at the centre of the house with Sephrenia and Vanion. Princess Danae sat on the ledge surrounding the fountain watching her kitten. Mmrr had discovered that there were goldfish swimming in the pool, and she sat with her tail twitching and her eyes wide with dreadful intent.

'I need to know something before I start,' Sparhawk said, looking directly at Sephrenia. 'How much does he know?' He pointed at Vanion.

'Just about everything, I'd say. I have no secrets from him.'

'That's not too specific, Sephrenia.' Sparhawk groped for a way to ask the question without revealing too much.

'Oh, *do* get to the point, Sparhawk,' Danae told him. 'Vanion knows who I am. He had a little trouble with it at first, but he's more or less reconciled to the idea now.'

'That's not entirely true,' Vanion disagreed. 'You're the one with the really serious problems though, Sparhawk. How are you managing the situation?'

'Badly,' Danae sniffed. 'He keeps asking questions, even though he knows he won't understand the answers.'

'Does Ehlana suspect?' Vanion asked seriously.

'Of course she doesn't,' the Child Goddess replied. 'Sparhawk and I decided that right at the beginning. Tell them what's been happening, Sparhawk – and don't be all night about it. Mirtai's bound to come looking for me soon.'

'It must be pure hell,' Vanion said sympathetically to his friend.

'Not entirely. I have to watch her, though. Once she had a swarm of fairies pollinating all the flowers in the palace garden.'

'The bees are too slow,' she shrugged.

'Maybe so, but people expect the bees to do it. If you turn the job over to the fairies, there's bound to be talk.' Sparhawk leaned back and looked at Vanion. 'Sephrenia's told you about the Lamorks and Drychtnath, hasn't she?'

'Yes. It's not just wild stories, is it?'

Sparhawk shook his head. 'No. We encountered some bronze-age Lamorks outside of Demos. After Ulath brained their leader, they all vanished – except for the dead. Oscagne's convinced that it's a diversion of some kind – rather like the games Martel was playing to keep us out of Chyrellos during the election of the Archprelate. We've been catching glimpses of Krager, and that lends some weight to Oscagne's theory, but you always taught us that it's a mistake to try to fight the last war over again, so I'm not locking myself into the idea that what's happening in Lamorkand is purely diversionary. I can't really accept the notion that somebody would go to all that trouble to keep the Church Knights out of Tamuli – not with the Atans already here.'

Vanion nodded. 'You're going to need someone to help you when you get to Matherion, Sparhawk. Tamul culture's very subtle, and you could make some colossal blunders without even knowing it.'

'Thanks, Vanion.'

'You're not the only one, though. Your companions aren't the most diplomatic men in the world, and Ehlana tends to jump fences when she gets excited. Did she *really* go head to head with Dolmant?'

'Oh, yes,' Danae said. 'I had to kiss them both into submission before I could make peace between them.'

'Who'd be the best to send, Sephrenia?' Vanion asked.

307

'Me.'

'That's out of the question. I won't be separated from you again.'

'That's very sweet, dear one. Why don't you come along then?'

He seemed to hesitate. 'I –'

'Don't be such a goose, Vanion,' Danae told him. 'You won't die the minute you leave Sarsos – any more than you did when you left my island. You're completely cured now.'

'I wasn't worried about that,' he told her, 'but Sephrenia can't leave Sarsos anyway. She's a member of the Council of Styricum.'

'I've been a member of the Council of Styricum for several centuries, Vanion,' Sephrenia told him. 'I've left here before – for long periods of time on occasion. The other members of the Council understand. They've all had to do the same thing themselves now and then.'

'I'm a little vague on this ruling council,' Sparhawk admitted. 'I knew that Styrics kept in touch with each other, but I hadn't realised it was quite so well-knit.'

'We don't make an issue of it,' Sephrenia shrugged. 'If the Elenes knew about it, they'd try to make some huge conspiracy out of it.'

'Your membership on the council keeps coming up,' Sparhawk noted. 'Is this council really relevant, or is it just some sort of ceremonial body?'

'Oh, no, Sparhawk,' Vanion told him. 'The council's very important. Styricum's a Theocracy, and the council's composed of the high priests – and priestesses – of the Younger Gods.'

'Being Aphrael's priestess isn't really a very taxing position,' Sephrenia smiled, looking fondly at the Child Goddess. 'She's not particularly interested in asserting herself, since she usually gets what she wants in other ways. I get certain advantages – like this house – but I

308

have to sit in on the meetings of the Thousand, and that can be tedious sometimes.'

'The Thousand?'

'It's another name for the Council.'

'There are a thousand Younger Gods?' Sparhawk was a bit surprised at that.

'Well, of *course* there are, Sparhawk,' Aphrael told him. 'Everybody knows that.'

'Why a thousand?'

'It's a nice number with a nice sound to it. In Styric it's *Ageraluon*.'

'I'm not familiar with the word.'

'It means ten times ten times ten – sort of. We had quite an argument with one of my cousins about it. He had a pet crocodile, and it had bitten off one of his fingers. He always had trouble counting after that. He wanted us to be *Ageralican* – nine times nine times nine, but we explained to him that there were already more of us than that, and that if we wanted to be *Ageralican*, some of us would have to be obliterated. We asked him if he'd care to volunteer to be one of them, and he dropped the idea.'

'Why would anyone want to have a pet crocodile?'

'It's one of the things we do. We like to make pets of animals you humans can't control. Crocodiles aren't so bad. At least you don't have to feed them.'

'No, but you have to count the children every morning. Now I understand why the question of whales keeps coming up.'

'You're really very stubborn about that, Sparhawk. I could really impress my family if I had a whale.'

'I think we're getting a little far afield,' Vanion said. 'Sephrenia tells me you've got some fairly exotic suspicions.'

'I've been trying to explain something I can't completely see yet, Vanion. It's like trying to describe a horse when all you've to work with is his tail. I've got a lot of bits and pieces and not too much more. I'm positive that everything that we've seen so far – and probably a lot of things we haven't – are all hooked together, and that there's one intelligence guiding it all. I think it's a God, Vanion – or Gods.'

'Are you sure your encounter with Azash didn't make you start seeing hostile divinities under beds and in dark closets?'

'I have it on the very best authority that only a God could raise an entire army out of the past. The authority who told me was quite smug about it.'

'Be nice, father,' Danae said primly. 'It's too complex, Vanion,' she explained. 'When you raise an army, you have to raise each individual soldier, and you have to know everything about him when you do that. It's the details that defeat human magicians when they try it.'

'Any ideas?' Vanion asked his friend.

'Several,' Sparhawk grunted, 'and none of them very pleasant. Do you remember that shadow I told you about? The one that was following me all over Eosia after I killed Ghwerig?'

Vanion nodded.

'We've been seeing it again, and this time *everybody* can see it.'

'That doesn't sound too good.'

'No, it doesn't. Last time, that shadow was the Troll-Gods.'

Vanion shuddered, and then the both of them looked at Sephrenia.

'Isn't it nice to be needed?' Danae said to her sister.

'I'll talk with Zalasta,' Sephrenia sighed. 'He's been keeping abreast of things here in Sarsos for the emperor. He probably knows a great deal about this, so I'll have him stop by tomorrow.'

There was a loud splash.

'I told you that was going to happen, Mmrr,' Danae said smugly to the wild-eyed kitten struggling to stay afloat in the fountain. Mmrr's problems were multiplied by the fact that the goldfish were ferociously defending their domain by bumping her paws and tummy with their noses.

'Fish her out, Danae,' Sparhawk told her.

'She'll get me all wet, father, and then mother will scold me. Mmrr got herself into that fix. Now let her get herself out.'

'She'll drown.'

'Oh, of course she won't, Sparhawk. She knows how to swim. Look at her. She's cat-paddling for all she's worth.'

'She's *what*?'

'Cat-paddling. You couldn't really call it dog-paddling, could you? She's not a dog, after all. We Styrics talk about cat-paddling all the time, don't we, Sephrenia?'

'*I* never have,' Sephrenia murmured.

CHAPTER 17

A large part of the fun came from the fact that her parents could not anticipate the Princess Danae's early-morning visits. They were certainly not a daily occurrence, and there were times when a whole week would go by without one. This morning's visit was, of course, the same as all the rest. Consistency is one of the more important divine attributes. The door banged open, and the princess, her black hair flying and her eyes filled with glee, dashed into the room and joined her parents in bed with a great, whooping leap. The leap was followed, as always, by a great deal of squirming and burrowing until Danae was firmly nestled between her parents.

She never paid these visits alone. Rollo had never really been a problem. Rollo was a well-mannered toy, anxious to please and almost never intrusive. Mmrr, on the other hand, could be a pest. She was quite fond of Sparhawk and she was a genius at burrowing. Having a sharp-clawed kitten climb up the side of one's bare leg before one is fully awake is a startling experience. Sparhawk gritted his teeth and endured.

'The birds are awake.' Danae announced it almost accusingly.

'I'm so happy for them,' Sparhawk said, wincing as the kitten lurking beneath the covers began to rhythmically flex her claws in his hip.

'You're grumpy this morning, father.'

'I was doing just fine until now. Please ask your cat not to use me for a pin-cushion.'

'She does it because she loves you.'

'That fills my heart. I'd still rather have her keep her claws to herself, though.'

'Is he always like this in the morning, mother?'

'Sometimes,' Ehlana laughed, embracing the little girl. 'I think it depends on what he had for supper.'

Mmrr began to purr. Adult cats purr with a certain decorous moderation. Kittens don't. On this particular morning, Danae's small cat sounded much like an approaching thunderstorm or a grist-mill with an off-centre wheel.

'I give up,' Sparhawk said. He threw back the covers, climbed out of bed and pulled on a robe. 'There's no sleeping with the three of you around,' he accused them. 'Coming, Rollo?'

His wife and daughter gave him a quick, startled glance then exchanged a worried look. Sparhawk scooped up Danae's stuffed toy and ambled out of the room, holding it by one hind leg. He could hear Ehlana and Danae whispering as he left. He plumped the toy into a chair. 'It's absolutely impossible, Rollo, old boy,' he said, making sure that his women-folk could hear him. 'I don't know how you can stand it.'

There was a profound silence from the bedroom.

'I think you and I should go away for a while, my friend,' Sparhawk went on. 'They're starting to treat us like pieces of furniture.'

Rollo didn't say anything, but then Rollo seldom did.

Sephrenia, who was standing in the doorway, however, seemed a bit startled. 'Aren't you feeling well, Sparhawk?'

'I'm fine, little mother. Why do you ask?' He hadn't really expected anyone to witness a performance intended primarily for his wife and daughter.

'You *do* realise that you're talking to a stuffed toy, don't you?'

Sparhawk stared at Rollo in mock surprise. 'Why, I believe you're right, Sephrenia. How strange that I didn't notice that. Maybe it has something to do with being rousted out of bed at the crack of dawn.' No matter how hard he tried to put a good face on this, it wasn't going to go very well.

'What on earth are you talking about, Sparhawk?'

'You see, Rollo?' Sparhawk said, trying to rescue *something*. 'They just don't understand – any of them.'

'Ah – Prince Sparhawk?' It was Ehlana's maid Alean. She had come into the room unnoticed, and her huge eyes were concerned. 'Are you all right?'

Things were deteriorating all around Sparhawk. 'It's a long, long story, Alean,' he sighed.

'Have you seen the princess, my Lord?' Alean was looking at him strangely.

'She's in bed with her mother.' There was really not much left for him to salvage from the situation. 'I'm going to the bath-house – if anybody cares.' And he stalked from the room with the tatters of his dignity trailing along behind him.

Zalasta the Styric was an ascetic-looking man with white hair and a long, silvery beard. He had the angular, uncompleted-looking face of all Styric men, shaggy black eyebrows and a deep, rich voice. He was Sephrenia's oldest friend, and was generally conceded to be the wisest and most powerful magician in Styricum. He wore a white, cowled robe and carried a staff, which may have been an affectation, since he was quite vigorous and did not need any aid when he walked. He spoke the Elenic language very well, although with a heavy Styric accent. They gathered that morning in Sephrenia's interior garden to hear the details of what was really going on in Tamuli.

'We can't be entirely positive if they're real or not,'

Zalasta was saying. 'The sightings have been random and very fleeting.'

'They're definitely Trolls, though?' Tynian asked him.

Zalasta nodded. 'No other creature looks quite like a Troll.'

'That's God's own truth,' Ulath murmured. 'The sightings could very well have been of real Trolls. Some time back they all just packed up and left Thalesia. Nobody ever thought to stop one to ask him why.'

'There have also been sightings of Dawn-men,' Zalasta reported.

'What are they, learned one?' Patriarch Emban asked him.

'Man-like creatures from the beginning of time, your Grace. They're a bit bigger than Trolls, but not as intelligent. They roam in packs, and they're very savage.'

'We've met them, friend Zalasta,' Kring said shortly. 'I lost many comrades that day.'

'There may not be a connection,' Zalasta continued. 'The Trolls are contemporary creatures, but the Dawn-men definitely come from the past. Their species has been extinct for some fifty aeons. There have also been some unconfirmed reports of sightings of Cyrgai.'

'You can mark that down as confirmed, Zalasta,' Kalten told him. 'They provided us with some entertainment one night last week.'

'They were fearsome warriors,' Zalasta said.

'They might have impressed their contemporaries,' Kalten disagreed, 'but modern tactics and weapons and equipment are a bit beyond their capabilities. Catapults and the charge of armoured knights seemed to baffle them.'

'Just exactly who *are* the Cyrgai, learned one?' Vanion asked.

'I gave you the scrolls, Vanion,' Sephrenia said. 'Didn't you read them?'

'I haven't got that far yet. Styric's a difficult language to read. Somebody should give some thought to simplifying your alphabet.'

'Hold it,' Sparhawk interrupted. He looked at Sephrenia. 'I've never seen you read anything,' he accused her. 'You wouldn't let Flute even touch a book.'

'Not an Elene book, no.'

'Then you *can* read?'

'In Styric, yes.'

'Why didn't you tell us?'

'Because it wasn't really any of your business, dear one.'

'You *lied!*' That shocked him for some reason.

'No, as a matter of fact I didn't. I *can't* read Elene – largely because I don't want to. It's a graceless language, and your writings are ugly – like spiders' webs.'

'You deliberately led us to believe that you were too simple to learn how to read.'

'That was sort of necessary, dear one. Pandion novices aren't really very sophisticated, and you had to have *something* to feel superior about.'

'Be nice,' Vanion murmured.

'I had to try to train a dozen generations of those great, clumsy louts, Vanion,' she said with a certain asperity, 'and I had to put up with their insufferable condescension in the process. Yes, Sparhawk, I *can* read, and I *can* count, and I *can* argue philosophy and even theology if I have to, and I *am* fully trained in logic.'

'I don't know why you're yelling at *me*,' he protested mildly, kissing her palms. 'I've always believed you were a fairly nice lady –' he kissed her palms again, 'for a Styric, that is.'

She jerked her hands out of his grasp and then saw the grin on his face. 'You're impossible,' she said, also suddenly smiling.

'We were talking about the Cyrgai, I believe,' Stragen said smoothly. 'Just exactly who are they?'

'They're extinct, fortunately,' Zalasta replied. 'They were of a race that appears to have been unrelated to the other races of Daresia – neither Tamul nor Elene, and certainly not Styric. Some have suggested that they might be distantly related to the Valesians.'

'I couldn't accept that, learned one,' Oscagne disagreed. 'The Valesians don't even have a government, and they have no concept of war. They're the happiest people in the world. They could not in any way be related to the Cyrgai.'

'Temperament is sometimes based on climate, your Excellency,' Zalasta pointed out. 'Valesia's a paradise, and central Cynesga's not nearly so nice. Anyway, the Cyrgai worshipped a hideous God named Cyrgon – and, like most primitive people do, they took their name from him. All peoples are egotistical, I suppose. We're all convinced that *our* God is better than all the rest and that *our* race is superior. The Cyrgai took that to extremes. We can't really probe the beliefs of an extinct people, but it appears that they even went so far as to believe that they were somehow of a different species from other humans. They also believed that all truth had been revealed to them by Cyrgon, so they strongly resisted new ideas. They carried the idea of a warrior society to absurd lengths, and they were obsessed with the concept of racial purity and strove for physical perfection. Deformed babies were taken out into the desert and left to die. Soldiers who received crippling injuries in battle were killed by their friends. Women who had too many female children were strangled. They built a city-state beside the Oasis of Cyrga in Central Cynesga and rigidly isolated themselves from other peoples and their ideas. The Cyrgai were terribly afraid of ideas. Theirs was perhaps the only culture in human history that idealised stupidity. They looked upon superior intelligence as a defect, and overly bright children were killed.'

'Nice group,' Talen murmured.

'They conquered and enslaved their neighbours, of course – mostly desert nomads of indeterminate race – and there was a certain amount of interbreeding, soldiers being what they are.'

'But that was perfectly all right, wasn't it?' Baroness Melidere added tartly. 'Rape is always permitted, isn't it?'

'In this case it wasn't, Baroness,' Zalasta replied. 'Any Cyrgai caught "fraternising" was killed on the spot.'

'What a refreshing idea,' she murmured.

'So was the woman, of course. Despite all their best efforts, however, the Cyrgai *did* produce a number of offspring of mixed race. In their eyes, that was an abomination, and the half-breeds were killed whenever possible. In time, however, Cyrgon apparently had a change of heart. He saw a use for these half-breeds. They were given some training and became a part of the army. They were called "Cynesgans", and in time they came to comprise that part of the army that did all of the dirty work and most of the dying. Cyrgon had a goal, you see – the usual goal of the militaristically inclined.'

'World domination?' Vanion suggested.

'Precisely. The Cynesgans were encouraged to breed, and the Cyrgai used them to expand their frontiers. They soon controlled all of the desert and began pushing at the frontiers of their neighbours. That's where *we* encountered them. The Cyrgai weren't really prepared to come up against Styrics.'

'I can imagine,' Tynian laughed.

Zalasta smiled briefly. It was an indulgent sort of smile, faintly tinged with a certain condescension. 'The priests of Cyrgon had certain limited gifts,' the Styric

318

went on, 'but they were certainly no match for what they encountered.' He sat tapping his fingertips together. 'Perhaps when we examine it more closely, that's our real secret,' he mused. 'Other peoples have only one God – or at the most, a small group of Gods. We have a thousand, who more or less get along with each other and agree in a general sort of way about what ought to be done. Anyway, the incursion of the Cyrgai into the lands of the Styrics proved to be disastrous for them. They lost virtually all of their Cynesgans and a major portion of their full-blooded Cyrgai. They retreated in absolute disorder, and the Younger Gods decided that they ought to be encouraged to stay at home after that. No one knows to this day which of the Younger Gods developed the idea, but it was positively brilliant in both its simplicity and its efficacy. A large eagle flew completely around Cynesga in a single day, and his shadow left an unseen mark on the ground. The mark means absolutely nothing to the Cynesgans or the Atans or Tamuls or Styrics or Elenes or even the Arjuni. It was terribly important to the Cyrgai, however, because after that day any Cyrgai who stepped over that line died instantly.'

'Wait a minute,' Kalten objected. 'We encountered Cyrgai just to the west of here. How did they get across the line?'

'They were from the past, Sir Kalten,' Zalasta explained, spreading his hands. 'The line didn't exist for them, because the eagle had not yet made his flight when they marched north.'

Kalten scratched his head and sat frowning. 'I'm not really all that good at logic,' he confessed, 'but isn't there a hole in that somewhere?'

Bevier was also struggling with it. 'I *think* I see how it works,' he said a little dubiously, 'but I'll have to go over it a few times to be sure.'

319

'Logic can't answer *all* the questions, Sir Bevier,' Emban advised. He hesitated. 'You don't have to tell Dolmant I said that, of course,' he added.

'It may be that the enchantment's no longer in force,' Sephrenia suggested to Zalasta. 'There's no real need for it, since the Cyrgai are extinct.'

'And no way to prove it either,' Ulath added, 'one way or the other.'

Stragen suddenly laughed. 'He's right, you know,' he said. 'There might very well be this dreadful curse out there that nobody even knows about because the people it's directed at all died out thousands of years ago. What finally happened to them, learned one?' he asked Zalasta. 'You said that they were extinct.'

'Actually, Milord Stragen, they bred themselves out of existence.'

'Isn't that a contradiction?' Tynian asked him.

'Not really. The Cynesgans had been very nearly wiped out, but now they were of vital importance, since they were the only troops at Cyrgon's disposal who could cross the frontiers. He directed the Cyrgai to concentrate on breeding up new armies of these formerly despised underlings. The Cyrgai were perfect soldiers who always obeyed orders to the letter. They devoted their attention to the Cynesgan women even to the exclusion of their own. By the time they realised their mistake, all the Cyrgai women were past child-bearing age. Legend had it that the last of the Cyrgai died about ten thousand years ago.'

'That raises idiocy to an art-form, doesn't it?' Stragen observed.

Zalasta smiled a thin sort of smile. 'At any rate, what used to be Cyrga is now Cynesga. It's occupied by a defective, mongrel race that manages to survive only because it sits astride the major trade routes between the Tamuls of the east and the Elenes of the west. The rest of the world looks upon these heirs of the invincible Cyrgai with the deepest contempt. They're sneaky, cowardly, thieving and disgustingly servile – a fitting fate for the offspring of a race that once thought it was divinely destined to rule the world.'

'History's such a gloomy subject,' Kalten sighed.

'Cynesga's not the only place where the past is returning to haunt us,' Zalasta added.

'We've noticed,' Tynian replied. 'The Elenes in western Astel are all convinced that Ayachin's returned.'

'Then you've heard of the one they call Sabre?' Zalasta asked.

'We ran across him a couple of times,' Stragen laughed. 'I don't think he poses much of a threat. He's an adolescent poseur.'

'He satisfies the needs of the western Astels, though,' Tynian added. 'They're not exactly what you'd call deep.'

'I've encountered them,' Zalasta said wryly. 'Kimear of Daconia and Baron Parok, his spokesman, are a bit more serious, though. Kimear was one of those men on horseback who emerge from time to time in Elene societies. He subdued the other two Elene Kingdoms in western Astel and founded one of those empires of a thousand years that spring up from time to time and promptly fall apart when the founder dies. The hero in Edom is Incetes – a bronze-age fellow who actually managed to hand to Cyrgai their first defeat. The one who does his talking for him calls himself Rebal. That's not his real name, of course. Political agitators usually go by assumed names. Ayachin, Kimear and Incetes appeal to the very simplest of Elene emotional responses – muscularity, primarily. I wouldn't offend you for the world, my friends, but you Elenes seem to like to break things and burn down other people's houses.'

'It's a racial flaw,' Ulath conceded.

'The Arjuni present us with slightly different problems,' Zalasta continued. 'They're members of the Tamul race, and their deep-seated urges are a bit more sophisticated. Tamuls don't want to rule the world, they just want to own it.' He smiled briefly at Oscagne. 'The Arjuni aren't very attractive as representatives of the race, though. Their hero is the fellow who invented the slave-trade.'

Mirtai's breath hissed sharply, and her hand went to her dagger.

'Is there some problem, Atana?' Oscagne asked her mildly.

'I've had experience with the slave-traders of Arjuna, Oscagne,' she replied shortly. 'Someday I hope to have more, and I won't be a child this time.'

Sparhawk realised that Mirtai had never told them the story of how she had become a slave.

'This Arjuni hero's of a somewhat more recent vintage than the others,' Zalasta continued. 'He was of the twelfth century. His name was Sheguan.'

'We've heard of him,' Engessa said bleakly. 'His slavers used to raid the training camps of Atan children. We've more or less persuaded the Arjuni not to do that any more.'

'That sounds ominous,' Baroness Melidere said.

'It was an absolute disaster, Baroness,' Oscagne told her. 'Some Arjuni slavers made a raid into Atan in the seventeenth century, and an imperial administrator got carried away by an excess of righteous indignation. He authorised the Atans to mount a punitive expedition into Arjuna.'

'Our people still sing songs about it,' Engessa said in an almost dreamy fashion.

'Bad?' Emban asked Oscagne.

'Unbelievable,' Oscagne replied. 'The silly ass who

authorised the expedition didn't realise that when you command the Atans to do something, you have to specifically prohibit certain measures. The fool simply turned them loose. They actually hanged the King of Arjuna himself and then chased all his subjects into the southern jungles. It took us nearly two hundred years to coax the Arjuni down out of the trees. The economic upheaval was a disaster for the entire continent.'

'These events are somewhat more recent,' Zalasta noted. 'The Arjuni have always been slavers, and Sheguan was only one of several operating in northern Arjuna. He was an organiser more than anything. He established the markets in Cynesga and codified the bribes that protect the slave-routes. The peculiar thing we face in Arjuna is that the spokesman's more important than the hero. His name is Scarpa, and he's a brilliant and dangerous man.'

'What about Tamul itself?' Emban asked, 'and Atan?'

'We both seem to be immune to the disease, your Grace,' Oscagne replied. 'It's probably because Tamuls are too egotistical for hero worship and because the Atans of antiquity were all so much shorter than their descendants that modern Atans overlook them.' He smiled rather slyly at Engessa. 'The rest of the world's breathlessly awaiting the day when the first Atan tops ten feet. I think that's the ultimate goal of their selective breeding campaign.' He looked at Zalasta. 'Your information's far more explicit than ours, learned one,' he complimented the Styric. 'The best efforts of the empire have unearthed only the sketchiest of details about these people.'

'I have different resources at my disposal, Excellency,' Zalasta replied. 'These figures from antiquity, however, would hardly be of any real concern. The Atans could quite easily deal with any purely military insurrection, but this isn't a totally military situation. Someone's been winnowing through the darker aspects of human imagination and spinning the horrors of folk-lore out of thin air. There are vampires and werewolves, ghouls, Ogres and once even a thirty-foot giant. The officials shrug these sightings off as superstitious nonsense, but the common people of Tamuli are in a state of abject terror. We can't be certain of the reality of *any* of these things, but when you mingle monsters with Trolls, Dawn-men and Cyrgai, you have total demoralisation. Then, to push the whole thing over the edge, the forces of nature have been harnessed as well. There have been titanic thunderstorms, tornadoes, earthquakes, volcanic eruptions and even isolated eclipses. The common people of Tamuli have become so fearful that they flee from rabbits and flocks of sparrows. There's no real focus to these incidents. They simply occur at random, and since there's no real plan behind them, there's no way to predict when and where they'll occur. That's what we're up against, my friends – a continent-wide campaign of terror – part reality, part illusion, part genuine magic. If it isn't countered – and very, very soon – the people will go mad with fear. The empire will collapse, and the terror will reign supreme.'

'And what was the *bad* news you had for us, Zalasta?' Vanion asked him.

Zalasta smiled briefly. 'You are droll, Lord Vanion,' he said. 'You may be able to gather more information this afternoon, my friends,' he told them all. 'You've been invited to attend the session of the Thousand. Your visit here is quite significant from a political point of view, and – although the council seldom agrees about anything – there's a strong undercurrent of opinion that we may have a common cause with you in this matter.' He paused, then sighed. 'I think you should be prepared for a certain amount of antagonism,' he cautioned. 'There's a reactionary faction in the council that begins

324

to foam at the mouth whenever someone even mentions the word "Elene". I'm sure they'll try to provoke you.'

'Something's happening that I don't understand, Sparhawk,' Danae murmured quietly a bit later. Sparhawk had retired to one corner of Sephrenia's little garden with one of Vanion's Styric scrolls and had been trying to puzzle out the Styric alphabet. Danae had found him there and had climbed up into his lap.

'I thought you were all-wise,' he said. 'Isn't that supposed to be one of your characteristics?'

'Stop that. Something's terribly wrong here.'

'Why don't you talk with Zalasta about it? He's one of your worshippers, isn't he?'

'Whatever gave you that idea?'

'I thought you and he and Sephrenia grew up together in the same village.'

'What's that got to do with it?'

'I just assumed that the villagers all worshipped you. It's sort of logical that you'd choose to be born in a village of your own adherents.'

'You don't understand Styrics at all, do you? That's the most tedious idea I've ever heard of – a whole village of people who all worship the same God? How boring.'

'Elenes do it.'

'Elenes eat pigs too.'

'What have you got against pigs?'

She shuddered.

'Who *does* Zalasta worship if he's not one of your adherents?'

'He hasn't chosen to tell us, and it's terribly impolite to ask.'

'How did he get to be a member of the Thousand then? I thought you had to be a high priest to qualify for membership.'

'He isn't a member. He doesn't want to be. He advises

them.' She pursed her lips. 'I really shouldn't say this, Sparhawk, but don't expect exalted wisdom from the council. High priests are devout, but that doesn't require wisdom. Some of the Thousand are frighteningly stupid.'

'Can you get any kind of clue about which God might be at the bottom of all these disturbances?'

'No. Whoever it is doesn't want any of the rest of us to know his identity, and there are ways we can conceal ourselves. About all I can say is that he's not Styric. Pay very close attention at the meeting this afternoon, Sparhawk. My temperament's Styric, and there may be things I'd overlook just because I'm so used to them.'

'What do you want me to look for?'

'I don't *know*. Use your rudimentary intuition. Look for false notes, lapses, any kind of clue hinting at the fact that someone's not entirely what he seems to be.'

'Do you suspect that there might be some member of the Thousand working for the other side?'

'I didn't say that. I just said that there's something wrong. I'm getting another of those premonitions like the one I had at Kotyk's house. Something's not what it's supposed to be here, and I can't for the life of me tell what it is. Try to find out what it is, Sparhawk. We really need to know.'

The council of the Thousand met in a stately marble building at the very centre of Sarsos. It was an imposing, even intimidating building that shouldered its way upward arrogantly. Like all public buildings, it was totally devoid of any warmth or humanity. It had wide, echoing marble corridors and huge bronze doors designed to make people feel tiny and insignificant.

The actual meetings took place in a large, semi-circular hall with tier upon tier of marble benches stair-stepping up the sides. There were ten of those tiers, naturally, and the seats on each tier were evenly spaced. It was all very logical. Architects are usually logical, since their buildings tend to collapse if they are not.

At Sephrenia's suggestion, Sparhawk and the other Elenes wore simple white robes to avoid those unpleasant associations in the minds of Styrics when they are confronted by armoured Elenes. The knights, however, wore chain-mail and swords under their robes.

The chamber was about half-full, since at any given time a part of the council was off doing other things. The members of the Thousand sat or strolled about talking quietly with each other. Some moved purposefully among their colleagues, talking earnestly. Others laughed and joked. Not a few were sleeping.

Zalasta led them to the front of the chamber where chairs had been placed for them in a kind of semi-circle.

'I have to take my seat,' Sephrenia told them quietly. 'Please don't take immediate action if someone insults you. There's several thousand years of resentment built up in this chamber, and some of it's bound to spill over.' She crossed the chamber to sit on one of the marble benches.

Zalasta stepped to the centre of the room and stood silently, making no attempt to call the assemblage to order. The traditional courtesies were obscure here. Gradually, the talking tapered off, and the Council members took their seats. 'If it please the Council,' Zalasta said in Styric, 'we are honoured today by the presence of important guests.'

'It certainly doesn't please *me*,' one member retorted. 'These "guests" appear to be Elenes for the most part, and I'm not all that interested in hob-nobbing with pig-eaters.'

'This promises to be moderately unpleasant,' Stragen

327

murmured. 'Our Styric cousins seem to be as capable of boorishness as we are.'

Zalasta ignored the ill-mannered speaker and continued. 'Sarsos is subject to the Tamul Empire,' he reminded them, 'and we benefit enormously from that relationship.'

'And the Tamuls make sure we pay for those benefits,' another member called.

Zalasta ignored that as well. 'I'm sure you'll all join with me in welcoming First Secretary Oscagne, the Chief of the Imperial Foreign Service.'

'I don't know what makes you so sure about that, Zalasta,' someone shouted with a raucous laugh.

Oscagne rose to his feet. 'I'm overwhelmed by this demonstration of affection,' he said dryly in perfect Styric.

There were cat-calls from the tiers of seats. The cat-calls died quite suddenly when Engessa rose to his feet and stood with his arms folded across his chest. He did not even bother to scowl at the unruly councillors.

'That's better,' Oscagne said. 'I'm glad that the legendary courtesy of the Styric people has finally asserted itself. If I may, I'll briefly introduce the members of our party, and then we'll place an urgent matter before you for your consideration.' He briefly introduced Patriarch Emban. An angry mutter swept through the chamber.

'That's directed at the Church, your Grace,' Stragen told him, 'not at you personally.'

When Oscagne introduced Ehlana, one council member on the top tier whispered a remark to those seated near him which elicited a decidedly vulgar laugh. Mirtai came to her feet like an uncoiling spring, her hands darting to her sheathed daggers.

Engessa said something sharply to her in the Tamul tongue.

She shook her head. Her eyes were blazing and her jaw was set. She drew a dagger. Mirtai may not have understood Styric, but she *did* understand the implications of that laugh.

Sparhawk rose to his feet. 'It's *my* place to respond, Mirtai,' he reminded her.

'You will not defer to me?'

'Not this time, no. I'm sorry, but it's a sort of formal occasion, so we should observe the niceties.' He turned to look up at the insolent Styric in the top row. 'Would you care to repeat what you just said a little louder, neighbour?' he asked in Styric. 'If it's so funny, maybe you should share it with us.'

'Well, what do you know,' the fellow sneered, 'a talking dog.'

Sephrenia rose to her feet. 'I call upon the Thousand to observe the traditional moment of silence,' she declared in Styric.

'Who died?' the loud-mouth demanded.

'You did, Camriel,' she told him sweetly, 'so our grief will not be excessive. This is Prince Sparhawk, the man who destroyed the Elder God Azash, and you've just insulted his wife. Did you want the customary burial – assuming that we can find enough of you to commit to the earth when he's done with you?'

Camriel's jaw had dropped, and his face had gone dead white. The rest of the Council also visibly shrank back.

'His name still seems to carry some weight,' Ulath noted to Tynian.

'Evidently. Our insolent friend up there seems to be having long, gloomy thoughts about mortality.'

'Councillor Camriel,' Sparhawk said quite formally, 'let us not interrupt the deliberations of the Thousand with a purely personal matter. I'll look you up after the meeting, and we can make the necessary arrangements.'

'What did he say?' Ehlana whispered to Stragen.

'The usual, your Majesty. I expect that Councillor Camriel's going to remember a pressing engagement on the other side of the world at any moment now.'

'Will the Council permit this barbarian to threaten me?' Camriel quavered.

A silvery-haired Styric on the far side of the room laughed derisively. 'You personally insulted a state visitor, Camriel,' he declared. 'The Thousand has no obligation to defend you under those circumstances. Your God has been very lax in your instruction. You're a boorish, loud-mouthed imbecile. We'll be well rid of you.'

'How *dare* you speak to me so, Michan?'

'You seem dazzled by the fact that one of the Gods is slightly fond of you, Camriel,' Michan drawled, 'and you overlook the fact that we all share that peculiar eminence here. My God loves me at least as much as your God loves you.' Michan paused. 'Probably more, actually. I'd guess that your God's having second thoughts about you at the moment. You must be a terrible embarrassment to him. But you're wasting valuable time. As soon as this meeting adjourns, I expect that Prince Sparhawk will come looking for you – with a knife. You *do* have a knife some place nearby, don't you, your Highness?'

Sparhawk grinned and opened his robe slightly to reveal his sword-hilt.

'Splendid, old fellow,' Michan said. 'I'd have been glad to lend you mine, but a man always works better with his own equipment. Haven't you left yet, Camriel? If you plan to live long enough to see the sun go down, you'd best get cracking.'

Councillor Camriel fled.

'What happened?' Ehlana demanded impatiently.

'If we choose to look at it in a certain light, we could

330

consider the Councillor's flight to be a form of apology,' Stragen told her.

'We do not accept apologies,' Mirtai said implacably. 'May I chase him down and kill him, Ehlana?'

'Why don't we just let him run for a while, Mirtai?' the queen decided.

'How long?'

'How long would you say he's likely to run, Milord?' Ehlana asked Stragen.

'The rest of his life probably, my Queen.'

'That sounds about right to me.'

The response of the Thousand to Zalasta's description of the current situation was fairly predictable, and the fact that all of the speeches showed evidence of much polishing hinted strongly that there had been few surprises in his presentation. The Thousand seemed to be divided into three factions. Predictably, there were a fair number of councillors who took the position that the Styrics could defend themselves and that they had no real reason to become involved. Styrics had strong suspicions where Elene promises were concerned, since Elene rulers tended to forget promises made to Styrics after a crisis had passed.

A second faction was more moderate. They pointed out the fact that the crisis here concerned the Tamuls rather than the Elenes, and that the presence of a small band of Church Knights from Eosia was really irrelevant. As the silvery-haired Michan pointed out, 'The Tamuls may not be our friends in every sense of the word, but at least they're not our enemies. Let's not overlook the fact that their Atans keep the Astels, the Edomish and the Dacites from our doorstep.' Michan was highly respected, and his opinion carried great weight in the council.

There was a third faction as well, a vocal minority so

rabidly anti-Elene that they even went so far as to suggest that the interests of Styricum might be better served by an alliance with the perpetrators of the outrages. Their speeches were not really intended to be taken seriously. The speakers had merely seized this opportunity to list long catalogues of grievances and to unleash diatribes of hatred and vituperation.

'This is starting to get tiresome,' Stragen finally said to Sparhawk, rising to his feet.

'What are you going to do?'

'Do? Why, I'm going to respond, old boy.' He stepped to the centre of the floor and stood resolutely in the face of their shouts and curses. The noise gradually subsided, more because those causing it had run out of things to say than because anyone was really curious about what this elegant blond Elene had to say. 'I'm delighted to discover that all men are equally contemptible,' Stragen told them, his rich voice carrying to every corner of the hall. 'I had despaired of ever finding a flaw in the Styric character, but I find that you're like all other men when you're gathered together into a mob. The outspoken and unconcealed bigotry you have revealed here this afternoon has lifted my despair and filled my heart with joy. I swoon with delight to find this cesspool of festering nastiness lurking in the Styric soul, since it proves once and for all that men are all the same, regardless of race.'

There were renewed shouts of protest. The protests were laced with curses this time.

Once again Stragen waited. 'I'm disappointed in you, my dear brothers,' he told them finally. 'An Elene child of seven could curse more inventively. Is this really the best the combined wisdom of Styricum can come up with? Is "Elene bastard" really all you know how to say? It doesn't even particularly insult me, because in my case it happens to be true.' He looked around, his expression urbane and just slightly superior. 'I'm also a thief and a murderer, and I have a large number of unsavoury habits. I've committed crimes for which there aren't even names, and you think your pallid, petty denunciations could distress me in any way? Does anyone have a meaningful accusation before I examine *your* failings?'

'You've enslaved us!' someone bellowed.

'Not me, old boy,' Stragen drawled. 'You couldn't *give* me a slave. You have to feed them, you know – even when they're not working. Now then, let's step right along here. We've established the fact that I'm a thief and a murderer and a bastard, but what are you? Would the word "snivellers" startle you? You Styrics whine a great deal. You've carefully stored up an inventory of the abuses you've suffered in the past several thousand years and you take a perverted pleasure in sitting in dark, smelly corners regurgitating them all, chewing them over and over like mouthfuls of stale vomit. You try to blame Elenes for all your troubles. Does it surprise you to discover that I feel no guilt about the plight of the Styrics? I have more than enough guilt for things I *have* done without beating my breast about things that happened a thousand years before I was born. Frankly, my friends, all these martyred expressions bore me. Don't you *ever* get tired of feeling sorry for yourselves? I'm now going to offend you even more by getting right to the point. If you want to snivel, do it in your own time. We're offering you the opportunity to join with us in facing a common enemy. It's just a courtesy, you understand, because we don't really need you. Keep that firmly in view. We don't need you. Actually, you'll encumber us. I've heard a few intellectual cripples here suggest an alliance with our enemy. What makes you think he'd *want* you as allies? The Elene peasantry would probably be overjoyed if you tried, though,

333

because that would give them an excuse to slaughter Styrics from here to the straits of Thalesia. Joining with us won't ensure a lessening of Elene prejudice, but joining with our enemies will almost guarantee that ten years from now there won't be a live Styric in any Elene kingdom in the world.'

He scratched thoughtfully at his chin and looked around. 'I guess that more or less covers everything,' he said. 'Why don't you talk it over amongst yourselves? My friends and I will be leaving for Matherion tomorrow. You might want to let us know what you've decided before we go. That's entirely up to you, of course. Words couldn't begin to express our indifference to the decisions of such an insignificant people.' He turned and offered his arm to Ehlana. 'Shall we leave, your Majesty?' he suggested.

'What did you say to them, Stragen?'

'I insulted them,' he shrugged, 'on as many levels as I possibly could. Then I threatened them with racial extinction and then invited them to sign on as allies.'

'All in one speech?'

'He was brilliant, your Majesty,' Oscagne said enthusiastically. 'He said some things to the Styrics that have needed saying for a long, long time.'

'I have certain advantages, your Excellency,' Stragen smiled. 'My character's so questionable that nobody expects me to be polite.'

'Actually, you're exquisitely courteous,' Bevier disagreed.

'I know, Sir Bevier, but people don't expect it of me, so they can't bring themselves to believe it.'

Both Sephrenia and Zalasta had icy, offended expressions on their faces that evening.

'I wasn't trying to be personally insulting,' Stragen assured them. 'I've heard any number of enlightened people say exactly the same thing. We sympathise with Styrics, but we find these interminable seizures of self-pity tedious.'

'You said many things that simply aren't true, you know,' Sephrenia accused him.

'Of course I did. It was a political speech, little mother. Nobody expects a politician to tell the truth.'

'You were really gambling, Milord Stragen,' Zalasta said critically. 'I nearly swallowed my tongue when you told them that the Elenes and the Tamuls were offering an alliance simply out of courtesy. When you told them that you didn't really need them, they might very well have decided to sit the whole affair out.'

'Not when he was holding all the rest of Styricum hostage, learned one,' Oscagne disagreed. 'It was a brilliant political speech. That not-so-subtle hint of the possibility of a new wave of Elene atrocities didn't really leave the Thousand any choice in the matter. What was the general reaction?'

'About what you'd expect, your Excellency,' Zalasta replied. 'Milord Stragen cut the ground out from under the Styric tradition of self-pity. It's very hard to play the martyr when you've just been told that it makes you look like a silly ass. There's a fit of towering resentment brewing among the Thousand. We Styrics are *terribly* fond of feeling sorry for ourselves, and that's been ruined now. No one ever really considered joining with the enemy – even if we knew who he was – but Stragen effectively bludgeoned us into going even further. Neutrality's out of the question now, since the Elene peasants would come to view neutrality as very nearly the same thing as actually joining with our unknown opponent. The Thousand will assist you, your Excellency. They'll do all they can do – if only to protect our brothers and sisters in Eosia.'

'You've put in a full day's work, Stragen,' Kalten said

admiringly. 'We could have been here for a month trying to persuade the Styrics that it was in their best interests to join us.'

'My day isn't finished yet,' Stragen told him, 'and the next group I have to try to persuade is much more hard-headed.'

'Might I be of some assistance?' Zalasta offered.

'I really rather doubt it, learned one. As soon as it gets dark, Talen and I have to pay a visit to the thieves of Sarsos.'

'There *are* no thieves in Sarsos, Stragen!'

Stragen and Talen looked at each other, and then they burst out with howls of cynical laughter.

'I just don't trust him, Sparhawk,' Ehlana said later that night when they were in bed. 'There's something about him that just doesn't ring true.'

'I think it's his accent, love. I felt the same way until I realised that while his Elene is perfect, his accent puts emphasis on the wrong words. Styric and Elene flow differently. Don't worry, though, Sephrenia would know if Zalasta weren't to be trusted. She's known him for a long, long time.'

'I still don't like him,' she insisted. 'He's so oily he gleams when the light hits him just right.' She raised one hand. 'And don't try to shrug it off as prejudice. I'm looking at Zalasta as a human being, not as a Styric. I just don't trust him.'

'That should pass after we get to know him better.'

There was a knock at the door. 'Are you busy?' Mirtai called. 'What would we be doing at this hour?' Ehlana called back impishly.

'Do you really want me to tell you, Ehlana? Talen's here. He has something you might want to know.'

'Send him in,' Sparhawk told her.

The door opened, and Talen came into the circle of

light of their single candle. 'It's just like old times, Sparhawk.'

'How so?'

'Stragen and I were coming back from our meeting with the thieves, and we saw Krager in the street. Can you believe that? It was good to see him again. I was actually starting to miss him.'

CHAPTER 18

'We simply don't have the time, Sparhawk,' Sephrenia said calmly.

'I'll *take* time, little mother,' he replied bleakly. 'It shouldn't take me too long. I'll stay here with Stragen, and we'll chase him down. Krager's not a Styric, so he shouldn't be hard to find. We can catch up with you after we've caught him and wrung every drop of information out of him. I'll squeeze him so hard that his hair will bleed.'

'And who's going to see to mother's safety while you're amusing yourself here, father?' Danae asked him.

'She's surrounded by an army, Danae.'

'*You're* her champion, father. Is that just some hollow title you can lay aside when something more amusing than protecting her life comes up?'

Sparhawk stared helplessly at his daughter. Then he slammed his fist against the wall in frustration.

'You'll break your hand,' Sephrenia murmured.

They were in the kitchen. Sparhawk had risen early and gone looking for his tutor to advise her of Talen's discovery and of his own plans to make Krager answer for a long, long list of transgressions. Danae's presence was really not all that surprising.

'Why didn't you rack him to death when you had your hands on him in Chyrellos, dear one?' Sephrenia asked calmly.

'*Sephrenia!*' Sparhawk was more startled by the cold-blooded way she said it than by the suggestion itself.

'Well, you should have, Sparhawk. Then he wouldn't

keep coming back to haunt us like this. You know what Ulath always says. Never leave a live enemy behind you.'

'You're starting to sound like an Elene, little mother.'

'Are you trying to be insulting?'

'Did banging your hand like that bring you to your senses, father?' Danae asked.

He sighed regretfully. 'You're right, of course,' he admitted. 'I guess I got carried away. Krager's continued existence offends me for some reason. He's a loose end with bits and pieces of Martel still hanging from him. I'd sort of like to tidy that part of my life up.'

'Can you really make somebody's hair bleed?' his daughter asked him.

'I'm not really sure. After I finally catch up with Krager, I'll let you know.' He nursed his sore knuckles. 'I guess we really should get on to Matherion. Sephrenia, just how healthy *is* Vanion, really?'

'Would you like a personal testimonial?' she asked him archly.

'That's none of my business, little mother. All I'm really asking is whether or not he's fit to travel.'

'Oh, yes,' she smiled. 'More than fit.'

'Good. I'll be delighted to hand the rewards and satisfactions of leadership back to him.'

'No. Absolutely not.'

'I beg your pardon?'

'Vanion carried that burden for too many years. That's what made him sick in the first place. You might as well accept the fact that you're the Pandion Preceptor now, Sparhawk. He'll advise you, certainly, but *you* get to make all the decisions. I'm not going to let you kill him.'

'Then you'll both be able to come with us to Matherion?'

'Of *course* they will, Sparhawk,' Danae told him. 'We decided that a long time ago.'

'It would have been nice if somebody'd thought to tell *me* about it.'

'Why? You don't have to know everything, father. Just do as we tell you to do.'

'What on earth ever possessed you to take up with this one, Sephrenia?' Sparhawk asked. 'Wasn't there *any* other God available – one of the Troll-Gods maybe?'

'*Sparhawk!*' Danae gasped.

He grinned at her.

'Zalasta will be coming with us as well,' Sephrenia said. 'He's been summoned back to Matherion anyway, and we really need his help.'

Sparhawk frowned. 'That might cause some problems, little mother. Ehlana doesn't trust him.'

'That's absolutely absurd, Sparhawk. I've known Zalasta all my life. I honestly think he'd die if I asked him to.'

'Has mother given you any reason for these suspicions?' Danae asked intently.

'Hate at first sight, maybe,' Sparhawk shrugged. 'His reputation as the wisest man in the world probably didn't help matters. She was probably predisposed to dislike him even before she met him.'

'And of course he's Styric.' There was a brittle edge to Sephrenia's voice.

'You know Ehlana better than that, Sephrenia. I think it's time we got you out of Sarsos. Some of the local opinions are starting to cloud your thinking.'

'Really?' Her tone was dangerous.

'It's very easy to dismiss any sort of animosity as simple prejudice, and that's the worst form of sloppy thinking. There are other reasons for disliking people too, you know. Do you remember Sir Antas?'

She nodded.

'I absolutely hated that man.'

'*Antas?* I thought he was your friend.'

'I couldn't stand him. My hands started to shake every time he came near me. Would you believe I was actually happy when Martel killed him?'

'*Sparhawk!*'

'You don't need to share that with Vanion, little mother. I'm not very proud of it. What I'm trying to say is that people sometimes hate us for personal reasons that have nothing at all to do with our race or class or anything else. Ehlana probably dislikes Zalasta just because she dislikes him. Maybe she doesn't like the way his eyebrows jut out. You should always consider the simplest explanation before you go looking for something exotic.'

'Is there anything else about me you'd like to change, Sir Knight?'

He looked her up and down gravely. 'You're really very small, you know. Have you ever considered growing just a bit?'

She almost retorted, but then she suddenly laughed. 'You can be the most disarming man in the world, Sparhawk.'

'I know. That's why people love me so much.'

'Now do you see why I'm so fond of these great Elene oafs?' Sephrenia said lightly to her sister.

'Of course,' Aphrael replied. 'It's because they're like big, clumsy puppies.' Her dark eyes grew serious. 'Not too many people know who I really am,' she mused. 'You two and Vanion are about the only ones who recognise me in this incarnation. I think it might be a good idea if we kept it that way. Our enemy – whoever he is – might make a slip or two if he doesn't know I'm around.'

'You'll want to tell Zalasta though, won't you?' Sephrenia asked her.

'Not yet, I don't think. He doesn't really need to

know, so let's just keep it to ourselves. When you trust someone, you're putting yourself in the position of also trusting everybody *he* trusts, and sometimes that includes people you don't even know. I'd rather not do that just yet.'

'She's growing very skilled at logic,' Sparhawk observed.

'I know,' Sephrenia sighed. 'She's fallen in with evil companions, I'm afraid.'

They left Sarsos later that morning, riding out through the east gate to be joined by the Church Knights, the Peloi and Engessa's two legions of Atans. The day was fair and warm, and the sky intensely blue. The newly-risen sun stood above the range of jagged, snow-capped peaks lying to the east. The peaks reared upward, and their soaring flanks were wrapped in the deep blue shadows of morning. The country lying ahead looked wild and rugged. Engessa was striding along beside Sparhawk, and his bronze face had a somewhat softer expression than it normally wore. He gestured toward the peaks. 'Atan, Sparhawk-Knight,' he said, 'my homeland.'

'A significant-looking country, Atan Engessa,' Sparhawk approved. 'How long have you been away?'

'Fifteen years.'

'That's a long exile.'

'It is indeed, Sparhawk-Knight.' Engessa glanced back at the carriage rolling along behind them. Zalasta had supplanted Stragen, and Mirtai, her face serene, sat holding Danae on her lap. 'We know each other, do we not, Sparhawk-Knight?' the Atan said.

'I'd say so,' Sparhawk agreed. 'Our people have many different customs, but we seem to have stepped around most of those.'

Engessa smiled slightly. 'You conducted yourself well

during our discussions concerning Atana Mirtai and Domi Kring.'

'Reasonable men can usually find reasons to get along with each other.'

'Elenes set great store in reason, do they not?'

'It's one of our quirks, I suppose.'

'I'll explain something about one of our customs to you, Sparhawk-Knight. I may not say it too clearly, because I am clumsy in your language. I'll rely on you to explain it to the others.'

'I'll do my very best, Atan Engessa.'

'Atana Mirtai will go through the Rite of Passage while she is in Atan.'

'I was fairly sure she would.'

'It is the custom of our people for the child to relive the memories of childhood before the rite, and it is important for her family to be present while that is done. I have spoken with Atana Mirtai, and her childhood was not happy. Many of her memories will be painful, and she will need those who love her near while she sets them aside. Will you tell Ehlana-Queen and the others what is happening?'

'I will, Engessa-Atan.'

'The Atana will come to you when she is ready. It is her right to choose those who will support her. Some of her choices may surprise you, but among my people, it is considered an honour to be chosen.'

'We will look upon it so, Engessa-Atan.'

Sparhawk briefly advised the others that Mirtai would be calling a meeting at a time of her own choosing, but he did not go into too much detail, since he himself did not know exactly what to expect.

That evening the Atan giantess moved quietly through the camp, her manner uncharacteristically diffident. She did not, as they might have expected, peremptorily command them to attend, but rather she

343

asked, one might almost say pleaded, and her eyes were very vulnerable. Most of her choices were the ones Sparhawk would have expected. They were the people who had been closest to Mirtai during her most recent enslavement. There were some surprises, however. She invited a couple of Pandions Sparhawk had not even known she was acquainted with as well as a couple of Kring's Peloi and two Atan girls from Engessa's legions. She also asked Emban and Oscagne to hear her story.

They gathered around a large fire that evening, and Engessa spoke briefly to them before Mirtai began. 'It is customary among our people for one to put childhood away before entering adulthood,' he told them gravely. 'Atana Mirtai will participate in the Rite of Passage soon, and she has asked us to be with her as she sets the past aside.' He paused, and his tone became reflective. 'This child is not like other Atan children,' he told them. 'For most, the childhood that is put away is simple and much like that of all others of our race. Atana Mirtai, however, returns from slavery. She has survived that and has returned to us. Her childhood has been longer than most and has contained things not usual – painful things. We will listen with love – even though we do not always understand.' He turned to Mirtai. 'It might be well to begin with the place where you were born, my daughter,' he suggested.

'Yes, Father-Atan,' she replied politely. Since Engessa had assumed the role of parent when they had first met, Mirtai's response was traditionally respectful. She spoke in a subdued voice that reflected none of her customary assertiveness. Sparhawk had the distinct impression that they were suddenly seeing a different Mirtai – a gentle, rather sensitive girl who had been hiding behind a brusque exterior.

'I was born in a village lying to the west of Dirgis,' she began, 'near the headwaters of the River Sarna.' She spoke in Elenic, since, with the exception of Oscagne, Engessa and the two Atan girls, none of her loved ones spoke Tamul. 'We lived deep in the mountains. My mother and father made much of that.' She smiled faintly. 'All Atans believe that they're special, but we mountain Atans believe that we're especially special. We're obliged to be the very best at everything we do, since we're so obviously superior to everybody else.' She gave them all a rather sly glance. Mirtai was very observant, and her offhand remark tweaked the collective noses of Styric and Elene alike. 'I spent my earliest years in the forests and mountains. I walked earlier than most and ran almost as soon as I could walk. My father was very proud of me, and he often said that I was born running. As is proper, I tested myself often. By the time I was five, I could run for half a day, and at six, from dawn until sunset.

'The children of our village customarily entered training very late – usually when we were nearly eight – because the training-camp in our district was very far away, and our parents did not want to be completely separated from us while we were still babies. Mountain Atans are very emotional. It's our one failing.'

'Were you happy, Atana?' Engessa asked her gently.

'Very happy, Father-Atan,' she replied. 'My parents loved me, and they were very proud of me. Ours was a small village with only a few children. I was the best, and my parents' friends all made much of me.'

She paused, and her eyes filled with tears. 'And then the Arjuni slavers came. They were armed with bows. They were only interested in the children, so they killed all of the adults. My mother was killed with the first arrow.'

Her voice broke at that point, and she lowered her head for a moment. When she raised her face, the tears were streaming down her cheeks.

345

Gravely, the Princess Danae went to her and held out her arms. Without apparently even thinking about it, Mirtai lifted the little girl up into her lap. Danae touched her tear-wet cheek and then softly kissed her.

'I didn't see my father die,' Mirtai continued. Her voice was choked, but then it rang out, and her tear-filled eyes hardened. 'I killed the first Arjuni who tried to capture me. They're ignorant people who can't seem to realise that children can be armed too. The Arjuni was holding a sword in his right hand, and he took my arm with his left. My dagger was very sharp, and it went in smoothly when I stabbed him under the arm with it. The blood came out of his mouth like a fountain. He fell back, and I stabbed him again, up under his breast-bone this time. I could feel his heart quivering on the point of my knife. I twisted the blade, and he died.'

'*Yes!*' Kring half-shouted. The Domi had been weeping openly, and his voice was hoarse and savage.

'I tried to run,' Mirtai went on, 'but another Arjuni kicked my feet out from under me and tried to grab my dagger. I cut the fingers off his right hand and stabbed him low in the belly. It took him two days to die, and he screamed the whole time. His screams comforted me.'

'*Yes!*' It was Kalten this time, and his eyes were also tear-filled.

The Atan girl gave him a brief, sad smile. 'The Arjuni saw that I was dangerous, so they knocked me senseless. When I woke up, I was in chains.'

'This all happened when you were only eight?' Ehlana asked the giantess in a half-whisper.

'Seven, Ehlana,' Mirtai corrected gently. 'I wasn't yet eight.'

'You actually killed a man at that age?' Emban asked her incredulously.

'Two, Emban. The one who screamed for two days

346

also died.' The Atana looked at Engessa, her glistening eyes a bit doubtful. 'May I claim that one as well, Father-Atan?' she asked. 'He might have died anyway of something else.'

'You may claim him, my daughter,' he judged. 'It was your knife-thrust that killed him.'

She sighed. 'I've always wondered about that one,' she confessed. 'It clouded my count, and I didn't like that.'

'It was a legitimate kill, Atana. Your count is unclouded.'

'Thank you, Father-Atan,' she said. 'It's a bad thing to be uncertain about so important a matter.' She paused, collecting her memories. 'I didn't kill again for almost half a year. The Arjuni took me south to Tiana. I did not cry at all during the journey. It is not proper to let your enemies see you grieve. At Tiana, my captors took me to the slave-market and sold me to a Dacite merchant named Pelaser. He was fat and greasy, he smelled bad, and he was fond of children.'

'He was a kindly master then?' Baroness Melidere asked her.

'I didn't say that, Melidere. Pelaser liked little boys and girls in a rather peculiar way. The Arjuni had warned him about me, so he wouldn't let me near any knives. I had to eat, however, so he gave me a spoon. He took me to his home at Verel in Daconia, and I spent the entire journey sharpening the handle of my spoon on my chains. It was a good metal spoon, and it took a very fine edge. When we got to Verel he chained me to the wall in a little room at the back of his house. The room had a stone floor, and I spent all my time working on my spoon. I grew very fond of it.' She bent slightly and slid her hand down into her boot. 'Isn't it pretty?' The implement she held up was a very ordinary-looking spoon with a wooden handle. She took it in both hands,

347

twisted the handle slightly and then pulled it off the shank of the spoon. The shank was thin and narrow, and it came to a needle-like point. It had been polished until it gleamed like silver. She looked at it critically. 'It's not quite long enough to reach a man's heart,' she apologised for her spoon. 'You can't kill cleanly with it, but it's good for emergencies. It looks so much like an ordinary spoon that nobody ever thinks to take it away from me.'

'Brilliant,' Stragen murmured, his eyes glowing with admiration. 'Steal us a couple of spoons, Talen, and we'll get to work on them immediately.'

'Pelaser came to my room one night and put his hands on me,' Mirtai continued. 'I sat very still, and so he thought I wouldn't resist. He started to smile. I noticed that he drooled when he smiled like that. He was still smiling – and drooling – when I stabbed both of his eyes out. Did you know that a man's eyes pop when you poke them with something sharp?'

Melidere made a slight gagging sound and stared at the calm-faced Atana in open horror.

'He tried to scream,' Mirtai went on in a chillingly clinical way, 'but I looped my chain around his neck to keep him quiet. I really wanted to cut him into little pieces, but I had to hold the chain in both hands to keep him from screaming. He began to struggle, but I just pulled the chain tighter about his neck.'

'Yes!' Rather astonishingly, it was Ehlana's doe-eyed maid Alean who cried her hoarse approval, and the quick embrace she gave the startled Atana was uncharacteristically fierce.

Mirtai touched the gentle girl's face fondly and then continued. 'Pelaser struggled quite a bit at first, but after a while, he stopped. He had knocked over the candle, and the room was dark, so I couldn't be sure he was dead. I kept the chain pulled tight around his neck until morning. His face was very black when the sun came up.'

'A fair kill, my daughter,' Engessa said to her proudly.

She smiled and bowed her head to him. 'I thought they would kill me when they discovered what I had done, but the Dacites of the southern towns are peculiar people. Pelaser wasn't well-liked in Verel, and I think many of them were secretly amused by the fact that one of the children he usually molested had finally killed him. His heir was a nephew named Gelan. He was very grateful that I'd made him rich by killing his uncle, and he spoke to the authorities on my behalf.' She paused and looked at the princess, who was still nestled in her lap holding the gleaming little dagger. 'Could you get me some water, Danae?' she asked. 'I'm not used to talking so much.'

Danae obediently slipped down and went over toward one of the cooking-fires.

'She might be a little young to hear about certain things,' Mirtai murmured. 'Gelan was a rather nice young man, but he had peculiar tastes. He gave his love to other young men instead of women.'

Sir Bevier gasped.

'Oh, dear,' Mirtai said. 'Are you truly *that* unworldly, Bevier? It's not uncommon, you know. Anyway, I got on quite well with Gelan. At least he didn't try to take advantage of me. He loved to talk, so he taught me to speak Elenic and even to read a bit. People in his circumstances lead rather tentative lives, and he needed a permanent friend. I had been taught that it was polite to listen when my elders spoke, and after a time he would pour out his heart to me. When I grew a little older, he bought me pretty gowns to wear, and sometimes he'd even wear them himself, although I think he was only joking. Some of his friends wore women's clothes, but nobody was really very serious about it. It's something they laughed about. It was about then that I started to go through that difficult time in a girl's life when she starts to become a woman. He was very gentle and understanding, and he explained what was happening so that I wasn't afraid. He used to have me wear my prettiest gowns, and he'd take me with him when he was doing business with people who didn't know his preferences. Daconia is an Elene Kingdom, and Elenes have some peculiar ideas about that sort of thing. They try to mix religion into it for some reason. Anyway, the fact that Gelan always had a young slave-girl with him quieted suspicions.'

Bevier's eyes had a stunned look in them.

'Maybe you should go help the princess look for that water, Bevier,' Mirtai suggested to him almost gently. 'This was a part of my childhood, so I have to talk about it at this time. You don't have to listen if it bothers you, though. I'll understand.'

His face grew troubled. 'I'm your friend, Mirtai,' he declared. 'I'll stay.'

She smiled. 'He's such a nice boy.' She said it in almost the same tone of voice Sephrenia had always used when saying exactly the same thing. Sparhawk was a bit startled at how shrewdly perceptive the Atan girl really was.

Mirtai sighed. 'Gelan and I loved each other, but not in the way that people usually think of when they're talking about a man and a woman. There are as many different kinds of love as there are people, I think. He had enemies, though – many enemies. He was a very sharp trader, and he almost always got the best of every bargain. There are small people in the world who take that sort of thing personally. Once an Edomish merchant became so enraged that he tried to kill Gelan, and I had to use my spoon to protect him. As I said before, the blade's not quite long enough to kill cleanly, so the incident was very messy. I ruined a very nice silk gown that evening. I told Gelan that he really ought to buy me some proper knives so that I could kill people without spoiling my clothes. The idea of having a twelve-year-old girl for a body-guard startled him at first, but then he saw the advantages of it. He bought me these.' She touched one of the silver-hilted daggers at her waist. 'I've always treasured them. I devised a way to conceal them under my clothes when we went out into the city. After I'd used them on a few people, the word got around, and his enemies quit trying to kill him.

'There were other young men like Gelan in Verel, and they used to visit each other in their homes where they didn't have to hide their feelings. They were all very kind to me. They used to give me advice and buy me pretty gifts. I was quite fond of them. They were all polite and intelligent, and they always smelled clean. I can't abide smelly men.' She gave Kring a meaningful look.

'I bathe,' he protested.

'Now and then,' she added a bit critically. 'You ride horses a great deal, Kring, and horses have a peculiar odour. We'll talk about regular bathing after I've put my brand on you.' She laughed. 'I wouldn't want to frighten you until I'm sure of you.' Her smile was genuinely affectionate. Sparhawk realised that what she was telling them was a part of the Rite of Passage, and that she would very likely never be this open again. Her typically Atan defences had all been lowered for this one night. He felt profoundly honoured to have been invited to be present.

She sighed then, and her face grew sad. 'Gelan had one very special friend whom he loved very much – a pretty young fellow named Majen. I didn't like Majen. He used to take advantage of Gelan, and he'd deliberately say and do things to hurt him. He was frivolous

351

and selfish and very, very vain about his appearance. He was also unfaithful, and that's contemptible. In time he grew tired of Gelan and fell in love with another meaningless pretty-boy. I probably should have killed them both as soon as I found out about it. I've always regretted the fact that I didn't. Gelan had foolishly given Majen the use of a rather splendid house on the outskirts of Verel and had told him that he'd made provisions in his will so that Majen would own the house if anything ever happened to him. Majen and his new friend wanted that house, and they plotted against Gelan. They lured him to the house one night and insisted that he come to them alone. When he got there, they killed him and dropped his body in the river. I cried for days after it happened, because I was really very fond of Gelan. One of his other friends told me what had really happened, but I didn't say anything or do anything right away. I wanted the two of them to feel safe and to think that they'd got away with the murder. Gelan's sister inherited me – along with all his other property. She was a nice enough lady, but awfully religious. She didn't really know how to deal with the fact that she owned me. She said she wanted to be my friend, but I advised her to sell me instead. I told her that I'd found out who had murdered Gelan and that I was going to kill them. I said that I thought it would probably be better if I belonged to somebody who was leaving Verel in order to avoid all the tedious business about unexplained bodies and the like. I thought she'd be tiresome about it, but she took it rather well. She was really quite fond of her brother, and she approved of what I was planning. She sold me to an Elenian merchant who was going to sail to Vardenais and told him that she'd deliver me to him on the morning of his departure. She'd made him a very good price, so he didn't argue with her.

'Anyway, on the night before my new owner was planning to sail, I dressed myself as a boy and went to the house where Majen and the other one were living. I waited until Majen left the house and went to the door and knocked. Majen's new friend came to the door, and I told him that I loved him. I'd lived with Gelan for six years, so I knew exactly how to behave to make the pretty fool believe me. He grew excited when I told him that, and he kissed me several times.' She sneered with the profoundest contempt. 'Some people simply cannot be faithful. Anyway, after he began to get very, very excited with the kissing, he started exploring. He discovered some things that surprised him very much. He was even more surprised when I sliced him across the belly just above his hips.'

'I *like* this part,' Talen said, his eyes very bright.

'You would,' Mirtai told him. 'You never like a story unless there's a lot of blood in it. Anyway, after I sliced the pretty boy open, all sorts of things fell out. He stumbled back into a chair and tried to stuff them back in again. People's insides are very slippery, though, and he was having a great deal of trouble.'

Ehlana made a choking sound.

'Didn't you know about insides?' Mirtai asked her. 'Get Sparhawk to tell you about it sometime. He's probably seen lots of insides. I left the young man sitting there and hid behind a door. Majen came home a while later, and he was dreadfully upset about his friend's condition.'

'I can imagine,' Talen laughed.

'He was even more upset, though, when I reached around from behind him and opened him up in exactly the same way.'

'Those are not fatal injuries, Atana,' Engessa said critically.

'I didn't intend for them to be, Father-Atan,' she

replied. 'I wasn't done with the two of them yet. I told them who I was and that what I'd just done to them was a farewell gift from Gelan. That was about the best part of the whole evening. I put Majen in a chair facing the chair of his friend so that they could watch each other die. Then I stuck my hands into them and jerked out several yards of those slippery things I told you about.'

'And then you just left them there?' Talen asked eagerly.

She nodded. 'Yes, but I set fire to the house first. Neither Majen or his friend managed to get enough of themselves put back inside to be able to escape. They screamed a great deal, though.'

'Good God!' Emban choked.

'A fitting revenge, Atana,' Engessa said to her. 'We will describe it to the children in the training-camps to provide them with an example of suitable behaviour.'

Mirtai bowed her head to him, then looked up. 'Well, Bevier?' she said.

He struggled with it. 'Your owner's sins were his own. That's a matter between him and God. What you did was the proper act of a friend. I find no sin in what you did.'

'I'm so glad,' she murmured.

Bevier laughed a bit sheepishly. 'That was a bit pompous, wasn't it?'

'That's all right, Bevier,' she assured him. 'I love you anyway – although you should keep in mind the fact that I have a history of loving some very strange people.'

'Well said,' Ulath approved.

Danae returned with a cup of water and offered it to Mirtai. 'Did you finish telling them the things you didn't want me to hear about?' she asked.

'I think I covered most of it. Thank you for being

so understanding – and for the water.' Nothing rattled Mirtai.

Ehlana, however, blushed furiously.

'It's getting late,' Mirtai told them, 'so I'll keep this short. The Elenian merchant who owned me took me to Vardenais and sold me to Platime. I pretended not to speak Elenic, and Platime misjudged my age because I was very tall. Platime's quite shrewd in some ways and ignorant in others. He simply couldn't understand the fact that an Atan woman can't be forced, and he tried to put me to work in one of his brothels. He took my daggers away from me, but I still had my spoon. I didn't kill *too* many of the men who approached me, but I *did* hurt them all quite seriously. Word got around, and the business in that brothel fell off. Platime took me out of there, but he didn't really know what to do with me. I wouldn't beg and I wouldn't steal, and he was really *very* disappointed when he found out that I'd only kill people for personal reasons. I *won't* be a paid assassin. Then the situation came up in the palace, and he gave me to Ehlana – probably with a great sigh of relief.' She frowned and looked at Engessa. 'That was the first time I'd ever been given away instead of sold, Father-Atan. Did Platime insult me? Should I go back to Cimmura and kill him?'

Engessa considered it. 'I don't think so, my daughter. It was a special case. You might even look upon it as a compliment.'

Mirtai smiled. 'I'm glad of that, Father-Atan. I sort of like Platime. He's very funny sometimes.'

'And how do you feel about Ehlana-Queen?'

'I love her. She's ignorant, and she can't speak a proper language, but most of the time she does what I tell her to do. She's pretty, and she smells nice and she's very kind to me. She's the best owner I've ever had. Yes. I love her.'

Ehlana gave a low cry and threw her arms around the golden woman's neck. 'I love you too, Mirtai,' she said in an emotion-filled voice. 'You're my dearest friend.' She kissed her.

'This is a special occasion, Ehlana,' the Atana said, 'so it's all right just this once.' She gently detached the queen's arms from around her neck. 'But it's not seemly to display so much emotion in public – and girls shouldn't kiss other girls. It might give people the wrong sort of ideas.'

CHAPTER 19

'Hang it all, Atan Engessa,' Kalten was saying, 'you heard the story the same as the rest of us. She said she hadn't even entered training when the Arjuni captured her. Where did she learn to fight the way she does? I've been training more or less constantly since Sparhawk and I were fifteen, and she throws me around like a rag doll anytime she feels like it.'

Engessa smiled slightly. It was still very early and a filmy morning mist drifted ghost-like among the trees, softening the dark outlines of their trunks. They had set out at dawn, and Engessa strode along among the mounted Pandions. 'I've seen you in a fight, Kalten-Knight,' the tall Atan said. He reached out and rapped one knuckle on Kalten's armour. 'Your tactics depend heavily on your equipment.'

'That's true, I suppose.'

'And your training has concentrated on the use of that equipment, has it not?'

'Well, to some degree, I suppose. We practise with our weapons and learn to take advantage of our armour.'

'And the sheer bulk of our horses,' Vanion added. Vanion was wearing his black armour for the journey. His choice of wardrobe had occasioned a spirited discussion between him and the woman he loved. Once she had removed herself from the restraining presence of all those Elenes, Sephrenia had become more vocal, and she had shown an astonishing aptitude for histrionics during the course of the conversation. Although she and Vanion had been talking privately, Sparhawk had been able to hear her comments quite clearly. Everyone in the house had heard her. Probably everyone in Sarsos had.

'At least half of your training has been in horsemanship, Kalten,' Vanion continued. 'An armoured knight without his horse is very much like a turtle on his back.'

'I've said much the same thing to my fellow-novices, Lord Vanion,' Khalad said politely. 'Most of them take offence when I say it to them though, so I usually have to demonstrate. That seems to offend them even more for some reason.'

Engessa chuckled. 'You train with your equipment, Kalten-Knight,' he repeated. 'So do we. The difference is that our bodies are our equipment. Our way of fighting is based on speed, agility and strength, and we can practise those without training grounds or large fields where horses can run. We practise all the time, and in the village where she was born, Atana Mirtai saw her parents and their friends improving their skills almost every hour. Children learn by imitating their parents. We see three- and four-year-olds wrestling and testing each other all the time.'

'There has to be more to it than that,' Kalten objected.

'Natural talent perhaps, Sir Kalten?' Berit suggested.

'I'm not *that* clumsy, Berit.'

'Was your mother a warrior, Kalten-Knight?' Engessa asked him.

'Of course not.'

'Or your grandmother, or your grandmother's grandmother? Back for fifty generations?'

Kalten looked confused.

'Atana Mirtai is descended from warriors on both sides of her family. Fighting is in her blood. She is gifted, and she can learn much just by watching. She can probably fight in a half dozen different styles.'

358

'That's an interesting notion, Atan-Engessa,' Vanion said. 'If we could find a horse big enough for her, she might make a very good knight.'

'*Vanion!*' Kalten exclaimed. 'That's the most unnatural suggestion I've ever heard!'

'Merely speculation, Kalten.' Vanion looked gravely at Sparhawk. 'We might want to give some thought to including a bit more hand-to-hand fighting in our training programme, Preceptor Sparhawk.'

'Please don't do that, Vanion,' Sparhawk replied in a pained tone. 'You're still the preceptor until the Hierocracy says otherwise. I'm just the interim preceptor.'

'All right, Interim Preceptor Sparhawk, when we get to Atan, let's pay some attention to their fighting style. We don't always fight on horseback, you know.'

'I'll put Khalad to work on it,' Sparhawk said.

'Khalad?'

'Kurik trained him, and Kurik was better at close fighting than any man I've ever known.'

'He was indeed. Good idea, Interim Preceptor Sparhawk.'

'Must you?' Sparhawk asked him.

They reached the city of Atana twelve days later – at least it *seemed* like twelve days. Sparhawk had decided to stop brooding about the difference between real and perceived time. Aphrael was going to tamper no matter what he did or said anyway, so why should he waste time worrying about it? He wondered if Zalasta could detect the manipulation. Probably not, he decided. No matter how skilled the Styric magician might be, he was still only a man, and Aphrael was divine. An odd thought came to Sparhawk one night, however. He wondered if his daughter could also make real time seem faster than it actually was instead of slower. After he thought about it for a while, though, he decided not to ask her. The whole concept gave him a headache.

Atana was a utilitarian sort of town in a deep green valley. It was walled, but the walls were not particularly high nor imposing. It was the Atans themselves who made their capital impregnable.

'Everything in the kingdom's named Atan, isn't it?' Kalten observed as they rode down into the valley. 'The kingdom, its capital, the people – even the titles.'

'I think Atan's more in the nature of a concept than a name,' Ulath shrugged.

'What makes them all so tall?' Talen asked. 'They belong to the Tamul race, but other Tamuls don't loom over everybody else like trees.'

'Oscagne explained it to me,' Stragen told him. 'It seems that the Atans are the result of an experiment.'

'Magic?'

'I don't know all that much about it,' Stragen admitted, 'but I'd guess that what they did went beyond what magic's capable of. Back before there was even such a thing as history, the Atans observed that big people win more fights than little people. That was in a time when parents chose the mates of their children. Size became the most important consideration.'

'What happened to short children?' Talen objected.

'Probably the same thing that happens to ugly children in *our* society,' Stragen shrugged. 'They didn't get married.'

'That's not fair.'

Stragen smiled. 'When you get right down to it, Talen, it's not really very fair when we steal something somebody else has worked for, is it?'

'That's different.'

Stragen leaned back in his saddle and laughed. Then he went on. 'The Atans prized other characteristics as well – ability, strength, aggressiveness and homicidal vindictiveness. It's strange how the combination worked out. If you stop and think about it, you'll realise that Mirtai's really a rather sweet girl. She's warm and affectionate, she really cares about her friends, and she's strikingly beautiful. She's got certain triggers built into her, though, and when somebody trips one of those triggers, she starts killing people. The Atan breeding programme finally went too far, I guess. The Atans become so aggressive that they started killing each other, and since such aggressiveness can't be restricted to one sex, the women were as bad as the men. It got to the point that there was no such thing in Atan as a mild disagreement. They'd kill each other over weather predictions.' He smiled. 'Oscagne told me that the world discovered just how savage Atan women were in the twelfth century. A large band of Arjuni slavers attacked a training camp for adolescent Atan females – the sexes are separated during training in order to avoid certain complications. Anyway, those half-grown Atan girls – most of them barely over six feet tall – slaughtered most of the Arjuni and then sold the rest to the Tamuls as eunuchs.'

'The slavers were eunuchs?' Kalten asked with some surprise.

'No, Kalten,' Stragen explained patiently. 'They weren't eunuchs until *after* the girls captured them.'

'Little girls did that?' Kalten's expression was one of horror.

'They weren't exactly babies, Kalten. They were old enough to know what they were doing. Anyway, the Atans had a very wise king in the fifteenth century. He saw that his people were on the verge of self-destruction. He made contact with the Tamul government and surrendered his people into perpetual slavery – to save their lives.'

'A little extreme,' Ulath noted.

'There are several kinds of slavery, Ulath. Here in

361

Atan, it's institutionalised. The Tamuls tell the Atans where to go and whom to kill, and they can usually find a reason to deny petitions by individual Atans to slaughter each other. That's about as far as it really goes. It's a good working arrangement. The Atan race survives, and the Tamuls get the finest infantry in the world.'

Talen was frowning. 'The Atans are terribly impressed with size, you said.'

'Well, it's *one* of the things that impresses them,' Stragen amended.

'Then why did Mirtai agree to marry Kring? Kring's a good warrior, but he's not much taller than I am, and I'm still growing.'

'It must be something else about him that impressed her so much,' Stragen shrugged.

'What do you think it is?'

'I haven't got the faintest idea, Talen.'

'He's a poet,' Sparhawk told them. 'Maybe that's it.'

'That wouldn't make *that* much difference to someone like Mirtai, would it? She *did* slice two men open and then burn them alive, remember? She doesn't sound to me like the kind of girl who'd get all gushy about poetry.'

'Don't ask *me*, Talen,' Stragen laughed. 'I know a great deal about the world, but I wouldn't even try to make a guess about why any woman chooses any given man.'

'Good thinking,' Ulath murmured.

The city had been alerted to their approach by Engessa's messengers, and the royal party was met at the gate by a deputation of towering Atans in formal attire, which in their culture meant the donning of unadorned, ankle-length cloaks of dark wool. In the midst of those giants stood a short, golden-robed Tamul. The Tamul had silver-streaked hair and an urbane expression.

'What are we supposed to do?' Kalten whispered to Oscagne.

'Act formal,' Oscagne advised. 'Atans adore formality. Ah, Norkan,' he said to the Tamul in the golden robe, 'so good to see you again. Fontan sends his best.'

'How is the old rascal?' Oscagne's colleague replied.

'Wrinkled, but he still hasn't lost his edge.'

'I'm glad to hear it. Why are we speaking in Elenic?'

'So that you can brief us all on local circumstances. How are things here?'

'Tense. Our children are a bit discontent. There's turmoil afoot. We send them to stamp it out, but it refuses to stay stamped. They resent that. You know how they are.'

'Oh my, yes. Has the emperor's sister forgiven you yet?'

Norkan sighed. 'Afraid not, old boy. I'm quite resigned to spending the rest of my career here.'

'You know how the people at court like to carry tales. Whatever possessed you to make that remark? I'll grant you that her Highness' feet are a bit oversized, but "big-footed cow" was sort of indiscreet, wouldn't you say?'

'I was drunk and a little out of sorts. Better to be here in Atan than in Matherion trying to evade her attentions. I have no desire to become a member of the imperial family if it means that I'd have to trudge along behind her as she clumps about the palace.'

'Ah, well. What's on the agenda here?'

'Formality. Official greetings. Speeches. Ceremonies. The usual nonsense.'

'Good. Our friends from the west are a bit unbridled at times. They're good at formality, though. It's when things become informal that they get into trouble. May I present the Queen of Elenia?'

'I thought you'd never ask.'

363

'Your Majesty,' Oscagne said, 'this is my old friend, Norkan. He's the imperial representative here in Atan, an able man who's fallen on hard times.'

Norkan bowed. 'Your Majesty,' he greeted Ehlana.

'Your Excellency,' she responded. Then she smiled. 'Are her Highness' feet *really* that big?' she asked him slyly.

'She skis with only the equipment God gave her, your Majesty. I could bear that, I suppose, but she's given to temper tantrums when she doesn't get her own way, and that sort of grates on my nerves.' He glanced at the huge, dark-cloaked Atans surrounding the carriage. 'Might I suggest that we proceed to what my children here refer to as the palace? The king and queen await us there. Is your Majesty comfortable speaking in public? A few remarks might be in order.'

'I'm afraid I don't speak Tamul, your Excellency.'

'Perfectly all right, your Majesty. I'll translate for you. You can say anything that pops into your head. I'll tidy it up for you as we go along.'

'How very kind of you.' There was only the faintest edge to her voice.

'I live but to serve, your Majesty.'

'Remarkable, Norkan,' Oscagne murmured. 'How *do* you manage to put both feet in your mouth at the same time?'

'It's a gift,' Norkan shrugged.

King Androl of Atan was seven feet tall, and his wife, Queen Betuana was only slightly shorter. They were very imposing. They wore golden helmets instead of crowns, and their deep blue silk robes were open at the front, revealing the fact that they were both heavily armed. They met the Queen of Elenia and her entourage in the square outside the royal palace of Atan, which was in actuality nothing more than their private dwelling. Atan ceremonies, it appeared, were conducted out of doors.

With the queen's carriage in the lead and her armed escort formed up behind, the visitors rode at a slow and stately pace into the square. There were no cheers, no fanfares, none of the artificial enthusiasm normally contrived for state visitors. Atans showed respect by silence and immobility. Stragen skilfully wheeled the carriage to a spot in front of the slightly raised stone platform before the royal dwelling, and Sparhawk dismounted to offer his queen a steel-encased forearm. Ehlana's face was radiantly regal, and her pleasure was clearly unfeigned. Though she occasionally spoke slightingly of ceremonial functions, pretending to view them as tedious, she truly loved ceremony. She took a deep satisfaction in formality.

Ambassador Oscagne approached the royal family of Atan, bowed and spoke at some length in the flowing, musical language of all Tamuls. Mirtai stood behind Ehlana, murmuring a running translation of his Excellency's words. Ehlana's eyes were very bright, and there were two spots of heightened colour on her alabaster cheeks, signs that said louder than words that she was composing a speech.

King Androl then spoke a rather brief greeting, and Queen Betuana added her somewhat lengthier agreement. Sparhawk could not hear Mirtai's translation, so for all he knew the Atan king and queen were discussing weather-conditions on the moon.

Then Ehlana stepped forward, paused for dramatic effect, and began to speak in a clear voice that could be heard throughout the square. Ambassador Norkan stood at the side of the stone platform and translated her words.

'My dear brother and sister of Atan,' she began, 'words cannot express my heartfelt joy at this meeting.'

365

Sparhawk knew his wife, and he knew that disclaimer to be fraudulent. Words *could* express her feelings, and she *would* tell everybody in the square all about them. 'I come to this happy meeting from the world's far end,' she went on, 'and my heart was filled with anxiety as I sailed across the wine-dark sea toward a foreign land peopled with strangers, but your gracious words of friendly – even affectionate – greeting have erased my childish fears, and I have learned here a lesson which I will carry all the days of my life. There are no strangers in this world, my dear brother and sister. There are only friends we have not yet met.'

'She's plagiarising,' Stragen murmured to Sparhawk.

'She does that now and then. When she finds a phrase she really likes, she sees no reason not to expropriate it.'

'My journey to Atan has been, of course, for state reasons. We of the royal houses of the world are not free to do things for personal reasons as others are.' She gave the Atan king and queen a rueful little smile. 'We cannot even yawn without its being subjected to extensive diplomatic analysis. No one ever considers the possibility that we might just be sleepy.'

After Norkan translated that, King Androl actually smiled.

'My visit to Atan, however, *does* have a personal reason as well as an official one,' Ehlana continued. 'I chanced some time ago upon a precious thing which belongs to the Atan people, and I have come half-round the world to return this treasure to you, though it is more dear to me than I can ever say. Many, many years ago, an Atan child was lost. That child is the treasure of which I spoke.' She reached out and took Mirtai's hand. 'She is my dear, dear friend, and I love her. The journey I have made here is as nothing. Gladly would I have travelled twice as far – ten times as far – for the joy I

366

now feel in re-uniting this precious Atan child with her people.'

Stragen wiped at his eyes with the back of his hand. 'She does it to me every time, Sparhawk,' he laughed, 'every single time. I think she could make rocks cry if she wanted to, and it always seems so simple.'

'That's part of her secret, Stragen.'

Ehlana was moving right along. 'As many of you may know, the Elene people have some faults – many faults, though I blush to confess it. We have not treated your dear child well. An Elene bought her from the soulless Arjuni who had stolen her from you. The Elene bought her in order to satisfy his unwholesome desires. This child of ours – for she is now as much my child as she is yours – taught him that an Atana may not be used so. It was a hard lesson for him. He died in the learning of it.'

A rumble of approval greeted the translation of that.

'Our child has passed through the hands of several Elenes – most with the worst of motives – and came at last to me. At first she frightened me.' Ehlana smiled her most winsome smile. 'You may have noticed that I am not a very tall person.'

A small chuckle ran through the crowd.

'I thought you might have noticed that,' she said, joining in their laughter. 'It's one of the failings of our culture that our menfolk are stubborn and short-sighted. I am not permitted to be trained in the use of weapons. I know it sounds ridiculous, but I've not even been allowed to kill my enemies personally. I was not accustomed to women who could see to their own defence, and so I was foolishly afraid of my Atan child. That has passed, however. I have found her to be steadfast and true, gentle and affectionate and very, very wise. We have come to Atan so that this dear child of ours may lay aside the silver of childhood and assume the gold

367

that is her just due in the Rite of Passage. Let us join our hands and our hearts, Elene and Atan, Styric and Tamul, in the ceremony which will raise our child to adulthood, and in that ceremony, may our hearts be united, for in this child, we are all made as one.'

As Norkan translated, an approving murmur went through the crowd of Atans, a murmur that swelled to a roar, and Queen Betuana, her eyes filled with tears, stepped down from the dais and embraced the pale blonde queen of Elenia. Then she spoke very briefly to the crowd.

'What did she say?' Stragen asked Oscagne.

'She advised her people that anyone who offered your queen any impertinence would answer to her personally. It's no idle threat, either. Queen Betuana's one of the finest warriors in all of Atan. I hope you appreciate your wife, Sparhawk. She's just scored a diplomatic coup of the highest order. How the deuce did she learn that the Atans are sentimentalists? If she'd talked for another three minutes, the whole square would have been awash with tears.'

'Our queen's a perceptive young woman,' Stragen said rather proudly. 'A good speech is always drawn on a community of interest. Our Ehlana's a genius when it comes to finding things she has in common with her audience.'

'So it would seem. She's ensured one thing, let me tell you.'

'Oh?'

'The Atans will give Atana Mirtai a Rite of Passage such as comes along only once or twice in a generation. She'll be a national heroine after an introduction like that. The singing will be tumultuous.'

'That's probably more or less what my wife had in mind,' Sparhawk told him. 'She loves to do nice things for her friends.'

'And not so nice things to her enemies,' Stragen added. 'I remember some of the plans she had for Primate Annias.'

'That's as it should be, Milord Stragen,' Oscagne smiled. 'The only real reason for accepting the inconveniences of power is to reward our friends and punish our enemies.'

'I couldn't agree more, your Excellency.'

Engessa conferred with King Androl, and Ehlana with Queen Betuana. No one was particularly surprised when Sephrenia served as translator for the queens. The small Styric woman, it appeared, spoke most of the languages in the known world. Norkan explained to Sparhawk and the others that the child's parents were much involved in the Rite of Passage. Engessa would serve as Mirtai's father, and Mirtai had rather shyly asked Ehlana to be her mother. The request had occasioned an emotional display of affection between the two of them. 'It's a rather touching ceremony, actually,' Norkan told them. 'The parents are obliged to assert that their child is fit and ready to assume the responsibilities of adulthood. They then offer to fight anyone who disagrees. Not to worry Sparhawk,' he added with a chuckle. 'It's a formality. The challenge is almost never taken up.'

'Almost never?'

'I'm teasing, of course. No one's going to fight your wife. That speech of hers totally disarmed them. They adore her. I hope she's quick of study, however. She'll have to speak in Tamul.'

'Learning a foreign language takes a long time,' Kalten said dubiously. 'I studied Styric for ten years and never did get the hang of it.'

'You have no aptitude for languages, Kalten,' Vanion told him. 'Even Elenic confuses you sometimes.'

'You don't have to be insulting, Lord Vanion.'

'I imagine Sephrenia will cheat a little,' Sparhawk

369

added. 'She and Aphrael taught me to speak Troll in about five seconds in Ghwerig's cave.' He looked at Norkan. 'When will the ceremony take place?' he asked.

'At midnight. The child passes into adulthood as one day passes into the next.'

'There's an exquisite kind of logic there,' Stragen noted.

'The hand of God,' Bevier murmured piously.

'I beg your pardon?'

'Even the heathen responds to that gentle inner voice, Milord Stragen.'

'I'm afraid I'm still missing the point, Sir Bevier.'

'Logic is what sets our God apart,' Bevier explained patiently. 'It's His special gift to the Elene people, and He reaches out with it to all others, freely offering its blessing to the unenlightened.'

'Is that really a part of Elene doctrine, your Grace?' Stragen asked the Patriarch of Ucera.

'Tentatively,' Emban replied. 'The view is more widely-held in Arcium than elsewhere. The Arcian clergy has been trying to have it included in the articles of the faith for the last thousand years or so, but the Deirans have been resisting. The Hierocracy takes up the question when we have nothing else to do.'

'Do you think it will ever be resolved, your Grace?' Norkan asked him.

'Good God no, your Excellency. If we ever settled the issue, we wouldn't have anything to argue about.'

Oscagne approached from the far side of the square. He took Sparhawk and Vanion aside, his expression concerned. 'How well do you gentlemen know Zalasta?' he asked them.

'I only met him once before we reached Sarsos,' Sparhawk replied. 'Lord Vanion here knows him much better than I.'

'I'm starting to have some doubts about this legendary

wisdom of his,' Oscagne said to them. 'The Styric enclave in eastern Astel abuts Atan, so he *should* know more about these people than he seems to. I just caught him suggesting a demonstration of prowess to the Peloi and some of the younger Church Knights.'

'It's not unusual, your Excellency,' Vanion shrugged. 'Young men like to show off.'

'That's exactly my point, Lord Vanion.' Oscagne's expression was worried. 'That's not done here in Atan. Demonstrations of that kind lead to bloodshed. The Atans look upon that sort of thing as a challenge. I got there just in time to avert a disaster. What was the man thinking of?'

'Styrics sometimes grow a bit vague,' Vanion explained. 'They can be profoundly absent-minded sometimes. I'll have Sephrenia speak with him and remind him to pay attention.'

'Oh, there's something else, gentlemen,' Oscagne smiled. 'Don't let Sir Berit wander around alone in the city. There are whole platoons of unmarried Atan girls lusting after him.'

'Berit?' Vanion looked startled.

'It's happened before, Vanion,' Sparhawk told him. 'There's something about our young friend that drives young women wild. It has to do with his eyelashes, I think. Ehlana and Melidere tried to explain it to me in Darsas. I didn't understand what they were saying, but I took their word for it.'

'What an astonishing thing,' Vanion said.

There were torches everywhere, and the faint, fragrant night breeze tossed their sooty orange flames like a field of fiery wheat. The Rite of Passage took place in a broad meadow outside the city. An ancient stone altar adorned with wild-flowers stood between two broad oaks at the centre of the meadow, and two bronze, basin-like oil-lamps flared, one on each end of the altar.

371

A lone Atan with snowy hair stood atop the city wall, intently watching the light of the moon passing through a narrow horizontal aperture in one of the battlements and down the face of a nearby wall, which was marked at regular intervals with deeply-scored lines. It was not the most precise way to determine the time, but if everyone agreed that the line of moonlight would reach a certain one of those scorings at midnight, precision was unimportant. As long as there was general agreement, it *was* midnight.

The night was silent except for the guttering of the torches and the sighing of the breeze in the dark forest surrounding the meadow.

They waited as the silvery line of moonlight crept down the wall.

Then the ancient Atan gave a signal, and a dozen trumpeters raised brazen horns to greet the new day and to signal the beginning of the Rite which would end Mirtai's childhood.

The Atans sang. There were no words, for this rite was too sacred for words. Their song began with a single deep rumbling male voice, swelling and rising as other voices joined it in soaring and complex harmonies.

King Androl and Queen Betuana moved with slow and stately pace along a broad, torchlit avenue toward the ageless trees and the flower-decked altar. Their bronze faces were serene, and their golden helmets gleamed in the torchlight. When they reached the altar, they turned, expectant.

There was a pause while the torches flared and the organ-song of the Atans rose and swelled. Then the melody subsided into a tightly controlled hum, scarcely more than a whisper.

Engessa and Ehlana, both in deep blue robes, escorted Mirtai out of the shadows near the city wall. Mirtai was all in white, and her raven hair was unadorned. Her eyes were modestly down-cast as her parents led her toward the altar.

The song swelled again with a different melody and a different counterpoint.

'The approach of the child,' Norkan murmured to Sparhawk and the others. The sophisticated, even cynical Tamul's voice was respectful, almost awed, and his world-weary eyes glistened. Sparhawk felt a small tug on his hand, and he lifted his daughter so that she might better see.

Mirtai and her family reached the altar and bowed to Androl and Betuana. The song sank to a whisper.

Engessa spoke to the king and queen of the Atans. His voice was loud and forceful. The Tamul tongue flowed musically from his lips as he declared his daughter fit. Then he turned, opened his robe and drew his sword. He spoke again, and there was a note of challenge in his voice.

'What did he say?' Talen whispered to Oscagne.

'He offered to do violence to anyone who objected to his daughter's passage.' Oscagne replied. His voice was also profoundly respectful, even slightly choked with emotion.

Then Ehlana spoke, also in Tamul. Her voice rang out like a silver trumpet as she also declared that her child was fit and ready to assume her place as an adult.

'She wasn't supposed to say that last bit,' Danae whispered in Sparhawk's ear. 'She's adding things.'

'You know your mother,' he smiled.

Then the Queen of Elenia turned to look at the assembled Atans, and her voice took on a flinty note of challenge as she also opened her robe and drew a silver-hilted sword. Sparhawk was startled by the professional way she held it.

Then Mirtai spoke to the king and queen.

'The child entreats passage,' Norkan told them.

King Androl spoke his reply, his voice loud and commanding, and his queen added her agreement. Then they too drew their swords and stepped forward to flank the child's parents, joining in their challenge.

The song of the Atans soared, and the trumpets added a brazen fanfare. Then the sound diminished again.

Mirtai faced her people and drew her daggers. She spoke to them, and Sparhawk needed no translation. He *knew* that tone of voice.

The song raised, triumphant, and the five at the altar turned to face the roughly-chiselled stone block. In the centre of the altar lay a black velvet cushion, and nestled on it there was a plain gold circlet.

The song swelled, and it echoed back from nearby mountains.

And then, out of the velvet black throat of night, a star fell. It was an incandescently brilliant white light streaking down across the sky. Down and down it arched, and then it exploded into a shower of brilliant sparks.

'Stop that!' Sparhawk hissed to his daughter.

'I didn't *do* it,' she protested. 'I might have, but I didn't think of it. How *did* they do that?' She sounded genuinely baffled.

Then, as the glowing shards of the star drifted slowly toward the earth filling the night with glowing sparks, the golden circlet on the altar rose unaided, drifting up like a ring of smoke. It hesitated as the Atan song swelled with an aching kind of yearning, and then, like a gossamer cobweb, it settled on the head of the child, and when Mirtai turned with exultant face, she was a child no longer.

The mountains rang back the joyous sound as the Atans greeted her.

CHAPTER 20

'They know nothing of magic.' Zalasta said it quite emphatically.

'That circlet didn't rise up into the air all by itself, Zalasta,' Vanion disagreed, 'and the arrival of the falling star at just exactly the right moment stretches the possibility of coincidence further than I'm willing to go.'

'Chicanery of some kind perhaps?' Patriarch Emban suggested. 'There was a charlatan in Ucera when I was a boy who was very good at that sort of thing. I'd be inclined to look for hidden wires and burning arrows.' They were gathered in the Peloi camp outside the city the following morning, puzzling over the spectacular conclusion of Mirtai's Rite of Passage.

'Why would they do something like that, your Grace?' Khalad asked him.

'To make an impression maybe. How would I know?'

'Who would they have been trying to impress?'

'Us, obviously.'

'It doesn't seem to fit the Atan character,' Tynian said, frowning. 'Would the Atans cheapen a holy rite with that kind of gratuitous trickery, Ambassador Oscagne?'

The Tamul Emissary shook his head. 'Totally out of the question, Sir Tynian. The rite is as central to their culture as a wedding or a funeral. They'd never demean it just to impress strangers – and it wasn't performed for our benefit. The ceremony was for Atana Mirtai.'

'Exactly,' Khalad agreed, 'and if there were hidden wires coming down from those tree-branches *she'd* have known they were there. They just wouldn't have done that to her. A cheap trick like that would have been an insult, and we all know how Atans respond to insults.'

'Norkan will be here in a little while,' Oscagne told them. 'He's been in Atan for quite some time. I'm sure he'll be able to explain it.'

'It cannot have been magic,' Zalasta insisted. It seemed very important to him for some reason. Sparhawk had the uneasy feeling that it had to do with the shaggy-browed magician's racial ego. So long as Styrics were the only people who could perform magic or instruct others in its use, they were unique in the world. If any other race could do the same thing, their importance would be diminished.

'How long are we going to stay here?' Kalten asked. 'This is a nervous kind of place. Some young knight or one of the Peloi is bound to make a mistake sooner or later. If somebody blunders into a deadly insult, I think all this good feeling will evaporate. We don't want to have to fight our way out of town.'

'Norkan will be able to tell us,' Oscagne replied. 'We don't want to insult the Atans by leaving too early either.'

'How far is it from here to Matherion, Oscagne?' Emban asked.

'About five hundred leagues.'

Emban sighed. 'Almost two more months,' he lamented. 'I feel as if this journey's lasted for years.'

'You *do* look more fit, though, your Grace,' Bevier told him.

'I don't *want* to look fit, Bevier. I want to look fat, lazy and pampered. I want to *be* fat, lazy and pampered – and I want a decent meal with lots of butter and gravy and delicacies and fine wines.'

'You *did* volunteer to come along, your Grace,' Sparhawk reminded him.

'I must have been out of my mind.'

376

Ambassador Norkan came across the Peloi campground with an amused expression on his face.

'What's so funny?' Oscagne asked him.

'I've been observing an exquisite dance, old boy,' Norkan replied. 'I'd forgotten just how profoundly literal an Elene can be. Any number of Atan girls have approached young Sir Berit and expressed a burning interest in western weaponry. They were obviously hoping for private lessons in some secluded place where he could demonstrate how he uses his equipment.'

'Norkan,' Oscagne chided him.

'Did I say something wrong, old chap? I'm afraid my Elenic's a bit rusty. Anyway, Sir Berit's arranged a demonstration for the entire group. He's just outside the city wall giving the whole bunch of them archery lessons.'

'We're going to have to have a talk with that boy,' Kalten said to Sparhawk.

'I've been told not to,' Sparhawk said. 'My wife and the other ladies want to keep him innocent. It seems to satisfy some obscure need.' He looked at Norkan. 'Maybe you can settle an argument for us, your Excellency.'

'I'm good at peace-making, Sir Sparhawk. It's not as much fun as starting wars, but the emperor prefers it.'

'What really happened last night, Ambassador Norkan?' Vanion asked him.

'Atana Mirtai became an adult,' Norkan shrugged. 'You were there, Lord Vanion. You saw everything I did.'

'Yes, I did. Now I'd like to have it explained. Did a star really fall at the height of the ceremony? And did the gold circlet really rise from the altar and settle itself on Mirtai's head?'

'Yes. Was there a problem with that?'

'Impossible!' Zalasta exclaimed.

'*You* could do it, couldn't you, learned one?'

'Yes, I suppose so, but I am Styric.'

'And these are Atans?'

'That's exactly my point.'

'We were also disturbed when we first encountered the phenomenon,' Norkan told him. 'The Atans are our cousins. So, unfortunately, are the Arjuni and the Tegans. We Tamuls are a secular people, as you undoubtedly know. We have a pantheon of Gods that we ignore except on holidays. The Atans only have one, and they won't even tell us what His name is. They can appeal to Him in the same way you Styrics appeal to your Gods, and He responds in the same fashion.'

Zalasta's face suddenly went white. 'Impossible!' he said again in a choked voice. 'We'd have known. There are Atans at Sarsos. We'd have felt them using magic.'

'But they don't do it at Sarsos, Zalasta,' Norkan said patiently. 'They only use it here in Atan and only during their ceremonies.'

'That's absurd!'

'I wouldn't tell *them* you feel that way. They hold you Styrics in some contempt, you know. They find the notion of turning a God into a servant a bit impious. Atans have access to a God, and their God can do the same sort of things other Gods do. They choose not to involve their God in everyday matters, so they only call on Him during their religious ceremonies – weddings, funerals, Rites of Passage, and a few others. They can't understand your willingness to insult your Gods by asking them to do things you really ought to do for yourselves.' He looked at Emban then with a sly sort of grin. 'It just occurred to me that your Elene God could probably do exactly the same thing. Have you ever thought of asking Him, your Grace?'

'Heresy!' Bevier gasped.

'Not really, Sir Knight. That word's used to describe somebody who strays from the teachings of his own

378

faith. I'm not a member of the Elene faith, so my speculations can't really be heretical, can they?'

'He's got you there, Bevier,' Ulath said. 'His logic's unassailable.'

'It raises some very interesting questions,' Vanion mused. 'It's entirely possible that the Church blundered when she founded the Militant Orders. We may *not* have had to go outside our own faith for instruction in magic. If we'd asked Him the right way, our own God might have given us the help we needed.' He coughed a bit uncomfortably. 'I'll trust you gentlemen not to tell Sephrenia I came up with that. If I start suggesting that she's unnecessary, she might take it the wrong way.'

'Lord Vanion,' Emban said quite formally. 'As the representative of the Church, I forbid you to continue this speculation. This is dangerous ground, and I want a ruling from Dolmant before we pursue the matter any further – and for God's sake, don't start experimenting.'

'Ah – Patriarch Emban,' Vanion reminded him rather mildly, 'I think that you're forgetting the fact that as the Preceptor of the Pandion Order, my rank in the Church is the same as yours. Technically speaking, you can't forbid me to do anything.'

'Sparhawk's the Preceptor now.'

'Not until he's been confirmed by the Hierocracy, Emban. I'm not trying to demean your authority, old boy, but let's observe the proprieties, shall we? It's the little things that keep us civilised when we're far from home.'

'Aren't Elenes fun?' Oscagne said to Norkan.

'I was just about to make the same observation myself.'

They met with King Androl and Queen Betuana later that morning. Ambassador Oscagne explained their mission in the flowing Tamul tongue.

'He's skirting around your rather unique capabilities, Sparhawk,' Sephrenia said quietly. A faint smile touched her lips. 'The emperor's officials seem a little unwilling to admit that they're powerless and that they had to appeal for outside help.'

Sparhawk nodded. 'We've been through it before,' he murmured. 'Oscagne was very concerned about that when he spoke to us in Chyrellos. It seems a little short-sighted in this situation, though. The Atans make up the Tamul army. It doesn't really make much sense to keep secrets from them.'

'Whatever made you think that politics made sense, Sparhawk?'

'I've missed you, little mother,' he laughed.

'I certainly *hope* so.'

King Androl's face was grave, even stern as Oscagne described what they had discovered in Astel. Queen Betuana's expression was somewhat softer – largely because Danae was sitting in her lap. Sparhawk had seen his daughter do that many times. Whenever there was a potential for tension in a situation, Danae started looking for laps. People invariably responded to her unspoken appeals to be held without even thinking about it. 'She does that on purpose, doesn't she?' he whispered to Sephrenia.

'That went by a little fast, Sparhawk.'

'Aphrael. She climbs into people's laps in order to control them.'

'Of course. Close contact makes it far more certain – and subtle.'

'That's the reason she's always remained a child, isn't it? So that people will pick her up and hold her and she can make them do what she wants?'

'Well, it's one of the reasons.'

'She won't be able to do that when she grows up, you know.'

'Yes, I *do* know, Sparhawk, and I'm going to be very interested to see how she handles the situation. Oscagne's coming to the point now. He's asking Androl for a report on any incidents similar to the ones you've encountered.'

Norkan stepped forward to translate for Androl, and Oscagne retired to the Elene side of the room to perform the same service. The Tamuls had perfected the tedious but necessary business of translation to make it as smooth and unobtrusive as possible.

King Androl pondered the matter for a few moments. Then he smiled at Ehlana and spoke to her in Tamul. His voice was very soft.

'Thus says the King,' Norkan began his translation. 'Gladly do we greet Ehlana-Queen once more, for her presence is like the sunshine come at last after a long winter.'

'Oh, that's *very* nice,' Sephrenia murmured. 'We always seem to forget the poetic side of the Atan nature.'

'Moreover,' Norkan continued his translation, 'glad are we to welcome the fabled warriors of the west and the wise-man of Chyrellos-Church.' Norkan was obviously translating verbatim.

Emban politely inclined his head.

'Clearly we see our common concern in the matter at hand, and staunchly will we join with the West-warriors in such acts as are needful.'

Androl spoke again, pausing from time to time for translation. 'Our minds have been unquiet in seasons past, for we have failed in tasks set for us by our Matherion-masters. This troubles us, for we are not accustomed to failure.' His expression was slightly mortified as he made that admission. 'I am sure, Ehlana-Queen, that Oscagne-Emperor-Speaker has told you of our difficulties in parts of Tamuli beyond our own borders. Shamed are we that he has spoken truly.'

Queen Betuana said something briefly to her husband.

'She told him to get on with it,' Sephrenia murmured to Sparhawk. 'It appears that his tendency to be flowery irritates her – at least that was the impression I got.'

Androl said something to Norkan in an apologetic tone.

'That's a surprise,' Norkan said, obviously speaking for himself now. 'The King just admitted that he's been keeping secrets from me. He doesn't usually do that.'

Androl spoke again, and Norkan's translation became more colloquial as the Atan king seemed to lay formality aside. 'He says that there have been incidents here in Atan itself. It's an internal matter, so he technically wasn't obliged to tell me about it. He says they've encountered creatures he calls "the shaggy ones". As I understand it, the creatures are even bigger than the tallest Atans.'

'Long arms?' Ulath asked intently. 'Flat noses and big bones in the face? Pointed teeth?'

Norkan translated into Tamul, and King Androl looked at Ulath with some surprise. Then he nodded.

'Trolls!' Ulath said. 'Ask him how many his people have seen at any one time.'

'Fifty or more,' came the reply.

Ulath shook his head. 'That's very unlikely,' he said flatly. 'You might find a single family of Trolls working together, but never fifty all at once.'

'He wouldn't lie,' Norkan insisted.

'I didn't say he did, but Trolls have never behaved that way before. If they had, they'd have driven us out of Thalesia.'

'It seems that the rules have changed, Ulath,' Tynian noted. 'Have there been any other incidents, your Excellency? Things that didn't involve Trolls?'

Norkan spoke to the king and then translated the reply. 'They've had encounters with warriors in strange armour and with strange equipment.'

'Ask him if they might have been Cyrgai,' Bevier suggested. 'Horse-hair-crested helmets? Big round shields? Long spears?'

Norkan posed the question, though his expression was baffled. It was with some amazement that he translated the reply. 'They were!' he exclaimed. 'They were Cyrgai! How's that possible?'

'We'll explain later,' Sparhawk said tersely. 'Were there any others?'

Norkan asked the questions quickly now, obviously excited by these revelations. Queen Betuana leaned forward slightly and took over for her husband.

'Arjuni,' Norkan said tersely. 'They were heavily armed and made no attempt to hide the way they usually do. And once there was an army of Elenes – mostly serfs.' Then his eyes went wide with astonishment. 'That's totally impossible! That's only a myth!'

'My colleague's losing his grip,' Oscagne told them. 'The queen says that once they encountered the Shining Ones.'

'Who are they?' Stragen asked.

'Norkan's right,' Oscagne replied. 'The Shining Ones are mythical creatures. It's another of those things I told you about back in Chyrellos. Our enemy's been sifting through folk-lore for horrors. The Shining Ones are like vampires, werewolves and Ogres. Would your Majesty object if Norkan and I pursued this and then gave you a summary?' he asked Ehlana.

'Go right ahead, your Excellency,' she agreed.

The two Tamuls began to speak more rapidly now, and Queen Betuana replied firmly. Sparhawk got the distinct impression that she was far more intelligent and forceful than her husband. Still holding Princess Danae in her lap, she answered the questions incisively, and her eyes were very intent.

'Our enemy seems to be doing the same things here in Atan that he's been doing elsewhere,' Oscagne told them finally, 'and he's been adding a few twists besides. The forces from antiquity behave the same as your antique Lamorks did back in Eosia and the way those Cyrgai and their Cynesgan allies did in the forest west of Sarsos. They attack; there's a fight, and then they vanish when their leader gets killed. Only their dead remain. The Trolls *don't* vanish. They all have to be killed.'

'What about these "Shining Ones"?' Kalten asked.

'There's no way to be sure about those,' Oscagne replied. 'The Atans flee from them.'

'They *what*?' Stragen's voice was startled.

'Everybody's afraid of the Shining Ones, Milord,' Oscagne told him. 'The stories about them make tales of vampires and werewolves and Ogres sound like bedtime stories.'

'Could you accept a slight amendment, your Excellency?' Ulath asked mildly. 'I don't want to alarm you, but Ogres *are* real. We see them all the time in Thalesia.'

'You're joking, Sir Ulath.'

'No, not really.' Ulath took off his horned helmet. 'These are Ogre-horns,' he said tapping the curved appurtenances on his headgear.

'Maybe what you have in Thalesia's just a creature you *call* an Ogre,' Oscagne said dubiously.

'Twelve feet tall? Horns? Fangs? Claws for fingers? That's an Ogre, isn't it?'

'Well –'

'That's what we've got in Thalesia. If they *aren't* Ogres, we'll settle for them until you can find us some real ones.'

Oscagne stared at him.

'They aren't all that bad, your Excellency. The Trolls give us more trouble – probably because they're meat eaters. Ogres eat anything. Actually, they prefer trees for dinner over people. They're particularly fond of maple trees for some reason – probably because they're sweet. A hungry Ogre will kick his way right through your house to get at a maple tree you've got growing in your backyard.'

'Is he actually serious?' Oscagne appealed to the others. Ulath sometimes had that effect on people.

Tynian reached over and rapped the Ogre-horns on Ulath's helmet with his knuckles. 'These feel fairly serious to me, your Excellency,' he said. 'And that raises some other questions. If Ogres are real, we might want to re-think our positions on vampires, werewolves and these Shining Ones as well. Under the circumstances, we might consider discarding the word "impossible" for the time being.'

'But you *are*, Mirtai,' Princess Danae insisted.

'It's a different kind of thing, Danae,' the Atana told her. 'It's symbolic in my case.'

'Everything's symbolic, Mirtai,' Danae told her. 'Everything we do means something else. There are symbols all around us. No matter how you want to look at it, though, we have the same mother, and that makes us sisters.' It seemed very important to her for some reason. Sparhawk was sitting with Sephrenia in the corner of a large room of King Androl's house. His daughter was busy asserting her kinship with Mirtai as Baroness Melidere and Ehlana's maid looked on.

Mirtai smiled gently. 'All right, Danae,' she gave in, 'if you want to think so, we're sisters.'

Danae gave a little squeal of delight, jumped into Mirtai's arms and smothered her with kisses.

'Isn't she a little darling?' Baroness Melidere laughed.

'Yes, Baroness,' Alean murmured. Then a small frown creased the girl's brow. 'I'll never understand that,' she said. 'No matter how closely I watch her, she always manages to get her feet dirty.' She pointed at Danae's grass-stained feet. 'Sometimes I almost think she's got a boxful of grass hidden among her toys, and she shuffles her feet in it when my back's turned just to torment me.'

Melidere smiled. 'She just likes to run barefoot, Alean,' she said. 'Don't you ever want to take off your shoes and run through the grass?'

Alean sighed. 'I'm in service, Baroness,' she replied. 'I'm not supposed to give in to that sort of whim.'

'You're so very proper, Alean,' the honey-eyed Baroness said. 'If a girl doesn't give in to her whims now and then, she'll never have any fun.'

'I'm not here to have fun, Baroness. I'm here to serve. My first employer made that very clear to me.' She crossed the room to the two 'sisters' and touched Danae's shoulder. 'Time for your bath, Princess,' she said.

'Do I *have* to?'

'Yes.'

'It's such a bother. I'll just get dirty again, you know.'

'We're supposed to make an effort to stay ahead of it, your Highness.'

'Do as she tells you, Danae,' Mirtai said.

'Yes, sister dear,' Danae sighed.

'That was an interesting exchange, wasn't it?' Sparhawk murmured to Sephrenia.

'Yes,' the small woman agreed. 'Has she been letting things slip that way very often?'

'I didn't quite follow that.'

'She's not really supposed to talk about symbols the way she just did when she's around pagans.'

386

'I wish you wouldn't use that word to describe us, Sephrenia.'

'Well, aren't you?'

'It sort of depends on your perspective. What's so important about symbols that she's supposed to hide them?'

'It's not the symbols themselves, Sparhawk. It's what talking about them that way reveals.'

'Oh? What's that?'

'The fact that she doesn't look at the world or think about it in the same way we do. There are meanings in the world for her that we can't even begin to comprehend.'

'I'll take your word for it. Are you and Mirtai sisters now, too? I mean, if she's Danae's sister and you are too, wouldn't you almost have to be?'

'All women are sisters, Sparhawk.'

'That's a generalisation, Sephrenia.'

'How perceptive of you to have noticed.'

Vanion entered the room. 'Where's Ehlana?' he asked.

'She and Betuana are conferring,' Sparhawk replied.

'Who's translating for them?'

'One of Engessa's girls from Darsas. What did you want to talk with her about?'

'I think we'll be leaving tomorrow. Engessa, Oscagne and I talked with King Androl. Oscagne feels that we should press on to Matherion. He doesn't want to keep the emperor waiting. Engessa's sending his legions back to Darsas, he'll be going on with us, largely because he speaks Elenic better than most Atans.'

'That doesn't disappoint me,' Mirtai said. 'He's my father now, and we really ought to get to know each other better.'

'You're enjoying this, aren't you, Vanion?' Sephrenia said it half-accusingly.

'I've missed it,' he admitted. 'I've been at the centre of things for most of my life. I don't think I was meant to sit on the back shelf.'

'Weren't you happy when there were just the two of us?'

'Of course I was. I'd have been perfectly content to spend the rest of my life alone with you, but we're not alone any more. The world's intruding upon us, Sephrenia, and we both have responsibilities. We still have time for each other, though.'

'Are you sure, Vanion?'

'I'll *make* sure, love.'

'Would you two like to be alone?' Mirtai asked them with an arch little smile.

'Later perhaps,' Sephrenia replied quite calmly.

'Won't we be a little under-manned without Engessa's Atans?' Sparhawk asked.

'King Androl's making arrangements,' Vanion said. 'Don't worry, Sparhawk. Your wife's almost as important to the rest of us as she is to you. We're not going to let anything happen to her.'

'We can discount the possibility of exaggeration,' Sephrenia said. 'The Atan character makes that very unlikely.'

'I'll agree there,' Sparhawk concurred. 'They're warriors, and they're trained to give precise reports.'

Vanion and Zalasta nodded. It was evening, and the four of them were walking together outside the city in order to discuss the situation apart from Norkan and Oscagne. It was not that they distrusted the two Tamuls. It was just that they wanted to be able to speak freely about certain things which Tamuls were culturally unprepared to accept.

'Our opponent is quite obviously a God,' Zalasta said firmly.

'He says it so casually,' Vanion noted. 'Are you so accustomed to confronting Gods that you're becoming blasé about it, Zalasta?'

Zalasta smiled. 'Just defining the problem, Lord Vanion. The resurrection of whole armies is beyond purely human capabilities. You can take my word for that. I tried it once and made a horrible mess of it. It took me weeks to get them all back into the ground again.'

'We've faced Gods before,' Vanion shrugged. 'We stared across a border at Azash for five hundred years.'

'Now who's blasé?' Sephrenia said.

'Just defining the solution, love,' he replied. 'The Church Knights were founded for just such situations. We really need to identify our enemy, though. Gods have worshippers, and our enemy's inevitably utilising his worshippers in this plan. We have to find out who he is so that we know who his adherents are. We can't disrupt his plans until we know whom to attack. Am I being obvious?'

'Yes,' Sparhawk told him, 'but logic always is right at first. I like the notion of attacking his worshippers. If we do that, he's going to have to stop what he's doing and concentrate on protecting his own people. The strength of a God depends entirely on his worshippers. If we start killing his people, we'll diminish him with every sword-stroke.'

'Barbarian,' Sephrenia accused.

'Can you make her stop doing that to me, Vanion?' Sparhawk appealed. 'She's called me both a pagan and a barbarian so far today.'

'Well, aren't you?' she said.

'Maybe, but it's not nice to come right out and say it like that.'

'It's the presence of the Trolls that has concerned me since you told me about it at Sarsos,' Zalasta told them.

'They are *not* drawn from the past, and they have but recently come to this part of the world from their ancestral home in Thalesia. I know little of Trolls, but it was my understanding that they are fiercely attached to their homeland. What could have provoked this migration?'

'Ulath's baffled,' Sparhawk replied. 'I gather that the Thalesians are so happy that the Trolls have left that they didn't pursue the matter.'

'Trolls don't habitually co-operate with each other,' Sephrenia told them. '*One* of them might have decided on his own to leave Thalesia, but he'd never have persuaded the rest to go with him.'

'You're raising a very unpleasant possibility, love,' Vanion said.

They all looked at each other.

'Is there any way they could have got out of Bhelliom?' Vanion asked Sephrenia.

'I don't know, Vanion. Sparhawk asked me the same question quite some time ago. I don't know what spell Ghwerig used to seal them inside the jewel. Troll-spells aren't the same as ours.'

'Then we don't *know* if they're still inside or if they've somehow managed to free themselves?'

She nodded glumly.

'The fact that the Trolls banded up and left their ancestral home all at the same time suggests that something with sufficient authority over them *commanded* them to leave,' Zalasta mused.

'That would be their Gods, all right.' Vanion's face was as glum as Sephrenia's. 'Trolls wouldn't obey anyone else.' He sighed. 'Well, we wanted to know who was opposing us. I think we may have just found out.'

'You're all full of light and joy today, Vanion,' Sparhawk said sourly, 'but I'd like something a little more concrete before I declare war on the Trolls.'

'How did you force the Troll-Gods to stop attacking

you in Zemoch, Prince Sparhawk?' Zalasta asked him.

'I used the Bhelliom.'

'It rather looks as if you'll have to use it again. I don't suppose you happened to bring it with you, did you?'

Sparhawk looked quickly at Sephrenia. 'You didn't tell him?' he asked with a certain surprise.

'It wasn't necessary for him to know, dear one. Dolmant wanted us all to keep it more or less to ourselves, remember?'

'I gather that it's not with you then, Prince Sparhawk,' Zalasta surmised. 'Did you leave it in some safe place in Cimmura?'

'It's in a safe place all right, learned one,' Sparhawk replied bleakly, 'but it's not in Cimmura.'

'Where is it then?'

'After we used it to destroy Azash, we threw it into the sea.'

Zalasta's face went chalk white.

'In the deepest part of the deepest ocean in the world,' Sephrenia added.

CHAPTER 21

'It is along the north coast, Ehlana-Queen,' Norkan translated Queen Betuana's reply. 'These shaggy ones you call Trolls have come across the winter ice in large groups for the past two years. At first our people thought they were bears, but it was not so. They avoided us at first, and the snow and fog of winter made it hard for our people to see them clearly. When there were more of them here, they grew bolder. It was not until one of them was killed that we realised they were not bears.'

King Androl was not present. Androl's intellectual gifts were not profound, and he much preferred to let his wife deal with state matters. The Atan King looked very impressive, but he was at his best in ceremonial situations where no surprises were likely to come up.

'Ask her if they've seen any Trolls farther south,' Sparhawk murmured to his wife.

'Why don't *you* ask her?'

'Let's keep things sort of formal, Ehlana. This is technically a conversation between the two of you. I don't think the rest of us are supposed to join in. Let's not take a chance of violating a propriety we don't know about.'

Ehlana posed the question, and Oscagne translated.

'No,' Norkan repeated Betuana's answer. 'The Trolls appear to have settled in the forests along the north slopes. So far as we know, they haven't come deeper into Atan.'

'Warn her that Trolls are very good at hiding in forests,' Ulath advised.

'So are we,' the reply was translated.

'Ask her if some advice on tactics would offend her,' the Genidian Knight said then. 'We Thalesians have had many experiences with Trolls – most of them bad.'

'We are always willing to listen to the voice of experience,' came the Atan queen's reply.

'When we encounter Trolls in Thalesia, we usually stay back a ways and shoot some arrows into them,' Ulath informed Ehlana. 'It's hard to kill them with arrows, because their fur and their hides are so thick, but it's a good idea to slow them down if you can. Trolls are much, much quicker than they look, and they have very long arms. They can snatch a man out of his saddle quicker than the man can blink.'

Ehlana went through the formality of repeating his words.

'What does the Troll do then?' Betuana's expression was curious.

'First he pulls off the man's head. Then he eats the rest of him. Trolls don't like to eat heads for some reason.'

Ehlana choked slightly on that.

'We do not use the bow in war,' Norkan translated Betuana's flowing Tamul. 'We only use it in the hunt for creatures we intend to eat.'

'Well,' Ulath said a bit dubiously, 'you *could* eat a Troll if you wanted to, I guess. I won't guarantee the flavour, though.'

'I refuse to repeat that, Sir Ulath!' Ehlana exclaimed.

'Ask her if javelins would be acceptable in the Atan culture,' Tynian suggested.

'Javelins would be quite all right,' Norkan replied. 'I've seen the Atans practising with them.'

Betuana spoke to him rapidly and at some length.

'Her Majesty's asked me to translate in narrative,' Norkan told them. 'The sun is well up, and she knows you should be on the road. Oscagne tells me that you're

393

planning to take the road leading to Lebas in Tamul proper. Atan society's organised along clan lines, and each clan has its own territory. You'll be passed along from clan to clan as you ride east. It's a breach of etiquette for one clan to intrude on the territory of another, and breaches of etiquette are avoided at all costs here in Atan.'

'I wonder why,' Stragen murmured.

'Oscagne,' Norkan said then, 'as soon as you reach civilisation, send me a score or so of imperial messengers with fast horses. Her Majesty wants to keep in close contact with Matherion during the crisis.'

'Very good idea,' Oscagne agreed.

Then Betuana rose, towering over all of them. She affectionately embraced Ehlana and then Mirtai, clearly indicating that it was time for them to continue their journey eastward.

'I will cherish the memory of this visit, dear Betuana,' Ehlana told her.

'And I will as well, dearly-loved sister-queen,' Betuana replied in almost flawless Elenic.

Ehlana smiled. 'I wondered how long you were going to hide your understanding of our language, Betuana,' she said.

'You knew?' Betuana seemed surprised.

Ehlana nodded. 'It's very hard to keep your face and your eyes from revealing your understanding while you're waiting for the translation. Why do you keep your knowledge of Elenic a secret?'

'The time the translator takes to convert your words into human speech gives me time to consider my reply,' Betuana shrugged.

'That's a very useful tactic,' Ehlana said admiringly. 'I wish I could use it in Eosia, but everybody there speaks Elenic, so I couldn't really get away with it.'

'Bandage your ears,' Ulath suggested.

'Does he *have* to do that?' Ehlana complained to Sparhawk.

'It's only a suggestion, your Majesty,' Ulath shrugged. 'Pretend to be deaf and have some people around to wiggle their fingers at you as if they were translating.'

She stared at him. 'That's absurd, Ulath. Do you have any idea of how awkward and inconvenient that would be?'

'I just said it was a suggestion, your Majesty,' he said mildly. 'I didn't say it was a good one.'

Following a formal farewell which was once again primarily for Mirtai's benefit, the queen and her party rode eastward out of Atana along the Lebas road. Once they were clear of the city, Oscagne, who had insisted on riding a horse that day, suggested to Sparhawk, Stragen and Vanion that they ride forward to confer with the other knights. They found them near the head of the column. Tynian was entertaining them with a much-embellished account of a probably imaginary amorous adventure.

'What's afoot?' Kalten asked when Sparhawk and the others joined them.

'Sparhawk and I conferred with Sephrenia and Zalasta last night,' Vanion replied. 'We thought we might share the fruits of our discussions – out of Ehlana's hearing.'

'That sounds ominous,' the blond Pandion observed.

'Not entirely,' Vanion smiled. 'Our conclusions are still a bit tenuous, and there's no point in alarming the queen until we're a bit more certain.'

'Then there *is* something to be alarmed about, isn't there, Lord Vanion?' Talen asked.

'There's always *something* to be alarmed about,' Khalad told his brother.

'We've sort of concluded that we're facing a God,' Vanion told them. 'I'm sure you've all more or less worked that out for yourselves.'

'Did you really have to invite me to come along this time, Sparhawk?' Kalten complained. 'I'm not very good at dealing with Gods.'

'Who is?'

'*You* weren't so bad at Zemoch.'

'Luck, probably.'

'This is the way our reasoning went,' Vanion continued. 'You've been seeing that shadow again, and the cloud. On the surface at least, they seem to be divine manifestations, and these armies out of the past – the Lamorks and the Cyrgai – couldn't have been raised by a mortal. Zalasta told us that he'd tried it once and that it all fell apart on him. If *he* can't do it, we can be fairly, sure that nobody else can either.'

'Logical,' Bevier approved.

'Thank you. Now then, the Trolls all left Thalesia a while back, and they've started to show up here in Atan. We more or less agreed that they wouldn't have done that unless they'd been commanded to by someone they'd obey. Couple that fact with the shadow, and it seems to point at the Troll-Gods. Sephrenia's not positive that they're permanently locked inside Bhelliom, so we more or less have to accept the fact that they've somehow managed to escape.'

'This isn't going to be one of the *good* stories, I gather,' Talen said glumly.

'It *is* a bit gloomy, isn't it?' Tynian agreed.

Vanion raised one hand. 'It gets worse,' he told them. 'We sort of agreed that all of this plotting involving ancient heroes, rabid nationalism and the like is somewhat beyond the capability of the Troll-Gods. It's not likely that they'd have a very sophisticated concept of politics, so I think we'll have to consider the possibility of an alliance of some kind. Someone – either human or immortal – is taking care of the politics, and the Troll-Gods are providing the muscle. They command the Trolls, and they can raise these figures from the grave.'

'They're being used?' Ulath suggested.

'So it would seem.'

'It doesn't wash, Lord Vanion,' the Thalesian said bluntly.

'How so?'

'What's in it for the Trolls? Why would the Troll-Gods ally themselves with somebody else if there weren't any benefits to the Trolls to come out of the arrangement? The Trolls can't rule the world, because they can't come down out of the mountains.'

'Why not?' Berit asked him.

'Their fur – and those thick hides of theirs. They *have* to stay where it's cool. If you put a Troll out in the summer sun for two days, he'll die. Their bodies are built to keep the heat *in*, not to get rid of it.'

'That *is* a fairly serious flaw in your theory, Lord Vanion,' Oscagne agreed.

'I think I might be able to suggest a solution,' Stragen told them. 'Our enemy – or enemies – want to re-arrange the world, right?'

'Well, at least the top part of it,' Tynian amended. 'Nobody I know of has ever suggested turning it all the way upside down and putting the peasantry in charge.'

'Maybe that comes later,' Stragen smiled. 'Our name-less friend out there wants to change the world, but he doesn't have quite enough power to pull it off by himself. He needs the power of the Troll-Gods to make it work, but what could he offer the Trolls in exchange for their help? What do the Trolls *really* want?'

'Thalesia,' Ulath replied moodily.

'Precisely. Wouldn't the Troll-Gods leap at an opportunity to wipe out the Elenes and Styrics in Thalesia and

397

return total possession of the peninsula to the Trolls? If someone's come up with a way to expel the Younger Styric Gods – or at least claims he has – wouldn't that be fairly enticing to the Troll-Gods? It was the Younger Gods who dispossessed them in the first place, and that's why they had to go hide. This is pure speculation, of course, but let's say this friend of ours came up with a way to free the Troll-Gods. Then he offered an alliance, promising to drive the Elenes and Styrics out of Thalesia – and possibly the north coasts of both continents as well – in exchange for the help he needs. The Trolls get the north, and our friend gets the rest of the world. If *I* were a Troll, that would sound like a very attractive bargain, wouldn't you say?'

'He may have hit on it,' Ulath conceded.

'His solution certainly answers *my* objection to the idea,' Bevier concurred. 'It may not be the *precise* arrangement between our friend and the Troll-Gods, but it's a clear hint that *something* could have been worked out. What's our course, then?'

'We have to break up the alliance,' Sparhawk replied.

'That's a neat trick when you don't know who one of the allies is,' Kalten told him.

'We *do* sort of know about *one* part of it, so we'll have to concentrate on that. Your theory narrows my options, Vanion. I guess I *will* have to declare war on the Trolls after all.'

'I don't quite understand,' Oscagne confessed.

'The Gods derive their strength from their worshippers, your Excellency,' Bevier explained. 'The more worshippers, the stronger the God. If Sparhawk starts killing Trolls, the Troll-Gods will notice it. If he kills enough of them, they'll withdraw from the alliance. They won't have any choice if they want to survive, and we found out at Zemoch that they're *very* interested in surviving, they went all to pieces when Sparhawk threatened to destroy Bhelliom and them along with it.'

'They became very co-operative at that point,' Sparhawk said.

'You gentlemen have a real treat in store for you,' Ulath told them. 'Fighting Trolls is very, *very* exhilarating.'

They set up their night's encampment that evening in a meadow beside a turbulent mountain stream that had carved a deep gorge in the mountains. The lower walls of the gorge were tree-covered, and they angled up steeply to the sheer cliffs rising a hundred or more feet to the rim of the cut. It was a good defensive position, Sparhawk noted as he surveyed the camp. Evening came early in these canyons, and the cooking fires flared yellow in the gathering dusk, their smoke drifting blue and tenuous downstream in the night breeze.

'A word with you, Prince Sparhawk?' It was Zalasta, and his white Styric robe gleamed in the half-light.

'Of course, learned one.'

'I'm afraid your wife doesn't like me,' the magician observed. 'She tries to be polite, but her distaste is fairly obvious. Have I offended her in some way?'

'I don't think so, Zalasta.'

A faintly bitter smile touched the Styric's lips. 'It's what my people call "the Elene complaint", then.'

'I rather doubt that. I more or less raised her, and I made her understand that the common Elene prejudice was without foundation. Her attitude sort of derives from mine, and the Church Knights are actually quite fond of Styrics – the Pandions particularly so, since Sephrenia was our tutor. We love her very much.'

'Yes. I've observed that.' The magician smiled. 'We ourselves are not without our failings in that area. Our prejudice against Elenes is quite nearly as irrational as yours against us. Your wife's disapproval of me must come from something else, then.'

399

'It may be something as simple as your accent, learned one. My wife's a complex person. She's very intelligent, but she *does* have her irrational moments.'

'It might be best if I avoided her, then. I'll travel on horseback from now on. Our close proximity in that carriage exacerbates her dislike, I expect. I've worked with people who've disliked me in the past and it's no great inconvenience. When I have leisure, I'll win her over.' He flashed a quick smile. 'I can be very winning when I set my mind to it.' He looked on down the gorge where the rapids swirled and foamed white in the gathering darkness. 'Is there any possibility that you might be able to retrieve the Bhelliom, Prince Sparhawk?' he asked gravely. 'I'm afraid we're at a distinct disadvantage without it. We need something powerful enough to achieve some measure of parity with a group of Gods. Are you at liberty to tell me where you were when you threw it into the sea? I might be able to aid you in its retrieval.'

'There weren't any restrictions placed on me about discussing it, learned one,' Sparhawk replied ruefully. 'There wasn't any need for that, since I haven't got the foggiest idea of where it was. Aphrael chose the spot, and she very carefully arranged things so that we couldn't identify the place. You might ask her, but I'm fairly sure she won't tell you.'

Zalasta smiled. 'She *is* a bit whimsical, isn't she?' he said. 'We all loved her in spite of that, however.'

'That's right, you grew up in the same village with her and Sephrenia, didn't you?'

'Oh, yes. I am proud to call them my friends. It was very stimulating trying to keep up with Aphrael. She had a very agile mind. Did she give you any reason for her desire to keep the location a secret?'

'Not in so many words, but I think she felt that the jewel was far too dangerous to be loosed in the world.

400

It's even more eternal than the Gods themselves, and probably more powerful. I can't pretend to even begin to understand where it originated, but it seems to be one of those elemental spirits that are involved in the creation of the universe.' Sparhawk smiled. 'That gave me quite a turn when I found out about it. I was carrying something that could create whole suns not six inches from my heart. I think I can understand Aphrael's concern about the Bhelliom, though. She told us once that the Gods can only see the future imperfectly, and she couldn't really see what might happen if the Bhelliom fell into the wrong hands. She and I took a very real chance of destroying the world to keep it out of the hands of Azash. She wanted to put it where nobody could ever use it again.'

'Her thinking is faulty, Prince Sparhawk.'

'I wouldn't tell *her* that, if I were you. She might take it as criticism.'

Zalasta smiled. 'She knows me, so she's not upset when I criticise her. If, as you say, the Bhelliom's one of those energies that's involved in the constructing of the universe, it must be allowed to continue its work. The universe will be flawed if it is not.'

'She said that this world won't last forever,' Sparhawk shrugged. 'In time, it'll be destroyed, and Bhelliom will be freed. The mind sort of shudders away from the notion, but I gather that the space of time stretching from the moment Bhelliom was trapped on this world until the moment the world burns away when our sun explodes is no more than the blinking of an eye to the spirit which inhabits it.'

'I sort of choke on the notions of eternity and infinity myself, Prince Sparhawk,' Zalasta admitted.

'I think we'll have to accept the notion that Bhelliom's lost for good, learned one,' Sparhawk told him. 'We're at a disadvantage, certainly, but I don't see any help for it. We're going to have to deal with this situation ourselves, I'm afraid.'

Zalasta sighed. 'You may be right, Prince Sparhawk, but we really need the Bhelliom. Our success or failure may hinge on that stone. I think we should concentrate our efforts on Sephrenia. We must persuade her to intercede with Aphrael. She has an enormous influence on her sister.'

'Yes,' Sparhawk agreed. 'I've noticed that. What were they like as children?'

Zalasta looked up into the gathering darkness. 'Our village changed a great deal when Aphrael was born,' he reminisced. 'We knew at once that she was no ordinary child. The Younger Gods are all very fond of her. Of all of them, she is the only child, and they've spoiled her outrageously over the aeons.' He smiled faintly. 'She's perfected the art of being a child. All children are lovable, but Aphrael is so skilled at making people love her that she can melt the hardest of hearts. The Gods always get what they want, but Aphrael makes us do what she wants out of love.'

'I've noticed that,' Sparhawk said wryly.

'Sephrenia was about nine when her sister was born, and from the moment she first saw the Child-Goddess, she committed her entire life to her service.' There was a strange note of pain in the magician's voice as he said it. 'Aphrael seemed to have almost no infancy,' he continued. 'She was born with the ability to speak – or so it seemed – and she was walking in an incredibly short period of time. It was not convenient for her to go through a normal babyhood, so she simply stepped over such things as teething and learning to crawl. She wanted to be a child, not a baby. I was several years older than Sephrenia and already deep into my studies, but I did observe them rather closely. It's not often that one has the opportunity to watch a God grow up.'

'Very rare,' Sparhawk agreed.

Zalasta smiled. 'Sephrenia spent every moment with her sister. It was obvious from the very beginning that there was a special bond between them. It's one of Aphrael's peculiarities that she adopts the subservient position of a young child. She's a Goddess, and she could command, but she doesn't. She almost seems to enjoy being scolded. She's obedient – when it suits her to be – but every so often she'll do something outrageously impossible – probably just to remind people who she really is.'

Sparhawk remembered the swarm of fairies pollinating the flowers in the palace garden in Cimmura.

'Sephrenia was a sensible child who always acted older than her years. I suspect Aphrael of preparing her sister for a lifelong task even before she herself was born. In a very real sense, Sephrenia became Aphrael's mother. She cared for her, fed her, bathed her – although that occasioned some truly stupendous arguments. Aphrael absolutely hates to be bathed – and she really doesn't need it, since she can make dirt go away whenever she wants to. I don't know if you noticed it, but her feet always have grass-stains on them, even when she's in a place where there is no grass. For some reason I can't begin to fathom, she seems to need those stains.' The Styric sighed. 'When Aphrael was about six or so, Sephrenia was obliged to become her mother in fact. The three of us were off in the forest, and while we were gone, a mob of drunken Elene peasants attacked our village and killed everyone there.'

Sparhawk drew in his breath sharply. 'That explains a few things,' he said. 'Of course it raises other things even more incomprehensible. After a tragedy like that, what could ever have persuaded Sephrenia to take on the chore of training generations of Pandion Knights?'

'Aphrael probably told her to,' Zalasta shrugged.

'Don't make any mistakes, Prince Sparhawk. Aphrael may *pretend* to be a child, but in truth she is not. She will obey when it suits her, but never forget that *she* is the one who makes the ultimate decisions, and she *always* gets what she wants.'

'What happened after your village was destroyed?' Sparhawk asked.

'We wandered for a time in the forest, and then another Styric village took us in. As soon as I was sure that the girls were settled in and safe, I left to pursue my studies. I didn't see them again for many years, and when I finally met them again, Sephrenia was the beautiful woman she is now. Aphrael, however, was still a child, not a day older than she had been when I left them.' He sighed again. 'The time we spent together when we were children was the happiest of my life. The memory of that time strengthens and sustains me when I am troubled.'

He looked up toward the sky where the first stars were beginning to come out. 'Please make my excuses, Prince Sparhawk. I think I'd like to be alone with my memories tonight.'

'I will, Zalasta,' Sparhawk replied, laying a friendly hand on the Styric's shoulder.

'We're fond of him,' Danae said.

'Why are you keeping your identity a secret from him then?'

'I'm not sure, father. Maybe it's just because girls need secrets.'

'That doesn't make sense, you know.'

'Yes, but I don't have to make sense. That's the nice thing about being universally adored.'

'Zalasta thinks we're going to need the Bhelliom.' Sparhawk decided to get right to the point.

'No.' Aphrael said it very firmly. 'I spent too much

404

time and effort getting it into a safe place to turn around and drag it out every time there's a change in the weather. Zalasta always wants to unleash more power than is really necessary in situations like this. If all we're facing is the Troll-Gods, we can manage without Bhelliom.' She held up one hand when he started to object. '*My* decision, Sparhawk,' she told him.

'I could always spank you and make you change your mind,' he threatened.

'Not unless I let you, you can't.' Then she sighed. 'The Troll-Gods aren't going to be a problem for much longer.'

'Oh?'

'The Trolls are doomed,' she said rather sadly, 'and once they're gone their Gods will be powerless.'

'Why are the Trolls doomed?'

'Because they can't change, Sparhawk. We may not always like it, but that's the way the world is. The creatures of this world must change – or die. That's what happened to the Dawn-men. The Trolls supplanted them because they couldn't change, and now it's the turn of the Trolls. Their nature is such that they need a great deal of room. A lone Troll needs fifty or so square leagues of range, and he won't share that range with any other Troll. There just isn't enough room left for them any more. There are Elenes in the world now as well, and you're cutting down trees to build your houses and to clear fields for your crops. The Trolls might have survived if they only had to live with Styrics. Styrics don't chop trees down.' She smiled. 'It's not that we're really all that fond of trees. It's just that we don't have very good axes. When you Elenes discovered how to make steel, you doomed the Trolls – and their Gods.'

'That lends some weight to the notion that the Troll-Gods may have allied themselves with someone else,' Sephrenia noted. 'If they can understand what's happening, they're probably getting desperate. Their survival depends on preserving the Trolls and their range.'

Sparhawk grunted. 'That might help to explain something that's been bothering me,' he said.

'Oh?' Sephrenia asked him.

'If there's someone involved as well as the Troll-Gods, it might account for the differences I've been feeling. I've been getting this nagging sense that things aren't quite the same as they were last time – jarring little discrepancies, if you take my meaning. The major discrepancy lies in the fact that these elaborate schemes with people like Drychtnath and Ayachin are just too subtle for the Troll-Gods to understand.' He made a rueful face. 'But that immediately raises another problem. How can this other one get the co-operation of the Troll-Gods if he can't explain what he's doing and why?'

'Would it offend your pride if I offered you a simpler solution?' Danae asked him.

'I don't think so.'

'The Troll-Gods know that others are smarter than they are, and the one you call "our friend" has a certain hold over them. He can always cram them back into Bhelliom and let them spend several million years in that box on the sea-bottom if they don't co-operate. Maybe he's just telling them what he wants them to do without bothering to explain it to them. The rest of the time, he could just be letting them blunder around making noise. All that crashing through the bushes would certainly help conceal what *he's* doing, wouldn't it?'

He stared at her for a long time. Then he laughed. 'I love you, Aphrael,' he said, lifting her in his arms and kissing her.

'He's such a nice boy,' the little Goddess beamed to her sister.

*   *   *

406

Two days later, the weather changed abruptly. Heavy clouds swept in off the Tamul sea several hundred odd leagues to the east, and the sky turned suddenly murky and threatening. To add to the gloom, one of those 'breakdowns in communications' so common in all government enterprises occurred. They reached a clan border marked by a several-hundred-yard-wide strip of open ground about noon only to find no escort awaiting them. The clan which had brought them this far could not cross that border, and, indeed, looked nervously back toward the safety of the forest.

'There are bad feelings between these two clans, Sparhawk-Knight,' Engessa advised gravely. 'It is a serious breach of custom and propriety for either clan to come within five hundred paces of the line between them.'

'Tell them to go on home, Atan Engessa,' Sparhawk told him. 'There are enough of us here to protect the queen, and we wouldn't want to start a clan war just for the sake of maintaining appearances. The other clan should be along soon, so there's no real danger.'

Engessa looked a bit dubious, but he spoke with the leader of their escort, and the Atans gratefully melted back into the forest.

'What now?' Kalten asked.

'How about some lunch?' Sparhawk replied.

'I thought you'd never think of that.'

'Have the knights and the Peloi draw up around the carriage and get some cooking fires going. I'll go tell Ehlana.' He rode back to the carriage.

'Where's the escort?' Mirtai asked brusquely. Now that she was an adult, Mirtai was even more commanding then she had been before.

'I'm afraid they're late,' Sparhawk told her. 'I thought we might as well have some lunch while we're waiting for them.'

'Absolutely splendid idea, Sparhawk,' Emban beamed.

'We thought you might approve, your Grace. The escort should be here by the time we finish eating.'

They were not, however. Sparhawk paced back and forth, chafing at the delay, and his patience finally evaporated. 'That's it!' he said loudly. 'Let's get ready to move out.'

'We're supposed to wait, Sparhawk,' Ehlana told him.

'Not out in the open like this, we're not. And I'm not going to sit here for two days waiting for some Atan clan-chief to mull his way through a message.'

'I think we'd better do as he says, friends,' Ehlana told the others. 'I know the signs, and my beloved's beginning to grow short-tempered.'

'-Er,' Talen added.

'You said what?' Ehlana asked him.

'Short-tempered-er. Sparhawk's always short-tempered. It's only a little worse now. You have to know him very well to be able to tell the difference.'

'Are you short-tempered-er right now, love?' she teased her husband.

'I don't think there is such a word, Ehlana. Let's get ready and move on out. The road's well-marked, so we can hardly get lost.'

The trees beyond the open space were dark cedars with swooping limbs that brushed the ground and concealed everything more than a few yards back into the forest. The clouds rolling in from the east grew thicker and the light back among the trees grew dim. The air hung motionless and sultry, and the whine of mosquitoes seemed to grow louder as they rode deeper into the woods.

'I love wearing armour in mosquito country,' Kalten said gaily. 'I have this picture of hordes of the little

408

blood-suckers sitting around with teeny little hammers trying to pound their beaks straight again.'

'They won't really try to bite you through the steel, Sir Kalten,' Zalasta told him. 'They're attracted by your smell, and I don't think any living creature finds the smell of Elene armour all that appetising.'

'You're taking all the fun out of it, Zalasta.'

'Sorry, Sir Kalten.'

There was a rumble far off to the east.

'The perfect end to a day gone sour,' Stragen observed, 'a nice rousing thunderstorm with lots of lightning, hail, driving rain and howling winds.'

Then, echoing down some unseen canyon back in the forest there came a hoarse, roaring bellow. Almost immediately there came an answer from the opposite direction.

Sir Ulath swore, biting off curses the way a dog tears at a piece of meat.

'What's wrong?' Sparhawk demanded.

'Didn't you recognise it, Sparhawk?' the Thalesian said. 'You've heard it before – back at Lake Venne.'

'What is it?' Khalad asked apprehensively.

'It's a signal that it's time for us to fort up! Those are Trolls out there!'

CHAPTER 22

'It's not perfect, friend Sparhawk,' Kring said a bit dubiously, 'but I don't think we've got time to look for anything better.'

'He's right about that, Sparhawk,' Ulath agreed. 'Time's definitely a major concern right now.'

The Peloi had ranged out into the surrounding forest in search of some defensible position. Given their nervousness about wooded terrain, Kring's horsemen had displayed a great deal of courage in the search.

'Can you give me some details?' Sparhawk asked the shaved-headed Domi.

'It's a blind canyon, friend Sparhawk,' Kring replied, nervously fingering the hilt of his sabre. 'There's a dried-up stream-bed running down the centre of it. From the look of it, I'd say that the stream runs full in the springtime. There seems to be a dry waterfall at the upper end. There's a cave at the foot of the dry falls that should provide some protection for the women, and it'll be a good place to defend if things get desperate.'

'I thought they already were,' Tynian noted.

'How wide is the mouth of the canyon?' Sparhawk asked intently.

'The canyon mouth itself is maybe two hundred paces across,' Kring told him, 'but when you go back in a ways, it narrows down to about twenty paces. Then it widens out again into a sort of a basin where the falls are.'

'The bad thing about a canyon is that you're down in a hole,' Kalten said. 'It won't take the Trolls too long to

410

go up to the canyon rim and start throwing rocks down on our heads.'

'Do we have any choice?' Tynian asked him.

'No, but I thought I'd point it out.'

'There's no place else?' Sparhawk asked the Domi.

'A few clearings,' Kring shrugged. 'A hill or two that I could spit over.'

'It looks like it's the canyon then,' Sparhawk said grimly. 'We'd better get there and start putting up some sort of fortification across that narrow place.'

They gathered closely around the carriage and pushed their way into the forest. The carriage jolted over the rough ground, and on several occasions fallen logs had to be dragged out of the way. After about five hundred yards, though, the ground began to slope upward and the trees thinned out.

Sparhawk pulled Faran in beside the carriage.

'There's a cave ahead, Ehlana,' he told his wife. 'Kring's men didn't have time to explore it, so we don't know how deep it is.'

'What difference would that make?' she asked him. Ehlana's face was even more pale than usual. The bellowing of the Trolls far back in the forest had obviously unnerved her.

'It might be very important,' he replied. 'When you get there, have Talen explore the place. If it goes back in far enough or branches out, you'll have a place to hide. Sephrenia's going to be with you, and she'll be able to block the entrance and hide any side-chamber so that the Trolls can't find you if they manage to get past us.'

'Why don't we all just go into the cave? You and Sephrenia can use magic to block the entrance, and we can just sit there until the Trolls get bored and go away.'

'According to Kring, the cave's not big enough. He's got men out looking for another one, but we *know* this

411

one's there. If something better turns up, we'll change the plan, but for right now this is the best we can manage. You'll take the other ladies, Patriarch Emban and Ambassador Oscagne and go inside. Talen will go in with you, and Berit and eight or ten other knights will cover the entrance to the cave. Please don't argue, Ehlana. This is one of those situations where *I* make the decisions. You agreed to that back in Chyrellos.'

'He's right, your Majesty,' Emban told her. 'We need a general right now, not a queen.'

'Am I encumbering you gentlemen?' she asked tartly.

'Not in the slightest, my Queen,' Stragen said smoothly. 'Your presence will inspire us to greater heights. We'll dazzle you with our prowess and our courage.'

'I'd be happy to simulate dazzlement if we could avoid this,' she said in a worried voice.

'I'm afraid you'd have to convince the Trolls on that score,' Sparhawk told her, 'and Trolls are very hard to convince – particularly if they're hungry.' Although the situation was grave, Sparhawk was not quite as desperately concerned about his wife's safety as he might normally have been. Sephrenia would be there to protect her, and if things grew truly desperate, Aphrael could take a hand in the matter as well. He knew that his daughter would not permit any harm to come to her mother, even if it meant revealing her identity.

The canyon had its drawbacks, there was no question about that. The most obvious was the one Kalten had raised. If the Trolls ever reached the canyon rim above them, the situation would quickly become untenable. Kalten made quite an issue of pointing that out. 'I told you so' figured prominently in his remarks.

'I think you're over-estimating the intelligence of Trolls, Kalten,' Ulath disagreed. 'They'll come straight

412

at us, because they'll be thinking of us as food, not as enemies. Supper's more important to them than a military victory.'

'You're just loaded with cheery thoughts today, aren't you, Ulath?' Tynian said dryly. 'How many of them do you think there are?'

'It's hard to say,' Ulath shrugged. 'I've heard ten different voices so far – probably the heads of families. There's probably a hundred or so of them out there at the very least.'

'It could be worse,' Kalten said.

'Not by very much,' Ulath disagreed. 'A hundred Trolls could have given Wargun's whole army some serious problems.'

Bevier, their expert on fortifications and defensive positions, had been surveying the canyon. 'There are plenty of rocks in the stream-bed for breastworks,' he observed, 'and whole thickets of saplings for stakes. Ulath, how long do you think we have before they attack?'

Ulath scratched at his chin. 'The fact that we're stopping gives us a bit more space,' he mused. 'If we were still moving, they'd attack right away, but now they'll probably take their time and gather their forces. I believe you might want to re-think your strategy though, Bevier. Trolls aren't going to shoot arrows at us, so breastworks aren't really necessary. Actually, they'd hinder *us* more than they would the Trolls. Our advantage lies in our horses – and our lances. You really want to keep Trolls at a distance if you possibly can. The sharpened stakes would be good, though. A Troll takes the easiest way to get at what he wants – us, in this case. If we can clutter up the sides of this narrow place and funnel them through so that only a few at a time can come at us, we'll definitely improve the situation. We don't want to take on more of them at any one time than we absolutely have to. What I'd really like is a dozen or so of Kurik's crossbows.'

'I have one, Sir Ulath,' Khalad volunteered.

'And many of the knights have longbows,' Bevier added.

'We slow them down with the stakes so that we can pick them off with arrows?' Tynian surmised.

'That's the best plan,' Ulath agreed. 'You don't want to go hand to hand with a Troll if you can possibly avoid it.'

'We'd better get at it, then,' Sparhawk told them.

The work was feverish for the next hour. The narrow gap was necked down even more with boulders from the stream-bed, and a forest of sharpened stakes, all slanting sharply outward, was planted to the front. There was a method to the planting of the stakes. They bristled so thickly along the sides of the gap as to be well-nigh impenetrable, but the corridor leading to the basin at the head of the canyon was planted only sparsely with them to encourage the monsters to follow that route. Kring's Peloi found a large bramble thicket, uprooted the thorn-bushes and threw them back among the thick-planted stakes at the sides to further impede progress.

'What's Khalad doing there?' Kalten asked, puffing and sweating with the large rock he carried in his arms.

'He's building something,' Sparhawk replied.

'This isn't really the time for the construction of camp improvements, Sparhawk.'

'He's a sensible young man. I'm sure he's usefully occupied.'

At the end of the hour, they stopped to survey the fruits of their labours. The gap had been narrowed to no more than eight feet wide, and the ground at the sides of the gap was dense with chest-high stakes angled so that they would keep the Trolls on the right path. Tynian, however, added one small embellishment. A number of his Alciones were driving pegs into the middle of the pathway and then sharpening the protruding ends.

'Trolls don't wear shoes, do they?' he asked Ulath.

'It'd take half a cow-hide to make shoes for a Troll,' Ulath shrugged, 'and they eat cows hide and all, so they're a little short of leather.'

'Good. We want to keep them in the centre of the canyon, but we don't want to make it *too* easy for them. Barefoot Trolls aren't going to run through *that* stubble-field – not after the first few yards, anyway.'

'I like your style, Tynian,' Ulath grinned.

'Could you gentlemen stand off to one side, please?' Khalad called. He had cut two fairly sturdy saplings off so that the stumps were about head high and had then lashed a third across them. Then he had strung a rope across the ends of the horizontal sapling and drawn it tight to form a huge bow. The bow was fully drawn, tied off to another stump at the rear, and it was loaded with a ten-foot javelin.

Sparhawk and the others moved off to the sides of the narrow cut, and Khalad released the bow by cutting the rope that held it drawn. The javelin shot forward with a sharp whistling sound and buried itself deep into a tree a good hundred yards down the canyon.

'I'm going to like that boy,' Kalten smiled. 'He's almost as good at this sort of thing as his father was.'

'The family shows a lot of promise,' Sparhawk agreed. 'Let's position our archers so that they have a clear shot at that gap.'

'Right,' Kalten agreed. 'What then?'

'Then we wait.'

'That's the part I hate the most. Why don't we grab something to eat? Just to pass the time, of course.'

'Of course.'

* * *

415

The storm which had been building to the east all morning was closer now, the clouds purplish-black and seething. There were flickers of lightning deep inside the cloud bank, and the thunder rolled from horizon to horizon, shaking the ground with every peal.

They waited. The air was dead calm and sultry and the knights were sweating uncomfortably in their armour.

'Can we think of anything else?' Tynian asked.

'I've contrived a few rudimentary catapults,' Bevier replied. 'They're hardly more than bent saplings, so they won't throw very big rocks, and their range is limited.'

'I'll take all the help I can get when it comes to fighting Trolls,' Ulath told him. 'Every one of them we knock down before they get to us is one less we'll have to fight.'

'Dear God!' Tynian exclaimed.

'What?' Kalten demanded with a certain alarm.

'I think I just saw one of them back at the edge of the forest. Are they all that big?'

'Nine feet or so tall?' Ulath asked quite casually.

'At least.'

'That's fairly standard for a Troll, and they weigh between thirty-five and fifty stone.'

'You're not serious!' Kalten said incredulously.

'Wait just a bit and you'll be able to weigh one for yourself.' Ulath looked around at them. 'Trolls are hard to kill,' he cautioned. 'Their hides are very tough, and their skull-bones are almost a half-inch thick. They can take a lot of punishment when they're excited. If we get in close, try to maim them. You can't really count on clean kills with Trolls, so every arm you chop off is one less the Troll can grab you with.'

'Will they have weapons of any kind?' Kalten asked.

'Clubs are about all. They aren't good with spears. Their arms aren't hooked on right for jabbing.'

'That's something, anyway.'

'Not very much,' Tynian told him.

They waited as the thunder moved ponderously toward them.

They saw several more Trolls at the edge of the forest in the next ten minutes, and the bellowing roars of those scouts were obviously summoning the rest of the pack. The only Troll Sparhawk had ever seen before had been Ghwerig, and Ghwerig had been dwarfed and grossly deformed. He quickly began to revise his assessment of the creatures. They were, as Ulath had stated, about nine feet tall, and they were covered with dark-brown, shaggy fur. Their arms were very long, and their huge hands hung below their knees. Their faces were brutish, with heavy brow-ridges, muzzle-like mouths and protruding fangs. Their eyes were small, deep-set and they burned with a dreadful hunger. They slouched along at the edge of the forest, not really trying to conceal themselves, and Sparhawk clearly saw that their long arms played a significant part in their locomotion, sometimes serving as an additional leg and sometimes grasping trees to help pull themselves along. Their movements were flowing, even graceful, and bespoke an enormous agility.

'Are we more or less ready?' Ulath asked them.

'I could stand to wait a little longer,' Kalten replied.

'How long?'

'Forty or fifty years sounds about right to me. What did you have in mind?'

'I've seen about fifteen different individuals,' the big Thalesian noted. 'They're coming out one by one to have a look, and that means that they're all more or less gathered just back under the trees. I thought I'd insult them for a while. When a Troll gets angry, he doesn't really

417

think. Of course Trolls don't have very much to think with in the first place. I'd like to provoke them into an ill-considered attack if possible. If I *really* insult them, they'll scream and howl and then come rushing out of those woods foaming at the mouths. They'll be easy targets for the bowmen at that point, and if a few of them get through, we can charge them with our horses and the lances. We should be able to kill quite a few of them before they come to their senses. I'd really like to whittle down their numbers, and enraged Trolls make easy targets.'

'Do you think we might be able to kill enough of them to frighten the rest away?' Kalten asked.

'I wouldn't count on it, but anything's possible, I suppose. I'd have sworn that you couldn't get a hundred Trolls to even walk in the same direction at the same time, so the situation here's completely new to me.'

'Let me talk with the others before we precipitate anything,' Sparhawk told him. He turned and walked back to where the knights and the Peloi waited with their horses. Vanion stood with Stragen, Engessa and Kring. 'We're about ready to start,' Sparhawk told them.

'Did you plan to invite the Trolls?' Stragen asked him. 'Or are we going to begin without them?'

'Ulath's going to see if he can provoke them into something rash,' Sparhawk replied. 'The stakes should slow them down enough so that our archers can work on them. We really want to thin them out a bit. If they manage to break through, we'll charge them with lances.' He looked at Kring. 'I'm not trying to insult you, Domi, but could you hold back a bit? Ulath tells us that Trolls take a lot of killing. It's a dirty business, but somebody's going to have to come along after we charge and kill the wounded.'

Kring's face clearly registered his distaste. 'We'll do

it, friend Sparhawk,' he agreed finally, 'but only out of friendship.'

'I appreciate that, Kring. As soon as Ulath enrages them enough to get them moving, those of us at the barricade will come back and get on our horses to join the charge. Oh, one thing – just because a Troll has a broken-off lance sticking out of him doesn't mean that he's out of action. Let's stick a few more in each one then – just to be on the safe side. I'll go advise the ladies that we're about to start, and then we'll get on with it.'

'I'll go with you,' Vanion said, and the two of them walked back up the canyon towards the cave-mouth.

Berit and a small group of young knights stood guard at the entrance to the cave. 'Are they coming?' the handsome young man asked nervously.

'We've seen a few scouts,' Sparhawk replied. 'We're going to try to goad them into an attack. If we have to fight them, I'd rather do it in the daylight.'

'And before that storm hits,' Vanion added.

'I don't think they'll get past us,' Sparhawk told the youthful knight, 'but stay alert. If things start to look tight, pull back inside the cave.'

Berit nodded.

Then Ehlana, Talen and Sephrenia emerged from the cave.

'Are they coming?' Ehlana asked, her voice slightly shrill.

'Not yet,' Sparhawk replied. 'It's just a question of time, though. We're going to try to goad them a bit. Ulath thinks he might be able to enrage some of them enough so that they'll attack before the rest are ready. We'd rather not have to face them all at once if we can avoid it.' He looked at Sephrenia. 'Are you up to a spell or two, Sephrenia?'

'That depends on the spell.'

419

'Can you block the cave mouth so that the Trolls can't get at you and the others?'

'Probably, and if not, I can always collapse it.'

'I wouldn't do that except as a last resort. Wait for Berit and his men to get inside with you, though.'

Talen's fine clothes were a bit mud-smeared. 'Any luck?' Sparhawk asked him.

'I found a place where a bear spent last winter,' the boy shrugged. 'It involved a bit of wriggling. There are a couple of other passageways I want to look at.'

'Pick the best one you can. If Sephrenia has to bring down the cave-mouth, I'd like to have you all back where it's safe.'

Talen nodded.

'Be careful, Sparhawk,' Ehlana said to him, embracing him fiercely.

'Always, love.'

Sephrenia had also embraced Vanion, her admonition echoing Ehlana's. 'Now go, both of you,' she added.

'Yes, little mother,' Sparhawk and Vanion said in unison.

The two knights started back down the canyon. 'You don't approve, do you, Sparhawk?' Vanion asked gravely.

'It's none of my business, my friend.'

'I didn't ask if it was any of your business, I asked if you approved. There wasn't any other way, you know. The laws of both our cultures prohibit our marrying.'

'I don't think the laws apply to you two, Vanion. You both have a special friend who ignores the laws when she chooses to.' He smiled at his old friend. 'Actually, I'm rather pleased about it. I got very tired of seeing the pair of you moping about the way you were.'

'Thanks, Sparhawk. I wanted to get that out into the open. I'll never be able to go back to Eosia, though.'

'I'd say that's no great a loss under the circumstances.

You and Sephrenia are happy, and that's all that matters.'

'I'll agree there. When you get back to Chyrellos, try to put the best face on it you can, though. I'm afraid Dolmant will burst into flames when he hears about it.'

'He might surprise you, Vanion.'

Sparhawk was a bit startled to discover that he still remembered a few words in Troll. Ulath stood in the centre of their narrow gap, bellowing at the forest in that snarling tongue.

'What's he saying?' Kalten asked curiously.

'It wouldn't translate very well,' Sparhawk replied. 'Trollish insults lean heavily in the direction of body-functions.'

'Oh. Sorry I asked.'

'You'd be a lot sorrier if I could translate,' Sparhawk said, wincing at a particularly vile imprecation Ulath had just hurled at the Trolls.

The Trolls, it appeared, took insults very seriously. Unlike humans, they seemed not to be able to shrug such things off as no more than a customary prelude to battle. They howled at each new sally from the big Genidian Knight. A number of them appeared at the edge of the wood, foaming at the mouth and stamping in rage.

'How much longer before they charge?' Tynian asked his tall blond friend.

'You can't always tell with Trolls,' Ulath replied. 'I don't think they're accustomed to fighting in groups. I can't say for sure, but I think one of them will lose his temper before the others, and he'll come rushing at us. I'm not positive if the others will follow.' He roared something else at the huge creatures at the forest's edge.

One of the Trolls shrieked with fury and broke into a shambling, three-legged run, brandishing a huge club

421

in his free hand. First one Troll, then several others, began to run after him.

Sparhawk glanced around, checking the positions of his archers. Khalad, he noted, had given his crossbow to another young Pandion and stood coolly sighting along the shaft of the javelin resting across the centre of his improvised engine.

The Troll in the lead was swinging wildly at the sharpened stakes with his club, but the springy saplings bent beneath his blows and then snapped back into place. The enraged Troll lifted his muzzle and howled in frustration.

Khalad cut the rope holding his over-sized bow drawn back. The limbs of the bow snapped forward with an almost musical twang, and the javelin shot forward in a long, smooth arc to sink into the Troll's vast, furry chest with a meaty-sounding 'chunk!'

The Troll jerked back and stood staring stupidly at the shaft protruding from his chest. He touched it with one tentative finger as if he could not even begin to understand how it had got there. Then he sat down heavily with blood pouring from his mouth. He grasped the shaft feebly with both hands and wrenched at it. A fresh gush of blood burst from his mouth, and he sighed and toppled over on one side.

'Good shot,' Kalten called his congratulations to Sparhawk's squire, who, with the help of two other young Pandions was already re-cocking the engine.

'Pass the word to the other archers,' Khalad called back. 'The Trolls stop when they come to those stakes. They don't seem to be able to understand them, and they make perfect targets when they're standing still like that.'

'Right.' Kalten went to the archers on one side of the canyon and Bevier to the other to pass the word along.

The half-dozen or so Trolls who had followed the first

one paid no attention to his fall and lunged on forward towards the field of sharpened stakes.

'We might have a problem, Sparhawk,' Tynian said. 'They're not used to fighting in groups, so they don't pay any attention to casualties. Ulath says that they don't die of natural causes, so they don't really understand what death's all about. I don't think they'll back away just because we kill all their comrades. It's not like fighting humans, I'm afraid. They'll make one charge, and they'll keep coming until they're all dead. We may have to adjust our tactics to take that into account.'

More Trolls came out of the trees, and Ulath continued to shout obscenities at them.

Kalten and Bevier returned. 'I just had a thought,' Kalten said. 'Ulath, will the females attack too?'

'Probably.'

'How do you tell the females from the males?'

'Are you having urges?'

'That's disgusting. I just don't want to kill women, that's all.'

'Women? These are Trolls, Kalten, not people. You can't tell a female from a male unless she's got cubs with her – or unless you get very, very close to her – and that's not a good idea. A sow will tear off your head just as quickly as a boar will.' The Genidian went back to shouting insults.

More Trolls joined the charge, and then, with a vast roar, the entire edge of the woods erupted with the monsters. They did not pause, but joined the loping charge.

'That's it,' Ulath said with a certain satisfaction. 'The whole pack's committed now. Let's go get our horses.'

They ran back to join the others as the several Cyrinics manning Bevier's improvised catapults and the Pandions working Khalad's engine began to launch missiles at the oncoming Trolls. The archers at the canyon walls

423

rained arrows into the shaggy ranks. Some Trolls fell, riddled with arrows, but others continued the charge, ignoring the shafts sticking out of them.

'I don't think we can count on their breaking and running just because their friends have been killed,' Sparhawk told Vanion and the others as he hauled himself onto Faran's back.

'Friends?' Stragen said mildly. 'Trolls don't have friends, Sparhawk. They aren't even particularly fond of their mates.'

'What I'm getting at is the fact that this is all going to be settled in one fight,' Sparhawk said to them. 'There probably won't be a second charge. They'll just keep coming until they break through or until they're all dead.'

'It's better that way, friend Sparhawk,' Kring said with a wolfish grin. 'Protracted fights are boring, wouldn't you say?'

'I wouldn't say that, would you, Ulath?' Tynian asked mildly.

The knights moved into formation, their lances at the ready as the Trolls continued their bellowing advance.

The first half-dozen or so Trolls that had been in the forefront of the charge were all down now, either dead or dying of arrow wounds, and the front rank of the bellowing horde was faltering as sheets of arrows struck them. The Trolls at the rear, however, simply ran over the top of their mortally wounded companions. Mouths agape and fangs dripping, they charged on and on.

The sharpened stakes served their purpose well. The Trolls, after a few futile efforts to break through the bristling forest, were forced into the narrow corridor where they were jammed together and milled impatiently behind the brutes who were leading the charge as Tynian's sharpened pegs protruding from the ground slowed the rushing advance of the leaders. Not even the most enraged creature in the world charges very well on sore paws.

Sparhawk looked around. The knights were drawn up into a column, four abreast, and their lances were all slightly advanced. The Trolls continued their limping charge up the gap until the first rank, also four abreast, reached the end of the stake-lined corridor where it opened out into the basin. 'I guess it's time,' he said. Then he rose up in his stirrups and roared 'Charge!'

The tactic Sparhawk had devised for the Church Knights was simple. They would charge four abreast into the face of the Trolls as soon as the creatures came out into the basin. They would drive their lances into the first rank of Trolls and then veer off, two-by-two, to the sides of the gap so that the next rank of four could make *their* charge. Once they had moved out of the way, they would return to the end of the column, take up fresh lances and proceed in an orderly fashion to the front rank again. It was, in effect, an endless charge. Sparhawk was rather proud of the concept. It probably wouldn't work against humans, but it had great potential in an engagement with Trolls.

Shaggy carcasses began to pile up at the head of the gap. A Troll, it appeared, was not guileful enough to play dead. He would continue to attack until he died or was so severely injured that he could not continue. After several ranks of the knights had struck the Troll-front, some of the brutes had as many as four broken-off lances protruding from them. Still the monsters came, clambering over the bleeding bodies of their fellows.

Sparhawk, Vanion, Kalten and Tynian made their second charge. They speared fresh Trolls in the raging front, snapped off their lances with well-practised twists of their arms and veered off to the sides.

'Your plan seems to be going well,' Kalten congratulated his friend. 'The horses have time to rest between charges.'

'That was part of the idea,' Sparhawk replied a bit smugly as he took a fresh lance from the rack at the rear of the column.

The storm was nearly on them now. The howling wind shrieked among the trees, and lightning staggered down in brilliant flashes from the purple clouds.

Then, from back in the forest there came a tremendous bellow.

'What in God's name was that?' Kalten cried. 'Nothing can make *that* much noise!'

Whatever it was, was huge, and it was coming toward them, crushing the forest as it came. The raging wind carried a foul, reptilian reek as it tore at the visored faces of the armoured knights.

'It stinks like a charnel-house!' Tynian shouted over the noise of the storm and the battle.

'Can you tell what it is, Vanion?' Sparhawk demanded.

'No,' the Preceptor replied. 'Whatever it is, it's big, though – bigger than anything I've ever encountered.'

Then the rain struck in driving sheets, obscuring the knights' vision and half-concealing the advancing Trolls. 'Keep at them!' Sparhawk commanded in a great voice. 'Don't let up!'

The methodical charges continued as the Trolls doggedly pushed through the mud into the killing zone. The strategy was going well, but it had not been without casualties. Several horses were down, felled by club strokes from wounded and enraged Trolls, and a few armoured knights lay motionless on the rain-swept ground.

426

Then the wind suddenly dropped, and the rain slackened as the calm at the centre of the storm passed over them.

'What's that?' Tynian shouted, pointing beyond the howling Trolls.

It was a single, incandescent spark, brighter than the sun, and it hung just over the edge of the forest. It began to grow ominously, swelling, surging, surrounded by a blazing halo of purplish light.

'There's something inside it!' Kalten yelled.

Sparhawk strained to see, squinting in the brilliant purple light that illuminated the battle-ground. 'It's alive,' he said tersely. 'It's moving.'

The ball of purple light swelled faster and faster, and blazing orange flames shot out from the edges of it.

There was someone standing in the centre of that fiery ball – someone robed and hooded and burning green. The figure raised one hand, opened it wide, and a searing bolt of lightning shot from that open palm. A charging Cyrinic Knight and his horse were blasted into charred fragments by the bolt.

And then, from behind that searing light, an enormous shape reared up out of the forest. It was impossible that anything alive could be so huge. The head left no doubt that the creature was reptilian. The huge head was earlessly sleek, scaly and had a protruding, lipless muzzle filled with row after row of back-curving teeth. It had a short neck, narrow shoulders and tiny forepaws. The rest of the body was mercifully concealed by the trees.

'We can't fight *that* thing!' Kalten cried.

The hooded figure within the ball of purple and orange fire raised its arm again. It seemed to clench itself, and then again the lightning shot from its open palm – and stopped, exploding in midair in a dazzling shower of sparks.

'Did you do that?' Vanion shouted at Sparhawk.

'Not me, Vanion. I'm not *that* fast.'

Then they heard the deep, resonant voice chanting in Styric. Sparhawk wheeled Faran to look.

It was Zalasta. The silvery-haired Styric stood partway up the steep slope on the north side of the canyon, his white robe gleaming in the storm's half-light. He had both arms extended over his head, and his staff, which Sparhawk had thought to be no more than an affectation, blazed with energy. He swung the staff downward, pointing it at the hooded figure standing in its fiery nimbus. A brilliant spark shot from the tip of the staff and sizzled as it passed over the heads of the Peloi and the armoured knights to explode against the ball of fire.

The figure in the fire flinched, and once more lightning shot from its open palm, directed at Zalasta this time. The Styric brushed it disdainfully aside with his staff and immediately responded with another of those brilliant sparks of light which shattered like the last on the surface of the ball of fire.

Again the hooded one inside its protecting fire flinched, more violently this time. The gigantic creature behind it screamed and drew back into the darkness.

The Church Knights, dumbfounded by the dreadful confrontation, had frozen in their tracks.

'We have our own work to attend to, gentlemen!' Vanion roared his reminder. 'Charge!'

Sparhawk shook his head to clear his mind. 'Thanks, Vanion,' he said to his friend. 'I got distracted there for a moment.'

'Pay attention, Sparhawk,' Vanion said crisply in precisely the same tone he had always used on the practice-field years before when Sparhawk and Kalten had been novices.

'Yes, my Lord Preceptor,' Sparhawk replied automatically in the self-same embarrassed tone he had used as a stripling. The two looked at each other, and then they both laughed.

'Just like old times,' Kalten said gaily. 'Well then, why don't we go Troll-hunting and leave the incidentals to Zalasta?'

The knights continued their endless charge and the two magicians continued their fiery duel overhead. The Trolls were no less savage now, but their numbers were diminished and the huge pile of their dead impeded their attack.

The bloody work on the ground went on and on while the air above the battleground sizzled and crackled with awful fire.

'Is it my imagination, or is our purple friend up there getting a little pale and wan?' Tynian suggested as they took up fresh lances once more.

'His fire's beginning to fade just a bit,' Kalten agreed. 'And he's taking longer and longer to work himself up to another thunderbolt.'

'Don't grow over-confident, gentlemen,' Vanion admonished them. 'We still have Trolls to deal with, and that oversized lizard's still out there in the forest.'

'I was trying very hard not to think about that,' Kalten replied.

Then, very suddenly, as suddenly as it had expanded, the ball of purple-orange fire began to contract. Zalasta stepped up his attack, the fiery sparks shooting from his staff in rapid succession to burst against the outer surface of that rapidly constricting nimbus like fiery hail.

Then the blazing orb vanished.

A cheer went up from the Peloi, and the Trolls faltered.

Khalad, his face strangely numb, set another javelin on his improvised engine and cut the rope to unleash his missile. The javelin sprang from the huge bow, and as it sped forward it seemed to ignite, and it blazed with light as it arced out higher and farther than any of the young man's previous shots had done.

The great lizard rearing up out of the forest roared, its awful mouth gaping. And then the burning javelin took it full in the chest. It sank deep, and the hideous creature shrieked a great cry of agony and rage, its tiny forepaws clutching futilely at the burning shaft. And then there was a heavy, muffled thud within the monster's body, a confined explosion that shook the very ground. The vast lizard burst open in a spray of bloody fire, and its ripped remains sank twitching back into the forest.

A nebulous kind of wavering appeared at the edge of the trees, a wavering very much like the shimmer of heat on a hot summer day, and then they all saw something emerging from that shimmer. It was a face only, brutish, ugly and filled with rage and frustration. The shaggy face sloped sharply back from its fang-filled muzzle, and the pig-like eyes burned in their sockets.

It howled – a vast howl that tore at the very air. It howled again, and Sparhawk recoiled. The wavering apparition was bellowing in Troll! Again it howled, its thunderous voice bending the trees around it like a vast wind.

'What in God's name is that?' Bevier cried.

'Ghworg,' Ulath replied tensely, 'the Troll-God of Kill.'

The immortal beast howled yet again, and then it vanished.

CHAPTER 23

All semblance of co-operation among the Trolls vanished with the disappearance of Ghworg. They were not, as Ulath had so frequently pointed out, creatures which normally ran in packs, and without the presence of the God to coerce them into semi-unity, they reverted to their customary antagonism toward each other. Their charge faltered as a number of very nasty fights broke out in their ranks. These fights quickly spread, and within moments there was a general brawl in progress out beyond the mouth of the canyon.

'Well?' Kalten asked Ulath.

'It's over,' the Genidian Knight shrugged, '– at least our part of it is. The riot among the Trolls themselves might go on for quite a while, though.'

Kring, it appeared, had reached the same conclusion, and his Peloi moved purposefully on the heaps of Trollish casualties, their sabres and lances at the ready.

Khalad was still standing behind his roughly constructed engine, his face blank and his eyes unseeing. Then he seemed to awaken. 'What happened?' he asked, looking around with some confusion.

'You killed that big reptile, my young friend,' Tynian told him. 'It was a spectacular shot.'

'I *did*? I don't remember even shooting at it. I thought it was out of range.'

Zalasta had come down from the sloping side of the canyon with a look of satisfaction on his beetle-browed face. 'I'm afraid I had to override your thoughts for a few moments there, young sir,' he explained to Sparhawk's squire. 'I needed your engine to deal with the thunder beast. I hope you'll forgive me, but there wasn't time to consult with you about it.'

'That's quite all right, learned one. I just wish I'd been able to see the shot. What kind of beast was it?'

'Its species roamed the earth millions of years ago,' the Styric replied. 'Before mankind or even the Trolls emerged. Our opponent appears to be very gifted in resurrecting the ancient dead.'

'Was that him inside that ball of fire?' Kalten asked.

'I can't be positive about that, Sir Kalten. It seems that we have many layers of enemies out there. If the one in the orb wasn't our main enemy, though, he was probably very high up in the opposing councils. He was most skilled.'

'Let's see to the wounded,' Vanion said crisply. Despite his protestations that Sparhawk was now in charge of the Pandions, the habit of command still ran deep in Vanion's blood.

'We might want to barricade that gap as well,' Ulath suggested, 'just to keep the surviving Trolls from paying us any unannounced visits during the night.'

'I'll go advise the ladies that the worst of this is over,' Sparhawk told them. He turned Faran and rode back to the cave. He was a bit surprised and more than a bit exasperated to find Ehlana and the rest of the party from the cavern standing out in the open. 'I told you to stay in the cave,' he reprimanded his wife sharply.

'You didn't really expect me to do it, did you?'

'Yes, as a matter of fact, I did.'

'Life's just filled with these little disappointments, isn't it?' Her tone was challenging.

'That will do, children,' Sephrenia said wearily. 'Domestic squabbles shouldn't be aired in public. Do your fighting in private.'

'We weren't fighting, were we, Sparhawk?' Ehlana said.

432

'We were just about to start.'

'I'm sorry, dear,' she apologised contritely. 'I couldn't bear to stay inside while you were in such terrible danger.' Then she made a wry face. 'Right now I'm going to have to choke down my royal pride and eat a large dish of crow. I've wronged Zalasta dreadfully. He saved the day for us, didn't he?'

'He certainly didn't hurt us,' Talen agreed.

'He was stupendous!' the queen exclaimed.

'He's very, very skilled,' Sephrenia said proudly. Perhaps unconsciously, she was holding Danae in her arms. Their centuries of sisterhood had made the small Styric woman's responses instinctive.

'What was that awful face at the edge of the woods?' Sir Berit asked with a shudder.

'Ulath says it was Ghworg, the Troll-God of Kill,' Sparhawk replied. 'I sort of remember him from the Temple of Azash back in Zemoch. I didn't really look at him that closely then, though. I was a little preoccupied at the time.' He made a face. 'Well, little mother,' he said to Sephrenia, 'it looks as if we might have been right. I'd say that Ghwerig's spell wasn't quite as iron-clad as we originally thought. The Troll-Gods are loose – at least Ghworg is. But what baffles me is why they didn't escape earlier. If they could get out at any time, why didn't they break free when I threatened to smash Bhelliom in the temple?'

'Maybe they needed help,' she shrugged. 'It's altogether possible that our enemy was able to enlist their aid by offering to help them escape their imprisonment. We'll ask Zalasta. He might know.'

More of the knights had been injured during the fight with the Trolls than Sparhawk had originally thought, and some fifteen of their number had been killed. As evening settled into the canyon, Engessa came to

Sparhawk, his eyes hard. 'I'll leave now, Sparhawk-Knight,' he said abruptly.

Sparhawk looked at him, startled.

'I must go have words with the clan of this region. Their failure to be at the boundary was inexcusable.'

'There was probably a reason for it, Atan Engessa.'

'No reason that *I'll* accept. I'll be back in the morning with enough warriors to protect Ehlana-Queen.'

'There are Trolls out there in the forest, you know.'

'They will not greatly inconvenience me, Sparhawk-Knight.'

'Just be careful, Atan Engessa. I'm getting very tired of burying friends.'

Engessa suddenly grinned at him. 'That's one of the good things about fighting Trolls, Sparhawk-Knight. You don't have to bury dead friends. The Trolls eat them.'

Sparhawk shuddered.

Zalasta was clearly the hero of the day. All of the Peloi and most of the Church Knights were obviously in awe of him. The vision of his explosive duel with the hooded figure in the blazing purple orb and the spectacular demise of the vast reptile was vividly etched on the minds of the entire party. He bore himself modestly, however, shrugging off his stunning accomplishments as if they were of no moment. He did, however, seem very pleased that Ehlana's animosity had dissolved and that she was now whole-heartedly cordial toward him. His somewhat stiff manner softened – Ehlana had that effect on people – and he became somehow less reserved and more human.

Engessa arrived the next morning with a thousand Atan clansmen. The faces of their officers clearly showed that Engessa had spoken firmly with them about their failure to be at the clan-border at the appointed time. The wounded knights were placed on litters borne by Atan warriors, and the much enlarged party moved slowly on back to the road and continued eastward toward Lebas in Tamul proper. Hindered as they were by the wounded, they did not make good time – or so it seemed. After what had apparently been two full days of travel, Sparhawk spoke very briefly with his daughter, advising her that he needed to talk with her at some point while the minds of the others were asleep. When the blank faces of his companions indicated that Aphrael was compressing time again, he rode back to the carriage.

'Please get right to the point, Sparhawk,' the little Goddess told him. 'It's very difficult this time.'

'Is it different somehow?'

'Of course it is. I'm extending the pain of the wounded, and that's very distasteful. I'm making them sleep as much as possible, but there are limits, you know.'

'All right then, how much of what happened back there was real?'

'How could I possibly know that?'

'You mean you can't tell?'

'Well, of *course* I can't, Sparhawk. When we create an illusion, *nobody* can tell. It wouldn't be much of an illusion if someone could detect it, would it?'

'You said "we". If it *was* an illusion, there was a God behind it then?'

'Yes – either directly or indirectly. If it was indirectly, though, someone has a great deal of influence with whatever God was involved. We don't surrender that much power very often – or very willingly. Don't beat around the bush, Sparhawk. What's bothering you?'

'I don't really know, Aphrael,' he confessed. 'Something about it didn't seem quite right.'

'Specifics, Sparhawk. I need something specific to work with.'

'It just seemed to me that it was overdone, that's all. I got a distinct feeling that someone was just showing off. It was adolescent.'

She considered that, her bow-like little mouth pouting. 'Maybe we *are* adolescent, Sparhawk. It's one of the dangers of our situation. There's nothing powerful enough to make us grow up, so we're at liberty to indulge ourselves. I've even noticed that in my own character.'

'You?'

'Be nice, father.' She said it almost absently, her small black brows knitted in concentration. 'It's certainly consistent,' she added. 'Back in Astel, that Sabre fellow showed a rather profound lack of maturity, and he was being rather tightly controlled. You may just have hit upon one of our weaknesses, Sparhawk. I'd rather you didn't apply the notion to me directly, but keep the idea that we're all just a bit immature sort of in the front of your mind. I won't be able to see it myself, I'm afraid. If it *is* one of our failings, I'm just as infected with it as the others. We all love to impress each other, and it's polite to be impressed when someone else is showing off.' She made a little face. 'It's automatic, I'm afraid. Keep a firm hold on your scepticism, Sparhawk. Your cold-eyed lack of gullibility might be very useful. Now please go back to sleep. I'm very busy right now.'

They crossed the summit of the mountains of Atan and moved on down the eastern slopes toward the border. The demarcation between Atan and Tamul was abrupt and clearly evident. Atan was a wilderness of trees and rugged peaks, Tamul was a carefully-tended park. The fields were excruciatingly neat, and even the hills seemed to have been artfully sculpted to provide pleasing prospects and vistas. The peasantry seemed

436

industrious, and they did not have that expression of hopeless misery so common on the faces of the peasants and serfs of the Elene Kingdoms.

'Organisation, my dear Emban,' Oscagne was telling the fat little churchman. 'The key to our success lies in organisation. All power in Tamul descends from the emperor, and all decisions are made in Matherion. We even tell our peasants when to plant and when to harvest. I'll admit that central planning has its drawbacks, but the Tamul nature seems to require it.'

'Elenes, unfortunately, are much less disciplined,' Emban replied. 'The Church would be happier with a more docile congregation, but we have to make do with what God gave us to work with.' He smiled. 'Oh, well, it keeps life interesting.'

They reached Lebas late one afternoon. It was a small, neat city with a distinctly alien-looking architecture that leaned strongly in the direction of artistic embellishment. The houses were low and broad, with graceful roofs that curved upward at the ends of their ridge-lines as if the architects felt that abrupt straight lines were somehow incomplete. The cobbled streets were broad and straight, and they were filled with citizens dressed in brightly coloured silks.

The entrance of the westerners created quite a stir, since the Tamuls had never seen Elene knights before. It was the Queen of Elenia, however, who astonished them the most. The Tamuls were a golden-skinned, dark-haired people, and the pale, blonde queen filled them with awe as her carriage moved almost ceremonially through the streets.

Their first concern, of course, was the wounded. Oscagne assured them that Tamul physicians were among the finest in the world. It appeared, moreover, that the ambassador held a fairly exalted rank in the empire. A house was immediately provided for the

injured knights, and a medical staff seemed to material-
ise at his command. Additional houses were provided
for the rest of their company, and those houses were
fully staffed with servants who could not understand a
single word of the Elenic language.

'You seem to throw a great deal of weight around,
Oscagne,' Emban said that evening after they had
eaten an exotic meal consisting of course after course of
unidentifiable delicacies and sometimes startling
flavours.

'I'm not the overweight one, my friend,' Oscagne
smiled. 'My commission is signed by the emperor, and
his hand had the full weight of the entire Daresian continent behind it. He's ordered that all of Tamuli do everything possible – and even impossible – to make the visit
of Queen Ehlana pleasant and convenient. No one ever
disobeys his orders.'

'They must not have reached the Trolls then,' Ulath
said blandly. 'Of course Trolls have a different view of
the world than we do. Maybe they thought Queen
Ehlana would be entertained by their welcome.'

'Does he have to do that?' Oscagne complained to
Sparhawk.

'Ulath? Yes, I think he does, your Excellency. It's
something in the Thalesian nature – terribly obscure,
I'm afraid, and quite possibly perverted.'

'*Sparhawk!*' Ulath protested.

'Nothing personal there, old boy,' Sparhawk grinned,
'Just a reminder that I haven't yet quite forgiven you for
all the times you've euchred me into doing the cooking
when it wasn't really my turn.'

'Hold still,' Mirtai commanded.

'You got some of it in my eye,' Talen accused her.

'It won't hurt you. Now hold still.' She continued to
daub the mixture onto his face.

'What is that, Mirtai?' Baroness Melidere asked curiously.

'Saffron. We use it in our cooking. It's a kind of a spice.'

'What are we doing here?' Ehlana asked curiously as she and Sparhawk entered the room to find the Atana spreading the condiment over Talen's face.

'We're modifying your page, my Queen,' Stragen explained. 'He has to go out into the streets, and we want him to be unobtrusive. Mirtai's changing the colour of his skin.'

'You could do that with magic, couldn't you, Sparhawk?' Ehlana asked.

'Probably,' he said, 'and if I couldn't, Sephrenia certainly could.'

'*Now* you tell me,' Talen said in a slightly bitter tone. 'Mirtai's been seasoning me for the past half-hour.'

'You smell good, though,' Melidere told him.

'I didn't set out to be somebody's supper. Ouch.'

'Sorry,' Alean murmured, carefully disengaging her comb from a snarl in his hair. 'I have to work the dye in, though, or it won't look right.' Alean was applying black dye to the young man's hair.

'How long will it take me to wash this yellow stuff off?' Talen asked.

'I'm not sure,' Mirtai shrugged. 'It might be permanent, but it should grow out in a month or so.'

'I'll get you for this, Stragen,' Talen threatened.

'Hold still,' Mirtai said again and continued her daubing.

'We have to make contact with the local thieves,' Stragen explained. 'The thieves at Sarsos promised that we'd get a definite answer here in Lebas.'

'I see a large hole in the plan, Stragen,' Sparhawk replied. 'Talen doesn't speak Tamul.'

439

'That's no real problem,' Stragen shrugged. 'The chief of the local thieves is a Cammorian.'

'How did *that* happen?'

'We're very cosmopolitan, Sparhawk. All thieves are brothers, after all, and we recognise the aristocracy of talent. Anyway, as soon as he can pass for a Tamul, Talen's going to the local thieves' den to talk with Caalador – that's the Cammorian's name. He'll bring him here, and we'll be able to talk with him privately.'

'Why aren't you the one who's going?'

'And get saffron all over my face? Don't be silly, Sparhawk.'

Caalador the Cammorian was a stocky, red-faced man with curly black hair and an open, friendly countenance. He looked more like a jovial innkeeper than a leader of thieves and cutthroats. His manner was bluff and good humoured, and he spoke in the typical Cammorian drawl and with the slovenly grammar that bespoke back-country origins. 'So yer the one ez has got all the thieves of Daresia so sore perplexed,' he said to Stragen when Talen presented him.

'I'll have to plead guilty on that score, Caalador,' Stragen smiled.

'Don't never do that, brother. Alluz try'n lie yer way outten thangs.'

'I'll try to remember that. What are you doing so far from home, my friend?'

'I mought ax you the same question, Stragen. It's a fur piece from here t' Thalesia.'

'And quite nearly as far from Cammoria.'

'Aw, that's easy explained, m' friend. I storted out in life ez a poacher, ketchin' rabbits an' sich in the bushes on land that weren't rightly mine, but that's a sore hard kinda work with lotsa' risk and mighty slim profit, so I tooken t' liftin' chickens outten hen-roosts – chickens not runnin' near ez fast ez rabbits, especial at night. Then I moved up t' sheep-stealing – only one night I had me a set-to with a hull passel o' sheep-dawgs which it wuz ez betrayed me real cruel by not stayin' bribed.'

'How do you bribe a dog?' Ehlana asked curiously.

'Easiest thang in the world, little lady. Y' thrun 'em some meat-scraps t' keep ther attention. Well, sir, them there dawgs tore into me somethin' fierce, an' I lit out – leavin', misfortunate-like, a hat which it wuz I wuz partial to an' which it wuz ez could be rekonnized ez mine by half the parish. Now, I'm jist a country boy at hort 'thout no real citified ways t' get me by in town, an' so I tooken t' sea, an' t' make it short, I fetched up on this yere furrin coast an' beat my way inland, the capting of the ship I wuz a-sailin' on wantin' t' talk t' me 'bout some stuff ez had turnt up missin' fum the cargo hold, y' know.' He paused. 'Have I sufficiently entertained you as yet, Milord Stragen?' he grinned.

'Very, very good, Caalador,' Stragen murmured. 'Convincing – although it was a trifle overdone.'

'A failing, Milord. It's so much fun that I get carried away. Actually, I'm a swindler. I've found that posing as an ignorant yokel disarms people. No one in this world is as easy to gull as the man who thinks he's smarter than you are.'

'Ohh.' Ehlana's tone was profoundly disappointed.

'Wuz yer Majesty tooken with the iggernent way I wuz atalkin'?' Caalador asked sympathetically. 'I'll do 'er agin, iff'n yer of a mind – of course it takes a beastly long time to get to the point that way.'

She laughed delightedly. 'I think you could charm the birds out of the bushes, Caalador,' she told him.

'Thank you, your Majesty,' he said, bowing with fluid grace. Then he turned back to Stragen. 'Your proposal has baffled our Tamul friends, Milord,' he said. 'The demarcation line between corruption and outright theft is very clearly defined in the Tamul culture. Tamul thieves are quite class-conscious, and the notion of actually co-operating with the authorities strikes them as unnatural for some reason. Fortunately, we Elenes are far more corrupt than our simple yellow brothers, and Elenes seem to rise to the top in our peculiar society – natural talent, most likely. *We* saw the advantages of your proposal immediately. Kondrak of Darsas was most eloquent in his presentation. You seem to have impressed him enormously. The disturbances here in Tamuli have been disastrous for business, and when we began reciting profit and loss figures to the Tamuls, they started to listen to reason. They agreed to co-operate – grudgingly, I'll grant you, but they *will* help you to gather information.'

'Thank God!' Stragen said with a vast sigh of relief. 'The delay was beginning to make me very, very nervous.'

'Y'd made promises t' yer queen, an' y' wuzn't shore iff'n y' could deliver, is that it?'

'That's very, very close, my friend.'

'I'll give you the names of some people in Matherion.' Caalador looked around. 'Private-like, if'n y' take my meanin',' he added. 'It's all vury well t' talk 'bout lendin' a helpin' hand an' sich, but 'taint hordly nach'ral t' be namin' no names right out in fronta no queens an' knights an' sich.' He grinned impudently at Ehlana. 'An' now, yer queenship, how'd y' like it iff'n I wuz t' spin y' a long, long tale 'bout my advenchoors in the shadowy world o' crime?'

'I'd be delighted, Caalador,' she replied eagerly.

Another of the injured knights died that night, but the two dozen sorely-wounded seemed on the mend. As Oscagne had told them, Tamul physicians were extraordinarily skilled, although some of their methods were

442

strange to Elenes. After a brief conference, Sparhawk and his friends decided to press on to Matherion. Their trek across the continent had yielded a great deal of information, and they all felt that it was time to combine that information with the findings of the Imperial government.

And so they set out from Lebas early one morning and rode south under a kindly summer sky. The countryside was neat, with crops growing in straight lines across weedless fields marked off with low stone walls. Even the trees in the woodlands grew in straight lines, and all traces of unfettered nature seemed to have been erased. The peasants in the fields wore loose-fitting trousers and shirts of white linen and tightly-woven, straw hats that looked not unlike mushroom-tops. Many of the crops grown in this alien countryside were unrecognisable to the Elenes – odd-looking beans and peculiar grains. They passed Lake Sama and saw fishermen casting nets from strange-looking boats with high prows and sterns, boats of which Khalad profoundly disapproved. 'One good gust of wind from the side would capsize them,' was his verdict.

They reached Tosa, some sixty leagues to the north of the capital, with that sense of impatience that comes near the end of every long journey.

The weather held fair, and they set out early and rode late each day, counting off every league put behind them. The road followed the coast of the Tamul sea, a low, rolling coast-line where rounded hills rose from broad beaches of white sand and long waves rolled in to break and foam and slither back out into deep blue water.

Eight days – more or less – after they left Tosa, they set up for the night in a park-like grove with an almost holiday air, since Oscagne assured them that they were no more than five leagues from Matherion.

'We could ride on,' Kalten suggested. 'We'd be there by morning.'

'Not on your life, Sir Kalten,' Ehlana said adamantly. 'Start heating water, gentlemen, and put up a tent we can use for bathing. The ladies and I are *not* going to ride into Matherion with half the dirt of Daresia caked on us – and string some lines so that we can hang our gowns out to air and to let the breeze shake the wrinkles out of them.' She looked around critically. 'And then, gentlemen, I want you to see to yourselves and your equipment. I'll inspect you before we set out tomorrow morning, and I'd better not find one single speck of rust.'

Kalten sighed mournfully. 'Yes, my Queen,' he replied in a resigned tone of voice.

They set out the following morning in a formal column with the carriage near the front. Their pace was slow to avoid raising dust, and Ehlana, gowned in blue and crowned with gold and diamonds, sat regally in the carriage, looking for all the world as if she owned everything in sight. There had been one small but intense disagreement before they set out, however. Her Highness, the Royal Princess Danae, had objected violently when told that she *would* wear a proper dress and a delicate little tiara. Ehlana did not cajole her daughter about the matter, but instead she did something she had never done before. 'Princess Danae,' she said quite formally, 'I am the queen. You *will* obey me.'

Danae blinked in astonishment. Sparhawk was fairly certain that no one had *ever* spoken to her that way before. 'Yes, your Majesty,' she replied finally in a suitably submissive tone.

Word of their approach had preceded them, of course. Engessa had seen to that, and as they rode up a long hill about mid-afternoon, they saw a mounted detachment of ceremonial troops wearing armour of black lacquered steel inlaid with gold awaiting them at the summit. The honour guard was drawn up in ranks on each side of the road. There were as yet no greetings, and when the column crested the hill, Sparhawk immediately saw why.

'Dear God!' Bevier breathed in awed reverence.

A crescent-shaped city embraced a deep blue harbour below. The sun had passed its zenith, and it shone down on the crown of Tamuli. The architecture was graceful, and every building had a dome-like, rounded roof. It was not so large as Chyrellos, but it was not the size which had wrung that reverential gasp from Sir Bevier. The city was dazzling, but its splendour was not the splendour of marble. An opalescent sheen covered the capital; a shifting rainbow-hued fire that blazed beneath the surface of its very stones, a fire that at times blinded the eye with its stunning magnificence.

'Behold!' Oscagne intoned quite formally. 'Behold the seat of beauty and truth! Behold the home of wisdom and power! Behold fire-domed Matherion, the centre of the world!'

PART FOUR

Matherion

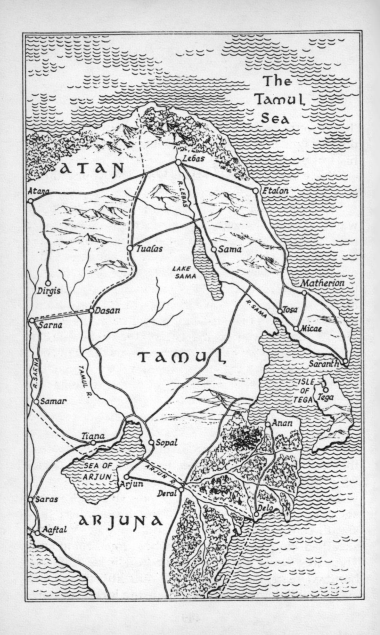

CHAPTER 24

'It's been that way since the twelfth century,' Ambassador Oscagne told them as they were escorted down the hill toward the gleaming city.

'Was it magic?' Talen asked him. The young thief's eyes were filled with wonder.

'You might call it that,' Oscagne said wryly, 'but it was the kind of magic one performs with unlimited money and power rather than with incantations. The eleventh and twelfth centuries were a foolish period in our history. It was the time of the Micaen Dynasty, and they were probably the silliest family to ever occupy the throne. The first Micaen emperor was given an ornamental box of mother-of-pearl – or nacre, as some call it – by an emissary from the Isle of Tega when he was about fourteen years old. History tells us that he would sit staring at it by the hour, paralysed by the shifting colours. He was so enamoured of the nacre he had his throne sheathed in the stuff.'

'That must have been a fair-sized oyster,' Ulath noted.

Oscagne smiled. 'No, Sir Ulath. They cut the shells into little tiles and fit them together very tightly. Then they polish the whole surface for a month or so. It's a very tedious and expensive process. Anyway, the second Micaen emperor took it one step further and sheathed the columns in the throne-room. The third sheathed the walls, and on and on and on. They sheathed the palace, then the whole royal compound. Then they went after the public buildings. After two hundred years, they'd cemented those little tiles all over every building in Matherion. There are low dives down

449

by the waterfront that are more magnificent than the Basilica of Chyrellos. Fortunately the dynasty died out before they paved the streets with it. They virtually bankrupt the empire and enormously enriched the Isle of Tega in the process. Tegan divers became fabulously wealthy plundering the sea floor.'

'Isn't mother-of-pearl almost as brittle as glass?' Khalad asked him.

'It is indeed, young sir, and the cement that's used to stick it to the buildings isn't all that permanent. A good wind-storm fills the streets with gleaming crumbs and leaves all the buildings looking as if they've got the pox. As a matter of pride, the tiles have to be replaced. A moderate hurricane can precipitate a major financial crisis in the empire, but we're saddled with it now. Official documents have referred to "Fire-domed Matherion" for so long that it's become a cliché. Like it or not, we have to maintain this absurdity.'

'It *is* breath-taking, though,' Ehlana marvelled in a slightly speculative tone of voice.

'Never mind, dear,' Sparhawk told her quite firmly.

'What?'

'You can't afford it. Lenda and I almost come to blows every year hammering out the budget as it is.'

'I wasn't seriously considering it, Sparhawk,' she replied. 'Well – not *too* seriously, anyway,' she added.

The broad avenues of Matherion were lined with cheering crowds that fell suddenly silent as Ehlana's carriage passed. The citizens stopped cheering as the Queen of Elenia went by because they were too busy grovelling to cheer. The formal grovel involved kneeling and touching the forehead to the paving-stones.

'What are they *doing*?' Ehlana exclaimed.

'Obeying the emperor's command, I'd imagine,' Oscagne replied. 'That's the customary sign of respect for the imperial person.'

450

'Make them stop!' she commanded.

'Countermand an imperial order? Me, your Majesty? Not very likely. Forgive me, Queen Ehlana, but I like my head where it is. I'd rather not have it displayed on a pole at the city gate. It *is* quite an honour, though. Sarabian's ordered the population to treat you as his equal. No emperor's ever done that before.'

'And the people who don't fall down on their faces are punished?' Khalad surmised with a hard edge to his voice.

'Of course not. They do it out of love. That's the official explanation, of course. Actually, the custom originated about a thousand years ago. A drunken courtier tripped and fell on his face when the emperor entered the room. The emperor was terribly impressed, and characteristically, he completely misunderstood. He awarded the courtier a dukedom on the spot. People aren't banging their faces on the cobblestones out of fear, young man. They're doing it in the hope of being rewarded.'

'You're a cynic, Oscagne,' Emban accused the ambassador.

'No, Emban, I'm a realist. A good politician always looks for the worst in people.'

'Someday they may surprise you, your Excellency,' Talen predicted.

'They haven't yet.'

The palace compound was only slightly smaller than the city of Demos in eastern Elenia. The gleaming central palace, of course, was by far the largest structure in the grounds. There were other palaces, however – glowing structures in a wide variety of architectural styles. Sir Bevier drew in his breath sharply. 'Good Lord!' he exclaimed. 'That castle over there is almost an exact replica of the palace of King Dregos in Larium.'

451

'Plagiarism appears to be a sin not exclusively committed by poets,' Stragen murmured.

'Merely a genuflection toward cosmopolitanism,
Milord,' Oscagne explained. 'We *are* an empire, after all,
and we've drawn many different peoples under our
roof. Elenes like castles, so we have a castle here to
make the Elene Kings of the western empire feel more
comfortable when they come to pay a call.'

'The castle of King Dregos certainly doesn't gleam in
the sun the way that one does,' Bevier noted.

'That was sort of the idea, Sir Bevier,' Oscagne smiled.

They dismounted in the flagstoned, semi-enclosed
court before the main palace, where they were met by
a horde of obsequious servants.

'What does he want?' Kalten asked, holding off a
determined-looking Tamul garbed in crimson silk.

'Your shoes, Sir Kalten,' Oscagne explained.

'What's wrong with my shoes?'

'They're made of steel, Sir Knight.'

'So? I'm wearing armour. Naturally my shoes are
made of steel.'

'You can't enter the palace with steel shoes on your
feet. Leather boots aren't even permitted – the floors,
you understand.'

'Even the floors are made of sea-shells?' Kalten asked
incredulously.

'I'm afraid so. We Tamuls don't wear shoes inside our
houses, so the builders went ahead and tiled the floors
of the buildings here in the imperial compound as well
as the walls and ceilings. They didn't anticipate visits
by armoured knights.'

'I can't take off my shoes,' Kalten objected, flush-
ing.

'What's the problem, Kalten?' Ehlana asked him.

'I've got a hole in one of my socks,' he muttered,
looking dreadfully embarrassed. 'I can't meet an

452

emperor with my toes hanging out.' He looked around at his companions, his face pugnacious. He held up one gauntleted fist. 'If anybody laughs, there's going to be a fight,' he threatened.

'Your dignity's secure, Sir Kalten,' Oscagne assured him. 'The servants have down-filled slippers for us to wear inside.'

'I've got awfully big feet, your Excellency,' Kalten pointed out anxiously. 'Are you sure they'll have shoes to fit me?'

'Don't be concerned, Kalten-Knight,' Engessa said. 'If they can fit *me*, they can certainly fit you.'

Once the visitors had been re-shod, they were escorted into the palace. There were oil lamps hanging on long chains suspended from the ceiling, and the lamplight set everything aflame. The shifting, rainbow-hued colours of the walls, floors and ceiling of the broad corridors dazzled the Elenes, and they followed the servants all bemused.

There were courtiers here, of course – no palace is complete without them – and like the citizens in the streets outside, they grovelled as the Queen of Elenia passed.

'Don't become too enamoured of their mode of greeting, love,' Sparhawk warned his wife. 'The citizens of Cimmura wouldn't adopt it no matter what you offered them.'

'Don't be absurd, Sparhawk,' she replied tartly. 'I wasn't even considering it. Actually, I wish these people would stop. It's really just a bit embarrassing.'

'That's my girl,' he smiled.

They were offered wine and chilled, scented water to dab on their faces. The knights accepted the wine enthusiastically, and the ladies dutifully dabbed.

'You really ought to try some of this, father,' Princess Danae suggested, pointing at one of the porcelain basins

453

of water. 'It might conceal the fragrance of your armour.'

'She has a point, Sparhawk,' Ehlana agreed.

'Armour's supposed to stink,' he replied, shrugging. 'If an enemy's eyes start to water during a fight, it gives you a certain advantage.'

'I knew there was a reason,' the little princess murmured.

Then they were led into a long corridor where mosaic portraits were inlaid into the walls, stiff, probably idealised representations of long-dead emperors. A broad strip of crimson carpet with a golden border along each edge protected the floor of that seemingly endless corridor.

'Very impressive, your Excellency,' Stragen murmured to Oscagne after a time. 'How many more miles is it to the throne-room?'

'You are droll, Milord.' Oscagne smiled briefly.

'It's artfully done,' the thief observed, 'but doesn't it waste a great deal of space?'

'Very perceptive, Milord Stragen.'

'What's this?' Tynian asked.

'The corridor curves to the left,' Stragen replied. 'It's hard to detect because of the way the walls reflect the light, but if you look closely, you can see it. We've been walking around in a circle for the past quarter of an hour.'

'A spiral, actually, Milord Stragen,' Oscagne corrected him. 'The design was intended to convey the notion of immensity. Tamuls are of short stature, and immensity impresses us. That's why we're so fond of the Atans. We're reaching the inner coils of the spiral now. The throne-room's not far ahead.'

The corridors of shifting fire were suddenly filled with a brazen fanfare as hidden trumpeters greeted the queen and her party. That fanfare was followed by an awful screeching punctuated by a tinny clanking noise. Mmrr, nestled in her little mistress' arms, laid back her ears and hissed.

'The cat has excellent musical taste,' Bevier noted, wincing at a particularly off-key passage in the 'music'.

'I'd forgotten that,' Sephrenia apologised to Vanion. 'Try to ignore it, dear one.'

'I *am*,' he replied with a pained expression on his face.

'You remember that Ogress I told you about?' Ulath asked Sparhawk, 'The one who fell in love with that poor fellow up in Thalesia?'

'Vaguely.'

'When she sang to him, it sounded almost exactly like that.'

'He went into a monastery to get away from her, didn't he?'

'Yes.'

'Wise decision.'

'It's an affectation of ours,' Oscagne explained to them. 'The Tamul language is very musical when it's spoken. Pretty music would seem commonplace, even mundane – so our composers strive for the opposite effect.'

'I'd say they've succeeded beyond human imagination,' Baroness Melidere said. 'It sounds like someone's torturing a dozen pigs inside an iron works.'

'I'll convey your observation to the composer, Baroness,' Oscagne told her. 'I'm sure he'll be pleased.'

'*I'd* be pleased if his song came to an end, your Excellency.'

The vast doors that finally terminated the endless-seeming corridor were covered with beaten gold, and they swung ponderously open to reveal an enormous, domed hall. Since the dome was higher than the surrounding structures, the illumination in the room came through inch-thick crystal windows high overhead. The sun poured down through those windows to set the walls and floor of Emperor Sarabian's throne room afire. The hall was of suitably stupendous dimensions, and the expanses of nacreous white were broken up by accents of crimson and gold. Heavy red velvet draperies hung at intervals along the glowing walls, flanking columnar buttresses inlaid with gold. A wide avenue of crimson carpet led from the huge doors to the foot of the throne, and the room was filled with courtiers, both Tamul and Elene.

Another fanfare announced the arrival of the visitors, and the Church Knights and the Peloi formed up in military precision around Queen Ehlana and her party. They marched with ceremonial pace down that broad, carpeted avenue to the throne of his Imperial Majesty, Sarabian of Tamul.

The ruler of half the world wore a heavy crown of diamond-encrusted gold, and his crimson cloak, open at the front, was bordered with wide bands of tightly-woven gold thread. His robe was gleaming white, caught at the waist by a wide golden belt. Despite the splendour of his throne-room and his clothing, Sarabian of Tamul was a rather ordinary-looking man. His skin was pale by comparison with the skin of the Atans, largely, Sparhawk surmised, because the emperor was seldom out of doors. He was of medium stature and build and his face was unremarkable. His eyes, however, were far more alert than Sparhawk had expected. When Ehlana entered the throne-room, he rose somewhat hesitantly to his feet.

Oscagne looked a bit surprised. 'That's amazing,' he said. 'The emperor never stands to greet his guests.'

'Who are the ladies gathered around him?' Ehlana asked in a quiet voice.

'His wives,' Oscagne replied, 'the Empresses of Tamuli. There are nine of them.'

'Monstrous!' Bevier gasped.

'Political expediency, Sir Knight,' the ambassador explained. 'An ordinary man has only one wife, but the emperor has to have one from each kingdom in the empire. He can't really show favouritism, after all.'

'It looks as if one of the empresses forgot to finish dressing,' Baroness Melidere said critically, staring at one of the imperial wives, a sunny-faced young woman who stood naked to the waist with no hint that her unclad state caused her any concern. The skirt caught around her waist was a brilliant scarlet, and she had a red flower in her hair.

Oscagne chuckled. 'That's our Elysoun,' he smiled. 'She's from the Isle of Valesia, and that's the costume – or lack of it – customary among the islanders. She's a totally uncomplicated girl, and we all love her dearly. The normal rules governing marital fidelity have never applied to the Valesian Empress. It's a concept the Valesians can't comprehend. The notion of sin is alien to them.'

Bevier gasped.

'Hasn't anyone ever tried to instruct them?' Emban asked.

'Oh, my, yes, your Grace,' Oscagne grinned. 'Churchmen from the Elene kingdoms of western Tamuli have gone by the score to Valesia to try to persuade the islanders that their favourite pastime is scandalous and sinful. The churchmen are filled with zeal right at first, but it doesn't usually last for very long. Valesian girls are all very beautiful and *very* friendly. Almost invariably, it's the Elenes who are converted. The Valesian religion seems to have only one commandment: "Be happy".'

'There are worse notions,' Emban sighed.

'Your *Grace*!' Bevier exclaimed.

'Grow up, Bevier,' Emban told him. 'I sometimes

457

think that our Holy Mother Church is a bit obsessive about certain aspects of human behaviour.'

Bevier flushed, and his face grew rigidly disapproving.

The courtiers in the throne-room, obviously at the emperor's command, once again ritualistically grovelled as Ehlana passed. Practice had made them so skilled that dropping to their knees, banging their foreheads on the floor and getting back up again was accomplished with only minimal awkwardness.

Ehlana, gowned in royal blue, reached the throne and curtseyed gracefully. The set look on her face clearly said that she would *not* grovel.

The emperor bowed in response, and an astonished gasp ran through the crowd. The imperial bow was adequate, though just a bit stiff. Sarabian had obviously been practising, but bowing appeared not to come naturally to him. Then he cleared his throat and spoke at some length in the Tamul language, pausing from time to time to permit his official translator to convert his remarks into Elenic.

'Keep your eyes where they belong,' Ehlana murmured to Sparhawk. Her face was serene, and her lips scarcely moved.

'I wasn't looking at her,' he protested.

'Oh, *really*?'

The Empress Elysoun had the virtually undivided attention of the Church Knights and the Peloi, and she quite obviously was enjoying it. Her dark eyes sparkled, and her smile was just slightly naughty. She stood not far from her Imperial husband, breathing deeply, evidently a form of exercise among her people. There was a challenge in the look she returned to her many admirers, and she surveyed them clinically. Sparhawk had seen the same look on Ehlana's face when she was choosing jewellery or gowns. He concluded that

Empress Elysoun was very likely to cause problems.

Emperor Sarabian's speech was filled with formalised platitudes. His heart was full. He swooned with joy. He was dumbstruck by Ehlana's beauty. He was quite overwhelmed by the honour she did him in stopping by to call. He thought her dress was very nice.

Ehlana, the world's consummate orator, quickly discarded the speech she had been preparing since her departure from Chyrellos and responded in kind. She found Matherion quite pretty. She advised Sarabian that her life had now seen its crown (Ehlana's life seemed to find a new crown each time she made a speech). She commented on the unspeakable beauty of the Imperial wives, (though making no mention of Empress Elysoun's painfully visible attributes). She also promised to swoon with joy, since it seemed to be the fashion here. She thanked him profusely for his gracious welcome. She did not, however, talk about the weather.

Emperor Sarabian visibly relaxed. He had clearly been apprehensive that the Queen of Elenia might accidentally slip something of substance into her speech which would have then obliged him to respond without consultation.

He thanked her for her thanks.

She thanked *him* for his thanks for her thanks.

Then they stared at each other. Thanks for thanks for thanks can only be carried so far without becoming ridiculous.

Then an official with an exaggeratedly bored look on his face cleared his throat. He was somewhat taller than the average Tamul, and his face showed no sign whatsoever of what he was thinking.

It was with enormous relief that Emperor Sarabian introduced his prime minister, Pondia Subat.

'Odd name,' Ulath murmured after the emperor's

remarks had been translated. 'I wonder if his close friends call him "Pondy".'

'Pondia is his title of nobility, Sir Ulath,' Oscagne explained. 'It's a rank somewhat akin to that of viscount, though not exactly. Be a little careful of him, my lords. He is *not* your friend. He also pretends not to understand Elenic, but I strongly suspect that his ignorance on that score is feigned. Subat was violently opposed to the idea of inviting Prince Sparhawk to come to Matherion. He felt that to do so would demean the emperor. I've also been advised that the emperor's decision to treat Queen Ehlana as an equal quite nearly gave our prime minister apoplexy.'

'Is he dangerous?' Sparhawk murmured.

'I'm not entirely certain, your Highness. He's fanatically loyal to the emperor, and I'm not altogether sure where that may lead him.'

Pondia Subat was making a few remarks.

'He says that he knows you're fatigued by the rigours of the journey,' Oscagne translated. 'He urges you to accept the imperial hospitality to rest and refresh yourselves. It's a rather neat excuse to conclude the interview before anyone says anything that might compel the emperor to answer before Subat has a chance to prompt him.'

'It might not be a bad idea,' Ehlana decided. 'Things haven't gone badly so far. Maybe we should just leave well enough alone for the time being.'

'I shall be guided by you, your Majesty,' Oscagne said with a florid bow.

Ehlana let that pass.

After another effusive exchange between their Majesties, the prime minister escorted the visitors from the hall. Just outside the door to the throne-room they mounted a flight of stairs and proceeded along a corridor directly to the far side of the palace, foregoing the pleasure of retracing their steps around and around the interminable spiral.

Pondia Subat, speaking through an interpreter, pointed out features of interest as they progressed. His tone was deliberately off-hand, treating wonders as commonplace. He was not even particularly subtle about his efforts to put these Elene barbarians in their place. He did not quite sneer at them, but he came very close. He led them along a covered walk-way to the gleaming Elene castle, where he left them in the care of Ambassador Oscagne.

'Is his attitude fairly prevalent here in Matherion?' Emban asked the ambassador.

'Hardly,' Oscagne replied. 'Subat's the leader of a very small faction here at court. They're arch-conservatives who haven't had a new idea in five hundred years.'

'How did he become prime minister if his faction is so small?' Tynian asked.

'Tamul politics are very murky, Sir Tynian. We serve at the emperor's pleasure, and he's in no way obliged to take our advice on any matter. Subat's father was a very close friend of Emperor Sarabian's sire, and the appointment of Subat as prime minister was more in the nature of a gesture of filial respect than a recognition of outstanding merit, although Subat's an adequate prime minister – unless something unusual comes up. Then he tends to go all to pieces. Cronyism's one of the major drawbacks of our form of government. The head of our church has never had a pious thought in his life. He doesn't even know the names of our Gods.'

'Wait a minute,' Emban said, his eyes stunned. 'Are you trying to say that ecclesiastical positions are bestowed by the emperor?'

'Of course. They *are* positions of authority, after all,

461

and Tamul emperors don't like to let authority of *any* kind out of their hands.'

They had entered the main hall of the castle, which, with the exception of the gleaming nacre that covered every exposed surface, was very much like the main hall of every Elene castle in the world.

'The servants here are Elenes,' Oscagne told them, 'so you should have no difficulty explaining your needs to them. I trust you'll excuse me now. I must go make my report to his Imperial Majesty.' He made a face. 'I'm not really looking forward to it, to be honest with you. Subat's going to be standing at his Majesty's elbow making light of everything I say.' He bowed to Ehlana, then turned and left.

'We've got problems here, I think,' Tynian observed. 'All this formality's going to keep us away from the emperor, and if we can't tell him what we've discovered, he's not likely to give us the freedom of movement we're going to need.'

'And the antagonism of the prime minister's going to make things that much worse,' Bevier added. 'It rather looks as if we've come half-way round the world to offer our help only to be confined in this very elaborate prison.'

'Let's feel things out a bit before we start getting obstreperous,' Emban counselled. 'Oscagne knows what he's doing, and he's seen almost everything we've seen. I think we can count on him to convey the urgency of the situation to Sarabian.'

'If you have no need of us, your Majesty,' Stragen said to Ehlana, 'Talen and I should go make contact with the local thieves. If we're going to be tied up in meaningless formalities here, we'll need some help in gathering information.'

'How do you plan to communicate with them?' Khalad asked him.

'Matherion's a very cosmopolitan place, Khalad. Caal-ador directed me to several Elenes who carry quite a bit of weight with the local thieves.'

'Do what you must, Stragen,' Ehlana told him, 'but don't cause any international incidents.'

'Trust me, your Majesty,' he grinned.

The royal apartments in the castle were high up in a central tower. The castle was purely ornamental, of course, but since it was a faithful reproduction of an Elene fort, the builders had unwittingly included defensive features they probably hadn't even recognised. Bevier was quite pleased with it. 'I could defend the place,' he judged. 'About all I'd need would be a few vats of pitch and some engines and I could hold this castle for several years.'

'Let's hope it doesn't come to that, Bevier,' Ehlana replied.

Later that evening, when Sparhawk and his extended family had said good night to the others and retired to the royal apartment, the Prince consort lounged in a chair by the window while the ladies did all those little things ladies do before going to bed. Many of those little ceremonies had clearly practical reasons behind them; others were totally incomprehensible.

'I'm sorry, Sparhawk,' Ehlana was saying, 'but it concerns me. If the Empress Elysoun's as indiscriminately predatory as Oscagne suggests, she could cause us a great deal of embarrassment. Take Kalten, for example. Can you believe that he'd decline the kind of offers she's likely to make – particularly in view of her costume?'

'I'll have a talk with him,' Sparhawk promised.

'By hand,' Mirtai suggested. 'Sometime it's a little hard to get Kalten's attention when he's distracted.'

'She's vulgar,' Baroness Melidere sniffed.

'She's very pretty though, Baroness,' Alean added,

'And she's not really flaunting her body. She knows it's there, of course, but I think she just likes to share it with people. She's generous more than vulgar.'

'Do you suppose we could talk about something else?' Sparhawk asked them in a pained tone.

There was a light knock on the door, and Mirtai went to see who was asking admittance. As always, the Atana had one hand on a dagger-hilt when she opened the door.

It was Oscagne. He was wearing a hooded cloak, and he was accompanied by another man similarly garbed. The two stepped inside quickly. 'Close the door, Atana,' the Ambassador hissed urgently, his usually imperturbable face stunned and his eyes wild.

'What's your problem, Oscagne?' she asked bluntly.

'Please, Atana Mirtai, close the door. If anybody finds out that my friend and I are here, the palace will fall down around our ears.'

She closed the door and bolted it.

A sudden absolute certainty came over Sparhawk, and he rose to his feet. 'Welcome, your Imperial Majesty,' he greeted Oscagne's hooded companion.

Emperor Sarabian pushed back his hood. 'How the deuce did you know it was me, Prince Sparhawk?' he asked. His Elenic was only slightly accented. 'I know you couldn't see my face.'

'No, your Majesty,' Sparhawk replied, 'but I could see Ambassador Oscagne's. He looked very much like a man holding a live snake.'

'I've been called a lot of things in my time,' Sarabian laughed, 'but never that.'

'Your Majesty is most skilled,' Ehlana told him with a little curtsey. 'I didn't see a single hint on your face that you understood Elenic. I could read it in Queen Betuana's face, but you didn't give me a single clue.'

'Betuana speaks Elenic?' He seemed startled. 'What

an astounding thing.' He removed his cloak. 'Actually, your Majesty,' he told Ehlana, 'I speak all the languages of the Empire – Tamul, Elenic, Styric, Tegan, Arjuni, Valesian and even the awful language they speak in Cynesga. It's one of our most closely guarded state secrets. I even keep it a secret from my government, just to be on the safe side.' He looked a bit amused. 'I gather that you'd all concluded that I'm not quite bright,' he suggested.

'You fooled us completely, your Majesty,' Melidere assured him.

He beamed at her. 'Delightful girl,' he said. 'I adore fooling people. There are many reasons for this subterfuge, my friends, but they're mostly political and not really very nice. Shall we get to the point here? I can only be absent for a short period of time without being missed.'

'We are, as they say, at your immediate disposal, your Majesty,' Ehlana told him.

'I've never understood that phrase, Ehlana,' he confessed. 'You don't mind if we call each other by name, do you? All those "your Majesties" are just *too* cumbersome. Where was I? Oh, yes – "immediate disposal". It sounds like someone running to carry out the trash.' His words seemed to tumble from his lips as if his tongue were having difficulty keeping up with his thoughts. 'The point of this visit, my dear friends, is that I'm more or less the prisoner of custom and tradition here in Matherion. My role is strictly defined, and for me to overstep certain bounds causes earthquakes that can be felt from here to the Gulf of Daconia. I could ignore those earthquakes, but our common enemy could probably feel them too, and we don't want to alert him.'

'Truly,' Sparhawk agreed.

'Please don't keep gaping at me like that, Oscagne,' Sarabian told the ambassador. 'I didn't tell you that I was really awake when most of you thought I was sleeping because it wasn't necessary for you to know before. Now it is. Snap out of it, man. The foreign minister has to be able to take these little surprises in his stride.'

'It's just taking me a little while to re-adjust my thinking, your Majesty.'

'You thought I was an idiot, am I right?'

'Well –'

'You were *supposed* to think so, Oscagne – you and Subat and all the other ministers. It's been one of my main defences – and amusements. Actually, old boy, I'm something of a genius.' He smiled at Ehlana. 'That sounds immodest, doesn't it? But it's true, nonetheless. I learned your language in three weeks, and Styric in four. I can find the logical fallacies in the most abstruse treaties on Elene theology, and I've probably read – and understood – just about everything that's ever been written. My most brilliant achievement, however, has been to keep all that a secret. The people who call themselves my government – no offence intended, Oscagne – seem to be engaging in some vast conspiracy to keep me in the dark. They only tell me things they think I'll want to hear. I have to look out of a window to get an accurate idea of the current weather. They have the noblest of motives, of course. They want to spare me any distress, but I really think that someone ought to tell me when the ship I'm riding in is sinking, don't you?'

Sarabian was still talking very fast, spilling out ideas as quickly as they came to him. His eyes were bright, and he seemed almost on the verge of laughing out loud. He was obviously tremendously excited. 'Now then,' he rushed on, 'we must devise a means of communicating without alerting everyone in the palace – down to and including the scullery boys in the kitchen – to what we're doing. I desperately need to know

466

what's *really* going on so that I can bring my towering intellect to bear on it.' That last was delivered with self-deprecating irony. 'Any ideas?'

'What are your feelings about magic, your Majesty?' Sparhawk asked him.

'I haven't formed an opinion yet, Sparhawk.'

'It won't work then,' Sparhawk told him. 'You have to believe that the spell's going to work, or it'll fail.'

'I might be able to *make* myself believe,' Sarabian said just a bit dubiously.

'That probably wouldn't do it, your Majesty,' Sparhawk told him. 'The spells would succeed or not depending on your mood. We need something a bit more certain. There are things we'll need to tell you that will be so important that we won't be able to just trust to luck.'

'My feelings exactly, Sparhawk. That defines our problem then. We need an absolutely certain method of passing information back and forth that can't be detected. My experience tells me that it has to be something so commonplace that nobody will pay any attention to it.'

'Exchange gifts,' Baroness Melidere suggested in an offhand way.

'I'd be delighted to send you gifts, my dear Baroness,' Sarabian smiled. 'Your eyes quite stop my heart, but –'

She held up one hand. 'Excuse me, your Majesty,' she told him, 'but nothing is more common than the exchange of gifts between ruling monarchs. I can carry little mementos from the queen to you, and the ambassador here can carry yours to her. After we've run back and forth a few times, nobody will pay any attention to us. We can conceal messages in those gifts, and no one will dare to search for them.'

'Where did you find this wonderful girl, Ehlana?' Sarabian demanded. 'I'd marry her in a minute – if I didn't already have nine wives – oh, incidentally, Sparhawk, I need to talk with you about that – privately, perhaps.' He looked around. 'Can anyone see any flaws in the baroness's plan?'

'Just one,' Mirtai said, 'but I can take care of that.'

'What is it, Atana?' the excited emperor asked.

'Someone may still have suspicions about this exchange of gifts – particularly if there's a steady stream of them. He might try to intercept Melidere, but I'll escort her back and forth. I'll personally guarantee that no one will interfere.'

'Excellent, Atana! Capital! We'd better get back, Oscagne. Subat misses me terribly when I'm not where he expects me to be. Oh, Sparhawk, please designate several of your knights to entertain my wife, Elysoun.'

'I beg your Majesty's pardon?'

'Young, preferably handsome and with lots of stamina – you know the type.'

'Are we talking about what I think we're talking about, your Majesty?'

'Of course we are. Elysoun enjoys exchanging gifts and favours too, and she'd be crushed if no one wanted to play with her. She's terribly shrill when she's unhappy. For the sake of my ears, please see to it, old boy.'

'Ah – how many, your Majesty?'

'A dozen or so should suffice, I expect. Coming, Oscagne?' And the emperor of Tamuli rushed to the door.

CHAPTER 25

'It's a characteristic of people with a certain level of intelligence, your Majesty,' Zalasta advised Ehlana. 'They talk very fast because their ideas are spilling over. Emperor Sarabian may not be *quite* as brilliant as he thinks he is, but his is a mind to be reckoned with. The amazing thing is that he's managed to keep it a secret from everybody in his government. Those people are usually so erratic and excitable that they trip themselves up.'

They were all gathered in the royal apartment to discuss the previous night's startling revelation. Ambassador Oscagne had arrived early, bringing with him a diagram of the hidden passageways and concealed listening posts inside the Elene castle which was their temporary home. A half-dozen spies had been rooted out and politely but firmly invited to leave. 'There's nothing really personal involved, your Majesty,' Oscagne apologised to Ehlana. 'It's just a matter of policy.'

'I understand completely, your Excellency,' she replied graciously. Ehlana wore an emerald green gown this morning, and she looked particularly lovely.

'Is your espionage system very well-developed, your Excellency?' Stragen asked.

'No, not really, Milord. Each bureau of the government has its spies, but they spend most of their time spying on each other. We're far more nervous about our colleagues than we are about foreign visitors.'

'There's no centralised intelligence service, then?'

'I'm afraid not, Milord.'

'Are we sure we cleaned all the spies out?' Emban asked, looking a bit nervously at the gleaming walls.

'Trust me, your Grace,' Sephrenia smiled.

'I didn't follow that, I'm afraid.'

'She wiggled her fingers, Patriarch Emban,' Talen said dryly. 'She turned all the spies we didn't catch into toads.'

'Well, not exactly,' she amended, 'but if there *are* any spies left hiding behind the walls, they can't hear anything.'

'You're a very useful person to have around, Sephrenia,' the fat little churchman observed.

'I've noticed that myself,' Vanion agreed.

'Let's push on here,' Ehlana suggested. 'We don't want to overuse our subterfuge, but we *will* want to exchange a few gifts with Sarabian just to make sure that no one's going to intercept our messages and to get the courtiers in the hallways accustomed to seeing Melidere trotting back and forth with trinkets.'

'I won't really trot, your Majesty,' Melidere objected. 'I'll swish – seductively. I've found that a man who's busy watching your hips doesn't pay too much attention to what the rest of you is doing.'

'Really?' Princess Danae said. 'I'll have to remember that. Can you show me how to swish, Baroness?'

'You're going to have to grow some hips first, Princess,' Talen told her.

Danae's eyes went suddenly dangerous.

'Never mind,' Sparhawk told her.

She ignored him. 'I'll get you for that, Talen,' she threatened.

'I doubt it, your Highness,' he replied impudently. 'I can still run faster than you can.'

'We have another problem,' Stragen told them. 'The absolutely splendid plan I conceived some months ago fell all to pieces on me last night. The local thieves aren't

470

going to be much help, I'm afraid. They're even worse than Caalador led us to believe back in Lebas. Tamul society's so rigid that my colleagues out there in the streets can't think independently. There's a certain way that thieves are supposed to behave here, and the ones we met last night are so hide-bound that they can't get around the stereotypes. The Elenes in the local thieves' community are creative enough, but the Tamuls are hopelessly inept.'

'That's certainly the truth,' Talen agreed. 'They don't even try to run when they're caught stealing. They just stand around waiting to be taken into custody. It's the most immoral thing I've ever heard of.'

'We might be able to salvage something out of it,' Stragen continued. 'I've sent for Caalador. Maybe he can talk some sense into them. What concerns me the most is their absolute lack of any kind of organisation. The thieves don't talk to the murderers; the whores don't talk to the beggars and nobody talks to the swindlers. I can't for the life of me see how they survive.'

'That's bad news,' Ulath noted. 'We were counting on the thieves to serve as our spy-network.'

'Let's hope that Caalador can fix it,' Stragen said. 'The fact that there's no central intelligence-gathering apparatus in the government makes those thieves crucial to our plans.'

'Caalador will be able to talk some sense into them,' Ehlana said. 'I have every confidence in him.'

'That's probably because you like to hear him talk,' Sparhawk told her.

'Speaking of talking,' Sephrenia said, 'I think our efforts here are going to be limited by the fact that most of you don't speak Tamul. We're going to have to do something about that.'

Kalten groaned.

'It won't be nearly as painful this time, dear one,' she

smiled. 'We don't really have the time for you to actually learn the language, so Zalasta and I are going to cheat.'

'Could you clarify that a bit for me, Sephrenia?' Emban said, looking puzzled.

'We'll cast a spell,' she shrugged.

'Are you trying to say that you can teach somebody a foreign language by magic?' he asked.

'Oh, yes,' Sparhawk assured him. 'She taught me to speak Troll in about five seconds in Ghwerig's cave, and I'd imagine that Troll's a lot harder to learn than Tamul. At least Tamuls are human.'

'We'll have to be careful, though,' the small Styric woman cautioned. 'If you all appear to be linguistic geniuses, it's going to look very curious. We'll do it a bit at a time – a basic vocabulary and a rudimentary grammar right at first, and then we'll expand on that.'

'I could send you instructors, Lady Sephrenia,' Oscagne offered.

'Ah – no, thanks all the same, your Excellency. Your instructors would be startled – and suspicious – if they suddenly found a whole platoon of extraordinarily gifted students. We'll do it ourselves in order to conceal what we're up to. I'll give our pupils here abominable accents right at first, and then we'll smooth things out as we go along.'

'Sephrenia?' Kalten said in a slightly resentful tone.

'Yes, dear one?'

'You can teach people languages by magic?'

'Yes.'

'Then why did you spend all those years trying to teach me Styric? When you saw that it wasn't going to work, why didn't you just wiggle your fingers at me?'

'Kalten, dear,' she said gently, 'why was I trying to teach you Styric?'

'So that I could perform magic tricks, I guess,' he

472

shrugged. 'That's unless you just enjoy making people suffer.'

'No, dear one. It was just as painful for me as it was for you.' She shuddered. 'More painful, probably. You *were*, in fact, trying to learn Styric so that you could work the spells, but in order to do that, you have to be able to *think* in Styric. You can't just mouth the words and make them come off the way you want them to.'

'Wait a minute,' he objected. 'Are you saying that people who speak other languages don't think the same way we do?'

'They may think the same way, but they don't think in the same words.'

'Do you mean to say that we actually think in words?'

'Of course we do. What did you think thoughts were?'

'I don't know. But we're all human. Wouldn't we all think the same way and in the same language?'

She blinked. 'And which language would that be, dear one?'

'Elenic, naturally. That's why foreigners aren't as clever as we are. They have to stop and translate their thoughts from Elenic into that barbarian gabble they call language. They do it just to be stubborn, of course.'

She stared at him suspiciously. 'You're actually serious, aren't you?'

'Of course. I thought everybody knew that's why Elenes are smarter than everybody else.' His face shone with blinding sincerity.

'Oh, dear,' she sighed in near-despair.

Melidere put on a lavender gown and swished off to the emperor's private apartments bearing a blue satin Elene doublet over one arm. Mirtai followed her. Mirtai did not swish. Melidere's eyes were ingenuously wide. Her expression was vapid. Her lower lip was adorably caught between her teeth as if she were breathless with

473

excitement. Emperor Sarabian's courtiers watched the swishing with great interest. Nobody paid the slightest attention to what she did with her hands.

She delivered the gift to the emperor with a breathy little speech, which Mirtai translated. The emperor responded quite formally. Melidere curtseyed and then swished back to the Elene castle. The courtiers still concentrated on the swishing – even though they had already had plenty of opportunity to observe the process.

'It went off without a hitch,' the Baroness reported smugly.

'Did they enjoy the swishing?' Stragen asked her.

'I turned the entire court to stone, Milord Stragen,' she laughed.

'Did she really?' he asked Mirtai.

'Not entirely,' the Atana replied. 'A number of them followed her so that they could see more. Melidere's a very good swisher. What was going on inside her gown looked much like two cats fighting inside a burlap sack.'

'We should use the talents God gave us, wouldn't you say, your Grace?' the blonde girl asked Emban with mock piety.

'Absolutely, my child,' he agreed without so much as cracking a smile.

Ambassador Oscagne arrived about fifteen minutes later bearing an alabaster box on a blue velvet cushion. Ehlana took the emperor's note out of the box and read aloud:

Ehlana,
  Your message arrived safely. I get the impression that the members of my court will not merely refrain from interfering with the baroness as she moves through the halls but will passionately defend her right to do so. How *does* the girl manage to move so many things all at the same time?
  – Sarabian

'Well,' Stragen asked the honey-blonde girl, 'how do you?'

'It's a gift, Milord Stragen.'

The visiting Elenes made some show of receiving instruction in the Tamul language for the next few weeks, and Oscagne helped their subterfuge along by casually advising various members of the government that he had been teaching the visitors the language during their long journey. Ehlana made a brief speech in Tamul at one of the banquets the prime minister had arranged for the guests in order to establish the fact that she and her party had already achieved a certain level of proficiency.

There were awkward moments, of course. On one occasion Kalten grossly offended a courtier when he smilingly delivered what he thought to be a well-turned compliment. 'What's the matter with him?' the blond Pandion asked, looking puzzled as the courtier stalked away.

'What were you trying to say to him?' Mirtai asked, stifling a laugh.

'I told him that I was pleased to see that he was smiling,' Kalten replied.

'That's not what you said.'

'Well, what *did* I say?'

'You said, "May all of your teeth fall out."'

'I used the wrong word for "smiling", right?'

'I'd say so, yes.'

The pretence of learning a new language provided the queen and her entourage with a great deal of leisure time. The official functions and entertainments they were obliged to attend usually took place in the evening, and that left the days generally free. They passed those hours in idle conversation – conducted for the most part in Tamul. The spell Sephrenia and Zalasta had woven gave them all a fairly complete understanding of vocabulary and syntax, but the smoothing out of pronunciation took somewhat longer.

As Oscagne had predicted he would, the prime minister threw obstacles in their paths at every turn. Insofar as he could, he filled their days with tedious and largely meaningless activities. They attended the openings of cattle-shows. They were awarded honorary degrees at the university. They visited model farms. He provided them with huge escorts whenever they left the imperial compound – escorts that usually took several hours to form up. Pondia Subat's agents put that time to good use, clearing the streets of precisely the people the visitors wanted to see. Most troublesome, however, was the fact that he severely restricted their access to Emperor Sarabian. Subat made himself as inconvenient as he possibly could, but he was unprepared for Elene ingenuity and the fact that many in their party were not entirely what they seemed to be. Talen in particular seemed to completely baffle the prime minister's agents. As Sparhawk had noticed long ago, it was quite nearly impossible to follow Talen in any city in the world. The young man had a great deal of fun and gathered a great deal of information.

On one drowsy afternoon, Ehlana and the ladies were in the royal apartments, and the queen's maid, Alean, was speaking as Kalten and Sparhawk quietly entered.

'It's not uncommon,' the doe-eyed girl was saying quietly. 'It's one of the inconveniences of being a servant.' As usual, Alean wore a severe dress of muted grey.

'Who was he?' Ehlana's eyes were like flint.

'It's not really important, your Majesty,' Alean replied, looking slightly embarrassed.

'Yes, Alean,' Ehlana disagreed, 'it is.'

476

'It was Count Osril, your Majesty.'

'I've heard of him.' Ehlana's tone was frosty.

'So have I.' Melidere's tone was just as cold.

'I gather that the Count's reputation is unsavoury?' Sephrenia asked.

'He's what's referred to as a rake, Lady Sephrenia,' Melidere replied. 'He wallows in debauchery of the worst kind. He boasts that he's saving God all the inconvenience of condemning him, since he was born to go to hell anyway.'

'My parents were country people,' Alean continued, 'so they didn't know about the count's reputation. They thought that placing me in service to him would give me the opportunity of a lifetime. It's the only real chance a peasant has for advancement. I was fourteen and very innocent. The count seemed friendly at first, and I considered myself lucky. Then he came home drunk one night, and I discovered why he'd been so nice to me. I hadn't received the kind of training Mirtai had, so there was nothing I could do. I cried afterward, of course, but all he did was laugh at my tears. Fortunately, nothing came of it. Count Osril customarily turned pregnant maids out with nothing but the clothes on their backs. After a few times, he grew tired of the game. He paid me my salary and gave me a good recommendation. I was fortunate enough to find employment at the palace.' She smiled a tight, hurt little smile. 'Since there were no after-effects, I suppose it doesn't really matter all that much.'

'It does to me,' Mirtai said bleakly. 'You have my word that he won't survive my return to Cimmura by more than a week.'

'If you're going to take that long, you'll miss your chance, Mirtai,' Kalten told her almost casually. 'Count Osril won't see the sunset of the day when *I* get back to Cimmura, I promise you.'

477

'He won't fight you, Kalten,' Sparhawk told his friend.

'He won't have any choice,' Kalten replied. 'I know any number of insults that no man can swallow – and if *they* don't work, I'll start slicing pieces off him. If you cut off a man's ears and nose, he almost has to reach for his sword – probably because he doesn't know what you plan to cut off next.'

'You'll get arrested.'

'That's no problem, Sparhawk,' Ehlana said, grimly. 'I'll pardon him.'

'You don't have to do that, Sir Kalten,' Alean murmured, her eyes downcast.

'Yes,' Kalten replied in a stony voice, 'as a matter of fact, I do. I'll bring you one of his ears after I've finished with him – just to prove that I've kept my promise.'

Sparhawk fully expected the gentle girl to react with violent revulsion to her protector's brutal offer. She did not, however. She smiled warmly at Sparhawk's friend. 'That would be *very* nice, Sir Kalten,' she said.

'Go ahead, Sephrenia,' Sparhawk said to his tutor. 'Roll your eyes and sigh. I might even agree with you this time.'

'Why should I do that, Sparhawk?' she asked. 'I think Sir Kalten's come up with a very appropriate course of action.'

'You're a savage, little mother,' he accused.

'So?'

Later that afternoon, Sparhawk and Kalten had joined the other knights in the gleaming great hall of the counterfeit Elene castle. The knights had put aside their formal armour and now wore doublets and hose. 'It wouldn't take very much,' Sir Bevier was saying. 'The walls are really very sturdy, and the fosse is already in place. The drawbridge is functional, though the capstans that raise it need some grease. All we really need to finish it off are sharpened stakes in the fosse.'

'And a few barrels of pitch?' Ulath suggested. 'I know how much you Arcians enjoy pouring boiling pitch on people.'

'Gentlemen,' Vanion said disapprovingly, 'if you start reinforcing the defences of this place, our hosts may take it the wrong way.' He thought about it for a moment. 'It might not hurt to quietly lay in a goodly supply of stakes, though,' he added, 'and maybe a number of barrels of lamp-oil. It's not quite as good as pitch, but it won't attract so much attention when we bring it inside. I think we might also want to start unobtrusively bringing in provisions. There are quite a lot of us, so concealing the fact that we're filling storerooms shouldn't be too hard. Let's keep it all fairly low-key, though.'

'What are you contemplating, Vanion?' Emban asked him.

'Just a few simple precautions, your Grace. Things are unstable here in Tamuli, and we have no way of knowing what might happen. Since we've got a perfectly good castle, we might just as well give it a few finishing touches – just in case.'

'Is it just my imagination, or does it seem to anybody else that this is a very, very long summer,' Tynian asked suddenly.

Sparhawk became very alert. Someone had been bound to notice that eventually, and if they really pursued the matter and started counting days, they'd be certain to uncover the fact that someone had been tampering with time. 'It's a different part of the world, Tynian,' he said easily. 'The climate's bound to be different.'

'Summer is summer, Sparhawk, and it's not supposed to last forever.'

'You can never tell about climate,' Ulath disagreed, 'particularly along a sea-coast. There's a warm current that runs up the west coast of Thalesia. It can be the dead of winter in Yosut on the east coast, and only mid-autumn in Horset.'

Good old Ulath, Sparhawk thought with some relief.

'It still seems a little strange to me,' Tynian said dubiously.

'Lots of things seem strange to you, my friend,' Ulath smiled. 'You've turned down any number of invitations I've sent you to go Ogre-hunting with me.'

'Why kill them if you're not going to eat them?' Tynian shrugged.

'You didn't eat any of those Zemochs you killed.'

'I didn't have a good recipe for cooking them.'

They all laughed and let the subject drop, and Sparhawk breathed a bit easier.

Talen came into the hall then. As usual, he had almost routinely shaken off the agents of the prime minister that morning and gone out into the city.

'Surprise, surprise,' he said dryly. 'Kroger's finally made it to Matherion. I was starting to worry about him.'

'*That* does it!' Sparhawk burst out, slamming his fist down on the arm of his chair. 'That man's starting to make me *very* tired.'

'We didn't really have the time to chase him down before, my Lord,' Khalad pointed out.

'Maybe we should have taken the time. I was sure of that when we saw him back in Sarsos. We're settled in now, though, so let's devote a little time and energy to rooting him out. Draw some pictures of him, Talen. Spread them around and promise a reward.'

'I know how to go about it, Sparhawk.'

'Do it then. I want to put my hands on that drunken little weasel. There's all kinds of information inside that sodden skin of his, and I'm going to wring him out until I've got the very last drop of it.'

'Testy, isn't he?' Tynian said mildly to Kalten.

'He's been having a bad day,' Kalten shrugged. 'He discovered a streak of brutality in his women-folk, and it upset him.'

'Oh?'

'There's a nobleman in Cimmura who needs killing. When I get home, I'm going to slice off his cods before I butcher him. The ladies all thought it was a wonderful idea. Their approval shattered a number of Sparhawk's illusions.'

'What's the fellow done?'

'It's a private matter.'

'Oh. Well, at least Sephrenia agreed with him.'

'No, as a matter of fact, she was even more blood-thirsty than the rest. She went so far as to offer some suggestions later on that even made Mirtai turn pale.'

'The fellow *really* must have done something awful.'

'He did indeed, my friend, and I'm going to give him hours and hours to regret it.' Kalten's blue eyes were like ice, and his nostrils were white and pinched with suppressed fury.

'I didn't do it, Kalten,' Tynian told him, 'so don't start looking at *me* like that.'

'Sorry,' Kalten apologised. 'Just thinking about it makes my blood boil.'

'Don't think about it then.'

Their accents were still rough; Sephrenia had seen to that, but their understanding of the Tamul language was very nearly perfect. 'Are we ready?' Sparhawk asked his tutor one evening.

'Unless you plan to make speeches, Prince Sparhawk,' Emperor Sarabian, who was paying them another of those whirlwind visits, said. 'Your accent is really vile, you know.'

'I'm going out there to listen, your Majesty,'

Sparhawk told him, 'not to talk. Sephrenia and Zalasta are hiding our proficiency behind the accents.'

'I wish you'd told me you could do this, Zalasta,' Sarabian said just a bit wistfully. 'You could have saved me months of time when I was studying languages, you know.'

'Your Majesty was keeping your studies a secret,' Zalasta reminded him. 'I didn't know you wanted to learn other tongues.'

'Caught by my own cleverness then,' Sarabian shrugged. 'Oh, well. What precisely are we planning?'

'We're going to winnow through your court, your Majesty,' Vanion told him. 'Your government's compartmentalised, and your ministers keep secrets from each other. That means that no one really has a grasp of the whole picture. We're going to fan out through the various compartments and gather up everything we can find. When we put it all together, we might be able to see some patterns starting to emerge.'

Sarabian made a sour face. 'It's my own fault,' he confessed.

'Please don't be cryptic, Sarabian,' Ehlana told him. The two monarchs were good friends by now, largely because the emperor had simply pushed all formalities aside and had spoken directly and had insisted that Ehlana do the same.

'I blundered, Ehlana,' he said ruefully. 'Tamuli's never faced a real crisis before. Our bureaucrats are more clever than the subject peoples, and they have the Atans to back them up. The imperial family's always been more afraid of its own government than of outsiders. We don't encourage co-operation between the various ministries. I seem to be reaping the fruit of a misguided policy. When this is all over, I think I'll fix it.'

'*My* government doesn't keep secrets from *me*,' Ehlana told him smugly.

'Please don't rub it in,' he said. 'What exactly are we looking for, Lord Vanion?'

'We observed a number of phenomena on our way to Matherion. Our guess is that we're facing an alliance of some sort. We know – or at least we have good evidence – about who *one* of the parties is. We need to concentrate on the other now. We're at a distinct disadvantage until we can identify him. If it's all right with you, your Majesty, Queen Ehlana and Prince Sparhawk will be spending a great deal of time with you. That means that you're going to have to have a long talk with your prime minister, I'm afraid. Pondia Subat's starting to be inconvenient.'

Sarabian raised one eyebrow questioningly.

'He's done everything he possibly can to make you inaccessible to us, Sarabian,' Ehlana explained.

'He was told not to do that,' Sarabian said bleakly.

'Apparently he didn't listen, your Majesty,' Sparhawk said. 'We have to wade through his people whenever we get near the main palace, and every time one of us so much as sticks his head out of a window, whole platoons of spies start to form up to follow us. Your prime minister doesn't approve of us, I gather.'

'It rather looks as if I'm going to have to explain some things to the esteemed Pondia Subat,' Sarabian said. 'I think he's forgotten the fact that his office isn't hereditary – *and* that his head's not so firmly attached that I can't have it removed if it starts to inconvenience me.'

'What charges would you bring against him, Sarabian?' Ehlana asked curiously.

'Charges? What on earth are you talking about, Ehlana? This is Tamuli. I don't need charges. I can have his head chopped off if I decide that I don't like his haircut. I'll take care of Pondia Subat, my friends. I can

483

promise his complete co-operation from now on – either his or that of his successor. Please continue, Lord Vanion.'

Vanion pushed on. 'Patriarch Emban will concentrate his attention on the prime minister,' he said, 'whoever he happens to be. Sir Bevier will spend his time with the faculty of the university. Scholars pick up a great deal of information, and governments tend to ignore their findings – until it's too late. Ulath, Kring and Tynian will observe the general staff of the army – the Tamul high command rather than the Atans. Atan Engessa will cover his own people. Milord Stragen and Talen will serve as liaison with the thieves of Matherion, and Alean and Khalad will circulate among the palace servants. Sephrenia and Zalasta will talk with the local Styric community and Melidere and Sir Berit will charm all the courtiers.'

'Isn't Sir Berit just a bit young?' Sarabian asked. 'My courtiers are a very sophisticated group of people.'

'Sir Berit has some special qualifications, your Majesty.' Melidere smiled. 'The younger women of your court – and some not quite so young – will do almost anything for him. He may have to sacrifice his virtue a few times, but he's a very dedicated young man, so I'm sure we can count on him.'

Berit blushed. 'Why do you always have to say things like that, Baroness?' he asked plaintively.

'I'm only teasing, Berit,' she said fondly.

'It's something that men don't understand, your Majesty,' Kalten told the emperor. 'Berit has a strange effect on young women for some reason.'

'Kalten and Mirtai will attend Sparhawk and the queen,' Vanion continued. 'We don't know exactly how far our opponents might be willing to go, so they'll provide you with some additional protection.'

'And you, Lord Vanion?' the emperor asked.

'Vanion and Oscagne are going to try to put it all together, Sarabian,' Ehlana replied. 'We'll all bring everything we find directly to them. They'll sort through it all and isolate the gaps so that we'll know where to concentrate further efforts.'

'You Elenes are a very methodical people,' Sarabian noted.

'It's an outgrowth of their dependency on logic, your Majesty,' Sephrenia told him. 'Their plodding search for corroboration is maddening sometimes, but it *does* get results. A well-trained Elene will spend half a day making observations before he'll allow himself to admit that it's raining.'

'Ah,' Emban said to her, 'but when an Elene says that it's raining, you can be absolutely sure that he's telling you the truth.'

'And what about you, your Highness?' Sarabian smiled down at the little girl in his lap. 'What part are you going to play in this grand scheme?'

'I'm supposed to distract you so that you don't ask too many questions, Sarabian,' Danae replied quite calmly. 'Your new friends are going to do things that aren't really proper, so I'm supposed to keep you from noticing.'

'*Danae!*' her mother exclaimed.

'Well, aren't you? You're going to lie to people and spy on them and probably kill anybody who gets in your way. Isn't that what you mean when you use the word "politics"?'

Sarabian laughed. 'I think she's got you there, Ehlana,' he chortled. 'Her definition of politics is a little blunt, but it's very close to the mark. She's going to make an excellent queen.'

'Thank you, Sarabian,' Danae said sweetly, kissing his cheek.

Then Sparhawk felt that sudden chill, and even

485

though he knew it was useless, his hand went to his sword-hilt as the flicker of darkness tugged at the very corner of his vision. He started to swear – half in Elenic and half in Tamul – as he realised that everything they had said had just been revealed to the shadowy presence that had been dogging their steps for all these months.

CHAPTER 26

'Please take my word for it, your Majesty,' Zalasta said to the sceptical Sarabian. 'It was most definitely *not* a normal phenomenon.'

'You're the expert, Zalasta,' Sarabian said dubiously. 'My instincts all tell me to look for a natural explanation first, though – a cloud passing in front of the sun, perhaps.'

'It's evening, Sarabian,' Ehlana pointed out. 'The sun's already gone down.'

'That *would* sort of weaken that particular explanation, wouldn't it? You've all seen this before then?'

'Most of us, your Majesty,' Oscagne assured him. 'I even saw it once myself – on shipboard – and there was nothing between me and the sun. I think we'll have to accept the testimony of our Elene friends here. They've had experiences with this particular manifestation before.'

'Stupid,' Sparhawk muttered.

'I beg your pardon?' Sarabian said mildly.

'Sorry, your Majesty,' Sparhawk apologised. 'I wasn't referring to you, of course. It's our visitor who's not very intelligent. If you set out to spy on someone, you don't announce your presence with drum-rolls and trumpet fanfares.'

'He's done it before, Sparhawk,' Patriarch Emban reminded him. 'He put in an appearance in Archimandrite Monsel's study in Darsas, if you remember.'

'Maybe he doesn't know he's doing it,' Kalten suggested. 'When he first went to work for Martel, Adus used to try to sneak around and spy on people. That's why Martel had to finally hire Krager.'

'Who's Adus?' Sarabian asked.

'A fellow we used to know, your Majesty,' Kalten replied. 'He wasn't of much use as a spy. Everybody for a hundred yards in any direction knew when Adus was around. He didn't believe in bathing, so he had a distinctive fragrance.'

'Is that at all possible?' Vanion asked Sephrenia. 'Could Kalten have *actually* come up with the right answer?'

'*Vanion!*' Kalten objected.

'Sorry, Kalten. That didn't come out exactly the way I'd intended. Seriously though, Sephrenia, could our visitor be unaware of the shadow he's casting?'

'Anything's possible, I suppose, dear one.'

'A visual stink?' Ulath suggested incredulously.

'I don't know if I'd use that exact term, but –' Sephrenia looked at Zalasta. 'Is it possible?'

'It would explain the phenomenon,' he replied after pondering the notion for a moment. 'The Gods are remarkable – not only in the depth of their understanding, but also in their limitations. It could very well be that our visitor doesn't know that we can smell him when he pays a call – if I may borrow Sir Ulath's metaphor. He may actually believe that he's totally invisible to us – that his spying is going unnoticed.'

Bevier was shaking his head. 'We always talk about it right after it happens,' he disagreed. 'He'd have heard us, so he has to know that he's giving himself away.'

'Not necessarily, Bevier,' Kalten disagreed. 'Adus didn't know that he smelled like a cesspool, and it's not really the sort of thing one admits to oneself. Maybe this shadow's the same sort of thing – a kind of socially unacceptable offensiveness, like bad breath or poor table-manners.'

'There's a fascinating idea,' Patriarch Emban laughed. 'We could extrapolate a complete book of divine etiquette from this one single incident.'

'To what purpose, your Grace?' Oscagne asked him.

'The noblest of purposes, your Excellency – the greater understanding of God. Isn't that why we're here?'

'I'm not sure that a dissertation on the table-manners of the Gods would significantly advance the sum of human knowledge, Emban,' Vanion observed. 'Might we prevail on your Majesty to smooth our way into the inner circles of your government?'

'Smooth or rough, Lord Vanion,' Sarabian grinned, 'I'll insert you into the ministries. After I've straightened Pondia Subat out, I'll take on the other ministers – one by one or row by row. I think it's time they all found out just exactly who's in charge here.' He suddenly laughed with delight. 'I'm *so* glad you decided to stop by, Ehlana. You and your friends have made me realise that I've been sitting on absolute power for all these years, and that it's never occurred to me to use it. I think it's time to pull it out, dust it off and wave it around just a bit.'

'Oh, dear,' Oscagne said, his face suddenly filled with chagrin. 'What have I done?'

'We got this yere problem, Stragen,' Caalador drawled in Elenic. 'These yere yaller brothers o' ourn ain't tooken with th' notion o' steppin' 'cross no social boundaries.'

'Please, Caalador,' Stragen said, 'spare me the folksy preamble. Get to the point.'

'T'aint really natch'ral, Stragen.'

'Do you mind?'

Stragen, Talen and Caalador were meeting in a cellar near the waterfront. It was mid-morning, and the local thieves were beginning to stir. 'As you've already discovered, the brotherhood here in Matherion's afflicted with a caste system,' Caalador continued. 'The thieves' guild doesn't talk to the swindlers, and the beggar's guild doesn't talk to the whores – except in the line of business, of course – and the murderer's guild is totally outcast.'

'Now that there's *real* on-natch-ral,' Talen observed.

'Don't do that, Talen,' Stragen told him. 'One of you is bad enough. I couldn't bear two. Why are the murderers so despised?'

'Because they violate one of the basic precepts of Tamul culture,' Caalador shrugged. 'They're paid assassins actually, and they don't bow and scrape to their victims before they cut their throats. The concept of courtesy overwhelms Tamuls. They don't really object to the notion of someone murdering noblemen for hire. It's the rudeness of it all that upsets them.' Caalador shook his head. 'That's one of the reasons so many Tamul thieves get caught and beheaded. It's considered impolite to run away.'

'Unbelievable,' Talen murmured. 'It's worse than we thought, Stragen. If these people don't talk to each other, we'll never get any information out of them.'

'I think I warned you not to expect too much here in Matherion, my friends,' Caalador reminded them.

'Are the rest of the guilds afraid of the murderers?' Stragen asked.

'Oh, yes,' Caalador replied.

'We'll start from there then. What's the general feeling about the emperor?'

'Awe, generally, and a level of adoration that hovers right on the verge of outright worship.'

'Good. Get in touch with the murderers' guild. When Talen brings you the word, have the cutthroats round up the heads of the other guilds and bring them to the palace.'

490

'What are we a-fixin' t' do here, m' friend?'

'I'll speak with the emperor and see if I can persuade him to make a speech to our brothers,' Stragen shrugged.

'Have you lost your mind?'

'Of course not. Tamuls are completely controlled by custom, and one of those customs is that the emperor can suspend customs.'

'Were you able to follow that?' Caalador asked Talen.

'I think he lost me on that sharp turn right there at the end.'

'Let's see if I've got this straight,' Caalador said to the blond Thalesian. 'You're going to violate every known propriety of the criminal culture here in Matherion by having the murderers kidnap the leaders of the other guilds.'

'Yes,' Stragen admitted.

'Then you're going to have them all taken to the palace compound, where they're absolutely forbidden to go.'

'Yes.'

'Then you're going to ask the emperor to make a speech to a group of people whose very existence he's not even supposed to know about.'

'That's more or less what I had in mind.'

'And the emperor's going to command them to suspend aeons-old custom and tradition and start co-operating with each other?'

'Is there some problem with that?'

'No, not really. I just wanted to be sure I had it all down straight in my mind, that's all.'

'See to it, would you, old boy?' Stragen asked. 'I'd probably better go talk with the emperor.'

Sephrenia sighed. 'You're being childish, you know,' she said.

Salla's eyes bulged. 'How *dare* you?' he almost screamed. The Styric elder's face had gone white.

'You forget yourself, Elder Salla,' Zalasta told the outraged man. 'Councillor Sephrenia speaks for the Thousand. Will you defy them? And the Gods they represent?'

'The Thousand are misguided!' Salla blustered. 'There can never be an accommodation between Styricum and the pig-eaters!'

'That's for the Thousand to decide,' Zalasta told him in a flinty tone.

'But look at what the Elene barbarians have done to us,' Salla said, his voice choked with outrage.

'You've lived out your whole life here in the Styric quarter in Matherion, Elder Salla,' Zalasta said. 'You've probably never even *seen* an Elene.'

'I can read, Zalasta.'

'I'm delighted to hear it. We're not really here for discussion, however. The High Priestess of Aphrael is conveying the instruction of the Thousand. Like it or not, you're compelled to obey.'

Salla's eyes filled with tears. 'They've murdered us!' he choked.

'You seem to be in remarkably good condition for a man who's been murdered, Salla,' Sephrenia told him. 'Tell me, was it painful?'

'You know what I mean, Priestess.'

'Ah, yes,' she said, 'that tiresome Styric compulsion to expropriate pain. Someone on the far side of the world stabs a Styric, and you start to bleed. You sit here in Matherion in protected luxury feeling sorry for yourself and secretly consumed with a gnawing envy that you're being denied martyrdom. Well, if you want to be a martyr so badly, Salla, I can arrange it for you.' Sephrenia was coldly angry with this babbling fool. 'The Thousand has made its decision,' she said flatly. 'I don't

492

really have to explain it to you, but I will – so that you can convey the decision to your followers – and you *will* explain it, Salla. You'll be very convincing about it, or I'll replace you.'

'I hold my position for life,' he declared defiantly.

'Precisely my point.' Her tone was ominous.

He stared at her. 'You wouldn't!' he gasped.

'Try me.' Sephrenia had wanted to say that to someone for years. She found it quite satisfying. 'It goes like this, Salla – feel free to stop me if I start going too fast for you. The Elenes are savages who are looking for an excuse to kill every Styric they see. If we *don't* assist them in this crisis, we'll be handing them that excuse on a velvet cushion. We *will* assist them, because if we don't, they'll slaughter every Styric on the Eosian continent. We don't want them to do that, do we?'

'But –'

'Salla, if you say "but" to me one more time, I'll obliterate you.' She was startled to discover just how enjoyable it was to behave like an Elene. 'I've given you the instruction of the Thousand, and the Thousand speaks for the Gods. The matter is not open for discussion, so quit trying to snivel or wriggle your way out of this. You will obey, or you will die. Those are your options. Choose quickly. I'm in a bit of a hurry.'

Even Zalasta seemed shocked at that.

'Your Goddess is cruel, councillor Sephrenia,' Salla accused.

She hit him before she even thought about it, her hand and arm seeming to move all on their own. She had spent generations with the Pandion Knights, and she knew how to get her shoulder behind the blow. It was more than an ineffectual slap. She caught him solidly on the point of the chin with the heel of her hand, and he reeled back, his eyes glazed.

Sephrenia began to intone the words of the deadly

incantation, her hands moving quite openly in the accompanying gestures.

'*I won't do that, Sephrenia!*' Aphrael's voice rang sharply in her mind.

'*I know,*' Sephrenia threw back the thought. '*I'm just trying to get his attention, that's all.*'

Salla gasped as he realised what she was doing. Then he screamed and fell to his knees, blubbering and begging for mercy.

'Will you do as I have commanded you to do?' she snapped.

'Yes, Priestess! Yes! Please don't kill me!'

'I have suspended the spell, but I have not cancelled it. I can finish it at any time. Your heart lies in my fist, Salla. Keep that firmly in mind the next time you feel an urge to insult my Goddess. Now get up and go do as you're told. Come along, Zalasta. The smell of self-pity in here nauseates me.'

'You've grown hard, Sephrenia,' Zalasta accused when they were back out in the narrow streets of the Styric quarter.

'I was bluffing, my old friend,' she told him. 'Aphrael would never have responded to the spell.' She touched her forearm gingerly. 'Do you happen to know where I might find a good physician, Zalasta? I think I've just sprained my wrist.'

'Not very impressive, are they?' Ulath suggested as he, Tynian and Kring walked back across the neatly-trimmed grounds of the imperial compound toward the Elene castle.

'Truly,' Kring agreed. 'They seem to spend all their time thinking about parades.' The three of them were returning from their meeting with the Imperial High Command. 'They're all show,' the Domi concluded. 'There's no substance to them.'

'Uniformed courtiers,' Ulath dismissed the Tamul general staff.

'I'll agree,' Tynian concurred. 'The Atans are the real military force in Tamuli. Decisions are made by the government, and the general staff simply passes those decisions on to the Atan commanders. I began to have some doubts about the effectiveness of the imperial army when they told me that rank is hereditary. I wouldn't want to rely on them in the event of an emergency.'

'That's God's own truth, friend Tynian,' Kring said. 'Their cavalry general took me to the stables and showed me what they call horses here.' He shuddered.

'Bad?' Ulath asked.

'Worse than bad, friend Ulath. Their mounts wouldn't even make good plough-horses. I wouldn't have believed that horses could get that fat. Anything faster than a walk would kill the poor beasts.'

'Are we agreed then?' Tynian asked them. 'The imperial army is totally useless?'

'I think you're flattering them, Tynian,' Ulath replied.

'We'll have to phrase our report rather carefully,' the Alcione Knight told his companions. 'We probably shouldn't offend the emperor. Could we say "under-trained"?'

'That's the truth certainly,' Kring answered.

'How about "unversed in modern tactics and strategy"?'

'No argument there,' Ulath grunted.

'"Poorly equipped"?'

'That's not exactly true, friend Tynian,' Kring disagreed. 'Their equipment is of very good quality. It's probably the best twelfth-century equipment I've ever seen.'

'All right,' Tynian laughed, 'how about "archaic weaponry"?'

'I could accept that,' the Domi conceded.

'You'd rather not mention "fat, lazy, stupid or inept",
I gather?' Ulath asked.

'That might be just a shade undiplomatic, Ulath.'

'True, though,' Ulath said mournfully.

Pondia Subat did not approve. Emban and Vanion
could sense that, although the prime minister's face and
manner remained diplomatically bland. Emperor Sarabian had, as promised, spoken at length with his prime
minister, and Pondia Subat was going out of his way to
be co-operative and to conceal his true feelings. 'The
details are very commonplace, my Lords,' he said deprecatingly, 'but then, the details of day-to-day government always are, aren't they?'

'Of course, Pondia,' Emban shrugged, 'but when
taken in the mass, the accretion of detail conveys the
sense of governing style, wouldn't you say? From what
I've seen so far this morning, I've already reached certain conclusions.'

'Oh?' Subat's tone was neutral.

'The guiding principle here seems to be the protection
of the emperor,' Emban told him. 'That principle's very
familiar to me, since it's identical to the one that domi-
nates our thinking in Chyrellos. The government of the
Church exists almost entirely to protect the Archprelate.'

'Perhaps, your Grace, but you'll have to admit that
there are differences.'

'Oh, of course, but the fact that Emperor Sarabian's
not as powerful as Archprelate Dolmant doesn't really
change things.'

Subat's eyes widened slightly, but he instantly gained
control of his expression.

'I realise that the concept is alien to you, Pondia,'
Emban continued smoothly, 'but the Archprelate speaks
for God, and that makes him the most powerful man on

496

earth. That's an Elene perception, of course, and it may have little or nothing to do with reality. So long as we all believe it, though, it *is* true. That's what those of us in church government do. We devote a great deal of our effort to making sure that all Elenes continue to believe that Dolmant speaks for God. So long as they believe that, the Archprelacy's safe.' The fat little churchman considered it. 'If you don't mind an observation, Pondia Subat, your central problem here in Matherion stems from the fact that you Tamuls have a secular turn of mind. Your church has been diminished, probably because you can't bring yourselves to accept the notion that any authority might equal or exceed that of the emperor. You've erased the element of faith from your national character. Scepticism is all very well and good, but it tends to get out of hand. After you've applied it to God – or your Gods – it starts to spill over, and people begin to question other things as well – the rightness of government, imperial wisdom, the justice of the tax system, that sort of thing. In the most perfect of worlds, the emperor would be deified, and church and state would become one.' He laughed in a self-deprecating little way. 'Sorry, Pondia Subat. I didn't mean to preach. It's an occupational compulsion, I suppose. The point is that both Tamuls and Elenes have made the same mistake. You didn't make your emperor a God, and we didn't make our archprelate an emperor. We've both cheated the people by placing an incomplete authority over them. They deserved better of us. But I can see that you're busy, and my stomach's telling me rather pointedly that it's lunch-time. We'll talk again – soon. Coming, Lord Vanion?'

'You don't actually believe what you just said, do you, Emban?' Vanion murmured as the two Elenes left the ministry.

'Probably not,' Emban shrugged, 'but we're going to

have to do something to widen the crack in that stone shell around Subat's mind. I'm sure that the emperor's offer to have his head docked opened his eyes a bit, but until he starts actually thinking instead of simply plodding along the well-worn paths of his preconceptions, we're not going to get anything out of him. Despite his general disapproval of us, he's still the most important man in the government, and I'd rather have him working for us than against us. Do you suppose we could step right along, Vanion? I'm definitely getting hungry.'

'It should be blue, though,' Danae was saying. She sat with Mmrr in Emperor Sarabian's lap, looking directly into his eyes.

'For an Elene, yes, but –' The Emperor sounded dubious.

'Right,' she agreed. 'Tamul skin tone would be better with –'

'But not red-red, though. More scarlet, perhaps even –'

'No. Maroon's too dark. It's a ball, not a –'

'We don't wear dark clothes at funerals. We wear –'

'Really? That's a very interesting notion. Why do you –?'

'It's considered insulting to –'

'The dead don't really mind, Sarabian. They're busy someplace else.'

'Can you even begin to follow them?' Ehlana murmured to Sparhawk.

'Sort of. They're both thinking about the same thing, so they don't have to finish sentences.'

Emperor Sarabian laughed delightedly. 'You're the most stimulating conversationalist I've ever met, your Royal Highness,' he said to the little girl in his lap.

'Thank you, your Imperial Majesty,' she replied. 'You're not so bad yourself, you know.'

'Danae!' Ehlana said sharply.

'Oh, mother. Sarabian and I are just getting to know each other.'

'I don't suppose –' Sarabian's tone was speculative.

'I'm afraid not, your Majesty,' Danae replied. 'I'm not being disrespectful, but the crown prince is much too young for me. People gossip when the wife's older than the husband. He's a sweet-natured baby, though. But I've already decided who I'm going –'

'You *have*? So young?'

'It avoids confusion later on. Girls get silly when they reach the marrying age. It's better to decide those things while you've still got your wits about you – isn't it, mother?'

Ehlana blushed suddenly.

'Mother started setting traps for my father when she was about my age,' Danae confided to the Emperor of Tamuli.

'Did you, Ehlana?' Sarabian asked.

'Well, yes, but it's not nice to talk about it in public.'

'He didn't mind being trapped, mother,' Danae said. 'At least not after he'd got used to the idea. All in all, they make a fairly good set of parents – except when mother starts throwing her rank around.'

'That will do, Princess Danae,' Ehlana said in her official tone.

'You see what I mean?' Danae grinned at the Emperor.

'Your daughter's going to be a remarkably gifted queen,' Sarabian complimented them. 'Elenia's going to be a lucky kingdom to have the two of you on the throne, one right after another. The problem with hereditary succession has always been those lamentable

499

lapses in talent. A great king or emperor is almost inevitably succeeded by a hopeless incompetent.'

'What's the customary procedure here in Tamuli, Sarabian?' Ehlana asked. 'I know that you have nine wives. Does your first-born become the crown Prince, no matter what the race of his mother?'

'Oh, no. Certainly not. The throne descends to the first-born son of the first wife. She's always a Tamul, since a Tamul princess is always the first one a crown prince marries. I was married at the age of two, actually. I married my other wives right after I was crowned emperor. It was a group ceremony – eight brides and one bridegroom. That eliminates jealousies and arguments about rank. I was absolutely exhausted the following morning.'

'You mean that –?'

'Oh, yes. It's required. It's another way to avoid those jealousies I mentioned. And it all has to be finished by sunrise.'

'How do they decide who's first?' Ehlana sounded very interested.

'I have no idea. Maybe they roll dice for the privilege. There were four royal bed-chambers on each side of a long corridor. I was obliged to go down that endless hallway and to pay a call on each of my new brides. It killed my grandfather. He wasn't a young man when he ascended the throne, and the exertion was too much for him.'

'Do you suppose we could change the subject?' Sparhawk asked.

'Prude,' Ehlana chided him.

'I wonder if Dolmant would let me have more than one husband,' Danae mused.

'Never mind,' Sparhawk told her very firmly.

The others arrived, and they all gathered around a large table set with a lunch consisting of unfamiliar delicacies. 'How did you find Subat, your Grace?' Sarabian asked the Primate of Ucera.

'We went to his offices, and there he was, your Majesty.'

'Emban,' Sephrenia chided the fat little churchman, who was looking suspiciously at an undefinable meat-course.

'Sorry, your Majesty,' Emban apologised. 'Your prime minister still seems to be a bit set in his ways.'

'You noticed,' Sarabian said dryly.

'We definitely noticed, your Majesty,' Vanion replied. 'His Grace here turned his thinking upside down for him just a bit, though. He suggested that what the world really needs is a Divine Emperor or an Imperial Archprelacy. Both offices are incomplete as they stand.'

'Me? A God? Don't be ridiculous, Emban. I've got enough problems with a government. Please don't pile a priesthood on top of it.'

'I wasn't really serious, your Majesty,' Emban replied. 'I just wanted to shake up his thinking a bit more. That talk you had with him opened his eyes, right enough, but we still have to open his mind.'

'What happened to your arm?' Vanion asked the woman he loved. Sephrenia had just turned back her sleeve to reveal her bandaged wrist.

'I sprained it,' she replied.

'On a stubborn Styric head,' Zalasta added, chuckling.

'*Sephrenia!*' Vanion stared at her.

'I used my Pandion training, dear one,' she smiled. 'Someone should have told me that I was supposed to lock my wrist, though.'

'You actually *hit* someone?' Kalten asked incredulously.

'She did indeed, Sir Kalten,' Zalasta grinned.

501

'She knocked him half-way across the room. She also threatened to kill him and even went so far as to begin the death spell. He grew very co-operative at that point.'

They all stared at her in disbelief.

'Oh, stop that,' she told them. Then she laughed softly. 'It was a great deal of fun actually. I've never bullied anyone before. It's very satisfying, isn't it?'

'*We* like it,' Ulath grinned.

'The Styrics will co-operate fully,' she told them.

'How was the army?' Emban asked Tynian.

'I don't think we should expect too much there, your Grace,' Tynian replied carefully, glancing at the emperor. 'Their function's primarily ceremonial.'

'They come from the very best families, Sir Knight,' Sarabian said defensively.

'That might be part of the problem, your Majesty – that and the fact that they've never had to actually fight anybody. We'll be depending on the Atans anyway, so we won't really need the Imperial Army.' He looked at Engessa. 'Is the local garrison up to standard, Atan Engessa?' he asked.

'A little soft, Tynian-Knight. I took them out for a run this morning, and they began to falter after twenty miles. I gave some orders. They'll be fit by the end of the week.'

'Things are falling into place,' Vanion approved.

'The palace servants have all the usual vices, Lord Vanion,' Khalad reported. 'They love to gossip. Alean's making much better progress than I am – probably because she's prettier.'

'Thank you,' the girl murmured, lowering her eye-lashes.

'It's no great compliment, Alean,' Talen told her. 'My brother's not a raving beauty – none of us are. Our faces are designed for wear, not for show.'

'I'd guess that by the end of the week we should have gained their confidence sufficiently to start picking up secrets,' Khalad surmised.

'You Elenes amaze me,' Sarabian marvelled. 'You all seem to have an absolute genius for intrigue.'

'This is a rather select group, your Majesty,' Emban told him. 'We knew before we left Chyrellos that our major task here would be the gathering of information. We chose people who were skilled at it.'

'I came across one of the scholars in the contemporary affairs department at the university,' Bevier reported. 'Most of the rest of the faculty has already established reputations based on this or that past event. Resting on one's laurels is one of the failings of academics. They can coast along on a single monograph for decades. Anyway, this fellow I mentioned is young and hungry. He's come up with a theory, and he's riding it for all he's worth. He's absolutely convinced that all the present turmoil's emanating from Arjuna – perhaps because no one else on the faculty's staked out that particular ground yet. He's also convinced that Scarpa's the man behind the entire conspiracy.'

'Who's Scarpa?' Kalten asked.

'Zalasta told us about him,' Ulath reminded him. 'He serves the same function in Arjuna as Sabre does in Astel and Gerrich does in Lamorkand.'

'Oh, yes, now I remember.'

'Anyway,' Bevier continued, 'our scholar's gathered a huge mass of corroborating evidence, some of it very shaky. He'll talk for hours about his theory to anybody willing to listen.'

'Is anybody else at the university working on any alternatives?' Emban asked him.

'Not actively, your Grace. They don't want to risk their reputations on false leads. Academic timidity's forcing them to take a wait-and-see position. My young enthusiast doesn't have a reputation, so he's willing to take some risks.'

'Stay with him, Bevier,' Vanion said. 'Even negative conclusions can help to narrow the search.'

'My feelings exactly, Lord Vanion.'

'Do you suppose I could impose on your Majesty?' Stragen asked the emperor.

'That's what a host is for, Milord,' Sarabian grinned. 'Impose to your heart's content.'

'You *did* know that there are criminals here in Matherion, didn't you?'

'You mean other than the members of my government?'

Stragen laughed. 'Score one for you, your Majesty,' he said. 'There's a world below the surface in every major city in the world,' he explained. 'It's a world of thieves, pickpockets, burglars, beggars, whores, swindlers and murderers. They eke out a precarious existence by preying on the rest of society.'

'We're aware that such people exist, of course,' Sarabian said. 'That's why we have policemen and prisons.'

'Yes, your Majesty. Those are some of the minor inconveniences in the criminal's life. What isn't generally known, however, is the fact that the criminals of the world co-operate with each other to some degree.'

'Go on.'

'I've had some contacts with those people in the past, your Majesty,' Stragen went on, choosing his words carefully. 'They can be very useful. There's almost nothing that goes on in a city that some criminal doesn't know about. If you make it clear that you're not interested in *their* activities, they'll usually sell you the information they've picked up.'

'A business arrangement then?'

'Precisely. It's something on the order of buying stolen goods. It's not very nice, but many people do it.'

504

'Of course.'

'Now, then. This co-operative spirit I mentioned doesn't exist here in Matherion. Tamuls don't co-operate very well for some reason. Each profession here keeps strictly to itself. They've even formed guilds, and they view other criminal professions with contempt and suspicion. We're going to have to break down those walls if those people are to be of any use to us.'

'That stands to reason, Milord.'

Stragen seemed to breathe a bit easier. 'I've made some arrangements, your Majesty,' he said. 'The leaders of the various criminal guilds are going to come here. They respect you enormously, and they'll obey if you tell them to do something.' He paused. 'That's as long as you don't command them to become honest, of course.'

'Of course. You can't ask a man to give up his profession, I suppose.'

'Exactly. What you *can* order them to do, though, your Majesty, is to abandon these caste barriers and start talking to each other. If they're going to be of any use, they're going to have to be willing to pass information to one central collecting point. If we have to contact the head of each guild, information would be stale long before we got our hands on it.'

'I see. Correct me if I'm wrong, Milord Stragen. What you want me to do is to organise the criminals of Matherion so that they can prey on honest citizens more effectively in exchange for unspecified information they may or may not be able to pick up in the street. Is that it?'

Stragen winced. 'I was afraid your Majesty might look at it that way,' he said.

'You needn't be fearful, Milord Stragen. I'll be happy to have a chat with these loyal criminals. The gravity of the current crisis over-rides my natural revulsion for

505

having dealings with knaves and rogues. Tell me, Milord, are you a good thief?'

'I guess I've underestimated your Majesty,' Stragen sighed. 'Yes, actually I'm a very good thief. I hate to sound immodest, but I'm probably the best thief in the world.'

'How's business?'

'Not so good lately, Emperor Sarabian. Times of turmoil are very bad for crime. Honest men grow nervous and start protecting their valuables. Oh, one thing, your Majesty. The criminals you'll be addressing will all be masked. They respect you enormously, but they'll probably want to hide their faces from you.'

'I can understand that, I suppose. I'm rather looking forward to speaking with your friends, Stragen. We'll put our heads together and come up with ways to circumvent the authorities.'

'That's not really a good idea, your Majesty,' Talen told him. 'Never let a thief get within ten feet of you.' He raised his hand to show Sarabian a jewelled bracelet.

The startled emperor looked quickly at his naked right wrist.

'Merely a demonstration, your Majesty,' Talen grinned. 'I wasn't really going to keep it.'

'Give him back the rest as well, Talen,' Stragen told the boy.

Talen sighed. 'Your eyes are unwholesomely sharp, Stragen.' He reached inside his doublet and took out several other jewels. 'The best plan is not to have anything of value on your person when you talk with thieves, your Majesty,' he advised.

'You're very good, Master Talen,' Sarabian complimented the boy.

'It's all in the wrist,' Talen shrugged.

'I absolutely love you Elenes,' Sarabian said. 'Tamuls are a dull, boring people, but you're full of surprises.'

506

He smiled archly at Melidere. 'And what startling revelations do you have for me, Baroness?' he asked her.

'Nothing really very startling, your Majesty,' she smiled. 'The swishing back and forth through the corridors has earned me several fairly predictable offers – and a fair number of pinches. Tamuls pinch more than Elenes, don't they? I've learned to keep my back to the wall, though. A pinch or two in the spirit of good clean fun is all right, I suppose, but the bruises take a long time to fade.'

Then they all looked at Berit. The young Pandion Knight blushed furiously. 'I haven't really got anything to report, my Lords and Ladies,' he mumbled.

'Berit,' Ehlana said gently, 'it's not nice to lie like that, you know.'

'It wasn't really anything, your Majesty,' he protested. 'It was all a misunderstanding, I'm sure – probably because I don't speak Tamul very well.'

'What happened, my young friend?' Sarabian asked him.

'Well, your Majesty, it was your wife, the empress Elysoun – the one with the unusual costume.'

'Yes, I'm acquainted with her.'

'Well, your Majesty, she approached me in one of the corridors and said that I was looking a bit tired – perhaps because I was keeping my eyes closed.'

'Why were you doing that?'

'Ah – well, her costume, you understand, your Majesty. I thought it might be impolite to stare.'

'In Elysoun's case, it's impolite not to. She's very proud of her attributes, and she likes to share them with people.'

Berit's blush deepened. 'Anyway,' he floundered on, 'she said I looked tired and told me that she had a very comfortable bed in her quarters that I could use if I wanted to get some rest.'

Kalten was gazing at the youthful knight with open-mouthed envy. 'What did you say?' he asked almost breathlessly.

'Well, I thanked her, of course, but I told her that I wasn't really sleepy.'

Kalten buried his face in his hands and groaned. 'There, there,' Ulath said, patting his shoulder comfortingly.

CHAPTER 27

'Well sir, yer Queenship,' Caalador was saying in his broad, colloquial drawl, 'these yere trinkets is purty thangs, I'll tell the world, but they ain't got no real practical use to 'em.' He offered Ehlana a pair of carved ivory figurines.

'They're gorgeous, Caalador,' she gushed.

'Is that guard gone?' Caalador muttered to Sparhawk.

Sparhawk nodded. 'Mirtai just shoved him out the door.'

'I thought he was planning to stay all day.'

'Did you have any trouble getting on the grounds?' Ehlana asked him.

'Not a bit, your Majesty.'

'I should hope not – not after the fuss I made.' She looked more closely at the figurines. 'These are really lovely Caalador,' she said. 'Where did you get them?'

'I had them stolen from the museum at the university,' he shrugged. 'They're ninth century Tegan – very rare and very valuable.' He grinned at her impishly. 'Iff'n yer Queenship's got this yere passion fer antikities, y' might's well git th' real thang.'

'I *love* to listen to this man talk,' Ehlana said.

Baroness Melidere escorted the others into the royal quarters.

'Any problems?' Stragen asked his brother thief.

'Got in slicker'n a weasel burrowin' into a hen-roost.'

'Please, Caalador, spare me.'

Caalador was serving the Queen of Elenia in the capacity of 'procurer of antiquities', and by her orders he was to be granted immediate access to her at any time. One or the other of the knights had escorted him onto the grounds several times during the past several weeks in order to familiarize the guards at the gates with his face, but this was the first time he had tried to gain entry by himself. Their assorted subterfuges were growing more and more subtle. 'Has anything meaningful turned up, Master Caalador?' Zalasta asked.

'I'm not entirely sure, learned one,' Caalador frowned. 'We keep running into something a little peculiar.'

'Oh?'

'All sorts of people are talking about something called "the Hidden City". They're the very people we've been watching, so we thought it might have some significance.'

'It *is* a bit unusual,' Zalasta agreed. 'It's not the sort of thing you'd expect to hear noised about on the streets.'

'It actually means something then?'

Zalasta nodded. 'It's an old Tamul platitude that has to do with the life of the mind. Are they saying, "The way to the Hidden City is long, but the rewards to be found there are treasures beyond price"?'

'That's it exactly, learned one. Two people meet on the street, one of them recites the first half, and the other recites the second.'

Zalasta nodded. 'The platitude's supposed to refer to the rewards of the search for knowledge and enlightenment. I'd suspect some other significance in this case, however. Are your people hearing it from anybody other than Tamuls?'

Caalador nodded. 'A couple of Elene merchants greeted each other with it on a street-corner just yesterday.'

'It sounds very much like a sign and countersign,' Vanion mused.

'I'd hate to concentrate all our efforts on something

510

like that to the exclusion of everything else,' Zalasta said cautiously.

'Aw, 'taint no big thang, yer sorcererership,' Caalador assured him. 'I'm up t' m' ears in beggars an' whores an' sneak thieves an' sich. I got what y' might call a embarrassment o' riches in that deportment.'

Zalasta looked puzzled.

'He says he's got more than enough people at his disposal, Zalasta,' Sephrenia translated.

'It's a colourful dialect, isn't it?' Zalasta observed mildly.

Ulath was frowning. 'I'm not entirely positive,' he said, 'but it seemed to me that I heard two of the palace guards talking about "the Hidden City" a few days ago. There might be more people involved than we thought.'

Vanion nodded. 'It may not lead anywhere,' he said, 'but it won't hurt anything if we all keep our ears open. If Caalador *has* stumbled across the password of the other side, it could help us to identify conspirators we might otherwise miss. Let's compile a sort of a list. Let's gather the names of all these people who hunger and thirst for the hidden city of the mind. If this *is* a sign and countersign, and if it's in any way connected to what we're looking for, let's have a group of names to work with.'

'You're starting to sound very much like a policeman, Lord Vanion,' Talen said, half accusingly.

'Can you ever forgive me?'

'Oh, by the way, I saw an old friend at the university,' Bevier told them with a faint smile. 'It seems that Baron Kotyk's brother-in-law's come to Matherion to expose the Department of Contemporary Literature to his unspeakable art.'

'Wouldn't "inflict" be a better word there, Bevier?' Ulath asked. 'I've heard some of Elron's poetry.'

'Who's Elron?' Sephrenia asked.

Sparhawk exchanged a long look with Emban. They were still bound by the oaths they had given Archimandrite Monsel. 'Ah –' he began, not quite sure how to proceed, 'he's an Astel – a sort of semi-aristocrat with literary pretensions. We're not sure just how much he's involved in the disturbances in Astel, but his opinions and sympathies seem to indicate that he's a strong supporter of the man known as Sabre.'

'Isn't it a coincidence that he just happens to have made the trip to Matherion at just about the same time that we're getting a strong odour of dead fish in the streets?' Tynian asked. 'Why would he come to the very centre of the culture of the godless yellow devils he professes to hate?'

'Unusual,' Ulath agreed.

'Anything that's unusual is suspicious,' Kalten asserted.

'That's a gross generalisation,' Sparhawk accused.

'Well, isn't it?'

'In this case you might be right. Maybe we'd better keep an eye on him. You'd better pull out your drawing pad again, Talen.'

'You know, Sparhawk,' the boy said, 'I could make a lot of money drawing these pictures if you weren't so set on making a Pandion of me and saddling me with all those high ideals.'

'Service is its own reward, Talen,' Sparhawk replied piously.

'Caalador,' Sephrenia said thoughtfully.

'Yes, yer sorceress-ship?'

'Please, don't do that,' she said wearily. 'There are a number of these so-called firebrands loose in Tamuli. Is it at all possible that some of the local thieves might have seen any of them?'

'I'll ask around, Lady Sephrenia, and I can send to the other kingdoms for people who've seen them if I

512

have to. I'm not sure how much good physical descriptions are going to be, though. If you say that a man's sort of medium, that's going to include about half the population almost by definition.'

'She can go beyond physical descriptions, Caalador,' Talen assured him. 'She'll wiggle her fingers at your witnesses and put an image of the person they've seen in a pail of water. I can draw a picture from that.'

'It might not be a bad idea to have pictures of these various patriots in circulation,' Sephrenia murmured. 'If Elron and Krager are here, others may decide to visit Matherion as well. If they're going to hold a convention, we should know about it, wouldn't you say?'

'Shouldn't you add a picture of Count Gerrich as well?' Danae suggested.

'But he's all the way across the world in Lamorkand, Princess,' Kalten pointed out.

'He's *still* one of the people involved, Kalten,' she said. 'If you're going to do something, do it right. How much is it going to cost? A few sheets of paper maybe? And the use of Talen's pencil for half an hour?'

'All right, include him. I don't care. I don't think he'll ever show up here, but go ahead and have Talen draw his picture, if you want.'

'Oh, thank you, Kalten. Thank you, thank you, thank you.'

'Isn't it nearly her nap-time?' Kalten asked sourly.

'Speaking of Krager,' Sparhawk said, 'have there been any new sightings of him?'

'Just those two I mentioned earlier,' Caalador replied. 'Is he the kind who's likely to go to ground?'

'That's Krager, all right,' Kalten said. 'He's perfectly at home with sewer rats – being at least half-rat himself. As long as there was someone around to fetch wine for him, he'd be quite happy to stay down a rat-hole for six months at a stretch.'

'I *really* want him, Caalador,' Sparhawk grated. 'My friends are all having a wonderful time telling me that they told me so.'

'I didn't follow that one,' Caalador said with a puzzled look.

'They all think I should have killed him. Even Sephrenia's all athirst for his blood.'

'Well, now, m' friend,' Caalador drawled, 'I kin make a *real* good case fer jist how forchoonate-like it wuz that y' din't kill 'im. You an' yer friends here all knows this yere Krager feller, an' he's some kinda high muckety-muck on t'other side – which it is that he wouldn't a' bin iffn y'd slit his weasand, now would he? We *knows* this yere Krager, an' we'll chase im' down sooner er later an' set fire t' his feet until he storts talkin'. If 'n he wuz t' be a absolute stranger, we wouldn't have no idea a-tall 'bout who we wuz a-lookin' fer, now would we?'

Sparhawk smiled beatifically around at his friends. 'See,' he said to them. 'I told you I knew what I was doing.'

Later that day, Sparhawk and Ehlana met with Emperor Sarabian and Foreign Minister Oscagne to discuss their findings to date. 'Is it at all possible that anyone in the government might have noticed people using this sign and counter-sign, your Excellency?' Sparhawk asked Oscagne.

'*Quite* possible, Prince Sparhawk.' Oscagne replied. 'The interior ministry's got spies everywhere, but their reports probably won't surface for six months to a year. They're great paper-shufflers over at Interior.'

'Subat's got his own spies,' Sarabian said moodily, 'but he wouldn't tell me if he's discovered anything. I doubt that he'd tell me if someone had cut the Isle of Tega adrift and towed it away.'

'All the traditions of the Prime Ministry tell him to

514

protect you, your Imperial Majesty,' Oscagne told him. 'Despite that little talk you had with him, you'll still probably have to pry information out of him. He devoutly believes that it's his duty to spare you the anguish of hearing unpleasant news.'

'If my house is on fire, I'd rather not be spared the anguish of finding out about it,' Sarabian said tartly.

'I have informants in the other ministries, your Majesty. I'll put them to work on it. Speaking of that, by the way, Interior's been getting a great many reports of disturbances – far more than we were experiencing previously. Kolata's at his wits end.'

'Kolata?' Sparhawk asked.

'The Minister of the Interior,' Sarabian said, 'the empire's chief of police. He's almost as good at keeping secrets from me as Subat is. What's afoot now, Oscagne?'

'The graveyards have been spitting out their dead, your Majesty. Someone's been digging up the recently deceased and re-animating them. They shamble about moaning and blank-eyed. Whole villages in Edom have been abandoned because of them. The werewolves are running in packs in Daconia, the vampires in the jungles of Arjuna are flocking up like migratory birds, and the Shining Ones are terrorising the region around Dasan. Add to that the fact that the Trolls are on the march in northern Atan and that the town of Sarna's been attacked twice by what appear to be Cyrgai, and we have some fair evidence that things may be coming to a head. In the past, these disturbances were sporadic and localised. Now they're becoming general.'

'Wonderful,' Sarabian said sourly. 'I think I'll just go into exile somewhere.'

'You'll miss all the fun, your Majesty,' Sparhawk told him.

'What fun?'

'We haven't even begun to take counter-measures yet. We might not be able to do too much about vampires and the like, but we can definitely move against the Trolls and the Cyrgai. Engessa's been training the local Atans in certain Elene tactics. I think Engessa's Atans might be able to deal with the Trolls and the Cyrgai,' Sparhawk said.

Sarabian looked a bit surprised. 'Atan Engessa's the commander of the garrison at Cenae in Astel,' he said. 'He doesn't have any authority here in Matherion.'

'As a matter of fact he does, your Majesty,' Sparhawk disagreed. 'I gather that he's received a special commission from King Androl – or Queen Betuana, more than likely. Other Atan commanders have been ordered to follow his suggestions.'

'Why doesn't anybody ever tell me these things?'

'Imperial policy, your Majesty,' Oscagne smiled. 'If you were to know too much, you might start interfering with the government.'

'Anyway,' Sparhawk continued, 'Engessa was very impressed with our tactics in the encounters we had on our way here. We've been training some of his Atans in Western techniques.'

'That's surprising,' Sarabian said. 'I wouldn't have expected Atans to listen to anybody when it came to military matters.'

'Engessa's a professional, your Majesty,' Sparhawk told him. 'Professionals are always interested in technical advances in weaponry and tactics. We rounded up some very large draught-horses so that we could mount a number of his Atans, and Kalten and Tynian have been giving them instruction with the lance. That's the safest way to deal with Trolls, we've found. Bevier's taken another group in hand, and he's teaching them how to construct and use siege-engines. When we encountered those Cyrgai outside Sarsos, Bevier's catapults broke up their phalanx. It's very hard to maintain a military formation when it's raining boulders. Oh, there's something else we should be aware of. Khalad found a tree outside town that was riddled with short steel arrows. Someone's been practising with a crossbow.'

'What's a crossbow?' Sarabian asked.

'It's a Lamork weapon, your Majesty.' Sparhawk scribbled a quick sketch. 'It looks something like this. The limbs are much stronger than those of an ordinary long-bow, so it has greater range and penetrating power. It's a serious threat to an armoured knight. Someone here in Matherion's working on a way to counter the advantage our armour gives us.'

'It's beginning to sound as if I'm hanging on to my throne by my fingertips,' Sarabian said. 'Could I appeal to you for political asylum, Ehlana?'

'I'd be delighted to have you, Sarabian,' she replied, 'but let's not give up on Sparhawk just yet. He's terribly resourceful.'

'As I was saying before,' Sparhawk continued, 'we can't do too much about the ghouls or werewolves or the Shining Ones or vampires, but I think we might be able to give the Trolls and the Cyrgai a few surprises. I'd like for the Atans to have a bit more training with mounted tactics and the use of Bevier's engines, and then I think it might be time to let our opponent know that he's not going to win this in a walk. I'd particularly like to decimate the Trolls. Our enemy's relying rather heavily on the Troll-Gods, and they'll leave the alliance if too many of their worshippers get killed. I think that early next week we might want to mount a couple of expeditions – one up into Troll-country and another down to Sarna. It's time to make our presence known.'

'And this local business?' Oscagne asked. 'All this fascination with the hidden city of the mind?'

'Caalador will keep working on that. We've got their password now, and that can open all kinds of doors for us. Vanion's drawing up a list of names. Before long, we'll know everybody in Matherion who's been talking about the Hidden City.' He looked at Sarabian. 'Have I your Majesty's permission to detain those people if necessary?' he asked. 'If we move first and round them all up before they can set their scheme in motion, we'll break the back of this plot before it gets too far along.'

'Detain away, Sparhawk,' Sarabian grinned. 'I've got lots of buildings we can use for prisons.'

'All right, young lady,' Sparhawk said quite firmly to his daughter a few days later. 'One of Caalador's beggars saw Count Gerrich in a street not far from here. How did you know that he'd be here in Matherion?'

'I didn't *know*, Sparhawk. I just had a hunch.' Danae was sitting calmly in a large chair, scratching her cat's ears. Mmrr was purring gratefully.

'A hunch?'

'Intuition, if that word makes you feel any better. It just didn't seem right that Krager and Elron would be here without the others being here as well – and that would logically include Gerrich, wouldn't it?'

'Don't confuse the issue by using the words ''logic'' and ''intuition'' in the same sentence.'

'Oh, Sparhawk, *do* grow up. That's all that logic really is – a justification for hunches. Have you ever known anyone who used logic to disprove something he already believed?'

'Well – not personally, maybe, but I'm sure there have *been* some.'

'I'll wait while you track one down. I'm an immortal, so time doesn't really mean all that much to me.'

'That's *really* offensive, Aphrael.'

'Sorry, father.' She didn't sound very contrite. 'Your

mind gathers information in hundreds of ways, Sparhawk – things you hear, things you see, things you touch and even things you smell. Then it puts all of that information together and jumps from there to a conclusion. That's all that hunches really are. Intuition is just as precise as logic, really, but it doesn't have to go through the long, tedious process of plodding along step by step to prove things. It leaps immediately from evidence to conclusion without all the tiresome intermediate steps. Sephrenia doesn't like logic because it's so boring. She already knows the answers you're so laboriously trying to prove – and so do you, if you'd be honest about it.'

'Folk-lore is full of these hunches, Aphrael – and they're usually wrong. How about the old notion that thunder sours milk?'

'That's a mistake in logic, Sparhawk, not a mistake in intuition.'

'Would you like to explain that?'

'You could just as easily say that sour milk causes thunder, you know.'

'That's absurd.'

'Of course it is. Thunder and sour milk are both effects, not causes.'

'You should talk to Dolmant. I'd like to see you try to explain that he's been wasting his time on logic all these years.'

'He already knows,' she shrugged. 'Dolmant's far more intuitive than you give him credit for being. He knew who I was the moment he saw me – which is a lot more than I can say for you, father. I thought for a while there that I was going to have to fly in order to persuade you.'

'Be nice.'

'I am. There are all sorts of things I didn't say about you. What's Krager up to?'

'Nobody knows.'

'We *really* need to find him, Sparhawk.'

'I *know*. I want him even more than you do. I'm going to enjoy wringing him out like a wet sock.'

'Be serious, Sparhawk. You know Krager. He'd tell you his whole life story if you even frowned at him.'

He sighed. 'You're probably right,' he conceded. 'It takes a lot of the fun out of it though.'

'You're not here to have fun, Sparhawk. Which would you rather have? Information or revenge?'

'Couldn't we come up with a way to have both?'

She rolled her eyes upward. 'Elenes,' she sighed.

Bevier took a detachment of newly-trained Atan engineers west toward Sarna early the next week. The following day Kalten, Tynian and Engessa took two hundred mounted Atans north toward the lands being ravaged by the Trolls. At Vanion's insistence the parties filtered out of Matherion in twos and threes to assemble later outside the city. 'There's no point in announcing what we're up to,' he said.

A few days after the departure of the two military expeditions, Zalasta left for Sarsos. 'I won't be very long,' he told them. 'We have a certain commitment from the Thousand, but I think I'd like to see some concrete evidence that they're willing to honour that commitment. Words are all well and good, but let's see some action – just as a demonstration of good faith. I know my brothers. Nothing in the world would please them more than being able to reap the benefits of allying themselves with us "in principle" without the inconvenience of actually being obliged to do anything to help. They're best suited to deal with these supernatural manifestations, so I'll pry them loose from their comfortable chairs in Sarsos and disperse them to these trouble-spots.' He smiled thinly at Vanion from under his beetling brows. 'Extensive travel might toughen them up a bit, my Lord,' he added. 'Perhaps we can avoid spraining any more of your ankles in demonstrations of how flabby and lazy they are.'

'I appreciate that, Zalasta,' Vanion laughed.

There were always more things to do than there was time for. The ceremonies and 'occasions' that surrounded the state visit by the Queen of Elenia filled their afternoons and evenings, and so Sparhawk and the others were obliged to work late and rise early in order to conduct their surreptitious operations in the city and the imperial compound. They all grew short-tempered from lack of sleep, and Mirtai began to badger Sparhawk about the condition of his wife's health. Ehlana *was*, in fact, beginning to develop dark circles under her eyes and an increasingly waspish disposition.

The break-through came about ten days after the departure of the expeditions to Sarna and to the newly-occupied lands of the Trolls. Caalador arrived early one morning with a kind of exultant tightness of his face and a large canvas sack in one hand. 'It was pure luck, Sparhawk,' he chortled when the two met in the royal apartment.

'We're due for some,' Sparhawk told him. 'What did you find?'

'How would you like to know the exact day and hour when this "Hidden City" business is going to come to a head?'

'I'd be moderately interested in that, yes. That self-congratulatory expression spread all over your face says that you've found out a few things.'

'I have indeed, Sparhawk, and it fell into my hand like an over-ripe peach.' Caalador slid into his drawl. 'Them there fellers on t' other side's mighty careless with wrote-down instructions. It seems that this yere cut-purse o' my acquaintance – enterprisin' young feller

521

with a real shorp knife – he slit open the purse o' this yere fat Dacite merchant, an' a hull fistful o' coins come slitherin' out, an' mixt in with them there silver an' brass coins they wuz this yere message, which it wuz ez hed bin passt onta him by one o' his feller-conspiracy-ers.' Caalador frowned. 'Maybe the right word there would have been "conspirytors",' he mused.

'Ehlana's still in bed, Caalador,' Sparhawk told him. 'You don't have to entertain *me* with that dialect.'

'Sorry. Just keeping in practice. Anyway, the note was quite specific. It said, "The day of the revelation of the Hidden City is at hand. All is in readiness. We will come to your warehouse for the arms at the second hour past sunset ten days hence." Isn't that interesting?'

'It is indeed, Caalador, but the note could be a week old.'

'No, actually it's not. Would you believe that the idiot who wrote it actually dated it?'

'You're not serious.'

'May muh tongue turn green if I ain't.'

'Can your cut-purse identify this Dacite merchant? I'd like to locate this warehouse and find out what kind of arms are stored there.'

'I'm way ahead of you, Sparhawk,' Caalador grinned. 'We tracked down the Dacite, and I called on my vast experience as a chicken-rustler to get inside his storehouse.' He opened the large bag he had brought with him and took out what appeared to be a newly-made crossbow. 'They wuz several hunnerd o' these in that there hen-roost o' his'n,' he said, 'along with a hull passel o' cheap swords – which wuz most likely forged in Lebros in Cammoria – which it is that's notorious fer makin' shoddy goods fer trade with backward folk.'

Sparhawk turned the crossbow over in his hands. 'It's not really very well-made, is it?' he noted.

'She'll prob'ly shoot, though – oncet anyway.'

'This explains that tree Khalad found with all the crossbow bolts stuck in it. It looks as if we've been anticipated. Our friend out there wouldn't really need crossbows unless he knew he was going to come up against men in armour. The long-bow's a lot more efficient against ordinary people. It shoots faster.'

'I think we'd better face up to something, Sparhawk,' Caalador said gravely. 'Several hundred crossbows means several hundred conspirators, not counting the ones who'll be using the swords, and that's fair evidence that the conspiracy's going to involve unpleasantness here in Matherion itself as well as out there in the hinterlands. I think we'd better be prepared for a mob – and for fighting in the streets.'

'You could very well be right, my friend. Let's see what we can do to defang that mob.'

He went to the door and opened it. As usual, Mirtai sat outside with her sword in her lap. 'Could you get Khalad for me, Atana?' he asked politely.

'Who's going to guard the door while I'm gone?' she asked him.

'I'll take care of it.'

'Why don't *you* go get him? I'll stay here and see to Ehlana's safety.'

He sighed. 'Please, Mirtai – as a special favour to me.'

'If anything happens to Ehlana while I'm gone, you'll answer to me, Sparhawk.'

'I'll keep that in mind.'

'Pretty girl, isn't she?' Caalador noted after the giantess had gone in search of Sparhawk's squire.

'I wouldn't make a point of noticing that too much when Kring's around, my friend. They're betrothed, and he's the jealous type.'

'Should I say that she's ugly, then?'

'That wouldn't really be a good idea either. If you do that *she'll* probably kill you.'

'Touchy, aren't they?'

'Oh, yes – both of them. Theirs promises to be a very lively marriage.'

Mirtai returned with Khalad a few minutes later. 'You sent for me, my Lord?' Kurik's son asked.

'How would you go about disabling this crossbow without making it obvious that it had been tampered with?' Sparhawk asked, handing the young man the weapon Caalador had brought with him.

Khalad examined the weapon. 'Cut the string almost all the way through – up here where it's attached to the end of the bow,' he suggested. 'It'll break as soon as anyone tries to draw it.'

Sparhawk shook his head. 'They might load the weapons in advance,' he said. 'Someone's going to try to use these on us, I think, and I don't want him to find out that they don't work until it's too late.'

'I could break the trigger-mechanism,' Khalad said. 'The bowman could draw it and load it, but he couldn't shoot it – at least he couldn't aim it at the same time.'

'Would it stay cocked until he tried to shoot it?'

'Probably. This isn't a very well-made crossbow, so he won't expect it to work very well. All you'd have to do is drive out this pin that holds the trigger in place and stick short steel pegs in the holes to hide the fact that the pin's gone. There's a spring that holds the bow drawn, but without the pin to provide leverage, the trigger won't release that spring. They'll be able to draw it, but they won't be able to shoot it.'

'I'll take your word for it. How long would it take you to put this thing out of action?'

'A couple of minutes.'

'You've got a few long nights ahead of you then, my friend. There are several hundred of these to deal with

– and you're going to have to do it quietly and in poor light. Caalador, can you slip my friend here into the Dacite merchant's warehouse?'

'If'n he kin move around sorta quiet-like, I kin.'

'I think he can manage. He's a country-boy the same as you are, and I'd guess that he's almost as skilled at making rabbit snares and stealing chickens.'

'Sparhawk!' Khalad protested.

'Those skills are too valuable to have been left out of your education, Khalad, and I knew your father, remember?'

'They knew we were coming, Sparhawk,' Kalten said angrily. 'We split up into small groups and stayed away from towns and villages, and they *still* knew we were coming. They ambushed us on the west shore of Lake Sama.'

'Trolls?' Sparhawk's voice was tense.

'Worse. It was a large group of rough-looking fellows armed with crossbows. They made the mistake of shooting all at the same time. If they hadn't, none of us would have made it back to tell you about it. They decimated Engessa's mounted Atans, though. He was seriously put out about that. He tore quite a number of the ambushers apart with his bare hands.'

A sudden cold fear gripped Sparhawk's stomach. 'Where's Tynian?' he asked.

'He's in the care of a physician. He caught a bolt in the shoulder, and it broke some things in there.'

'Is he going to be all right?'

'Probably. It didn't improve his temper very much though. He uses his sword almost as well with his left hand as he does with his right. We had to restrain him when the ambushers broke and ran. He was going to chase them down one by one, and he was bleeding like a stuck pig. I think we've got spies here in this imitation castle, Sparhawk. Those people couldn't have laid that ambush without some fairly specific information about our route and our destination.'

'We'll sweep those hiding-places again.'

'Good idea, and this time let's do a bit more than reprimand the people we catch for bad manners. A spy can't creep through hidden passages very well with two broken legs.' The blond Pandion's face was grim. 'I get to do the breaking,' he added. 'I want to be sure that there aren't any miraculous recoveries. A broken shin-bone heals in a couple of months, but if you take a sledge-hammer to a man's knees, you'll put him out of action for much, much longer.'

Bevier, who led the survivors of *his* detachment back into Matherion two days later, took Kalten's suggestion a step further. *His* notion involved amputations at the hip. The devout Cyrinic Knight was *very* angry about being ambushed and he used language Sparhawk had never heard from him before. When he had calmed himself finally, though, he contritely sought absolution from Patriarch Emban. Emban not only forgave him, but granted an indulgence as well – just in case he happened across some new swear-words.

A thorough search of the opalescent castle turned up no hidden listeners, and they all gathered to confer with Emperor Sarabian and Foreign Minister Oscagne the day after Sir Bevier's return. They met high in the central tower, just to be on the safe side, and Sephrenia added a Styric spell to further ensure that their discussions would remain private.

'I'm not accusing anyone,' Vanion said, 'so don't take this personally. Word of our plans is somehow leaking out, so I think we should all pledge that no hint of what we discuss here should leave this room.'

'An oath of silence, Lord Vanion?' Kalten seemed surprised. That Pandion tradition had fallen into disuse in the past century.

'Well,' Vanion amended, 'something on that order, I suppose, but we're not all Pandion Knights here, you know.' He looked around. 'All right then, let's summarise the situation. The plot here in Matherion quite obviously goes beyond simple espionage. I think we'd better face up to the probability of an armed insurrection directed at the imperial compound. Our enemy seems to be growing impatient.'

'Or fearful,' Oscagne added. 'The presence of Church Knights – *and* Prince Sparhawk – here in Matherion poses some kind of threat. His campaign of random terror, civil disturbance and incipient insurrection in the subject kingdoms was working fairly well, but it appears that something's come up that makes that process too slow. He has to strike at the centre of imperial authority now.'

'And directly at *me*, I gather,' Emperor Sarabian added.

'That's unthinkable, your Majesty,' Oscagne objected. 'In all the history of the empire, no one *ever* directly confronted the emperor.'

'Please, Oscagne,' Sarabian said, 'don't treat me like an idiot. Any number of my predecessors have met with "accidents" or fallen fatally ill under peculiar circumstances. Inconvenient emperors *have* been removed before.'

'But never right out in the open, your Majesty. That's *terribly* impolite.'

Sarabian laughed. 'I'm sure that the three government ministers who threw my great-great-grandfather from the top of the highest tower in the compound were all exquisitely courteous about it, Oscagne. We're going to have an armed mob in the streets then, all enthusiastically howling for my blood?'

'I wouldn't discount the possibility, your Majesty,' Vanion conceded.

'I hate this,' Ulath said sourly.

'Hate what?' Kalten asked him.

'Isn't it obvious? We've got an Elene castle here. It might not be *quite* as good as one that Bevier would have designed, but it's still the strongest building in Matherion. We've got three days until the streets are going to be filled with armed civilians. We don't have much choice. We *have* to pull back inside these walls – fort up until the Atans can restore order. I *detest* sieges.'

'I'm sure we won't have to go *that* far, Sir Ulath,' Oscagne protested. 'As soon as I heard about that message Master Caalador unearthed, I sent word to Norkan in Atana. There are ten thousand Atans massed twenty leagues from here. The conspirators aren't going to move until after dark on the appointed day. I can have the streets awash with seven-foot tall Atans before noon of that same day. The attempted coup will fail before it ever gets started.'

'And miss the chance to round them all up?' Ulath said. 'Very poor military thinking, your Excellency. We've got a defensible castle here. Bevier could hold this place for two years at least.'

'Five,' Bevier corrected. 'There's a well inside the walls. That adds three years.'

'Even better,' Ulath said. 'We work on our fortifications here very quietly, and mostly at night. We bring in barrels of pitch and naphtha. Bevier builds siege-engines. Then, just before the sun goes down, we move the entire government and the Atan garrison inside the castle. The mob will storm the imperial compound and rage through the halls of all those impressive buildings here in the grounds. They won't encounter any resistance – until they come here. They'll try to storm our walls, and they'll be over-confident because nobody will

528

have tried to fight them in any of the other buildings. They won't really be expecting a hail-storm of large boulders or sheets of boiling pitch dumped in their faces. Add to that the fact that their crossbows won't work because Khalad's been breaking the triggers in that Dacite warehouse for the last two nights, and you've got a large group of people with a serious problem. They'll mill around out there in confusion and chagrin, and then, probably about midnight, the Atans will enter the city, come to the imperial compound and grind the whole lot of them right into the ground.'

'Yes!' Engessa exclaimed enthusiastically.

'It's a brilliant plan, Sir Ulath,' Sarabian told the big Thalesian. 'Why are you so dissatisfied with it?'

'Because I don't like sieges, your Majesty.'

'Ulath,' Tynian said, wincing slightly as he shifted his broken shoulder, 'don't you think it's time that you abandoned this pose? You're as quick to suggest forting-up as any of the rest of us when the situation calls for it.'

'Thalesians are *supposed* to hate sieges, Tynian. It's a part of our national character. We're supposed to be impetuous, impatient and more inclined toward brute force than toward well-considered endurance.'

'Sir Ulath,' Bevier said, smiling slightly, 'King Wargun's father endured a siege at Heid that lasted for seventeen years. He emerged from it none the worse for wear.'

'Yes, but he didn't *enjoy* it, Bevier. That's my point.'

'I think we're overlooking an opportunity, my friends,' Kring noted. 'The mob's going to come to the imperial compound here, right?'

'If we've guessed their intentions correctly, yes,' Tynian agreed.

'*Some* of them are going to be all afire with political fervour – but not really very many, I don't think. Most of them are going to be more interested in looting the various palaces.'

Sarabian's face blanched. 'Hell and night!' he swore. 'I hadn't even thought of that!'

'Don't be too concerned, friend Emperor,' the Domi told him. 'Whether it's politics or greed that brings them, they'll almost all come into the grounds. The walls around the compound are high and the gates very imposing. Why don't we let them come in – but then make sure they don't leave? I can hide men near the gate-house. After the mob's in the grounds, we'll close the gates. That should keep them all more or less on hand to greet the Atans when they arrive. The loot will bring them in, and the gates will keep them in. They'll loot, right enough, but loot isn't really yours until you've escaped with it. We'll catch them all this way, and we won't have to dig any of them out of rabbit-holes later.'

'That's got real possibilities, you know that, Kring?' Kalten said admiringly.

'I'd have expected no less of him,' Mirtai said. 'He *is* a brilliant warrior, after all – *and* my betrothed.'

Kring beamed.

'One last touch, perhaps,' Stragen added. 'I think we all have a burning curiosity about certain things, and we've compiled this list of the names of people who might have answers to some of our most urgent questions. Battles are chancy, and sometimes valuable people get killed. I think there are some out there in Matherion who should be removed to safety before the fighting starts.'

'Good idea, Milord Stragen,' Sarabian agreed. 'I'll send out some detachments on the morning of the big day to round up those we'd like to keep alive.'

'Ah – perhaps that might not be the best way to go at it, your Majesty. Why not let Caalador attend to it? As a group, policemen tend to be obvious when they arrest people – uniforms, chains, marching in step – that sort of thing. Professional murderers are much more unobtrusive. You don't have to put chains on a man when you arrest him. A dagger-point held discreetly to his side is just as effective, I've found.'

Sarabian gave him a shrewd look. 'You're speaking from experience, I gather?' he speculated.

'Murder *is* a crime, your Majesty,' Stragen pointed out, 'and as a leader of criminals, I should have *some* experience in all branches of the field. Professionalism, you understand.'

CHAPTER 28

'It was definitely Scarpa, Sparhawk,' Caalador assured the big Pandion. 'We didn't have to rely entirely on the drawing. One of the local whores is from Arjuna, and she's had business-dealings with him in the past. She positively identified him.' The two of them were standing atop the castle wall where they could speak privately.

'That seems to be everybody but Baron Parok of Daconia then,' Sparhawk noted. 'We've seen Krager, Gerrich, Rebal of Edom, this Scarpa from Arjuna, and Elron from Astel.'

'I thought the conspirator from Astel was called Sabre,' Caalador said.

Sparhawk silently cursed his careless tongue. 'Sabre keeps his face hidden,' he said. 'Elron's a sympathizer – more than that, probably.'

Caalador nodded. 'I've known some Astels,' he agreed, '*and* some Dacites, too. I wouldn't be positive that Baron Parok's not lurking in the shadows somewhere. They're definitely all gathering here in Matherion.' He looked thoughtfully out over the gleaming nacreous battlements at the fosse below. 'Is that ditch down there going to be all that much a barrier?' he asked. 'The sides are so gently sloped that there's lawn growing on them.'

'It gets more inconvenient when it's filled with sharpened stakes,' Sparhawk replied. 'We'll do that at the last minute. Has there been any influx of strangers into Matherion? All those assorted patriots have large followings. A mob gathered off the streets is one thing, but a horde drawn from most of Tamuli would be something else entirely.'

'We haven't seen any unusual number of strangers here in town,' Caalador said, 'and there aren't any large gatherings out in the countryside – at least not within five leagues in any direction.'

'They could be holding in place farther on out,' Sparhawk said. 'If *I* had a supporting army out there someplace, *I* wouldn't bring them in until the last minute.'

Caalador turned and looked pointedly at the harbour. 'That's our weakness right there, Sparhawk. There could be a fleet hiding in coves and inlets along the coast. We'd never see them coming until they showed up on the horizon. I've got pirates and smugglers scouring the coasts, but –' He spread his hands.

'There's not very much we can do about it, I'm afraid,' Sparhawk said. 'We've got an army of Atans close at hand though, and they'll be inside the city soon after the uprising starts. Do your people have the hiding places of these assorted visitors fairly well-pinpointed? If things go well, I'd like to sweep them all up at once if possible.'

'They don't seem to have lighted in specific places yet, Sparhawk. They're all moving around quite a bit. I've got people following them. We could pick them up early, if you'd like.'

'Let's not expose our preparations. If we can catch them on the day of the uprising, fine. If not, we can chase them down later. I'm not going to endanger our counter-measures just for the pleasure of their company. Your people are doing very well, Caalador.'

'Their performance is a bit forced, my friend,' Caalador admitted ruefully. 'I've had to gather a large number of burly ruffians with clubs to keep reminding the Tamul criminals that we're all working together in this affair.'

'Whatever it takes.'

'Her Majesty's suggestion has some advantages, Lord Vanion,' Bevier said after giving it some thought. 'It's what the fosse was designed for originally anyway. It's supposed to be a moat, not just a grassy ditch.'

'It completely exposes the fact that we're preparing to defend the castle, Bevier,' Vanion objected. 'If we start pumping the moat full of water, everybody in Matherion will know about it within the hour.'

'You didn't listen to the whole plan, Vanion,' Ehlana said patiently. 'We've been attending balls and banquets and various other entertainments ever since we arrived here. It's only proper that I respond to all those kindnesses, so I'm planning a grand entertainment to pay my social obligations. It's not my fault that it's going to take place on the night of the uprising, is it? We have an Elene castle, so we'll have an Elene party. We'll have an orchestra on the battlements, coloured lanterns and buntings on the walls and festive barges in the moat – complete with canopies and banquet tables. I'll invite the emperor and his whole court.'

'That would be extremely convenient, Lord Vanion,' Tynian said. 'We'd have everybody we want to protect right close at hand. We wouldn't have to go looking for them, and we wouldn't alert anybody to what we're doing by chasing cabinet ministers across the lawns.'

Sparhawk's squire was shaking his head.

'What is it, Khalad?' Ehlana asked him.

'The bottom of the ditch hasn't been prepared to hold water, your Majesty. We don't know how porous the sub-soil is. There's a very good chance that the water you pump in will just seep into the ground. Your moat could be empty again a few hours after you fill it.'

'Oh, bother!' Ehlana fretted. 'I didn't think of that.'

'I'll take care of it, Ehlana,' Sephrenia smiled. 'A good

plan shouldn't be abandoned just because it violates a few natural laws.'

'Would you have to do that *before* we started to fill the moat, Sephrenia?' Stragen asked her.

'It's easier that way.'

He frowned.

'What's the problem?' she asked.

'There are those three tunnels that lead under the fosse to connect with the hidden passageways and listening posts inside the castle.'

'Three that we know about, anyway,' Ulath added.

'Exactly my point. Wouldn't we all feel more secure if all those tunnels – the ones we know about *and* the ones we don't – are flooded before the fighting starts?'

'Good point,' Sparhawk said.

'I can wait to seal the bottom of the moat until after you've flooded the tunnels,' Sephrenia told them.

'What do you think, Vanion?' Emban asked.

'The preparations for the queen's party *would* cover a lot of activity,' Vanion conceded. 'It's a very good plan.'

'I like all of it except the barges,' Sparhawk said. 'I'm sorry, Ehlana, but those barges would just give the mob access to our walls. They'd defeat the whole purpose the moat was designed for in the first place.'

'I'm getting to that, Sparhawk. Doesn't naphtha float on top of water?'

'Yes, but what's that got to do with it?'

'A barge isn't just a floating platform, you know. It's got a hold under the deck. Now, suppose we fill the holds with casks of naphtha. Then, when the trouble starts, we throw boulders down from the battlements and crack the barges open like eggshells. The naphtha will spread out over the water in the moat, we set fire to it and surround the castle with a wall of flame. Wouldn't that sort of inconvenience people trying to attack the castle?'

535

'You're a *genius*, my Queen!' Kalten exclaimed.

'How nice of you to have noticed that, Sir Kalten,' she replied smugly. 'And the beautiful part about the whole thing is that we can make all of our preparations right out in the open without sneaking around at night and losing all that sleep. This grand party gives us the perfect excuse to do almost anything to the castle in the name of decoration.'

Mirtai suddenly embraced her owner and kissed her. 'I'm proud of you, my mother,' she said.

'I'm glad you approve, my daughter,' Ehlana said modestly, 'but you really ought to be more reserved, you know. Remember what you told me about girls kissing girls.'

'We found two more tunnels, Sparhawk,' Khalad reported as his lord joined him on the parapet. Khalad was wearing a canvas smock over his black leather vest.

Sparhawk looked out at the moat where a gang of workmen were driving long steel rods into the soft earth at the bottom of the ditch. 'Isn't that a little obvious?' he asked.

'We have to have mooring stakes for the barges, don't we? The tunnels are all about five feet below the surface. Most of the workmen with the sledge-hammers don't know what they're really looking for, but I've got a fair number of knights down in the ditch with them. The ceilings of those tunnels will be very leaky when we start to fill the moat.' Khalad looked out across the lawn. Then he cupped his hands around his mouth. 'Be careful with that barge!' he bellowed in Tamul. 'If you spring her seams, she'll leak!'

The foreman of the Tamul work-crew laboriously pulling the broad-beamed barge across the lawn on rollers looked up. 'It's very heavy, honoured sir,' he called back. 'What have you got inside of it?'

'Ballast, you idiot!' Khalad called back. 'There are going to be a lot of people on that deck tomorrow night. If the barge capsizes and the emperor falls in the moat, we'll all be in trouble.'

Sparhawk looked inquiringly at his squire.

'We're putting the naphtha casks in the barges inside the construction sheds,' Khalad explained. 'We decided to do that more or less in private.' He looked at his lord. 'You don't necessarily have to tell your wife I said this, Sparhawk,' he said, 'but there were a few gaps in her plan. The naphtha was a good idea – as far as it went, but we've added some pitch as well, just to make sure it catches on fire when we want it to. Naphtha casks are also very tight. They won't do us much good if they just sink to the bottom of the moat when we break open the barges. I'm going to put a couple of Kring's Peloi in the hold of each barge. They'll take axes to the casks at the last minute.'

'You think of everything, Khalad.'

'Somebody has to be practical in this group.'

'Now you sound like your father.'

'There is one thing though, Sparhawk. Your party-goers are going to have to be very, very *careful*. There'll be lanterns – and probably candles as well – on those barges. One little accident could start the fire quite a bit sooner than we'd planned, and – ah, actually, we're a bit ahead of schedule, your Highness,' he said in Tamul for the benefit of the half dozen labourers who were pulling a two-wheeled cart along the parapet. The cart was filled with lanterns which the labourers were hanging from the battlements. 'No, no, no!' Khalad chided them. 'You can't put two green ones side by side like that. I've told you a thousand times – white, green, red, blue. Do it the way I told you to do it. Be creative in your own time.' He sighed exaggeratedly. 'It's *so* hard to get good help these days, your Highness,' he said.

'You're overacting, Khalad,' Sparhawk muttered.

'I know, but I want to be sure they're getting the point.'

Kring came along the parapet rubbing his hand over his scarred head. 'I need a shave,' he said absently, 'and Mirtai's too busy to attend to it.'

'Is that a Peloi custom, Domi?' Sparhawk asked. 'Is it one of the duties of a Peloi woman to shave her man's head?'

'No, actually it's Mirtai's personal idea. It's hard to see the back of your own head, and I used to miss a few places. Shortly after we were betrothed, she took my razor away from me and told me that from now on, *she* was going to do the shaving. She does a very nice job, really – when she isn't too busy.' He squared his shoulders. 'They absolutely refused, Sparhawk,' he reported. 'I knew they would, but I put the matter before them the way you asked. They *won't* be locked up inside your fort during the battle. If you stop and think about it, though, we'll be much more useful ranging around the grounds on horseback anyway. A few score mounted Peloi will stir that mob around like a kettle-full of boiling soup. If you want confusion out there tomorrow night, we'll give you lots of confusion. A man who's worried about getting a sabre across the back of the head isn't going to be able to concentrate on attacking a fort.'

'Particularly when his weapon doesn't work,' Khalad added.

Sparhawk grunted. 'Of course we're assuming that the warehouse full of crossbows Caalador found was the only one,' he added.

'I'm afraid we won't find that out until tomorrow night,' Khalad conceded. 'I disabled about six hundred of those things. If twelve hundred crossbowmen come into the palace grounds we'll know that half of their weapons are going to work. We'll have to take cover at that point. You there!' he shouted suddenly, looking upward. '*Drape* that bunting! Don't stretch it tight that way!' He shook his fist at the workman leaning precariously out of a window high up in one of the towers.

Although he was obviously quite young, the scholar Bevier escorted into Ehlana's presence was almost totally bald. He was very nervous, but his eyes had that burning glaze to them that announced him to be a fanatic. He prostrated himself before Ehlana's throne-like chair and banged his forehead on the floor.

'Don't do that, man,' Ulath rumbled at him. 'It offends the queen. Besides, you'll crack the floor tiles.'

The scholar scrambled to his feet, his eyes fearful.

'This is Emuda,' Bevier introduced him. 'He's the scholar I told you about – the one with the interesting theory about Scarpa of Arjuna.'

'Oh, yes,' Ehlana said in Tamul. 'Welcome, Master Emuda. Sir Bevier has spoken highly of you.' Actually, Bevier had not, but a queen is allowed to take certain liberties with the truth.

Emuda gave her a fawning sort of look. Sparhawk moved in quickly to cut off a lengthy, rambling preamble. 'Correct me if I'm wrong about this, Master Emuda,' he said, 'but our understanding of your theory is that you think that Scarpa's behind all these disturbances in Tamuli.'

'That's a slight over-simplification, Sir – ?' Emuda looked inquiringly at the tall Pandion Knight.

'Sparhawk,' Ulath supplied.

Emuda's face went white, and he began to tremble violently.

'I'm a simple sort of man, neighbour,' Sparhawk told him. 'Please don't confuse me with complications. What sort of evidence do you have that lays everything at Scarpa's door?'

'It's quite involved, Sir Sparhawk,' Emuda apologised.

'Un-involve it. Summarise, man. I'm busy.'

Emuda swallowed very hard. 'Well, uh –' he faltered. 'We know – that is, we're fairly certain – that Scarpa was the first of the spokesmen for these so-called "heroes from the past".'

'Why do you say "so-called", Master Emuda?' Tynian asked him. Sir Tynian still had his right arm in a sling.

'Isn't it obvious, Sir Knight?' Emuda's tone was just slightly condescending. 'The notion of resurrecting the dead is an absurdity. It's all quite obviously a hoax. Some henchman is dressed in ancient clothing, appears in a flash of light – which any country-fair charlatan can contrive – and then starts babbling gibberish, which the "spokesman" identifies as an ancient language. Yes, it's clearly a hoax.'

'How clever of you to have unmasked it,' Sephrenia murmured. 'We all thought it was magic of some kind.'

'There's no such thing as magic, madame.'

'Really?' she replied mildly. 'What an amazing thing.'

'I'd stake my reputation on that.'

'How courageous of you.'

'You say that Scarpa was the first of these revolutionaries to appear?' Vanion asked him.

'By more than a year, Sir Knight. The first reports of his activities began to appear in diplomatic dispatches from the capital at Arjuna just over four years ago. The next to emerge was Baron Parok of Daconia, and I have a sworn statement from a ship-captain that Scarpa sailed from Kaftal in southwestern Arjuna to Ahar in Daconia. Ahar is Baron Parok's home, and he began *his* activities about three years ago. The connection is obvious.'

'It *would* seem so, wouldn't it?' Sparhawk mused.

'From Ahar I have documented evidence of the travels of the two. Parok went into Edom, where he actually

540

stayed in the home town of Rebal – that connection gave me a bit of trouble, since Rebal isn't using his real name. We've identified his home district, though, and the town Parok visited is the district capital. I think I'm safe in assuming that a meeting took place during Parok's visit. While Parok was in Edom, Scarpa travelled all the way up into Astel. I can't exactly pinpoint his travels there, but I know he moved around quite a bit just to the north of the marches on the Edomish-Astellian border, and that's the region where Sabre makes his headquarters. The disturbances in Edom and Astel began some time after Scarpa and Parok had journeyed into those kingdoms. The evidence of connection between the four men is all very conclusive.'

'What about these reports of supernatural events?' Tynian asked.

'More hoaxes, Sir Knight.' Emuda's expression was offensively superior. 'Pure charlatanism. You may have noticed that they always occur out in the countryside where the only witnesses are superstitious peasants and ignorant serfs. Civilised people would not be fooled by such obvious trickery.'

'I wondered about that,' Sparhawk said. 'Are you sure about this timetable of yours? Scarpa was the first to start stirring things up?'

'Definitely, Sir Sparhawk.'

'Then he contacted the others and enlisted them? Perhaps a year and a half later?'

Emuda nodded.

'Where did he go when he left Astel after recruiting Sabre?'

'I've lost track of him for a time there, Sir Sparhawk. He went into the Elene Kingdoms of Western Tamuli about two and a half years ago and didn't return to Arjuna until eight or ten months later. I have no idea of where he was during that interim. Oh, one other thing.

541

The so-called vampires began to appear in Arjuna at almost precisely the same time that Scarpa began telling the Arjuni that he'd been in contact with Sheguan, their national hero. The traditional monsters of the other kingdoms also put in *their* appearance at the same time these other revolutionaries began *their* campaigns. Believe me, your Majesty,' he said earnestly to Ehlana, 'if you're looking for a ringleader, Scarpa's your man.'

'We thank you for this information, Master Emuda,' she said sweetly. 'Would you please provide Sir Bevier with your supporting data and describe your findings to him in greater detail? Pressing affairs necessarily limit the time we can spend with you, fascinating though we find your conclusions.'

'I shall be happy to share the entire body of my research with Sir Bevier, your Majesty.'

Bevier rolled his eyes ceilingward and sighed.

They watched the enthusiast lead poor Bevier from the room.

'I'd hate to have to take *that* case into any court – civil *or* ecclesiastical,' Emban snorted.

'It *is* a bit thin, isn't it?' Stragen agreed.

'The only thing that makes me pay any attention to him at all is that timetable of his,' Sparhawk said. 'Dolmant sent me to Lamorkand late last winter to look into the activities of Count Gerrich. While I was there, I heard all the wild stories about Drychtnath. It seems that our prehistoric Lamork started making appearances at a time that coincides almost exactly with the period when our scholarly friend lost track of Scarpa. Emuda's such a complete ass that I sort of hate to admit it, but he may just have hit upon the right answer.'

'But it's for all the wrong reasons, Sparhawk,' Emban objected.

'I'm only interested in his answers, your Grace,' Sparhawk replied. 'As long as they're the right answers, I don't care *how* he got them.'

'It's just too risky to do it any earlier, Sparhawk,' Stragen said later that day.

'You two are taking a lot of chances,' Sparhawk objected.

'It's a hull lot more chancy t' stort out earlier, Sparhawk,' Caalador drawled. 'Iff'n we wuz t' grab th' leaders sooner, them ez is left could jist call it all off, an' all these traps o' ourn wouldn't ketch no rabbits. We gotta wait 'till they open that warehouse an' stort passin' out them there weepons.'

Sparhawk winced. 'Weepons?'

'The word wouldn't appear in that particular dialect,' Caalador shrugged. 'I had to countrify it up – just for the sake of consistency.'

'You switch back and forth like a frog on a hot rock, my friend.'

'I know. Infuriating, isn't it? It goes like this, Sparhawk. If we pick up the conspirators any time before they start arming the mob, they'll be able to suspend operations and go to ground. They'll wait, reorganise and then pick another day – which it is that we won't know nuthin' about. On the other hand, once they pass out the weapons, it'll be too late. There'll be thousands in the streets – most of them about half-drunk. Our friends in the upper councils could no more stop them than stop the tide. The sheer momentum of this attempted coup will be working for *us* instead of for our shadowy friends.'

'They can still go to ground and just feed the mob to the wolves, you know.'

Caalador shook his head. 'Tamul justice is a bit abrupt, and an attack on the emperor is going to be viewed as the worst sort of bad manners. Several hundred people are going to be sent to the headsman's block. Recruitment after that will be virtually impossible. They have no choice. Once they start, they *have* to follow through.'

'You're talking about some very delicate timing, you know.'

'Aw, that's easy tuk care of, Sparhawk,' Caalador grinned. 'There's this yere temple right smack dab in the middle o' town. It's more'n likely all fulla cobwebs an' dust, on accounta our little yella brothers don't take ther religion none too serious-like. There's these yere priests ez sits around in there, drinkin' an' carousin' an' sich. When they gits therselves all beered-up an' boistrous-like, they usual decides t' hold services. They got this yere bell, which it is ez must weigh along 'bout twenty ton 'er so. One o' them there drunk priests, he wobbles over t' that there bell an' he takes up this yere sledge-hammer an' he whacks the bell a couple licks with it. Makes the awfullest sound you ever *did* hear. Sailors bin known t' hear it 'bout ten leagues out t' sea. Now, there ain't no special time set fer when they goes t' whackin' on that there bell. Folks here in Matherion don't pay no attention t' it, figgerin' that it's jist the priests enjoyin' therselves.' Even Caalador could apparently tire of the exaggerated dialect. 'That's the beauty of it, Sparhawk,' he said, lapsing into normal speech. 'The sound of that bell is random, and nobody takes any special note of it. Tomorrow night, though, it's going to be profoundly significant. As soon as that warehouse opens, the bell's going to peal out its message of hope and joy. The murderers sitting almost in the laps of the people we want to talk with will take that as their orders to move. We'll have the whole lot rounded up in under a minute.'

'What if they try to resist?'

'Oh, there'll be some losses,' Caalador shrugged. 'You

can't make an omelette without breaking eggs. There are several dozen people we want to pick up, so we can afford to lose a few.'

'The sound of the bell will *also* alert *you*, Sparhawk,' Stragen pointed out. 'When you hear it start ringing, you'll know that it's time to move your wife's party inside.'

'But you can't *do* this, your Majesty!' the minister of the interior protested shrilly the next morning as tons of water began to gush into the moat from the throats of the huge pipes strewn across the lawn of the imperial compound.

'Oh?' Ehlana asked innocently. 'And why is that, Minister Kolata?'

'Uh, well, uh, there's no sub-foundation under the moat, your Majesty. The water will just sink into the ground.'

'Oh, that's all right, Minister Kolata. It's only for one night. I'm sure the moat will stay full enough until after the party.'

Kolata stared with chagrin at a sudden fountain-like eruption of air and muddy water out in the centre of the moat.

'My goodness,' Ehlana said mildly, looking at the sudden whirlpool funnelling down where the eruption had taken place. 'There must have been an old abandoned cellar under there.' She laughed a silvery little laugh. 'I'd imagine that the rats who lived in there were *very* surprised, wouldn't you agree, your Excellency?'

Kolata looked a bit sick. 'Uh, would you excuse me, your Majesty?' he said, and he turned to hurry across the lawn without waiting for a reply.

'Don't let him get away, Sparhawk,' Ehlana said coolly. 'I strongly suspect that Lord Vanion's list wasn't as complete as we might have hoped. Why don't you invite the minister of the interior into the castle so that you can show him our other preparations?' She tapped one finger thoughtfully against her chin. 'And you might ask Sir Kalten and Sir Ulath to join you when you get around to showing his Excellency the torture-chamber. Emperor Sarabian's excellent minister of the interior might want to add a few names to Vanion's list.'

It was the cool and unruffled way she said it that chilled Sparhawk's blood the most.

'He's beginning to feel more than a little offended, Sparhawk,' Vanion said soberly as the two of them watched Khalad's workmen 'decorating' the vast gates of the imperial compound. 'He's not stupid, and he knows that we're not telling him everything.'

'It can't be helped, Vanion. He's just too erratic to be let in on all the details.'

'Mercurial might be a more diplomatic term.'

'Whatever. We don't really know him all that well, Vanion, and we're operating in an alien society. For all we know, he keeps a diary and writes everything down. That could be a Tamul custom. It's entirely possible that our whole plan could be available to the chambermaid who makes up his bed every morning.'

'You're speculating, Sparhawk.'

'These ambushes out in the countryside weren't speculation.'

'Surely you don't suspect the emperor.'

'*Somebody* passed the word of our expeditions along to our enemy, Vanion. We can apologise to the emperor *after* this evening's entertainment is concluded.'

'Oh, that's just *too* obvious, Sparhawk!' Vanion burst out, pointing at the heavy steel lattice Khalad's work-men were installing on the inside of the gates.

'It won't be visible when they open the gates all the way, Vanion, and Khalad's going to hang bunting on the lattice to conceal it. Did Sephrenia have any luck when she tried to contact Zalasta?'

'No. He must still be too far away.'

'I'd be a lot more comfortable if he were here. If the Troll-Gods put in an appearance tonight, we could be in very serious trouble.'

'Aphrael can deal with them.'

'Not without revealing her true identity, she can't, and if that comes out, my wife's going to find out some things I'd rather she didn't know. I'm not so fond of Sarabian that I'm willing to risk Ehlana's sanity just to keep him on his throne.'

The sun crept slowly down the western sky, moving closer and closer to the horizon. Although he knew it to be an absurdity, it seemed to Sparhawk that the blazing orb was plummeting to earth like a shooting star. There were so many details – so many things that had yet to be done. Worse yet, many of those tasks could not even be commenced until after the sun went down and gathering darkness concealed them from the hundreds of eyes that were certainly out there watching.

It was early evening when Kalten finally came to the royal apartment to announce that they had gone as far as they could go until after dark. Sparhawk was relieved to know that at least *that* much had been completed on time.

'Was the minister of the interior at all forthcoming?' Ehlana asked from her chair near the window where Alean and Melidere were involved in the extended process known as 'doing her hair'.

'Oh, yes, your Majesty,' Kalten replied with a broad grin. 'He seems even more eager to talk than your cousin Lycheas was. Ulath can be very persuasive at times. Kolata seemed to be particularly upset by the leeches.'

'Leeches?'

Kalten nodded. 'It was right after Ulath offered to stuff him head-down into a barrelful of leeches that Kolata developed this burning desire to share things with us.'

'Dear God!' the queen shuddered.

It was the general opinion of all the guests present that evening that the Queen of Elenia's party was absolutely *the* crowning event of the season. The lanterns illuminating the mother-of-pearl battlements were spectacular, the gay buntings – several thousand yards of *very* expensive silk – were festive, and the orchestra on the battlements, playing traditional Elene airs rather than the discordant cacophony that passed for music in Sarabian's court, lent a pleasantly archaic quality to the entire occasion. It was the barges moored in the moat, however, that drew the most astonished comment. The idea of dining out of doors had never occurred to the Tamuls, and the notion of floating dining-rooms ablaze with candle-light and draped with brightly-coloured silk bunting was quite beyond the imagination of the average member of the emperor's court.

The candles caused the knights no end of concern. The thought of open flame so close to the hidden cargo of the barges was sufficient to make strong men turn pale.

Since the party was taking place around the Elene castle, and the hostess was herself an Elene, the ladies of the Emperor's court had quite nearly exhausted the creative talents of every dressmaker in Matherion in their efforts to 'dress Elene'. The results were not uniformly felicitous, however, since the dressmakers of Matherion were obliged to rely on books for inspiration, and many of the books in the library of the university were several hundred years old and the gowns depicted on their pages were terribly out of fashion.

Ehlana and Melidere *were* in fashion, however, and they were the absolute centre of attention. Ehlana's gown was of regal blue, and she wore a diamond and ruby-studded tiara nestled in her pale-blonde hair. Melidere was gowned in lavender. It seemed to be her favourite colour. Mirtai was defiantly not in fashion. She wore the blue sleeveless gown she had worn at her owner's wedding, and *this* time, she *was* visibly armed. Rather surprisingly, Sephrenia also wore an Elene gown – of snowy white, naturally – and Vanion was obviously smitten by her all over again. The knights of the queen's escort wore doublets and hose, much against Sparhawk's better judgement. Their armour, however, was close at hand.

After the members of the imperial court had made their appearance and had begun to circulate on the barges, there was a pause, and then a brazen Elene fanfare. 'I had to offer violence to the musicians to get them to greet the emperor properly,' the elegantly-garbed Stragen muttered to Sparhawk.

'Oh?'

'They were very insistent that the emperor should be greeted by that dreadful noise they call music around here. They became much more co-operative after I sliced the smock off one of the trumpeters with my rapier.' Stragen's eyes suddenly widened. 'For God's sake, man!' he hissed at a servant placing a large platter of steaming beef on one of the tables, 'be careful of those candles!'

'He's a Tamul, Stragen,' Sparhawk pointed out when the servant gave the Thalesian a blank stare. 'You're trying to talk to him in Elenic.'

'Make him be careful, Sparhawk! A single tongue of fire in the wrong place on any of these barges could broil us all alive!'

Then the emperor and his nine wives appeared on

the drawbridge and came down the carpeted steps to the first barge.

Everyone bowed to the emperor, but no one looked at him. All eyes were locked on the radiantly smiling Empress Elysoun of Valesia. She had modified the customary Elene costume to accommodate her cultural tastes. Her scarlet gown was really quite lovely, but it had been altered so that those attributes Elene ladies customarily concealed and Valesian ladies flaunted were nestled on two frilly cushions of snowy lace and were thus entirely, even aggressively, in full view.

'Now *that* is what you might call a fashion statement,' Stragen murmured.

'That it is, my friend,' Sparhawk chuckled, adjusting the collar of his black velvet doublet, 'and everybody's listening to her. Poor Emban appears to be quite nearly on the verge of apoplexy.'

In a kind of formal little ceremony, Queen Ehlana escorted Sarabian and his empresses across the bridges that stepped from barge to barge. The Empress Elysoun was obviously looking for someone, and when she saw Berit standing off to one side on the second barge, she altered course and bore down upon him with all sails set – figuratively speaking, of course. Sir Berit looked at first apprehensive, then desperate, as Elysoun more or less pinned him to the rail of the barge without so much as laying a hand on him.

'Poor Berit,' Sparhawk said sympathetically. 'Stay close to him, Stragen. I don't know for sure if he can swim. Be ready to rescue him if he jumps into the moat.'

After the emperor had been given the grand tour, the banquet began. Sparhawk had judiciously spaced out the knights among the diners. The knights were not really very interesting dinner companions, since they all concentrated almost exclusively on the candles and the lanterns. 'God help us if a wind comes up,' Kalten muttered to Sparhawk.

'Truly,' Sparhawk agreed fervently. 'Ah – Kalten, old friend.'

'Yes?'

'You're supposed to be keeping an eye on the candles, not the front of the Empress Elysoun's gown.'

'What front?'

'Don't be vulgar, and remember what you're supposed to be doing here.'

'How are we going to herd this flock of over-dressed sheep inside when that bell rings?' Kalten shifted uncomfortably. His green satin doublet was buttoned very tightly across his stomach.

'If we've timed it right, the feasters will be finishing up the main course at just about the same time as our friends out in the city start distributing the weapons. When that bell rings, Ehlana's going to invite all the revellers into the castle dining-room where the dessert course is set upon more tables.'

'Very clever, Sparhawk,' Kalten said admiringly.

'Go congratulate my wife, Kalten. It was her idea.'

'She's really awfully good at this sort of thing, you know that? I'm glad she decided to come along.'

'I'm still of two minds about that,' Sparhawk grunted.

The feast went on, and there were toasts by the dozen. The feasters heaped praise upon the Queen of Elenia. Since the revellers were totally unaware of the impending climax of the evening, there were many inadvertent ironies in the compliments.

Sparhawk scarcely tasted his dinner, and he picked at his food, his eyes constantly on the candles and his ears alert for the first sound of the bell which would announce that his enemies were on the move.

Kalten's appetite, however, seemed unaffected by the impending crisis.

'How can you stuff yourself that way?' Sparhawk asked his friend irritably.

'Just keeping up my strength, Sparhawk. I'm likely to burn up a lot of energy before the night's out. If you're not busy, old boy, would you mind passing that gravy down this way?'

Then from somewhere near the centre of the gleaming, moon-drenched city of Matherion, a deep-toned bell began to boom, announcing that the second half of the evening's entertainment had begun.

CHAPTER 29

'Why didn't you *tell* me, Ehlana?' Sarabian demanded. The emperor's face was livid with suppressed fury, and his heavy gold crown was slightly askew.

'Please calm yourself, Sarabian,' the blonde queen suggested. 'We didn't find out until mid-morning today, and there was no possible way to get the information to you without taking the chance of compromising it.'

'Your snake-hipped baroness could have carried a message to me,' he accused, smacking his palm down on the battlement. They were on the parapet, ostensibly admiring the view.

'My fault there, your Majesty,' Sparhawk apologised. 'I'm more or less in charge of security, and Minister Kolata's the man who controls the police in Tamuli – both the overt police and the ones who hide in the bushes. There was no way we could be absolutely sure that our subterfuge involving the baroness had been successful. The information that we had discovered the minister's involvement was just too sensitive to risk. This attempt on your government tonight *has* to go off as planned. If our enemy gets the slightest hint that we know what he's up to, he'll postpone things until another day, and we won't have any idea of which day it's going to be.'

'I'm still very put out with you, Sparhawk,' Sarabian complained. 'I can't fault your reasoning, but you've definitely bruised my feelings here.'

'We're supposed to be watching the play of lights on the waters of the moat, Sarabian,' Ehlana reminded the emperor. 'Please at least glance over the battlements once in a while.' Their position on the parapet gave

553

them privacy, *and* a good vantage-point from which to watch for the approach of the mob.

'The news about Kolata's involvement in this business is really distressing,' Sarabian fretted. 'He controls the police, palace security and all the spies inside the empire. Worse than that, he has a certain amount of authority over the Atans. If we lose them, we're in very serious trouble.'

'Engessa's trying to sever that connection, your Majesty,' Sparhawk told him. 'He sent runners to the Atan forces outside the city to advise the commanders that the agents of the ministry of the interior aren't to be trusted. The commanders will pass that on to Androl and Betuana.'

'Are we safe here in the event that Atan Engessa's runners are intercepted?'

'Sir Bevier assures us that he can hold this castle for five years, Sarabian,' Ehlana told him, 'and Bevier's the expert on sieges.'

'And when the five years runs out?'

'The Church Knights will be here long before then, your Majesty,' Sparhawk assured him. 'Caalador has his instructions. If things go awry, he'll get word to Dolmant in Chyrellos.'

'You people are still making me very, very nervous.'

'Trust me, your Majesty,' Sparhawk said.

Kalten came puffing up the stairs to the parapet. 'We're going to need more wine, Sparhawk,' he said. 'I think we made a mistake when we set those wine-casks in the courtyard. The queen's guests are lingering down there, and they're swilling down Arcian red like water.'

'May I draw on your wine-cellars, Sarabian?' Ehlana asked sweetly.

Sarabian winced. 'Why are you pouring all that drink into them?' he demanded. 'Arcian red's very expensive here in Matherion.'

'Drunk people are easier to manage than sober ones, your Majesty,' Kalten shrugged. 'We'll let them continue to carouse down there in the courtyard and inside the castle until the fighting starts. Then we'll push the stragglers on inside the castle with the others and keep them drinking. When they wake up tomorrow morning, most of them won't even know there's been a battle.'

The party in the courtyard was growing noisier. Tamul wines were not nearly as robust as Elene vintages, and the wits of the revellers had become fuddled. They laughed a great deal and walked about the yard unsteadily with silly grins on their faces. Queen Ehlana looked critically down from the parapet. 'How much longer would you say it's going to take them to be totally incapacitated, Sparhawk?' she asked.

'Not much longer,' he shrugged. He turned and looked out towards the city. 'I don't want to seem critical, Emperor Sarabian, but I have to point out that your citizenry is profoundly unimaginative. Your rebels out there are carrying torches.'

'So?'

'It's a cliché, your Majesty. The mob in every bad Arcian romance ever written carries torches.'

'How can you be so cool, man?' Sarabian demanded. 'If someone made a loud noise behind me right now, I'd jump out of my skin.'

'Professional training, I guess. I'm more concerned that they might *not* reach the imperial compound than that they *will*. We *want* them to come here, your Majesty.'

'Shouldn't you raise the drawbridge?'

'Not yet. There are conspirators here in the compound as well as out there in the streets. We don't want to give away the fact that we know they're coming.'

Khalad thrust his head out of the turret at the corner of the battlements and beckoned to his lord.

555

'Will you excuse me, your Majesties?' Sparhawk asked politely. 'I have to go put on my work-clothes. Oh, Ehlana, why don't you signal Kalten that it's time to push those stragglers inside and lock them in the dining room with the others?'

'What's this?' Sarabian asked.

'We don't want them underfoot when the fighting starts, Sarabian,' the queen smiled. 'The wine should keep them from noticing that they're locked in the dining room.'

'You Elenes are the most cold-blooded people in the world,' Sarabian accused as Sparhawk moved off down the parapet toward the turret where Khalad was waiting with the suit of black armour.

When he returned about ten minutes later, he was dressed in steel. He found Ehlana talking earnestly with Sarabian. 'Can't you talk with her?' she was saying. 'The poor young man's on the verge of hysteria.'

'Why doesn't he just do what she wants him to? Once they've entertained each other, she'll lose interest.'

'Sir Berit's a very young knight, Sarabian. His ideals haven't been tarnished yet. Why doesn't she chase after Sir Kalten or Sir Ulath? They'd be happy to oblige her.'

'Sir Berit's a challenge to Elysoun, Ehlana. Nobody's ever turned her down before.'

'Doesn't her rampant infidelity bother you?'

'Not in the slightest. It doesn't really mean anything in her culture, you see. Her people look upon it as a pleasant but unimportant pastime. I sometimes think you Elenes place far too much significance on it.'

'Can't you make her put some clothes on?'

'Why? She's not ashamed of her body, and she enjoys sharing it with people. Be honest, Ehlana, don't you find her quite attractive?'

'I think you'd have to ask my husband about that.'

'You don't *really* expect me to answer that kind of

question, do you?' Sparhawk said. He looked out over the battlements. 'Our friends out there seem to have found their way to the palace compound,' he noted as the torch-bearing rioters began to stream through the gate onto the grounds.

'The guards are supposed to stop them,' Sarabian said angrily.

'The guards are taking their orders from Minister Kolata, I expect,' Ehlana shrugged.

'Where's the Atan Garrison then?'

'We've moved them inside the castle here, your Majesty,' Sparhawk advised him. 'I think you keep overlooking the fact that we *want* those people in the grounds. It wouldn't make much sense to impede their progress.'

'Isn't it about time to raise the drawbridge?' Sarabian seemed nervous about that.

'Not yet, your Majesty,' Sparhawk replied coolly. 'We want them *all* to be inside the compound first. At that point, Kring will close the gates. *Then* we'll raise the drawbridge. Let them take the bait before we spring the trap on them.'

'You sound awfully sure of yourself, Sparhawk.'

'We have all the advantages, your Majesty.'

'Does that mean that nothing can possibly go wrong?'

'No, something can always go wrong, but the probabilities are remote.'

'You don't mind if I worry a little bit anyway, do you?'

'Go right ahead, your Majesty.'

The mob from the streets of Matherion continued to stream unimpeded through the main gate of the Imperial grounds and fanned out rapidly, shouting excitedly as they crashed their way into the various palaces and administration buildings. As Kring had anticipated, many emerged from the gleaming buildings burdened down with assorted valuables they had looted from the interiors.

There was a brief flurry of activity in front of the castle when one group of looters reached the drawbridge and encountered a score of mounted knights under the command of Sir Ulath. The knights were there to provide cover for the Peloi who had been hidden in the holds of the barges during the earlier festivities and who had fallen to work on the naphtha casks with their axes as soon as the revellers had retired to the castle yard. A certain amount of glistening seepage from the sides of the barges indicated that the axemen crossing the decks of the festive vessels in the moat toward the drawbridge had done their work well. When the mob reached the outer end of the drawbridge, Ulath made it abundantly clear to them that he was in no mood to receive callers. The survivors decided to find other places to loot.

The courtyard had been cleared, and Bevier and his men were moving their catapults into place on the parapet. Engessa's Atans had moved up onto the parapets with the Cyrinics and were crouched down out of sight behind the battlements. Sparhawk looked around. Everything seemed in readiness. Then he looked at the gates of the compound. The only revolutionaries coming in now were the lame and the halt. They crutched their way along vigorously, but they had lagged far behind their companions. Sparhawk leaned out over the battlements. 'We might as well get started, Ulath,' he called down to his friend. 'Why don't you ask Kring to close the gates? Then you should probably come inside.'

'Right!' Ulath's face was split with a broad grin. He lifted his curled Ogre-horn to his lips and blew a hollow-sounding blast. Then he turned and led his knights across the drawbridge back into the castle.

The huge gate at the entrance to the palace grounds moved ponderously, slowly, swinging shut with a dreadful kind of inexorability. Sparhawk noted that several of those still outside stumped along desperately on their crutches, trying for all they were worth to get inside before the gate closed. 'Kalten,' he yelled down into the courtyard.

'What?' Kalten's tone was irritable.

'Would you like to let those people out there know that we're not receiving any more visitors tonight?'

'Oh, all right. I *suppose* so.' Then the blond Pandion grinned up at his fellow-knight and he and his men began turning the capstan that raised the drawbridge.

'Clown,' Sparhawk muttered.

The significance of the simultaneous closing of the gate and raising of the drawbridge did not filter through the collective mind of the mob for quite some time. Then sounds of shouted commands and even occasional clashes of weapons from nearby buildings announced that at least *some* of the rebels were beginning, however faintly, to see the light.

Tentatively, warily, the torch-bearing mob began to converge on the pristinely white Elene castle, where the gaily-coloured silk buntings shivered tremulously in the night breeze and the lantern and candle-lit barges bobbed sedately in the moat.

'Hello, the castle!' a bull-voiced fellow in the front rank roared in execrable Elenic. 'Lower your drawbridge, or we'll storm your walls!'

'Would you please reply to that, Bevier?' Sparhawk called to his Cyrinic friend.

Bevier grinned and carefully shifted one of his catapults. He sighted carefully, elevated his line of sight so that the catapult was pointed almost straight up, and then he applied the torch to the mixture of pitch and naphtha in the spoon-like receptacle at the end of the catapult-arm. The mixture took fire immediately.

'I command you to lower your drawbridge!' the

unshaven knave out beyond the moat bellowed arrogantly.

Bevier cut the retaining rope on the catapult-arm. The blob of dripping fire sizzled as it shot almost straight up into the air, then it slowed and seemed to hang motionless for a moment. Then it fell.

The ruffian who had been demanding admittance gaped at Bevier's reply as it majestically rose into the night sky and then fell directly upon him like a comet. He vanished as he was engulfed in fire.

'Good shot!' Sparhawk called his compliment.

'Not bad,' Bevier replied modestly. 'It was sort of tricky, because he was so close.'

'I noticed that.'

Emperor Sarabian had gone very pale, and he was visibly shaken. 'Did you *have* to do that, Sparhawk?' He demanded in a choked voice as the now-frightened mob fled back across the lawns to positions that may or may not have been out of Sir Bevier's range.

'Yes, your Majesty,' Sparhawk replied calmly. 'We're playing for time here. The bell that started to ring an hour or so ago was a sort of general signal. Caalador's cutthroats took the ring-leaders into custody when it rang, Ehlana moved the party-goers inside the castle, and the Atan legions outside the city started to march as soon as they heard it. That loud-mouth who's presently on fire at the edge of the moat is a graphic demonstration of just how truly unpleasant things are going to get if the mob decides to insist on being admitted. It's going to take some serious encouragement to persuade them to approach us again.'

'I thought you said you could hold them off.'

'We can, but why risk lives if you don't have to? You'll note that there was no cheering or shouts when Bevier shot his catapult. Those people out there are staring at an absolutely silent, apparently unmanned castle that

560

almost negligently obliterates offensive people. That's a terrifying sort of thing to contemplate. This is the part of the siege that frequently lasts for several years.' Sparhawk looked down the parapet. 'I think it's time for us to move inside that turret, your Majesties,' he suggested. 'We can't be positive that Khalad disabled *all* the crossbows – or that somebody in the mob hasn't repaired a few. I'd have a great deal of trouble explaining why I was careless enough to let one of you get killed. We can see what's going on from the turret, and I'll feel much better if you've both got nice thick stone walls around you.'

'Shouldn't we rupture those barges now, dear?' Ehlana asked him.

'Not just yet. We've got the potential for inflicting a real disaster on the besiegers there. Let's not waste it.'

Some few of the crossbows in the hands of the mob functioned properly, but not very many. There seemed to be a great deal of swearing about that.

A serious attempt to re-open the gates of the compound fell apart when the Peloi, their sabres flashing and their shrill, ululating war cries echoing back from the walls of nearby opalescent palaces charged across the neatly-clipped lawns to savage the crowd clustered around the gate.

Then, because once the Peloi have been unleashed they are very hard to rein in again, the tribesmen from the marches of eastern Pelosia sliced back and forth through the huddled mass cowering on the grass. The palace guards who had joined the mob made some slight effort to respond, but the Peloi horsemen gleefully rode them down.

Sephrenia and Vanion entered the turret. The small Styric woman's white gown gleamed in the shaft of moonlight that streamed in through the door. 'What are you thinking of, Sparhawk?' she demanded angrily.

'This isn't a safe place for Ehlana and Sarabian.'

'I think it's as safe as I can manage, little mother. Ehlana, what would you say if I told you that you had to go inside?'

'I'd say no, Sparhawk. I'd crawl out of my skin if you locked me up in some safe room where I couldn't see what's going on.'

'I sort of thought you might feel that way. And you, Emperor Sarabian?'

'Your wife just nailed my feet to the floor, Sparhawk. How could I possibly run off and hide while she's standing up here on the wall like the figurehead on a warship?' The emperor looked at Sephrenia. 'Is this insane foolhardiness a racial characteristic of these barbarians?' he asked her.

She sighed. 'You wouldn't *believe* some of the things they're capable of, Sarabian,' she replied, throwing a quick smile at Vanion.

'At least *someone* in that mob's still thinking coherently, Sparhawk,' Vanion said to his friend. 'He's just realised that there are all sorts of unpleasant implications in the fact that they can't get in here or out of the compound. He's out there trying to whip them up by telling them that they're doomed unless they take this castle.'

'I hope he's *also* telling them that they're doomed if they try,' Sparhawk replied.

'I'd imagine that he's glossing over that part. I had some misgivings about you when you were a novice, my friend. You and Kalten seemed like a couple of wild colts, but now that you've settled down, you're really quite good. Your strategy here has been brilliant, you know. You actually haven't embarrassed me too much this time.'

'Thanks, Vanion,' Sparhawk said dryly.

'No charge.'

The rebels approached the moat tentatively, their faces filled with apprehension and their eyes fixed on the night sky, desperately searching for that first flicker of fire which would announce that Sir Bevier was sending them greetings. The chance passage of a shooting-star across the velvet throat of night elicited screams of fright, followed by a vast nervous laugh.

The gleaming, brightly-lit castle, however, remained silent. No soldiers lined the battlements. No globs of liquid fire sprang into the night sky from within those nacreous walls.

The defenders crouched silently behind the battlements and waited.

'Good,' Vanion muttered after a quick glance out of one of the embrasures in the turret. 'Someone saw the potential of those barges. They've clapped together some scaling ladders.'

'We *have* to rupture those barges now, Vanion!' Ehlana exclaimed urgently.

'You didn't tell her?' Vanion asked Sparhawk.

'No. The concept might have been difficult for her to accept.'

'You'd better take her back inside the castle then, my friend. What's going to happen next is likely to upset her a great deal.'

'*Will* you two stop talking about me as if I weren't even here?' Ehlana burst out in exasperation. 'What are you going to do?'

'You'd better tell her,' Vanion said bleakly.

'We can start that fire at any time, Ehlana,' Sparhawk said as gently as he could. 'In a situation like this, fire's a weapon. It's not tactically practical to waste it by setting it off before your enemies are around to receive its benefits.'

She stared at him, the blood draining from her face. 'This wasn't what I'd planned, Sparhawk!' she said vehemently. 'The fire's supposed to keep them away from the moat. I didn't want you to burn them alive with it.'

'I'm sorry, Ehlana. It's a military decision. A weapon's useless unless you demonstrate your willingness to employ it. I know it's hard to accept, but if we take your plan to its ultimate application, it may save lives in the long run. We're outnumbered here in Tamuli, and if we don't establish a certain reputation for ruthlessness, we'll be over-run the next time there's a confrontation.'

'You're a monster!'

'No, dear. I'm a soldier.'

She suddenly started to cry.

'Would you take her inside now, little mother?' Sparhawk asked Sephrenia. 'I think we'd all rather she didn't see this.'

Sephrenia nodded and took the weeping queen to the stairway leading down from the turret.

'You might want to go too, your Majesty,' Vanion suggested to Sarabian. 'Sparhawk and I are more or less accustomed to this sort of unpleasantness. You don't have to watch, though.'

'No, I'll stay, Lord Vanion,' Sarabian said firmly.

'That's up to you, your Majesty.'

A sheet of crossbow bolts rattled against the battlements like hail. It appeared that the rebels had been repairing the results of Khalad's tampering. Then, fearfully, splashing in panicky desperation, swimmers leapt from the edge of the moat and struggled their way to the barges to slip the mooring lines. The barges were quickly pulled to shore, and the rebels, their makeshift scaling-ladders already raised, swarmed on board and began to pole their way rapidly across the moat to the sheer castle-wall.

Sparhawk stuck his head out through the doorway of the turret. 'Kalten!' he hissed to his friend who was crouched down on the parapet not far from the

564

urret. 'Pass the word! Tell the Atans to get ready!'

'Right.'

'But tell them not to move until they hear the signal.'

'I know what I'm doing, Sparhawk. Quit treating me ike an idiot.'

'Sorry.'

The urgent whisper sped around the battlements.

'Your timing's perfect, Sparhawk,' Vanion said ensely in a low voice. 'I just saw Kring's signal from he compound wall. The Atans are outside the gate.' He paused. 'You're having an unbelievable run of good uck, you know. Nobody could have guessed in advance hat the mob would start up the wall and the Atans would arrive at precisely the same time.'

'Probably not,' Sparhawk agreed. 'I think we might want to do something nice for Aphrael the next time we see her.'

In the moat below, the barges bumped against the castle walls, and the rebels began their desperate scramble up the ladders towards the ominously silent battlements.

Another urgent whisper slithered back around the parapet.

'The barges are all up against the wall now, Sparhawk!' Kalten whispered hoarsely.

'All right.' Sparhawk drew in a deep breath. 'Tell Ulath to give the signal.'

'Ulath!' Kalten shouted, no longer even bothering to whisper. 'Toot your horn!'

'*Toot?*' Ulath's voice was outraged. Then his Ogrehorn rang out its message of pain and death.

From around the parapet, great boulders were lifted, teetered a moment on the battlements and then plummeted down onto the swarming decks of the barges below. The barges ruptured, splintered and began to sink. The viscous mixture of naphtha and pitch spread

565

out across the surface of the moat. The spreading slick was rainbow-hued and, Sparhawk absently thought, really rather pretty.

The towering Atans rose from their places of conceal ment, took up the lanterns conveniently hanging from the battlements and hurled them down into the moat like a hundred flaring comets.

The rebels who had leaped from the sinking barges and who were struggling in the oily water below screamed in terror as they saw flaming death raining down on them from above.

The moat exploded. A sheet of blue fire shot across the naphtha-stained water, and it was immediately fol lowed by towering billows of sooty orange flame and dense black smoke. There were volcano-like eruptions from the sinking barges as the deadly, unspilled naph tha still in their holds took fire. The flames belched upward to sear the rebels still clinging to the scaling ladders. They fell or jumped from the burning ladders, streaking flame as they plunged into the inferno below.

The screams were dreadful. Some few of the burning men reached the far bank of the moat and ran blindly across the tidy lawns of the compound, shrieking and dripping fire.

The rebels who had stood at the brink of the moat impatiently awaiting their turn to cross the intervening water to scale the walls recoiled in horror from the sud den conflagration that had just made the gleaming castle of the Elenes as unreachable as the far side of the moon.

'Ulath!' Sparhawk roared. 'Tell Kring to open the gate!'

Once more the Ogre-horn sang.

The massive gates of the compound swung slowly open, and the golden Atan giants, running in perfect unison, swept into the imperial compound like an ava lanche.

CHAPTER 30

'I don't *know* how they did it, Sparhawk,' Caalador replied with a dark scowl. 'Krager himself hasn't been seen for days. He's a slippery one, isn't he?' Caalador had come in from the city and located Sparhawk on the parapet.

'That he is, my friend. What about the others? I wouldn't have thought that Elron could have managed something like that.'

'Neither would I. He was doing everything but wearing a sign reading "conspirator" on his forehead – all that swirling of his cape and exaggerated tip-toeing through back alleys.' Caalador shook his head. 'Anyway, he was staying in the house of a local Edomish nobleman. We know he was inside, because we watched him go in through the front door. We were watching every single door and window, so we know he didn't come back out, but he wasn't inside when we went to pick him up.'

There was a crash from a nearby palace as the Atans broke in the doors to get at the rebels hiding inside.

'Did your people check the house for hidden rooms or passages?' Sparhawk asked.

Caalador shook his head. 'They stood the Edomish noble barefoot in a brazier of hot coals instead. It's faster that way. There was no place to hide in that house. I'm sorry, Sparhawk. We picked up all the second-raters without a hitch, but the leaders –' He spread his hands helplessly.

'Somebody was probably using magic. They've done it before.'

'Can you really do that sort of thing with magic?'

'*I* can't, but I'm sure Sephrenia knows the proper spells.'

Caalador looked out over the battlements. 'Well, at least we broke up this attack on the government. That's the main thing.'

'I'm not so sure,' Sparhawk disagreed.

'It *was* fairly important, Sparhawk. If they'd succeeded, all of Tamuli would have flown apart. As soon as the Atans finish mopping up, we'll be able to start questioning survivors – and those underlings we *did* manage to catch. They might be able to direct us to the important plotters.'

'I sort of doubt it. Krager's very good at this sort of thing. I think we'll find that the underlings don't actually have a lot of information. It's a shame. I *really* wanted to have a little talk with Krager.'

'You always get that tone of voice when you talk about him.' Caalador observed. 'Is there something personal between you two?'

'Oh, yes, and it goes back a long, long ways. I've missed any number of opportunities to kill him – usually because it wasn't convenient. I was usually too busy concentrating on the man who employed him, and that may have been a mistake. Krager always makes sure that he's got just enough information to make him too valuable to kill. The next time I come across him, I think I'll just ignore that.'

The Atans were efficiency personified as they rounded up the rebels. They offered the armed insurgents one opportunity to surrender each time they surrounded a group, and they didn't ask twice. By two hours past midnight, the imperial compound was quiet again. A few Atan patrols searched the grounds and buildings for any rebels who might have gone into hiding, but there was little in the way of significant activity.

Sparhawk was bone-tired. Though he had not physically participated in the suppression of the rebellion, the tension had exhausted him more than a two-hour battle might have. He stood on the parapet looking wearily down into the compound, watching without much interest as the grounds-keepers, who had been pressed into service for the unpleasant task, cringingly pulled the floating dead out of the moat.

'Why don't you go to bed, Sparhawk?' It was Khalad. His bare, heavy shoulders gleamed in the torchlight. His voice and appearance and brusque manner were so much like his father's that Sparhawk once again felt that brief, renewed pang of sorrow.

'I just want to be sure that there won't be any bodies left floating in the moat when my wife wakes up tomorrow morning. People who've been burned to death aren't very pretty.'

'I'll take care of that. Let's go to the bath-house. I'll help you out of your armour, and you can soak in a tub of hot water for a while.'

'I didn't really exert myself very much this evening, Khalad. I didn't even work up a sweat.'

'You don't have to. That smell's so ingrained into your armour that five minutes after you put it on, you smell as if you haven't bathed for a month.'

'It's one of the drawbacks of the profession. Are you sure you want to be a knight?'

'It wasn't my idea in the first place.'

'Maybe when this is all over, the world will settle down enough so that there won't be any need for armoured knights any more.'

'Of course, and maybe someday fish will fly too.'

'You're a cynic, Khalad.'

'What *is* he doing up there?' Khalad demanded irritably, looking up toward the towers soaring over the castle.

'Who's doing what where?'

'There's somebody up in the very top of that south tower. This is the fourth time I've caught a flicker of candle-light through that window.'

'Maybe Tynian or Bevier put one of their knights up there to keep watch,' Sparhawk shrugged.

'Without telling you? Or Lord Vanion?'

'If it worries you so much, let's go take a look.'

'You don't sound very concerned.'

'I'm not. This castle's absolutely secure, Khalad.'

'I'll go have a look after I get you ready for bed.'

'No, I'll go along.'

'I thought you were certain that the castle's secure.'

'It never hurts to be careful. I don't want to have to tell your mothers that I made a mistake and got you killed.'

They went down from the battlements, crossed the courtyard and went into the main building.

There were loud snores coming from behind the bolted door of the main dining hall. 'I'd imagine that there are going to be some monumental headaches emerging from that room in the morning,' Khalad laughed.

'We didn't force our guests to drink so much.'

'They'll accuse us of it, though.'

They started up the stairway that led to the top of the south tower. Although the main tower and the north tower had been constructed in the usual fashion with rooms stacked atop each other, the south tower was little more than a hollow shell with a wooden stairway rising up through a creaking scaffolding. The architect had evidently added this structure primarily for the purposes of symmetry. The single room in the entire tower was at the very top, a room floored with wooden beams roughly adzed square.

'I'm getting too old to be climbing stairs in full

armour,' Sparhawk puffed when they were about half-way up.

'You're out of condition, Sparhawk,' Khalad told his lord bluntly. 'You're spending too much time on your backside talking about politics.'

'It's part of my job, Khalad.'

They reached the door at the top of the stairs. 'You'd better let me go in first,' Sparhawk murmured, sliding his sword out of its scabbard. Then he reached out and pushed the door open.

A shabby-looking man sat at a wooden table in the centre of the room, his face lit by a single candle. Sparhawk knew him. The years of hard drinking had not been kind to Krager. His hair had thinned even more in the six or so years since Sparhawk had last seen him, and the puffy pouches under his eyes were even more pronounced. The eyes themselves, nearsighted and watery, were discoloured and seemed to be overlaid with a kind of yellow stain. The hand in which he held his wine-cup palsied, and a continual tic shuddered in his right cheek.

Sparhawk moved without even stopping to think. He levelled his sword at Martel's threadbare former underling and lunged.

There was no feeling of resistance as the sword plunged into Krager's chest and emerged from his back.

Krager flinched violently, and then he laughed in his rusty, drink-corroded voice. 'God, that's a startling experience!' he said conversationally. 'I could almost feel the blade running through me. Put your sword away, Sparhawk. You can't hurt me with it.'

Sparhawk pulled the sword out of Krager's substantial-appearing body and swept it back and forth through the man's head.

'Please don't do that, Sparhawk,' Krager said, closing his eyes. 'It's really very unnerving, you know.'

'My compliments to your magician, Krager,' Sparhawk said flatly. 'That's really a very convincing illusion. You look so real that I can almost smell you.'

'I see that we're going to be civilised about this,'
Krager said, taking a drink of his wine. 'Good. You're
growing up, Sparhawk. Ten years ago, you'd have
chopped the room into kindling before you'd have
finally been willing to listen to reason.'

'Magic?' Khalad asked Sparhawk.

Sparhawk nodded. 'And fairly sophisticated too.
Actually Krager's sitting in a room a mile or more away
from here. Someone's projecting his image into this
tower. We can see him and hear him, but we can't touch
him.'

'Pity,' Khalad murmured, fingering the hilt of his
heavy dagger.

'You've really been very clever this time, Sparhawk,'
Krager said. 'Age seems to be improving you – like a
good wine.'

'You're the expert on that, Krager.'

'Petty, Sparhawk. Very petty.' Krager smirked.
'Before you engage in an orgy of self-congratulation,
though, you ought to know that this was just another
of those tests a friend of mine mentioned to you a while
back. I told my associates all about you, but they wanted
to see for themselves. We arranged a few entertainments
for you so that you could demonstrate your prowess –
and your limitations. The catapults definitely confused
the Cyrgai, and your mounted tactics against the Trolls
were almost brilliant. You also did remarkably well in
an urban setting here in Matherion. You really surprised
me on that score, Sparhawk. You caught on to our sign
and counter-sign much faster than I'd thought you
would, and you intercepted the message about the
warehouse in a remarkably short period of time. That
Dacite merchant only had to walk through town three

572

times before your spy stole the note from him. I'd have expected you to fail miserably when faced with a conspiracy instead of an army in the field. My congratulations.'

'You've been drinking for too many years, Krager. Your memory's starting to slip. You're forgetting what happened in Chyrellos during the election. As I recall, we countered just about every one of the schemes Martel and Annias cooked up there as well.'

'That wasn't really a very great accomplishment, Sparhawk. Martel and Annias weren't really very challenging opponents. I tried to tell them that their plots weren't sophisticated enough, but they wouldn't listen. Martel was too busy thinking about the treasure-rooms under the Basilica, and Annias was so blinded by the Archprelate's mitre that he couldn't see anything else. You really missed your chance there, Sparhawk. I've always been your most serious opponent. You had me right in your hands, and you let me go just for the sake of a few crumbs of information and some exaggerated testimony before the Hierocracy. Very poor thinking there, old boy.'

'This evening's festivities weren't really designed to succeed then, I gather?'

'Of course not, Sparhawk. If we'd really wanted to take Matherion, we'd have brought in whole armies.'

'I'm sure there's a point to all this,' Sparhawk said to the illusion. 'Do you suppose we could step right along? I've had a tiring day.'

'The tests have all been designed to oblige you to commit your resources, Sparhawk. We needed to know what kinds of responses you had at your command.'

'You haven't seen them all yet, Krager – not by half.'

'Khalad, isn't it?' Krager said to Sparhawk's squire. 'Tell your master that he should practise a bit more before he tries lying. He's really not very convincing –

oh, convey my regards to your mother. She and I always got on well.'

'I sort of doubt that,' Khalad replied.

'Be realistic, Sparhawk,' Krager went on. 'Your wife and daughter are here. Do you *really* expect me to believe that you'd hold anything back if you thought they were in danger?'

'We used what was necessary, Krager. You don't have to send out a whole regiment to step on a bug.'

'You're so much like Martel was, Sparhawk,' Krager observed. 'You two could almost have been brothers. I used to despair of ever nursing him through his adolescence. He was a hopeless innocent when he started out, you know. About all he had was a towering resentment – directed primarily at you and Vanion – and at Sephrenia, of course, although to a lesser degree. I had to raise him from virtual infancy. God, the hours I spent patiently grinding away all those knightly virtues.'

'Reminisce on your own time, Krager. Get to the point. Martel's history now. This is a new situation, and he's not around any more.'

'Just renewing our acquaintance, Sparhawk. You know, "the good old days" and all that. I've found a new employer, obviously.'

'I gathered as much.'

'When I was working for Martel, I had very little direct contact with Otha and almost none with Azash Himself. That situation might have had an entirely different outcome if I'd had direct access to the Zemoch God. Martel was obsessed with revenge, and Otha was too sunk in his own debauchery for either of them to think clearly. They were giving Azash very poor advice as a result of their own limitations. I could have given him a much more realistic assessment of the situation.'

'Provided you were ever sober enough to talk.'

'That's beneath you, Sparhawk. Oh, I'll admit that I

take a drink now and then, but never so much that I lose sight of the main goals. Actually, it turned out better for me in the long run. If I'd been the one advising Azash, He'd have beaten you. Then I'd have been inextricably involved with Him, and I'd have been destroyed when He confronted Cyrgon – that's my new employer's name, by the way. You've heard of Him, I suppose?'

'A few times.' Sparhawk forced himself to sound casual.

'Good. That saves us a lot of time. Pay attention now, Sparhawk. We're getting to the significant part of this little chat. Cyrgon wants you to go home. Your presence here on the Daresian continent is an inconvenience – nothing more, really. Just an inconvenience. If you had Bhelliom in your pocket, we might take you seriously, but you don't – and so we don't. You're all alone here, my old friend. You don't have the Bhelliom, and you don't have the Church Knights. You've only got the remnants of Ehlana's honour guard and a hundred of those mounted apes from Pelosia. You're hardly worth even noticing. If you go home, Cyrgon will give you His pledge not to move against the Eosian continent for a hundred years. You'll be long dead by then, and so will everybody you care about. It's not really a bad offer, you know. You get yourself a hundred years of peace just by getting on a ship and going back to Cimmura.'

'And if I don't?'

'We'll kill you – *after* we've killed your wife and your daughter and everybody else in the whole world you care about. There's another possibility, of course. You could join us. Cyrgon could see to it that you lived longer than even Otha did. He specifically told me to make you that offer.'

'Thank Him for me – if you ever see Him again.'

'You're declining, I gather?'

'Obviously. I haven't seen nearly as much of Daresia

as I want to see, so I think I'll stay for a while, and I'm sure I wouldn't care for the company of you and Cyrgon's other hirelings.'

'I told Cyrgon you'd take that position, but He insisted that I make the offer.'

'If he's so all-powerful, why's He trying to bribe me?'

'Out of respect, Sparhawk. Can you believe that? He respects you because you're Anakha. The whole concept baffles Him, and He's intrigued by it. I honestly believe He'd like to get to know you. You know how childish Gods can be at times.'

'Speaking of Gods, what's behind this alliance He's made with the Troll-Gods?' Then Sparhawk thought of something. 'Never mind, Krager, I've just worked it out for myself. A God's power is dependent on the number of worshippers he has. The Cyrgai are extinct, so Cyrgon's no more than a squeaky little voice making hollow pronouncements in a ruin somewhere in central Cynesga – all noise and no substance.'

'Someone's been telling you fairy-tales, Sparhawk. The Cyrgai are far from extinct – as you'll find out to your sorrow if you stay in Tamuli. Cyrgon made the alliance with the Troll-Gods in order to bring the Trolls to Daresia. Your Atans are very impressive, but they're no match for Trolls. Cyrgon's very sentimental about His chosen people. He'd rather not lose them needlessly in skirmishes with a race of freaks, so He made an arrangement with the Troll-Gods. The Trolls will get the pleasure of killing – and eating – the Atans.' Krager drained the rest of his wine. 'This is starting to bore me, Sparhawk, and my cup's gone empty. I told Cyrgon I'd present you with His offer. He's giving you the chance to live out the rest of your life in peace. I'd advise you to take it. He won't make the offer again. Really, old boy, why should you care what happens to the Tamuls? They're nothing but yellow monkeys, after all.'

'Church policy, Krager. Our Holy Mother takes the long view. Tell Cyrgon to take His offer and stick it up His nose. I'm staying.'

'It's your funeral, Sparhawk,' Krager laughed. 'I might even send flowers. I've had all the entertainment of knowing a pair of anachronisms – you and Martel. I'll drink to your memories from time to time – if I remember you at all.'

And then the illusion of the shabby scoundrel vanished.

'So that's Krager,' Khalad said in a chill tone. 'I'm glad I got the chance to meet him.'

'What exactly have you got in mind, Khalad?'

'I thought I might kill him just a little bit. Fair's fair, Sparhawk. You got Martel, Talen got Adus, so Krager's mine.'

'Sounds fair to me,' Sparhawk agreed.

'Was he drunk?' Kalten asked.

'Krager's always a little drunk,' Sparhawk replied. 'He wasn't so far gone that he got careless, though.' He looked around. 'Would everybody like to say "I told you so" right here and now?' he asked them. 'Let's have it out of the way right at the start, so I don't have it hanging over my head. Yes, it probably would have been more convenient if I'd killed him the last time I saw him, but if we hadn't had his testimony to the Hierocracy at the time of the election, Dolmant probably wouldn't be the Archprelate right now.'

'I might be able to learn to live with that,' Ehlana murmured.

'Be nice,' Emban told her.

'Only joking, your Grace.'

'Are you sure you repeated what he said verbatim?' Sephrenia asked Sparhawk.

'It was very close, little mother,' Khalad assured her.

She frowned. 'It was contrived. I'm sure you all realise that. Krager didn't really tell us anything we didn't already know – or could have guessed.'

'The name Cyrgon hadn't come up before, Sephrenia,' Vanion disagreed.

'And it may very well never come up again,' she replied. 'I'd need a lot more than Krager's unsubstantiated word before I'll believe that Cyrgon's involved.'

'Well, *somebody's* involved,' Tynian noted. 'Somebody had to be impressive enough to get the attention of the Troll-Gods, and Krager doesn't quite fit that description.'

'Not to mention the fact that Krager can't even pronounce "magic", much less use it,' Kalten added. 'Could just any Styric have cast that spell, little mother?'

Sephrenia shook her head. 'It's very difficult,' she conceded. 'If it hadn't been done exactly right, Sparhawk's sword would have gone right through the real Krager. Sparhawk would have started the thrust in that room up in the tower, and it would have finished up in a room a mile away sliding through Krager's heart.'

'All right then,' Emban said, pacing up and down the room with his pudgy hands clasped behind his back. 'Now we know that this so-called uprising tonight wasn't intended seriously.'

Sparhawk shook his head. 'No, your Grace, we *don't* know that for certain. Regardless of what he says, Krager learned much of his style from Martel, and trying to shrug a failure off by pretending that the scheme wasn't really serious in the first place is exactly the sort of thing Martel would have done.'

'You knew him better than I did,' Emban shrugged. 'Can we *really* be sure that Krager and the others are working for a God – Cyrgon or maybe some other one?'

'Not really, Emban,' Sephrenia replied. 'The Troll-Gods are involved, and *they* could be doing the things

578

we've encountered that are beyond the capability of a human magician. There's a sorcerer out there, certainly, but we can't be certain that there's a God – other than the Troll-Gods – involved as well.'

'But it *could* be a God, couldn't it?' Emban pressed.

'Anything's possible, your Grace,' she shrugged.

'That's what I needed to know,' the fat little churchman said. 'It rather looks as if I'm going to have to make a flying trip back to Chyrellos.'

'That went by me a little fast, your Grace,' Kalten confessed.

'We're going to need the Church Knights, Kalten,' Emban said. 'All of them.'

'They're committed to Rendor, your Grace,' Bevier reminded him.

'Rendor can wait.'

'The Archprelate may feel differently about that, Emban,' Vanion told him. 'Reconciliation with the Rendors has been one of our Holy Mother's goals for over half a millennium now.'

'She's patient. She'll wait. She's going to *have* to wait. This is a crisis, Vanion.'

'I'll go with you, your Grace,' Tynian said. 'I won't be of much use here in Tamuli until my shoulder heals anyway, and I'll be able to clarify the military situation to Sarathi much better than you will. Dolmant's had Pandion training, so he'll understand military terminology. Right now we're standing out in the open with our breeches down – begging your Majesty's pardon for the crudity of that expression,' he apologised to Ehlana.

'It's an interesting metaphor, Sir Tynian,' she smiled, 'and it conjures up an absolutely enthralling image.'

'I'll agree with the Patriarch of Ucera,' Tynian went on. 'We definitely have to have the Church Knights here in Tamuli. If we *don't* get them here in a hurry, this whole situation's going to crumble right in our hands.'

'I'll send word to Tikume,' Kring volunteered. 'He'll send us several thousand mounted Peloi. We don't wear armour or use magic, but we know how to fight.'

'Will you be able to hold out here until the Church Knights arrive, Vanion?' Emban asked.

'Talk to Sparhawk, Emban. He's in charge.'

'I wish you wouldn't keep doing that, Vanion,' Sparhawk objected. He thought for a moment. 'Atan Engessa,' he said then, 'how hard was it to persuade your warriors that it's not really unnatural to fight on horseback? Can we persuade any more of them?'

'When I tell them that this Krager-drunkard called them a race of freaks, they'll listen to me, Sparhawk-Knight.'

'Good. Krager may have helped us more than he thought then. Are *you* convinced that it's best to attack Trolls with warhorses and lances, my friend?'

'It was most effective, Sparhawk-Knight. We haven't encountered the Troll-beasts before. They're bigger than we are. That may be difficult for my people to accept, but once they do, they'll be willing to try horses – if you can find enough of those big ones.'

'Did Krager happen to make any references to the fact that we've been using thieves and beggars as our eyes and ears?' Stragen asked.

'Not in so many words, Milord,' Khalad replied.

'That puts an unknown into our equation then,' Stragen mused.

'Please don't do that, Stragen,' Kalten pleaded. 'I absolutely *hate* mathematics.'

'Sorry. We don't know for certain whether Krager's aware that we've been using the criminals of Matherion as spies. If he *is* aware of it, he could use it to feed us false information.'

'That spell they used sort of hints that they know, Stragen,' Caalador noted. 'That explains how it was that

580

we saw the leaders of the conspiracy go into a house and never come out. They used illusions. They wouldn't have done that if they hadn't known we were watching.'

Stragen stuck out his hand and wobbled it from side to side a bit dubiously. 'It's not set in stone yet, Caalador,' he said. 'He may not know just exactly how well-organised we are.'

Bevier's expression was profoundly disgusted. 'We've been had, my friends,' he said. 'This was all an elaborate ruse – armies from the past, resurrected heroes,vampires and ghouls – all of it. It was a trick with no other purpose than to get us to come here without the entire body of the Church Knights at our backs.'

'Then why have they turned round and told us to go home, Sir Bevier?' Talen asked him.

'Maybe they found out that we were a little more effective than they thought we'd be,' Ulath rumbled. 'I don't think they really expected us to break up that Cyrgai assault or exterminate a hundred Trolls or break the back of this coup-attempt the way we did. It's altogether possible that we surprised them and even upset them more than a little. Krager's visit could have been sheer bravado, you know. We might not want to get over-confident, but I don't think we should get *under*-confident either. We're professionals, after all, and we've won every encounter so far. Let's not give up the game and run away just because of a few windy threats by a known drunkard.'

'Well said,' Tynian murmured.

'We don't have any choice, Aphrael,' Sparhawk told his daughter later when they were alone with Sephrenia and Vanion in a small room several floors above the royal apartments. 'It's going to take Emban and Tynian at least three months to get back to Chyrellos and then

581

nine months for the Church Knights to come overland to Daresia. Even then, they'll still be present only in the western kingdoms.'

'Why can't they come by boat?' The princess sounded a bit sulky, and she was holding Rollo tightly to her chest.

'There are a hundred thousand Church Knights, Aphrael,' Vanion reminded her, 'twenty-five thousand in each of the four orders. I don't think there are enough ships in the world to transport that many men and horses. We can bring in some – ten thousand perhaps – by ship, but the bulk of them will have to come overland. We won't be able to count on even that ten thousand for at least six months – the time it's going to take Emban and Tynian to reach Chyrellos and then come back by ship with the knights and their horses. Until they arrive, we're all alone here.'

'With your breeches down,' she added.

'Watch your tongue, young lady,' Sparhawk scolded her.

She shrugged that off. 'My instincts all tell me that it's a very bad idea,' she told them. 'I went to a lot of trouble to find a safe place for Bhelliom, and the first time there's a little rain-shower, you all want to run to retrieve it. Are you *sure* you're not exaggerating the danger? Ulath might have been right, you know. Everything Krager said to you could have been sheer bluster. I still think you can handle it without Bhelliom.'

'I disagree,' Sephrenia told her. 'I know Elenes better than you do, Aphrael. It's not in their nature to exaggerate dangers. Quite the reverse, actually.'

'The whole point here is that your mother may be in danger,' Sparhawk told his daughter. 'Until Tynian and Emban bring the Church Knights to Tamuli, we're seriously over-matched. Even as stupid as they are, it was only the Bhelliom that gave us any advantage over the

582

Troll-Gods last time. *You* couldn't even deal with them, as I recall.'

'That's a hateful thing to say, Sparhawk,' she flared.

'I'm just trying to get you to look at this realistically, Aphrael. Without the Bhelliom, we're all in serious danger here – and I'm not just talking about your mother and all our friends. If Krager was telling the truth and we *are* matched up against Cyrgon, He's at least as dangerous as Azash was.'

'Are you *sure* all of these flimsy excuses aren't coming into your head because you want to get your hands on Bhelliom again, Sparhawk?' she asked him. 'Nobody's really immune to its seduction, you know. There's a great deal of satisfaction to be had in wielding unlimited power.'

'You know me better than that, Aphrael,' he said reproachfully. 'I don't go out of my way looking for power.'

'If it *is* Cyrgon, His first step would be to exterminate the Styrics, you know,' Sephrenia reminded the little Goddess. 'He hates us for what we did to His Cyrgai.'

'Why are you all joining forces to bully me?' Aphrael demanded.

'Because you're being stubborn,' Sparhawk replied. 'Throwing Bhelliom into the sea was a very good idea when we did it, but the situation's changed now. I know that it's not in your nature to admit that you made a mistake, but you did, you know.'

'Bite your tongue!'

'We have a new situation here, Aphrael,' Sephrenia said patiently. 'You've told me again and again that you can't fully see the future, so you couldn't really have foreseen all of what's happening here in Tamuli. You didn't *really* make a mistake, baby sister, but you have to be flexible. You can't let the world fly all to pieces

583

just because you want to maintain a reputation for infal-libility.'

'Oh, all *right!*' Aphrael gave in, flinging herself into a chair and starting to suck her thumb as she glared at them.

'Don't do that,' Sparhawk and Sephrenia told her in unison.

She ignored them. 'I want all three of you to know that I'm really very put out with you for this. You've been very impolite and very inconsiderate of my feel-ings. I'm ashamed of you. Go ahead. I don't care. Go ahead and get the Bhelliom if you think you absolutely *have* to have it.'

'Ah – Aphrael,' Sparhawk said mildly, 'we don't know where it is, remember?'

'That's not my fault,' she replied in a sulky little voice.

'Yes, actually it is. You were very careful to make sure that we *didn't* know where we were when we threw it into the sea.'

'That's a spiteful thing to say, father.'

A horrible thought suddenly occurred to Sparhawk. 'You *do* know where it is, don't you?' he asked her anxiously.

'Oh, Sparhawk, don't be silly! Of *course* I know where it is. You didn't think I'd let you put it someplace where I couldn't find it, did you?'